About the Author

George Fairbrother held a variety of jobs before turning his hand to writing. His interest in politics and history was inspired, from afar, by the works of Alan Bleasdale, Peter Flannery, Ken Loach and many others.

When not working at the computer, he enjoys spending time outdoors, organic gardening, cooking, walking, listening to Status Quo, and reading Patrick O'Brian.

The Enemy Within

George Fairbrother

The Enemy Within

Olympia Publishers
London

www.olympiapublishers.com
OLYMPIA PAPERBACK EDITION

A CIP catalogue record for this title is
available from the British Library.

ISBN: 978-1-78830-518-1

This is a work of fiction.
Names, characters, places and incidents originate from the writer's
imagination. Any resemblance to actual persons, living or dead, is
purely coincidental.

First Published in 2020

Olympia Publishers
Tallis House
2 Tallis Street
London
EC4Y 0AB

Printed in Great Britain

Dedication

...for when the boat comes in...

PROLOGUE
KNIGHTSBRIDGE, WEST LONDON
CHRISTMAS 1994

"Guess what, bonny lad! Ha'way man, I've done it again. Guess what, My Lord, I should've said!"

"Christmas again, God help us. And with your rather quaint obsession for meeting deadlines, I have no doubt you're about to tell me that the third instalment will soon be gracing our Christmas stockings."

"Spot on, old marra."

"And you're about to dazzle me with the title?"

"Are you ready for it?"

"I'm suitably agog with anticipation!"

"Here it is. *A New Britain — Thatcher and the End of Consensus; Volume Three.* What do you think?"

"Well, I must admit, I had moderately high hopes that this title would be an improvement. I thought the names you came up with for the first two volumes were God-awful. But it's fair to say you've set a new standard of deplorability with this one."

"How kind you are. But now, finally, please, can we talk about the Banqueting Club?"

"That's not my club. I'm not a member of that one. I know nothing about it."

"Bollocks, man! Every time I raise it, we go through the same ridiculous charade, year in, year out, argue back and forth until you suddenly have to go the gents. Then you come back and change the subject, and I let you get away with it. Not this time, bonny lad. It's time to lay our cards on the table. Everything we know."

"Why? What good will it do anyone?"

"Because your family is up to their eyeballs in it, and has been for generations. Half of them have been actually part of it, the other half have fought it, or tried to escape it. Either way, like it or not, the Most Worshipful Order of Liege Knights; Liege *Nutters* more like; of Charles the First, the Banqueting Club, with all their sins, is *your* family history. And now you have the dynasty to consider. Unless you've secretly discovered the secret to eternal life — which wouldn't surprise me, by the way — Rick's going to be the Second Viscount Armstrong one day, then young James eventually. Don't you think they have a right to know the truth? It'll all come out; these family secrets always do. I'm sure if Dickie Billings knew all about that so-called secret society, other people did too. Better for Rick, James and Ellie to find out from us, than from a grubby tabloid, or from a political rival or jealous corporate competitor determined to bring them down."

"It's all ancient history."

"That's where you're completely wrong, old marra. I felt like that once as well, as you know, and abandoned thirty-four years of investigations; a few months after the end of the Miners' Strike, it was. I convinced myself there was nothing to it. I didn't pick up on it again until after Sir Dick shuffled off and left me all his papers. From what I discovered from Dick's memoirs I was wrong to have given up so easily, back in '85. I was dead wrong."

"Sorry, just say that again."

"Say what again?"

"Just that last bit, what you said."

"Which part? Oh, you mean when I said that I was wrong?"

"Yes. Say that again."

"I was wrong."

"There, you have no idea how good that feels! Music to my ears. I've been waiting forty-four years to hear those three beautiful little words uttered from your lips. This calls for a celebration."

"I might have been wrong about the Banqueting Club, but not about too much else, bonny lad."

"I thought it was too good to be true; your self-righteousness has no limits. Dick Billings was certainly right about that, God rest him. Ah well, you were always way too eager to embrace any tired old conspiracy theory. Especially if it involved the Conservative side. Not so keen on digging into the sins of your Labour and union *marras* though, were you? Didn't hear too much from you at the time about Scargill and the Libyan connection, did we?"

"That's because it was all a load of shite, man! And you know fine well I went just as hard after Labour and union stupidity as I did after your lot. When I was political editor for Sir Eddie Donoghue, our newsroom was famous for being fair, balanced and objective."

"Well, to a certain degree, perhaps. You went a bit mad during the Miners' Strike though, didn't you? Sir Eddie copped one hell of a battering over the biased, anti-government activism that you tried to pass off as objective reporting."

"Well, okay. I'll concede that, to a point. But if, *and only if*, you admit that some of your actions as Home Secretary left a lot to be desired. Especially, and I hope you'll forgive me for saying this, after Eileen was killed at Brighton."

"Well. Yes. Granted. Perhaps we both might have gone a little too far, in the heat of battle."

"Just on that little matter of my documentary on the strike, the one that got your lot so angry —"

"The first one or the second one?"

"The first one."

"What about it?"

"Remember when I politely asked you to get the government attack dogs to leave Sir Eddie alone, and you graciously complied?"

"Politely asked me? When you blackmailed the government, you mean. I had no choice but to comply with your demands."

"Ha'way, man, I wouldn't call it blackmail, as such. Perhaps a little robust arm-twisting. But there was one thing I always wondered?"

"Oh?"

"I was left alone after that as well. One minute I'm being lambasted in the House of Commons and across the Tory press as an enemy of the people, a Labour stooge and a red traitor, then... nothing. I was well prepared for the onslaught to intensify once Eddie was out of the line of fire, but things went very quiet. And not once was there any hint of my preferred access to Number Ten and the Cabinet questioned. This series of books, the first two of which have been universally critically acclaimed I'd remind you, wouldn't have been possible without the access I was granted, which was largely down to you."

"As ever, your modesty is breathtaking."

"I've often wondered why that was the case."

"Why what was the case?"

"Why I was left alone after the documentary, when the Tory attacks still clearly had some way to run. Dick Billings was only just warming up. He didn't want to go after Sir Eddie personally, for obvious reasons, but he had no such reservations when it came to me. And neither did most of your Cabinet colleagues."

"Perhaps what it came down to was that you simply weren't anywhere near as important as you thought you were, and you just weren't worth the effort."

"Well, you always say just the right things. But I know that I owe you a belated thanks, for saving my bacon for the second time. First my life, then my career."

"Don't drag me into your revisionist history sermon. But I know you've tried to look out for me as well, in your ham-fisted way."

"Ah bollocks, man. It was me that changed the subject this time. Back onto what we were talking about. Now. Think of Rick. He's spent his life distancing himself from your politics, and from the weight of his own family history; the burden that you've had to shoulder for your entire adult life. But whether he likes it or not, in a few years' time he's going to be taking your seat in the Lords; the Second Viscount Armstrong. And what a fine fellow to keep that chamber of somnambulant rogues in line. No offence intended."

"None taken. It's a reasonably accurate definition."

"And look at young James, doing very well in Austin Wells's constituency office. I think by the next election your grandson will be ready to stand in his own right. I hope he stands in your old constituency. In fact, I'm encouraging him to do so, and so is Austin. Let's face it, it's no longer safe Conservative territory, certainly not like it was for the forty-two years you held it, and your father before, and old Great Uncle Piers, and on and on —"

"Yes, yes. We can dispense with the historical commentary."

"Stonebridge South-east could very easily fall to Labour next time round. Imagine that, back in the Armstrong family once again, but with a Labour MP."

"It's just too horrible to contemplate. But, having said that, James at least has some brains, a miracle after his Comprehensive education, so he might at least be able to keep some of the fringe lunatics of the Left at bay."

"You mean like me?"

"I was thinking more of his future parliamentary colleagues, but if the cap fits… sorry, if the *flat* cap fits —"

"Very droll, My Lord. But it's not the first time your family's changed political allegiances, is it? At least this time it's taken generations, but there was someone in your ancestral history that managed it in the space of one career."

"I don't follow."

"Who was the General in Cromwell's New Model Army? Another James Armstrong, wasn't it? There's been quite a few of those down the years."

"What about him?"

"According to my research, he spent years fighting for the parliamentarian armies, then just as the corpse of Old Noll was being dug up, cheerfully sliced into little pieces and distributed around London, your James Armstrong suddenly — and rather conveniently — remembered that he'd been a royalist all along and was scrambling madly to pay homage to Charles the Second."

"Demonstrates sound judgement. If he hadn't, the dynasty would have ended before it even started. But the Armstrongs haven't always been Tories, you know, that's a myth. Some previous generations dabbled in Whiggery, years before Robert Peel's time."

"Dabbled in *what*?"

"Whiggery."

"By, that's a relief. I thought you said —"

"Thought I said what?"

"Never mind. Never mind. But you've done it again. Changed the subject."

"Ancient history, like I said."

"Wrong again. Let's think of the dangers of the Banqueting Club for future generations. Yours is a high achieving, famous family, old marra. I'd go as far as to say that you're the patriarch of the most powerful family in the country. You're still very influential in the Lords, and everyone knows you still quietly control what's left of the Thatcherite faction, along with the Baroness herself. And as for Rick, there's no question about his status. He is without doubt one of the most powerful businessmen, if not *the* most. And it's not just the lads. How old is Ellie now? Eight? Nine?"

"She's just turned ten."

"She's either going to follow her brother and grandfather into politics, or her father to the heights of corporate success. Or maybe even her mother into the arts. Do you really want to send these unsuspecting, bonny young people out into the lion's den, totally naïve and unaware? Completely unsuspecting, proud of their da' and granda', and of the preceding generations of war heroes and statesmen; totally secure in their glorious family history. Then one day, out of the blue, some muckraking journalist, or a political or corporate rival, crawls out of the woodwork and throws all this up in their faces. Everything they believed about their great family history, turned to ashes in front of their eyes. I think you know how that feels, bonny lad. I've seen the effect on you. Is that what you want for them?"

"No."

"My beautiful Dolly, God rest her; we weren't blessed as you were, Norman, but I've had the great joy of watching Rick's growing success, year after year. It's been one of the great honours of my life to work for him these past few years. He's the only reason I'm still at it, by the way, at the grand old age of seventy-two."

"You're seventy-six!"

"Well, be that as it may. Look at what Rick has achieved, *and* he's managed to keep his fundamental decency and humanity along the way. Not even Eddie Donoghue could have dreamed what's been possible. Satellite television across Europe, an airline flying all the major routes to the US, Europe and Asia; a global twenty-four-hour news channel beamed into homes around the world. Local television, a record label, investments in film production, magazines and newspapers. Mobile phones. As you know, Rick's been recently talking to people in California. Silicon Valley. Computers all networked together forming an information super-motorway, around the world. It will revolutionise how business is done, how we get our news, and even our entertainment. I don't really understand it, but Rick says it will be a big thing in the future. The internetwork. Rick's all over that."

"There's no doubt he's achieved miracles; to rescue the remnants of Sir Eddie's conglomerate after the '87 crash. With a little quiet help. But much as I love nothing more than celebrating the achievements of my son, now who's changed the subject?"

"That's where you're wrong. This is exactly the point I've been trying to make. The dynasty is secure. For the moment. But it's not just Rick. Your wonderful grandchildren, young James, and now Ellie growing up faster than we can keep up with. We couldn't have loved those bairns any more if they were our own, Dolly and me. But now it's up to you, Norman, with my help. We can't let them down. Look, Norman, man, if you'd prefer to let sleeping dogs lie, I completely understand. I'll never mention anything to do with the Banqueting Club in your presence again. But Rick at least deserves to know the truth, and he can make the decision about what to tell Sally, James and Ellie. And when. I can tell him, if you'd prefer. I can sit him down and take him through what I've learned, from the Billings Papers, and from all my other investigations over the past forty-three years. You know what Eileen would've said about this. And Dolly."

"Well, there might be something in what you say. I'll consider it."

"Good. We also have Godfrey to consider. He's involved in this as well, don't forget, through no fault of his own. We must be mindful of how he feels about it all."

"Lord Powell has always been a realist. You don't rise to the top of the Civil Service without a deep understanding and acceptance of how the world works. He's demonstrated that time and again."

"I suppose I could ask him, come to think of it. I'm having lunch with him at the Savoy next week."

"Since when do Peers that are former civil servants — the keepers of the nation's secrets — consort with broken-down old lobby correspondents?"

"We've become good friends over the years, since he was your Permanent Secretary at the Home Office. And since when do hard-line old Thatcherite Tory Lords invite decrepit socialists to their homes for off the record briefings and a bit' craic?"

"Touché, Comrade. I'm sure Sir Archie Prentice once mentioned to me something about keeping your friends close and your enemies closer. Apparently, it's a quote from a film."

"*The Godfather*, or was it the second one? I'm not sure. Or the third."

"I wouldn't know anything about that. The last film I sat through and enjoyed was *Reach for the Sky;* Kenneth More playing dear old Dougie Bader. Marvellous."

"You really should get out more."

"People have been telling me that for years, but I don't think I'm missing much. My grandson James spent most of his teenage years trying in vain to get me to appreciate what he called the new wave comedians. Ben Mayall, Rik somebody or other. Alexis Sales, not sure who she was. Just grotty

18

unwashed revolting youths swearing, berating Margaret and beating each other up. The BBC might just as well have stuck a camera in one of these inner-city council estates and could have filmed all of that behaviour going on every day, without wasting the hard-earned money of the long-suffering licence payers. That's not entertainment. Now, *Dad's Army*: that was entertainment. And *The Two Ronnies. Steptoe. The Good Life.* I don't mind *On the Up*, with Joan Sims and that rough chap from *Minder*. Actually, here's one I liked recently. *You Rang, M'Lord.* Written by the pair that did *Dad's Army*. That was very good. What were we talking about before you got me off the track?"

"I told you that I'm meeting Lord Powell for lunch at the Savoy."

"The Savoy? My goodness me; oh, hail the great champion of the working man. I think Michael Foot was right about you when he called you a class traitor."

"In fairness, it was *sources close to* Michael Foot that made that comment. And the Savoy was Godfrey's choice, not mine."

"Well, that makes it perfectly all right then."

"Now, are we going to tell Rick about the Banqueting Club, and your family's involvement?"

"Yes, you're right. For once. When the time is right, we'll put him in the picture."

"I can't help thinking that's your best decision since you decided to resign as Home Secretary."

"I'm not quite sure how I should take that."

"But I must warn you, there are parts of what I've learned that... let's just say that these matters are not going to be comfortable for you to hear. And that's an understatement.

You need to prepare yourself. People are not always as they seem."

"I came to the realisation years ago that my family history wasn't quite what I had always believed. But I've never run away from a fight, nor from a difficult truth, and I'm not going to start now."

"No fears for steady men, old marra."

"There aren't many of us left."

...By March of 1985, the year-long Miners' Strike had ended, but its all-pervading shadow was set to lengthen and, for better or worse, influence the course of events politically, socially and economically long into the future. The popular view was that it represented the last great ideological battle between defiant bitter-enders of the Keynesian quest for full employment through a mixed economy, and the free market Monetarist crusaders of Thatcherism. Like all good epics, there was a hero and a villain. Leading the free marketeers was, of course, the Conservative Prime Minister Mrs Thatcher, strongly supported by her Dry faction, which included the unapologetically hard-line Home Secretary Sir Norman Armstrong, and abrasive Chief Whip and Party Chairman Sir Dick Billings. This formidable force was pitted against the National Union of Mineworkers, under the direction of Arthur Scargill. Mrs Thatcher derided Scargill as "the enemy within" while Mr Scargill had formed his opinion of the Thatcher Government quite early, making comparisons to Nazis and promising to oppose a second-term Thatcher government as vigorously as he could. Unfortunately for Mr Scargill, the Thatcher Government went on to achieve a massive majority, and a crushing mandate, for its second term, which it was determined to put to good use.

So, which was the hero, which was the villain? Of course, it depends whom you ask. Neither had universal support, even from their own respective sides. Moderate Tories questioned the extent of the pit closures and the actions of the police, in particular the Home Secretary's own unit, known as Armstrong's Army, which had, during the strike, arguably become a direct instrument of the State. Nine months into the strike, former Conservative Prime Minister Harold Macmillan, by then the Earl of Stockton, and once described by post-war Labour Prime Minister Clement Attlee as "by far the most radical man I've known in politics", made a notable speech in the House of Lords, lamenting the widening divisions within the country:

"...It breaks my heart to see — and I cannot interfere — what is happening in our country today. This terrible strike, by the best men in the world, who beat the Kaiser's and Hitler's armies and never gave in. It is pointless, and we cannot afford that kind of thing... Then there is the growing division of comparative prosperity in the South and an ailing North and Midlands. We used to have battles and rows, but they were quarrels. Now there is a new kind of wicked hatred that has been brought in by different kinds of people..."

Mr Scargill himself had strong critics within both the union movement and the Labour Party, particularly Michael Foot's successor as leader, Neil Kinnock, who remained consistently critical of the absence of a national ballot, stating, "A ballot would have been won for the strike. What it would have done is guarantee unity right across the mining labour force. The strike was ruined the minute it was politicised, and in the mind of Arthur Scargill it was always a political struggle... He fed himself the political illusion that as long as the miners were united, they had the right to destabilise and overthrow the democratically elected government. The miners didn't deserve him; they deserved much, much better. My view is Margaret Thatcher and Arthur Scargill deserved each other. But no-one else did."

Whether the two main protagonists deserved each other or not, by any objective evaluation, the end of the strike signalled a crushing defeat for Mr Scargill and, by default, for the wider trade union movement; a comprehensive final victory for the forces of Thatcherism. Although opinion polls continued to seesaw back and forth between both major parties, it was clear that the victors enjoyed strong public support. But, when the victory celebrations died down, and the harsh reality of the aftermath was there to be confronted in real human terms, what was the true cost of victory, or the real price of defeat? To take from an old Chinese proverb, one might argue that it is still too early to say.

A freer market generally, and a more democratic system of industrial relations? Perhaps. But to achieve this, was the breakdown of trust between many communities and their police a price worth paying? And what about the lives lost on and near the picket lines? Let us also consider the economic and social devastation that befell pit villages and towns where the dominant employer was the mine, many of which progressively fell silent under the National Coal Board's programme of closures. Labour MP Austin Wells, then a senior NUM spokesman, often referred to the knock-on effect; that for every one hundred mining jobs lost around eighty to ninety others would follow, in related industries and in mining communities. He argued that the cost of closing pits was greater than for subsidising them to remain operating. Mrs Thatcher unsurprisingly maintained the opposite view, stating; "I'm always sympathetic, of course, about the loss of jobs. But, how are you going to get new jobs in coal? You're not going to get it by keeping open pits which put up the price of coal for all that wish to buy it." Mrs Thatcher also defended her resolute stance, alleging that the NUM had been hijacked by a "ruthless manipulating few". On the subject of negotiations with union leadership, she said, "I will never negotiate with people who use coercion and violence to achieve their objective. They are the enemies of democracy; they are not interested in the future of democracy; they're trying to kill democracy for their own purpose."

Political and ideological arguments all ultimately became academic. The reality of the Government-National Coal Board victory could not be denied. The industrial war might have been over, but the legal fight was just beginning. The ensuing court cases would expose injustice and police malpractice on a scale not seen since the dark days of institutionalised corruption surrounding the West End rackets, or what had more recently been exposed by Operation Countryman. A number of stellar reputations would be severely dented, none more so than that of Metropolitan Police Commissioner, "Honest Ron" Coburn.

Although he would remain the perpetual shining hero of the business lobby and the driest factions of the Tory Party, Home Secretary Sir Norman Armstrong's stubborn defence of the indefensible would lead to his increasing unpopularity throughout the country, as the government rampaged towards its troubled, third and final term in power...

From:
A New Britain — Thatcher and the End of Consensus (Volume III) by Alf Burton
© 1994 Donoghue Publishing and Broadcasting

CHAPTER ONE
SPRING 1985

Gwynne Fielding, a steadfast and dedicated lawyer, whose already crippling workload and anxiety levels were increasing exponentially as the first of the Orgreave trials rapidly approached, was far more used to spending time inside Her Majesty's Prisons than Alf Burton was. She therefore took the security checks, the rather cold, unwelcoming demeanour of the officers, and the dank, depressing nature of the surroundings in her stride. The outer door closed behind them with a loud and ominous, echoing clang; followed by another, and then another, prompting Alf to gulp. A man could easily disappear in a place like this without trace, he contemplated, earnestly hoping that the guards would remember to let them out at the end of their visit. How people lived and worked in these conditions, day in, day out, was beyond him.

Gwynne was there to visit her client, Garry Parker, a former miner from Headleyton, a pit village that had fought an ultimately unsuccessful battle against the closure of their mine, the economic and social heart of their community; and, like many others, was now facing a frighteningly bleak future. The strike itself might have been over, but its sinister shadow remained. Long standing, local family businesses were going to the wall one after the other, while the ranks of the skilled unemployed grew, and residual hatreds and animosities ate painfully away at the remnants of the once united community like an untreated cancer.

As Gwynne and Alf made to enter the visiting area, an officer stood in their way.

"I'm sorry, Miss Fielding, but I'm afraid it's just not possible," the officer stated firmly, standing in front of her with his arms folded.

"Actually, it's *Ms* Fielding, and I have a legal appointment with my client," she replied politely, but with equal inflexibility. "Surely I don't have to remind you —"

"I can't let you in, I'm sorry. The prison governor is on his way."

There followed a few moments of increasingly tense silence, during which Gwynne Fielding glared at the officer with such unrelenting intensity and personal rancour that Alf actually began to feel sorry for him.

The governor duly arrived, and Gwynne immediately turned her attention to him. "What's going on, Mr Barrett? I've booked this conference with my client in accordance with all the procedures, and I'd remind you even under this current government regime, prisoners on remand awaiting trial still have some rights. If you stand in my way, I'll have a court order before you can —"

"I'm not standing in the way of your legal appointment, Ms Fielding," Barrett assured her, holding up his hands; a gesture of peace in an attempt to stem the inevitable verbal onslaught, which he felt was just warming up. "But Mr Burton isn't on the list, I can't let him go in with you."

"He's here assisting me."

"I'm afraid I can't let him in."

Gwynne was about to open her mouth again, but Alf intervened. "Ah well, no bother," he replied, shrugging his shoulders. "Perhaps I could make a phone call, please, Governor?"

The governor had been warned not to underestimate Mr Burton, and not to be taken in by his generally dishevelled appearance and unthreatening demeanour of absent-minded, benign friendliness. "Mr Burton, I know you have a lot of influence; that you work for Sir Eddie Donoghue, and that you're friends with Commissioner Coburn, but the Metropolitan Police has no jurisdiction over these kinds of matters, inside HM Prisons. And neither does the media organisation that you work for, no matter how close your boss is to the government. Rules are rules. You can't just get around them by phoning up your powerful chums."

"Ha'way man, it's nowt like that," Alf reassured the prison governor with a kindly smile. "I just need to organise a lift back to the railway station. I don't want to cause any bother."

Governor Barrett sighed with relief. "Of course, come this way."

The three walked along the corridor, their footsteps echoing, to the governor's office.

"Just dial zero for the outside line," Barrett told him, handed him the receiver, and then made to leave.

"No need to gan away, Governor," Alf told him. "This isn't a private call."

He dialled, then waited a few seconds. "Ah, good morning, bonny lass. May I speak to Mr Davenport, please? It's Alf Burton speaking."

"Who's this Mr Davenport?" Barrett whispered to Gwynne Fielding.

"I'm not sure," she replied, "but I think we're both about to find out."

The Governor began to look a little nervous.

"Roger! What fettle, bonny lad? It's Alf. Is the Home Secretary available? He isn't? What about Mr Seymour? Miss Best? No? Oh well, not to worry." Governor Barrett appeared to relax, noting that neither Sir Norman Armstrong, his Special Minister of State nor his Parliamentary Private Secretary were going to take Alf's call. That'll teach him, the jumped-up Geordie tosser, coming in here and lording it all over... Then the governor's face fell, as Alf continued, "The Permanent Secretary is free? Champion! Can you put me through to Sir Godfrey please? Thanks, Roger. Tirra!"

Sir Godfrey Powell was also a name of which Governor Barrett was well aware. The permanent head of the Home Office, the most senior civil servant in that department, and more powerful, in some ways, than even the Home Secretary himself. When Alf greeted Sir Godfrey like an old friend, the Governor immediately realised the game was up. He offered a broad smile and a thumbs up.

"I'm terribly sorry to have troubled you, bonny lad," Alf said. "There's been a bit of a misunderstanding here, but it seems to have been resolved. Thanks for taking my call, and I'll be in touch about that other little matter soon."

Even Gwynne Fielding was impressed. She knew Alf by his reputation as a fearless, crusading journalist and political commentator, and had appreciated the support he'd given to her and her clients via his radio programme and widely read, influential newspaper columns. But this little exchange demonstrated just how close Alf still was to the very top. Clearly his personal friendships remained solid despite his ongoing and increasingly bitter ideological fight with the government, and she offered a silent prayer of thanks that he was on her side.

The governor summoned an officer to take Alf and Gwynne back to the visiting area to meet her client. Once he was alone, he closed his office door and immediately made a phone call.

"Sir Archie Prentice, please," he said as soon the call was answered, and waited anxiously to be put through.

***

Alf and Gwynne were shown to a table amongst several in the visiting area. As this was outside normal visiting times, the room was deserted. Within a few moments Garry Parker was escorted in and took his seat opposite.

"Garry, this is Mr Burton," Gwynne said, and the two men shook hands across the table.

"Oh aye, I know who you are," Garry replied. "Thanks for all you're doing for us, Mr Burton, on the radio and in the papers. And that documentary you made on the strike last year. Finally, the truth. I'll bet you copped it over that!" Alf nodded. If only you knew the half of it, he thought.

"How are you bearing up?" Gwynne asked.

"It's not so bad," Garry replied. "There are some good lads in my wing; we all get on fine. Everyone looks out for each other — it's a bit like being at the pit. It's not as bad as you might think, apart from the food, and being away from home. But it's much worse for the family on the outside."

"They're being taken care of, Garry, rest assured," Gwynne told him. "Austin Wells is making sure that they're getting regular food parcels and other necessaries. Remember the series of concerts late last year, by Austin's brother's rock band, the Forgotten North? A huge amount was raised; not just cash, but a lot of essentials were donated as well. There's still quite a war chest. Even though Austin is no longer working directly with the NUM, he's still taking a strong interest in welfare matters."

"The idea of charity goes against the grain, Miss Fielding. I've always paid my own way. Never had a day unemployed in my life."

"Everyone's in the same boat, Garry, man," Alf said. "All the old certainties are gone. Everyone just has to pull together now. There's nothing else for it."

"Well, if you say so, Mr Burton. Whatever can be done to take care of things at home, I'm grateful for. Miss Fielding knows that. I have my routine here, comforting in a way. It's funny how you find common ground with people that you would've run a mile from on the outside. There's a few right nutters." Garry looked around to see that they weren't being overheard by any hovering officers. "There's an old guy, must be seventy-five or even eighty. A real gentleman, nice to talk to. Loves old American cars, so we chat about them. So one day he says to me, 'Garry son, the thing that bugs me, is that I'm in this time on a sex offence. I'm not a nonce, after all, a man has his dignity. I mean, I done all them murders,' so I said, 'What you mean *all them* murders?'" Garry's sudden and raucous laugh reverberated in the empty visiting room. "So you see," he continued, "the bugger's a serial killer, but he's all indignant about being fitted up as a nonce!" Garry laughed some more. "He also said to me, quite seriously, that if you want to get rid of a body, you plant a tree over it. And then there's the old professor, not sure what he's in for, reads a lot, he reckons that the bubonic plague is rife in Newcastle, but no one catches it because the rats only come out when everyone is asleep. And the blagger that told me that his first job was on a factory office, and he and his mate dropped the safe out of an upstairs window onto the back of the little lorry they'd stolen for the job. And the fucker went right through the back of the lorry and hit the ground, meaning they had to escape without the safe or their getaway lorry, on a pair of stolen bicycles!" Garry laughed again but stopped as he noticed that Gwynne Fielding was smiling politely, and that Alf's expression was hovering somewhere between puzzlement, pity and severe discomfort. Garry looked suddenly embarrassed. "I'm sorry, Miss Fielding, Mr Burton. Your sense of what's polite and what isn't tends to change, given the type of conversations you have in here. What's the line in that song by the Forgotten North? Something about resolution failing, moral compass bent. Second verse of *Winter of Discontent*. He's a great songwriter that Freddie Wells, better than that electronic shite and new romantic crap. Anyway, I think my moral compass might be bending slightly. I guess it's the company I keep." Garry stopped again. "I'm talking bollocks, sorry."

"You're just getting through your days as easily as you can, Garry, no one is judging," Gwynne reassured him. "It's the smart way to do it. I don't think there's anything wrong with your moral compass either."

"There's a few of life's little tragedies in here, Miss Fielding. Especially some of the younger lads. Never had a chance, some of the stories —"

"There's an old saying, Garry, I tell it to all my clients who find themselves banged up, whether for ten days or ten years. Do your own time and no one else's. It's very easy to get dragged into other people's problems; you just can't afford to let yourself become involved."

After a brief moment of brooding silence, Gwynne came to the point of their visit.

"It would help us, and you of course, Garry," she said, "if you would tell Alf the whole truth about what happened at the flyover that day. And who was there with you. Alf is going to do everything he can to help us, but he needs to be convinced that you're innocent; I've told him what I think, of course, but he needs to hear it from you. The best way to do this would be for you to tell him everything that you've told me. From the beginning."

Garry took a deep breath. "The lads heard that scab lorry drivers were going to crash the pickets at Headleyton Colliery, that afternoon," he explained. "I heard what was being planned; stupid and dangerous, I thought, so I drove to the flyover to try and talk the lads out of it. By the time I got there it was all over. The minicab was on its roof down the embankment, and there were two bodies on the grass by the car."

"What had happened?" Alf asked, although he already knew the answer.

"They saw the first lorry coming, it was a fair distance behind the cab. They balanced the lump of concrete on the safety rail of the bridge, but they couldn't hold it and it fell, hitting the minicab. They felt terrible, no one wanted this to happen. They just wanted to scare the shite out the scab-gobshite-bastard lorry driver."

Alf looked at Garry sceptically. A lump of concrete dropped on a busy road demonstrated much more sinister motives than just wanting to scare someone, he thought, but he allowed his expression to remain impassive. Garry himself realised that his tone had become angry and combative. He leaned back in his uncomfortable plastic chair and apologised again. "You have to understand that people weren't thinking straight. We were all skint, man. Going crackers. People weren't in their right minds."

"But you initially told the polis that you were never there at all, on the flyover," Alf countered. "Now you're saying you *were* there, but not until after the concrete block had already been dropped."

"Aye. That's the truth of it."

"What did you do then?" Alf asked.

"Told the lads to make themselves scarce. Then so did I."

"When did the polis feel your collar?"

"Not for weeks, just after Orgreave, it was."

"Were you there? At Orgreave?"

"I was with the flying pickets. I got away down the railway embankments just as the heavy mob were heading towards the village."

Alf had also been at Orgreave, with his film crew. It still kept him awake nights. "Back to the Headleyton incident. Why did the polis get you in the end, and none of the others?"

"I couldn't say."

"Why were there no other witnesses?" Alf asked. "There must have been traffic going past on the flyover itself. They would have been close enough to get a good look at your faces and easily recognise who was there."

"There was a detour. The flyover was closed to traffic because of cracks in the concrete," Garry explained. "It was built a few years ago by a London firm, Donoghue Constructions. They build tower blocks and office high-rises mostly. Most of them get condemned very soon after they're built, from what I hear."

Alf nodded. Several years ago, he had written a series of articles exposing the corruption of local authorities by Donoghue bagmen, and the second-rate, cheaply built structures that inevitably followed. Donoghue Constructions was a division of the same conglomerate that also controlled Donoghue Publishing and Broadcasting, Alf's direct employer. However, as Sir Eddie Donoghue steadfastly refused to interfere in the editorial stance of his newspapers, radio and television stations, on the occasions that Alf's investigations exposed some of his own company's shortcomings, the tycoon just had to grin and bear it.

"This is where it gets a little murky," Gwynne Fielding interrupted, consulting some notes in her file. "There are statements from two police officers that place Garry on the flyover when the concrete was dropped."

"Bollocks," Garry said. "There were nae polis anywhere near. I should know. I was looking out for them the whole time. And if they were close enough to recognise me, why didn't they arrest me, and the other lads, right away? And why didn't they go to help the lads in the accident? There was nae polis anywhere, I'm certain of it."

"I still don't understand how the polis came to arrest you, and no one else," Alf persisted.

"I don't rightly know. One day I just opened my front door, and the next thing I know I'm in the back of the van on the way to the station, with a black eye and split lip for my trouble."

"Do you know if they were local officers?"

"They weren't. The local lads had been going around asking questions, but no one was talking. Don't get me wrong, there was a lot of sympathy for the cab driver; he was a local as well, born and bred. Not quite so much for the undercover copper though. The local force was obviously making no progress, so the flying squad was called in. You know, the ones they call Armstrong's Army. They marched in like a bunch of Saturday night yobs and the next thing I know, I'm on the way to the nick."

"What are the charges again?" Alf asked, directing his question to Gwynne.

"Two counts of murder," Gwynne told him, "but the CPS are already talking about accepting a plea for manslaughter; if Garry gives up the other people on the bridge. Oh yes, and they've also thrown in their old favourite, riot, for good measure."

"Life sentences, however it turns out," Garry said, his shoulders sagging as the true nature of his predicament was laid out before him in chilling, clinical reality.

Following their meeting — the officers did remember to let them out, much to Alf's relief — Gwynne drove him to the station to catch his train back to London.

"Do you believe him?" Gwynne asked.

"No," Alf replied. "If you just want to scare someone, you smash their car windows, or slash the tyres when it's parked in the street and they're safely asleep inside their house. We saw a lot of that during the strike, as you know. You don't drop a thumping great block of concrete onto a busy bypass road during peak traffic. What did they think was going happen?"

"I mean, do you believe his story that he didn't arrive on the flyover until afterwards?"

"I'm not convinced," Alf admitted. "But you clearly are."

"There's a disturbing pattern with some of these police statements," she replied. "I'm seeing it with the Orgreave files as well. I'll have a better idea once we have the officers concerned on the stand for cross-examination. I've got my clients a great silk named Valerie Smedley."

"What do you mean by a disturbing pattern?"

"I think some of them don't reflect the whole truth of what happened," Gwynne said.

"Tactfully put," Alf said, then countered, "but it's a big chance to take. If they're making things up, they risk perjury charges, surely?"

"I think it's a tactic, Alf, particularly in Garry's case. I don't think there were police anywhere near the flyover. I think that the police plan was to wear him down over the twelve months and more between his arrest and his trial, hoping he'd lose his nerve and give up the names of the others. Then they'd withdraw the murder charges and accept a guilty plea for riot. Either way, as Garry pointed out, it's a potential life sentence."

Alf recalled the legal definition of riot as articulated by the Home Secretary himself, for Alf's highly controversial television documentary of the Miners' Strike that had been aired on nationwide television late the previous year. Another of his efforts that had made life deeply uncomfortable for his friend and employer, Sir Eddie Donoghue, who otherwise enjoyed a close and mutually advantageous relationship with the Conservative government.

"A riot," Sir Norman Armstrong had read in a prepared statement, "is where three or more people gather and have in their minds a common purpose they intend to achieve by the use of force, behaving to terrorise someone of ordinary strength of character."

A concrete block dropped through your windscreen neatly fits into that definition, Alf thought. One way or the other, Garry's goose was well and truly cooked. Reflecting on Garry's prison anecdotes, he asked, "Do they normally put remand prisoners in with serial murderers?"

"They can do anything they want to do," Gwynne replied, thought for a moment, then continued. "Alf, I know how well connected you are. Is there anything you can tell me that you think might help? The Orgreave trials are almost upon us; then Garry's is soon after. I feel that I'm running out of time, and the stakes are so high."

Alf could sympathise with Gwynne, whom he'd first met at the Rotherham Police Station on the evening following the Orgreave confrontations, and there had been an immediate mutual liking and professional respect between them. Her Orgreave defendants were also facing riot charges, with potential life sentences, and Gwynne was feeling the crushing burden of responsibility. Their lives were very much in her hands.

"I would've cracked up months ago if I was doing your job, bonny lass," Alf told her, and received a faint smile in return. Alf weighed up carefully what he could tell her.

By now they had arrived at the railway station and were sitting shoulder to shoulder in Gwynne's Mini Clubman. It started to rain.

"Strictly between us, and off the record."

"Of course," Gwynne replied.

"I'm not sure just how receptive to any kind of deal the government is going to be over Garry's case. The undercover police officer that was killed along with the cab driver was the former bodyguard of Sir Norman Armstrong himself."

"My God!" Gwynne gasped. "The Home Secretary's own security man?"

"I'm afraid so. He was very well liked by all the senior Home Office politicians and officials. And also by at least one very senior and powerful civil servant, the administrator of a department that no one acknowledges actually exists, if you get my meaning. Have you ever heard of Sir Archie Prentice?"

"No," Gwynne replied.

"Almost nobody has," Alf replied. "But I've learned, over the years, not to underestimate what he, and certain parts of the government, are capable of. I only mention him, Gwynne lass, to emphasise how important it is that you be very careful. With whom you meet, and in what you say to people. Be particularly careful about what you say on the phone. To tell you the truth, you're probably not doing yourself any favours by being in my company."

Gwynne found herself scanning the station car park through the windows, which she noticed with some amusement had fogged up, as if they were two breathless teenagers parked up for a quiet snog. Were they being watched, even now? Gwynne only just managed to stem tears of hopelessness and felt every ounce of the weight of her responsibilities. Not only was the late detective a favourite of the Home Secretary, whose personal and political power just seemed to grow unchecked, but was also very well placed within the hierarchy of the security services. These were the last people you wanted to make real enemies of, she reflected ruefully, although it was now probably too late for both of them on that score.

"So," Gwynne contemplated, her steady voice in stark contrast to how she felt. "They'll be in no mood for mercy. There'll be no favourable sentencing recommendation from the CPS under any circumstances."

"No."

"And we're bound to end up with a pro-police, anti-union Tory judge. It'll be a fix. It's inevitable."

"I can't disagree."

"How much do you know about the police unit, Armstrong's Army?"

"No more than you, bonny lass. They're made up from officers drawn from a number of forces, to be deployed, as we've seen close up, at the Home Secretary's discretion. I've been told there's a secret operations manual that has been drawn up, setting out military-style tactics and methods in extensive detail. I'm trying to get hold of a copy, but so far I haven't had any luck. I was hoping that a young police officer I met at Orgreave would make contact, off the record, but he never did."

"Why would he want to talk to you?" Gwynne asked.

"I stopped him from knocking the shite out of a young woman who was helping an injured man on the roadside. Then he was about to have a crack at my film crew. And me. I managed to talk him down. He was in a hell of a mess, you could tell. He was caught up in the overwhelming atmosphere of violence, as if he'd lost control of himself. When he started to calm down, he seemed to be appalled at what he, and his marras, were doing. I gave him my card, but he never made contact."

"Could you identify him? Did you happen to get his number?" Gwynne felt she was probably clutching at the last elusive straw, but to be able to flip a police officer and get some inside information, testimony even, would be just too wonderful for words. To have actual, credible confirmation of what they suspected; what they knew was going on, and to have him in court under oath, with Valerie Smedley's forensic cross-examination —

"None of the Armstrong's Army lads had their numbers visible," Alf replied. "They weren't that silly."

"I know. I was just hoping against hope," Gwynne replied, deflated.

"A senior officer from Thames Valley was brought in last year, my sources tell me," Alf continued, "on the request of the Met Commissioner, to try and bring them into line. Even within the government there were concerns that they were becoming a law unto themselves."

"A lot of good that did," Gwynne scoffed. "They're worse than ever. So much for Commissioner 'Honest Ron' Coburn and his lifelong mission against police misconduct. All this is happening right under his nose. He's either complicit, or if he's not, he's too stupid to see the reality."

"I've known Ron Coburn for years, since the sixties, when as a young DCI he took on the Soho crime barons and galloping corruption within the Met. He's certainly not stupid, and I don't believe he's complicit."

"I suppose he has to answer to the Home Secretary, Armstrong," Gwynne commiserated. "I can't think that it would be easy, having to work for that inhuman monster."

"Actually, Sir Norman's not like that at all. I've known him for thirty-five years, ever since he was first elected in 1950, and I was an angry, Tory-hating young lobby correspondent. We hit it off straight away. In a manner of speaking."

"Oh sorry, Alf. No offence intended. Of course, you're a friend of the family. You introduced me to his son at the benefit concert at Headleyton."

"None taken, bonny lass. None taken. We used to be very good friends, Norman and I, as strange as that sounds; an old socialist like me and the hardest of hard-line Thatcherites."

"The quintessential odd couple, if ever there was one. Did you say used to be?"

"We fell out last year. We're back on speaking terms, more or less, but it hasn't been the same. It's just that... since Brighton —" Alf took a moment to compose himself. It was hard to talk about this even now, many months on. "Since his wife, Eileen, Lady Armstrong, was killed in the bombing, he's changed, for the worse. He was always tough, always blindly conservative in every sense, infuriatingly so. Thatcherism really is his religion. But underneath, there was, is, a decent man, and a good friend. Unfortunately, now —"

Gwynne remembered the news coverage of the IRA bombing of the Conservative Party conference the previous October. She also remembered the Prime Minister's defiant speech afterward, and as much as she despised Mrs Thatcher and everything that she, and Sir Norman, stood for, there was no doubt about the Prime Minister's strength and leadership. If only they could incorporate some compassion and humanity at the same time, she thought.

Gwynne also reflected on the news coverage of the deaths and injuries at the Grand Hotel. Lady Eileen Armstrong had been fêted as a tireless worker in her husband's own constituency, a loving wife, mother and grandmother; with a commitment to her local community that had transcended politics and attracted friends and admirers everywhere she went. Alf had written a loving obituary in his regular newspaper column, *Westminster Watch*, and Gwynne could see that his own feelings of loss were still raw. Lady Eileen Armstrong was, by all accounts, a beautiful person in every sense. Perhaps Alf was right. The Home Secretary couldn't be such a monster after all, if someone like Lady Eileen could have loved him for forty years, and Alf Burton could be his friend for almost as long.

"How is Rick taking it?" she asked.

"Very, very badly. He and his wife Sally had just welcomed their second child, only a couple of months before the bombing. I don't believe he's spoken to his father very much, if at all, since the funeral. He's taken his family off to Australia while he's personally supervising the Forgotten North's tour, which I think then goes on to New Zealand. I don't think Rick plans to be back much before the end of summer." Gwynne reflected on the unexpected human face of what, on the surface, appeared a wholly inhuman government.

So, she contemplated, as she watched Alf's train disappear into the mist from the deserted platform; her clients fighting for their very lives; a merciless, enraged, grief-stricken Home Secretary intent on revenge, and the might of the entire government, including a fanatical, Machiavellian intelligence boss, lined up against them.

"No pressure," she sighed, and walked back to her car as the rain got heavier.

CHAPTER TWO

It was generally unheard of for a senior civil servant to give private, off the record briefings to lobby correspondents, but when Alf Burton arrived at 50 Queen Anne's Gate, he was immediately ushered into the private office of the Permanent Secretary of the Home Office, Sir Godfrey Powell.

"It's good of you to spare me the time, Sir Godfrey," Alf said as soon as they were seated at a conference table adjacent to the Permanent Secretary's own oversized desk.

"I think you'd better just call me Godfrey."

"Thank you, I will."

"And I think I should be thanking you, for sparing *me* the time." A not entirely comfortable silence fell, as they carefully considered how best to move things forward. The matter that brought them together on this particular morning, although deeply personal for Sir Godfrey, could have much wider ramifications. Both were aware of the significance and, despite their combined experience, peerless professional reputations and undisputed individual courage, were feeling the heavy burden of responsibility; combined with a nervous foreboding of future unknowns.

"Your little problem, or obstacle, the other day," Godfrey asked, for no other reason than to start the conversation flowing. "I take it, whatever it might have been, was resolved satisfactorily in the end?"

"Oh aye. Just disappeared as soon as you answered the phone, funnily enough."

"Good, good." Godfrey knew perfectly well that Alf had visited Garry Parker along with the troublesome, firebrand solicitor Gwynne Fielding. Not only had he seen the government surveillance reports but had received a rather testy phone call from Sir Archie Prentice. The call had been polite because Sir Godfrey's senior position meant that even shadowy manipulators and blackmailers like Prentice had to tread carefully. When the intelligence chief had asked what Burton had been playing at, and why Sir Godfrey had been phoned in the first place, the Permanent Secretary politely but firmly instructed Prentice to mind his own business. It wasn't a phrase the intelligence chief heard too often, but in this case there was nothing he could do.

As a courtesy, Sir Godfrey went on to inform the Home Secretary, who surprisingly didn't seem too displeased at all that his old friend and RAF Commanding Officer had been put in his place. Sir Godfrey also confided some personal matters and received a discreet blessing from Sir Norman to proceed as he thought best.

"Perhaps, as you were the one who asked to see me, Alf," Godfrey encouraged, "you should open the batting, as it were."

"Good idea, bonny lad," Alf replied, relieved. "Obviously everything is off the record. You have my word that anything we talk about today will be in the strictest confidence."

"I have no doubt of that."

"And also," Alf continued, "I'm not quite sure how to put this, but I promise that I'll be discreet. I'm aware that certain people are keeping, shall we say, a fatherly eye on me at the moment, if you get my meaning."

The two men shared the smile of fellow conspirators. "I understand," Sir Godfrey assured him. "Let me just say, that I wouldn't entrust this to anyone else."

"I appreciate that, Sir Godfrey, that is, Godfrey, bonny lad. Okay then. Let's bash on. Our mutual friend, Commodore O'Malley, related to me the suspicions of your father, God rest him, regarding the death of your elder brother during the war."

"How is the Commodore, by the way?" Godfrey asked.

"In cracking fettle," Alf replied. "Looks and acts ten years younger, since he married Florrie Tweedle."

"I'm glad to hear it," Godfrey replied. "I think my father was worried that Florrie might prove a little too much for him. Please pass on my best when next you see them."

"I'll be sure to do that, Godfrey, man."

Godfrey stood up, walked the short distance to his desk, and gathered up a sheaf of handwritten pages. He handed them to Alf. "For reasons that I think will become very clear, I won't allow these papers to leave my office. But I'm perfectly happy for you to read them here and make whatever notes you think necessary."

"Champion. And don't worry, my shorthand is unintelligible to anyone but me. It sometimes even confounds me, to tell you the truth."

Alf read through the papers carefully, making his scribbly notes as he went. While he was concentrating, Godfrey made a quick phone call, then returned to the conference table and waited patiently for Alf to finish.

"Do you have enough to be getting on with?" Godfrey asked, as soon as Alf closed his notebook.

"Oh aye, most definitely. Is there anything you'd like to add?"

"I don't think so," Godfrey replied.

"Very good. Now I won't be working on this full time, of course."

"Of course. You're heavily committed, between your radio programme, newspaper columns and investigative work. I'm aware that you're very good at playing the long game. So am I."

Alf smiled. "Well, I've been working on this for thirty-four years, on and off. By the way, as much as I think I'd quite enjoy your company, it's probably best that we don't meet too often."

"I was thinking the same thing."

"I suggest that if we really need to speak face to face, we coordinate a visit out to Stonebridge House and catch up with Jim and Florrie O'Malley. Otherwise I can get a message to you using Sir Eddie's personal driver. He's one hundred percent reliable, and discreet. I borrow him for special jobs, from time to time."

"Agreed," said the Permanent Secretary, and the two men rose and shook hands. "Oh, and by the way," Godfrey continued. "I thought it might be prudent for you to have a pretext for being here, so I made sure that Miss Best would be available for an interview. She's in her office now."

"Champion. Now, there's just one small thing that you might be able to do, to help set the wheels in motion, like."

Godfrey listened to Alf's request. "I'm sure that won't be a problem," he said, and made a short note on his writing pad. "Just one more thing, Alf. Off the record."

"Oh aye?"

"These trials coming up. The Orgreave rioters and then the Garry Parker murder trial. How are things looking, do you think? For us here at the Home Office?"

"Off the record, and speaking frankly," Alf replied, "there will be some questions raised over the, shall we say, accuracy, of the police statements. My opinion, for what it's worth, is that the Orgreave lads will get off. Riot charges were a massive overreach. I'm not so sure about Parker though. I haven't made up my mind about him."

"I see."

"The biggest problems for your department will arise as much from the Home Secretary's own behaviour, as from the polis. As you know, Godfrey, Norman and I have been friends since 1950, so I mean no disrespect when I say this. It was very unwise of him to be so closely associated with the Orgreave battles. Actually, it was plain crackers. *The Sun* might have loved it, the Home Secretary at the front of the police lines like a modern-day Churchill, in riot gear, made a memorable front page, but the rest of the country isn't so sure. And he shouldn't have been making prejudicial public statements about the charges while the matter was still pending. I did warn him. More than once. I'm sure that the defence will be arguing in court that he's nullified the defendants' chances of a fair trial. Gwynne Fielding has said as much, publicly."

Godfrey thought carefully. "So, if you were the Home Office press secretary, what would you be advising?"

"Disband your flying squad, Armstrong's Army. They're a political liability, and, excuse my language, a bunch of out of control, bullying, violent, unaccountable bastards. And the true extent of their thuggish behaviour and procedural malpractices are going to be laid bare during the upcoming trials. The damage to Norman, Charles Seymour and to Janice Best, as well as to Commissioner Coburn's reputation for honesty and fighting corruption, is going to be devastating. Their reputations are going to be left in tatters, unless you act now. I would go so far as to say that Janice will struggle to hold on to her seat at the next election. Get ahead of the game. Set up an independent, public inquiry. The outcome won't be pretty, but at least you'll be able to say that it was your own initiative. It might go some way to minimising the damage."

The Permanent Secretary nodded thoughtfully. "Thank you, Alf. I'll consider it. That is, I'll consider passing on your suggestion to the Home Secretary."

"Best leave me well out of it," Alf advised. As he stood up to leave the office, he hesitated, and said, "I haven't really spoken to Norman since... I've phoned him at Knightsbridge a couple of times, but I got the impression he really didn't want to talk. Is he, that is, how is he...? Is he going all right, do you think? Considering."

"It's hard to say," Sir Godfrey replied. "He's working harder than ever; very much on top of things, as you would expect. He's still very polite and considerate to the staff, although more demanding, I think. But there's something not quite right. It's as if he's closed the shutters and won't let anyone see in."

"I just wish I could do something to help," Alf lamented.

"We all do, but I think the best we can do is to keep doing our jobs and be there for him if and when he needs us. Sir Dick Billings, of all people, seems to be getting through to him, and offering support, as far as he can."

Alf nodded. "And another thing," he added. "No one has seen too much of Norman in the past few months. Officially, I mean. It's understandable, of course, but people are starting to think that Charles Seymour is the Home Secretary. Charles is a smooth operator, but always comes across as cold and calculating. And superior. Norman is a much better communicator, and people tend to warm to his avuncular toughness in a way that they never would with Seymour. I think if Norman could take on a higher public profile, it might not be too late to turn things around, politically."

Godfrey nodded his agreement, as Alf continued. "Look, if you can convince Norman to come on my show, I'll give him a good run. I won't go easy, but I'll give him a little elbow room, to get himself back into the saddle, before I wind him up. Then we can have a good old set-to, on the radio, just like the old days. Blow out a few cobwebs. It might be just what he needs."

"I'll pass it on."

"Thanks, Godfrey." Thoughts of his old friend, and Eileen, had dampened his mood. Alf bade a melancholy farewell to the Permanent Secretary, then went off to meet with Sir Norman's Parliamentary Private Secretary, Janice Best.

Sir Godfrey walked to the window and gazed distractedly out. There was no chance of disbanding Armstrong's Army in the foreseeable future, he thought. They were about to move their operations north, to Tyneside, and the Speers-Donoghue shipyard. Within the next few weeks, secret plans for massive, progressive job losses were to be made public. The active and famously militant Amalgamated Fitters and General Shipyard Workers Union was, without doubt, going to fight back with everything at their disposal, and the baton-wielding skirmishers of the Home Secretary's flying squad were going to be once again on the frontline.

"God help the workers," Godfrey muttered. "And God help us as well." He returned to his desk, and to more pressing problems, a multitude of which confronted the head of a major government department each and every hour of every day. But there was one in particular. Sir Archie Prentice himself. Sir Godfrey was aware that Sir Norman had been urging the Cabinet Secretary, Sir Peregrine Walsingham, to do something to at least try to rein in the intelligence chief's most egregious excesses; in particular, his obsession with phone tapping and generally eavesdropping on just about anyone who was exercising their democratic right and opposing the government. This, of course, included a number of prominent NUM officials, including Arthur Scargill, Austin Wells and Kim Howells; media personalities like Alf Burton and Roland Moreland; and probably Labour MPs Tony Benn, Terry Patchett, Don Dixon and God only knew who else. Godfrey was a realist, and understood as much as the next senior civil servant that these tactics were necessary in the interests of national security. He fully agreed with the Home Secretary's frequently stated mantra, that the national interest trumps everything. But in Godfrey's judgement, Sir Archie was becoming a dangerous menace, and now his unconstrained bungling had nearly created a scandal of monumental proportions, engulfing the government's sequestration agent and their search for funds the National Union of Mineworkers had apparently hidden offshore following adverse court judgements, in order to evade the Treasury confiscators.

In the course of events, Sir Archie's small army of earwiggers and lurking peeping toms had uncovered where, and under what false identities, certain NUM funds had been secretly stashed. What followed was, in Godfrey's view, a harebrained scheme of epic stupidity, and how someone as measured and careful as the Cabinet Secretary had got mixed up in it remained a mystery.

Sir Peregrine Walsingham and Sir Archie had paid a discreet visit to one of the senior partners in the City accounting firm tasked with the complicated job of untangling the NUM finances, and provided him with invaluable assistance toward following the missing money trail. They did not, of course, disclose how they had come by this helpful information. But the partner was no fool, and having promised his complete discretion, couldn't help excitedly telling his colleagues at the next partners' meeting how he was cooperating with not only the nation's most senior civil servant of all, but someone he was convinced was an actual, *genuine* spy! Suddenly, being a rather unremarkable number cruncher was in a different league of excitement and prestige altogether.

This breathless revelation in itself posed no real threat; the partners were all old school and unfailingly discreet, people the combative Chief Whip and Conservative Party Chairman, Sir Dick Billings, would have sneeringly derided as the "come dine at my club old boy types". But when the firm became embroiled in court proceedings in Dublin, in the course of their pursuit of one cache of NUM money, the judge began to ask some very pointed questions about just how the accountants had uncovered certain critical information in the first place. There suddenly loomed a very real danger that uncomfortable truths might have to be disclosed in open court. This was obviously fraught with all kinds of hazards; not only exposing the government's questionable tactics, but also the very existence of Archie's department which had, thus far and by some miracle, remained an intact secret, even after a number of his agents had been found to be cheerfully and blatantly cooperating with the Russians several years earlier.

The Cabinet Secretary had seen the danger immediately and was also very aware that they had potentially exposed the government, and the Prime Minister herself, to myriad political difficulties. Sir Peregrine duly circulated a confidential memo to a number of his close colleagues, in which he offered to take full responsibility, and be named publicly, thereby deflecting the blame from the Prime Minister and the Cabinet. Godfrey's own stake in these proceedings was high. Inasmuch as the Cabinet Secretary was there to support, advise and protect the Prime Minister, Sir Godfrey's own role was the same when applied to the Home Secretary, Sir Norman Armstrong. Not that Sir Norman needed protection from anyone, Godfrey mused, but he knew his responsibilities, and was determined that his own department, and Secretary of State, were going to come out of this mess unscathed.

Godfrey glanced again at the Cabinet Secretary's memo, which read:

"Although I'm not particularly concerned about my own name becoming public, I am mindful of the conclusions that may be drawn, not only by the government's political enemies but by the nation at large, about the involvement of Sir Archibald Prentice, and about the activities in which his department was engaged in connection with the NUM dispute. The case for legitimate use of interception to seek to discover what assistance the NUM was receiving from overseas in terms of the covert movement of funds could be easily made, but it would be more difficult to justify the use of information obtained by interception, to assist the searches of the sequestrators."

Sir Godfrey returned the memo to his top drawer and considered the measured use of massive understatement as Sir Peregrine had calmly laid out the political dangers caused by an unaccountable and apparently uncontrollable security service.

As usual, when crises reached the irrevocable point of extremis, the Home Secretary himself was called upon to do what he could. Had he still been Chief Whip, Sir Norman could have quietly slipped into Dublin, remaining there largely unnoticed while he set things to rights. As Home Secretary, this was going to be impossible, so it was decided, following discussions with Godfrey, and with Attorney-General Sir Michael Havers, that Sir Norman's talented Principal Private Secretary, Roger Davenport, would go instead, hold a meeting with lawyers on both sides, try to negotiate their way out of looming disaster, and see if some accommodation could be agreed upon to prevent delicate matters being aired in open court.

Fortunately, in the end, intervention was not required, thanks to the fact that lawyers for the NUM advised that there would now be a more cooperative approach toward the administrators' search for any offshore hidden funds, so matters were largely settled out of court, to everyone's intense relief. Sir Norman subsequently confided to his Permanent Secretary that this wasn't the first time that the chaps had been forced to rally around and rescue one of Sir Archie's ill-fated schemes that had gone belly-up and threatened to create a major public scandal.

Sir Godfrey's own patience was now finally running out, especially as he could see his own department being dragged into Archie's incompetent scheming with greater regularity. He was aware that some tact would be required; the Cabinet Secretary, Sir Norman Armstrong, Metropolitan Police Commissioner Ron Coburn and Archie himself were all RAF comrades from the war, and their tight little cabal was widely known as the Winged Mafia. He was also aware that very few people were brave enough to come out into open conflict with Prentice, as he had an extensive and wide-ranging dirt file on members of Her Majesty's Government, Opposition and Civil Service that made the one held by the Chief Whip look like a *Janet and John* story.

Fortunately for Sir Godfrey, both his personal and professional lives were without blemish, and therefore he was one of the few people at the top of government with nothing to fear. It was time, he now firmly believed, to take steps.

Not only was Prentice a serial blunderer, Godfrey thought indignantly, but one with such elevated self-importance that he felt sufficiently emboldened to ring Sir Godfrey himself, the Permanent Secretary of one of the top four government departments, and scold him like a schoolmaster telling off a rebellious boy, for accepting a phone call from Alf Burton. Godfrey wasn't having any part of that, feeling his anger rising at the mere memory. He picked up his telephone.

"The Cabinet Secretary, please," he instructed, and waited to be put through.

***

The top floor of Padraig Donoghue House, Fleet Street, contained the London studios of City Radio, as well as a television studio and control room. The TV studios were currently used for preparing London content for Donoghue Publishing and Broadcasting's regional ITV franchises, including a nightly political wrap for their local news services, prepared by national political editor Roland Moreland. They were soon going to be broadcasting into London itself through a new subscription cable television service, which after seemingly endless delays, arising from both technical and financial constraints, was soon going live. Or so frequent internal memos claimed.

One floor down was the executive floor. An entire corner was taken up by the inner sanctum of Sir Eddie Donoghue himself, where he was insulated from the world by a small army of personal assistants who allowed only a chosen few direct access. Sir Eddie's daughter, Erin, also worked in Eddie's private suite, which neighboured the boardroom, the executive dining room, and the offices of the Burton Unit, set up several months earlier for investigative and in-depth political reporting.

The remainder of the floor was taken up by Armstrong and Cox Public Relations, whose remit was to work almost exclusively for the Donoghue group, extolling the virtues of their construction, transport, shipping, and media divisions, as well as their struggling new airline, Erin Airways. Their small fleet was based at Birmingham Airport, the pride of which was a Boeing 747, previously owned by Freddie Laker and a progression of other airlines around the world, diminishing in size, importance, and financial stability, as the jet had aged. Erin Airways was currently flying a small number of

Mediterranean routes to tourist destinations but was struggling to break even. Customer satisfaction generally remained low, due to frequent delays and cancellations as the second, third and fourth-hand fleet could barely keep up with the schedule and required constant attention by engineers. Sir Eddie's efficiency consultant, Chester "The Chainsaw" Peacock, already living up to his name by relentlessly and ruthlessly trimming expenditure right across the group, was insisting that Erin Airways needed to be flying out of Heathrow, across the Atlantic, to survive. Sir Eddie's close personal friend, Sir Dick Billings, the Conservative Party Chairman and Chief Whip, was lobbying hard to expedite the privatisation of British Airways to level the competitive playing field, and in the meantime, to provide Erin Airways with coveted slots at Heathrow. Sir Dick's critics, and he had many even on his own side of politics, now openly referred to him as the Secretary of State for Eddie Donoghue. Any criticism was, of course, done in whispers, as Dick, an energetic octogenarian and Father of the House, was powerful, relentlessly confrontational, perpetually ill-tempered and rigidly unforgiving; while Sir Eddie was the largest individual donor to the Conservative cause, and an employer of many, many thousands across his various businesses.

One floor down from the lavishly decorated and equipped executive offices was the much more modestly appointed, and significantly more cramped, editorial floor. Projecting a general air of being under siege, the perpetual haze of cigarette smoke, orders constantly barked across the room; the noise of clattering typewriters, word processors and telexes, and the almost constant jangling of telephones made it not a workplace for the faint of heart. From here, the Donoghue broadsheet, the

Daily Focus, was produced seven days a week, and shipped nationwide, along with packaged London and foreign news for a number of local smaller circulation papers around the country. The journalists, editors and sub-editors worked in a labyrinth of partitioned cubicles, the largest of which was occupied by Roland Moreland, whose own editorial responsibilities encompassed the entire media group's political coverage.

Roland had just completed scripting his summary of London political news and was due upstairs at the studio for a pre-record that afternoon, but first, he was due at a lunch meeting in the executive dining room. Other invitees were Erin Donoghue, Alf Burton, and Terry Cox, joint managing director of Armstrong and Cox PR. Sitting next to Eddie, Roland noted with interest as he entered the dark panelled plushness of the dining room, was Sir Dick Billings himself.

As soon as lunch was served, they were left alone. As usual, the commanding portrait of Padraig Donoghue, Sir Eddie's father and from whose stable of influential newspapers the current multibillion pound group of Donoghue companies had evolved, regarded them suspiciously from the wall beyond the head of the long table.

"Thanks for coming," Sir Eddie said genially. "Do you have everything you need?"

"There's no brown sauce," Alf observed.

"Oh, sorry, Alf." Eddie obligingly used the intercom to order the missing condiment and, knowing Alf's propensity for unintentionally spraying sauce around like a garden sprinkler, also called for a number of additional napkins. With lunch served, and wine bottles available on the table, Sir Dick having placed one next to his own glass for easily available refills, Eddie got straight to the point.

"I need to tell you all about something that we're about to announce publicly. It's extremely important that none of this leaks before the official announcement in a couple of days. Do I have your solemn promise that you'll honour this?" Eddie looked around at the gathering, and all those present nodded their assent.

"Right. This is not easy. It's not easy to talk about, and it won't be easy to do. But there's no alternative. The long-term survival of our group depends on it." Eddie took a deep breath. "We're restructuring the shipyard. The first phase will be the cancellation of the nightshift and the outsourcing of a number of non-core manufacturing areas. During the course of this year we intend to shed three thousand jobs, and probably the same again next year, leaving a workforce of just over two thousand, while we introduce greater automation and improve efficiencies and work practices. Now, this is going to create a number of challenges. As you know, towards the end of 1983, we had plans to close the yard entirely and redevelop the site. For a number of reasons this did not occur. Now that we're more or less stuck with the yard, we need to make changes. It's old, overstaffed and outdated. We all know that it's been a very difficult couple of years; I don't mind telling you that there were times I wondered if we'd be able to keep it all going. But we've turned the corner, our future is looking very bright, but the consequences are that we need to be guided by Mr Peacock's recommendations."

Alf nodded ruefully. He was well aware that the large number of banks up to their eyes in Eddie's struggling, debt-ridden conglomerate had made it a condition of their ongoing support that Chester Peacock be brought in to consult on cuts and efficiencies. You don't have a lad nicknamed "The Chainsaw" running riot without blood being spilt along the way, he reflected.

"Now, these manpower reductions are going to be a challenge to manage," Eddie continued. "The dynamic is very different this time, because, unlike our intentions last time, the yard is not closing altogether. We need to keep it working. There's a lot at stake at the minute. We have the MoD contracts in the form of the fisheries protection vessels, as well as a new container ship and tanker for our own line, and a major refit of our last cruise liner, the *Calcutta Queen III*. With so much money around, the market for custom-made ocean-going yachts is also really taking off — all the new yuppie millionaires and even billionaires want one to show off."

And no doubt use as some kind of tax avoidance scam, Alf thought bitterly, as he dabbed at some brown sauce he'd spilt on the highly polished tabletop. Cruising the oceans in pampered luxury at the expense of the poor sods working every hour God sent to put food on the table. Three and half million unemployed in this country, probably more, and this is what it's come to —

"We've taken our first order," Eddie continued, "and once she's launched, the next client will want one bigger and better, and more expensive; it's human nature. For the first time in years, I genuinely think the yard has a future for the long term. It's been there for one hundred and forty-five years; it could very well be there for another hundred and forty-five, but not with its current structure. The union is going to do everything they can to fight against us."

"The government, and the Prime Minister personally, are right behind you on this, Eddie," Sir Dick said, as he hacked his way through a large, rare steak, washed down with frequent and noisy gulps from his wine glass. "I can tell you that the Ministry of Defence will stand by you, and will accept any delays resulting from industrial action in the interests of the wider benefits of another union being fucked right royally up the —" Dick stopped himself, suddenly remembering that Erin Donoghue was present. "What I mean to say, is, another bunch of parasite bolshie revolutionaries getting what's coming to them." Dick pointedly looked in Alf's direction with a superior smile and emptied his glass again. "In addition to this," Dick continued, "Charles Seymour at the Home Office has promised —"

"Thanks, Dick," Eddie interrupted, and hastily changed tack. The less said about Armstrong's Army the better at this stage, he thought. "This is how the announcement will be handled. There's a special board meeting tomorrow afternoon, where Mr Peacock will lay out the plans in detail, and the financial projections. The General Manager of the shipyard will be present and will be advised then and there. He'll handle the notification of employees at a local level. The following day, I'll go on the radio to make our public announcement. Roland, I'd be happy to pre-record an interview with you, which can then be broadcast through the City Radio network. I'll also do a sit-down in the studio for our regional TV news. Terry, I'll need your PR people to coordinate with the BBC, and also London Weekend or Thames, for any radio and television spots you can get me. Alf, I understand this is going to be personally awkward for you, given your family's connection with the yard, so I'd be happy for you to cover the union response and the local angle however you see fit. I understand we're going to take a beating, it's inevitable, which is why I'm going to take full, personal responsibility for the decision, in public. I'm just hoping, Alf, you'll be a little nicer to us that you were to the government over the Miners' Strike."

"Fat chance of that," Sir Dick mumbled. "Once a pinko union lickspittle —"

There was a ripple of quiet laughter. Alf's television documentary, *Strike!* had gone out the previous year and had resulted in a vicious backlash from the government and had, as a result, led to some very difficult times, personally and business-wise, for Sir Eddie. Alf himself had come under sustained attack, but despite his own crushing array of problems, Eddie had remained loyal throughout, refusing to throw his most senior reporter under the bus. "We fucking well stick together in this company," Eddie had assured his inner circle at a crisis meeting several months earlier.

Alf sighed. For better or worse, he owed his gaffer the same loyalty, whatever his personal feelings. Maybe his critics were right after all. Had he really sold his working-class, socialist soul? The Speers-Donoghue shipyard was in his own home town of Jarrow; generations of his family had worked there, and still did. Alf had thus far made an art form out of carefully managing his own divided loyalties, politically and personally. Of knowing when to keep his opinions to himself, no matter how difficult, for pragmatic reasons. Since the rippling aftermath of the Miners' Strike had proven to be far more devastating than even he had predicted, he was feeling increasingly conflicted and torn between two worlds. One was his northern working-class reality of a dying industrial heritage; closing pits and crumbling towns, unemployment, poverty, and a desperate longing to be back in the loving, protective embrace of Clement Attlee and Nye Bevan. The other was his own success, achieved through decades of hard work and commitment, and his place in the materialistic, false, rarefied world of conspicuous 1980s corporate excess. Like it or not, he was a spectacular success in Thatcher's Britain. Not unlike rising to the top in ancient Rome, he often thought, and with a comparable moral compass. We all know what happened there, he reflected. The Britain of the mid-1980s was like being on an out-of-control fairground ride. You couldn't make it stop, and you couldn't get off because it was going too fast. But at some point, the machinery was going to break up under the strain, throwing people high into the air, only to come crashing down onto hard ground. We'll all get it in the end, he thought gloomily, one way or the other. Only a matter of time.

Sir Eddie continued, "Any questions?"

There were none, and lunch concluded in a nervous silence. As they went their separate ways, Alf approached Sir Dick. "I understand you've been keeping an eye on Norman. How is he?"

"Who fucking well knows?" Dick grumbled. "He's shut everyone out. On the surface he's just the same. We've all tried, but even his little boys' club, the Winged Mafia, can't seem to break through." Dick glared at Alf for a brief moment. Eventually he said, "So I take it you're not having any more success than the rest of us?"

"I'm afraid not," Alf replied.

Dick reached across the table and picked up each wine bottle in turn, hoping to find some dregs to at least partially refill his glass. When he discovered they were all empty, he grunted with annoyance.

"Godfrey Powell suggested the best thing that we could do is just to keep doing our jobs, and be there for him if he needs us," Alf said.

Dick looked at Alf in surprise, and Alf regretted his indiscretion immediately. It was highly unusual for a journalist, even one as famous and successful as Alf, to have any contact with a senior civil servant. Officially, at least. This had made Dick suspicious, but Alf was relieved when he chose not to pursue it.

"Probably sound advice," Dick admitted, as they were approached by one of Eddie's assistants.

"Excuse me, Alf," she said, "Sir Dick, do you have time to see Sir Eddie in his office before you go?"

"Yes," Dick replied, "I'll be right there." He offered his wine glass to the assistant. "Any chance of another?" he asked hopefully.

"Before you go," Alf asked the Tory Chief Whip and Party Chairman, "I have a slot on my radio programme on Friday. Would you like to come on and discuss the current state of the opinion polls?"

"I'd rather stick burning splinters into my eyeballs, you pinko limp-dick," Sir Dick Billings growled, then set off for Eddie's office. Alf sighed. Like Christmas 1914 on the Western Front, the sweet, all-too-brief truce was over, and it was back to their respective trenches.

Not long after Alf had returned to his own office, he had a visit from Terry Cox, who was looking distinctly nervous.

"I'm not really sure what I should be doing about his," he confided. "Rick always handles this tricky political stuff. I just do fluff like grand openings and corporate booze-ups."

"Don't sell yourself short, bonny lad," Alf reassured him. "You've done great work for Erin Airways. That whole fiasco surrounding the emergency landing at Birmingham would have been much worse if not for your intervention."

"Well, thank you, but Rick knows exactly how to handle these controversial issues. He has all the contacts, and knows how to put a long campaign together much better than me. Look at his success with the Forgotten North. And their series of concerts raising money for the strikers; that was a masterclass in planning and implementation. I couldn't have done that. Erin is meeting with her dad this afternoon, to find out exactly what our role is going to be. I'm feeling a bit lost, to tell you the truth. Actually, I'm scared shitless."

Perhaps a bit more attention to work, and less attention to your conference room wine bar might be a good way to re-focus, Alf thought. Not to mention the constant parade of new secretaries and assistants whose roles seemed to involve little more than spending as much of the day as possible doing sod-all. And the twenty-four-hour-a-day party that seems to be going on in your offices, he contemplated further. But what went on behind the closed doors of the Armstrong and Cox suite was none of his business, Alf conceded inwardly. Money was being made hand over fist, and Rick clearly had no issue, as he been in contact only spasmodically over the previous months that he had been abroad.

"It's time Rick came home, for all kinds of reasons," Alf said. "Leave it with me. In the meantime, if you need any help, just ask."

When Terry had gone back to his own office, having been voluble in his gratitude, Alf reached into his desk drawer for a copy of the Forgotten North's Australian tour itinerary that Rick had given him before he left. He scanned the list of dates and venues: Thebarton Theatre, Adelaide, Festival Hall, Melbourne. Newcastle Working Men's Club — there's a nice little comforting piece of home on the other side of the world, he thought. Where in God's name was Wagga Wagga? Was that really a place after all? He remembered it as the home town of Tony Hancock's dopey Australian sidekick on the wireless, but always thought the name had been made up.

Alf observed that it was an uncharacteristically easy schedule, allowing for additional dates to be added along the way, interviews and television appearances, but more importantly, frequent opportunities to enjoy the clean white sand and blue surf of the Australian summer. It was a schedule designed by someone who wanted to spend as long as possible away from home. Understandable, Alf accepted, but even after the most heartbreaking of tragedies, life went on. Rick had responsibilities; it was time to re-join the human race. The summer was well and truly over, on the other side of the world anyway. And his father needed him.

Having spent quite some time with pencil and paper trying to work out the time difference, Alf decided to spend the evening at home, then return to Fleet Street by cab in the early hours.

In the quiet nocturnal solitude of his office on the executive floor, with only the distant hum of a cleaner's Hoover for company, Alf phoned an old friend from the *Sydney Morning Herald*. Laurie Turner was their Federal Politics correspondent, based in Canberra, and someone Alf had first met a decade earlier when they had jointly reported on the controversial dismissal of Australian Labor Prime Minister, Gough Whitlam, by the nation's Governor General, Sir John Kerr. Laurie had been present on the steps of Canberra's Parliament House to capture the former Prime Minister's defiant statement to a rally of his supporters, "Well may we say God save the Queen," Gough Whitlam boomed. "Because nothing will save the Governor General!"

A couple of years later, Laurie had spent some time in London at the *Daily Focus* as part of an exchange programme and had since publicly credited his time with Alf as an essential element in honing his much-envied skills as a member of the Canberra press gallery.

"G'day-Alf-yer-big-pommie-prick," Laurie cried joyfully as soon as he heard Alf's voice. "Fuck me, what time is it over there? You must be up early. Or late!"

"What fettle, bonny lad?" Alf replied.

"Never a dull moment. And you?"

"Same here. I need a favour."

"Anything, old mate. Anytime."

"I need to get in touch with Rick Armstrong. He's managing the Forgotten North tour."

"I've been reading all about that. What a hoot. I remember you introduced me to his father at the House of Commons, when they were still in Opposition. Must have been '78, I reckon. Bloody hell, Alf, Rick's boys don't like Maggie much, do they? And they don't mind telling everybody." Laurie suddenly changed tone. "Jesus, the bombing. We ran your piece here, and your obituary for Mrs Armstrong, sorry, Lady Armstrong. And Mrs Tebbit so badly hurt. Mr Berry, and all the others. Sorry mate, I should have phoned you at the time. You were friends, of course. It must be —"

"We're moving on as best we can, bonny lad," Alf interrupted, sensing Laurie's discomfort. "But if you could find Rick for me, I'd appreciate it."

"No worries. Let me make couple of phone calls and I'll get right back to you."

Within half an hour, Alf's phone buzzed. It was the night-duty switchboard operator. "Mr Burton, there's an international call for you, from someone named, um, I think he said... Lozz."

Alf smiled. "That's Laurie Turner from Canberra. You can put him straight through, thanks, bonny lass."

"Righto, yer big ugly bastard," Laurie said affectionately, as soon as he was on the line. "I phoned an old mate at 2SM. The boys are staying at the Sebel Townhouse in Sydney. All the top celebrities stay there. I've been told that the cleaners make a fortune from all the cocaine dust they vacuum up from the carpets. Rick's boys have been playing the local pub circuit in the city, then they're going down the 'Gong for a couple of nights. It sounds like they're sort of making it up as they go."

What was 2SM? Alf wondered. A government department? The Australian equivalent of Archie Prentice's sinister yet unnamed operation? No, he suddenly remembered with some relief; it was a leading Sydney rock music radio station, that's right. And where, or what, was the 'Gong? Wollongong perhaps? He'd vaguely heard of that. Could it be near Wagga Wagga? Alf promised himself that as soon as he had a spare minute he would nip along to their research department and have a look at some maps.

But Rick needed to get a grip. Playing a series of one-nighters in pubs on the other side of the world, in places with names that you couldn't even begin to pronounce or understand, seemed a retrograde step after consecutive hits, platinum records and sold out gigs at premier venues like the Birmingham NEC and Wembley Arena. He carefully wrote down the number of the hotel and expressed his thanks.

"Anytime, Alfo!" Laurie said cheerily. "Must go, Hawkie's about to give a press conference. Seeya-ron!"

It took Alf a couple of moments to translate Lozz's farewell. See you *later* on, he must have meant. Alf chuckled out loud. And Norman Armstrong often complained that what he generalised as "Northern" was a different language!

Alf was aware that "Hawkie" was Australia's hugely popular and raffish Prime Minister, Bob Hawke, who had once famously told the nation, during marathon celebrations following Australia's win at the America's Cup yacht race, that any employer who sacked someone for not turning up to work the next morning, would be a "bum". And not the American understanding of that word either, Alf surmised, noting that the general condition of the Prime Minister that night, plain for all to see on national television, would have made it quite difficult for him to arise bright and early for work himself.

Alf had expressed an opinion that Hawke was populist lightweight, a closet Tory in spite of his union background; perfectly suited to an out of the way country with no international relevance or influence like Australia. But Laurie had contradicted that assertion forcefully. Beneath the rough and ready exterior, Laurie had assured Alf, was a genuine international statesman and reforming Prime Minister who would leave his mark not only on their own rapidly evolving country, but on the world as well.

"God save us all from reforming Prime Ministers," Alf muttered, then wondered if the assembled reporters at Laurie's press conference would actually refer to their Prime Minister as "Hawkie", right to his face. Alf wouldn't be at all surprised. He contemplated how that might translate to their own situation; Maggie, can you tell us the current status of talks with the Russians, oh and by the way, Mags, how's your new marra, Mr Gorbachev? No, Gorbo, it would be. Nige, old cock, what's the current rate of inflation? How are things at the Foreign Office, Geoff?

Still snickering away as he thought of gleefully slapping Cabinet Ministers like Michael Heseltine or Leon Brittan on their backs and saying, *"How yer goin', yer big ugly prick?"*, he phoned the Sebel Townhouse and by a stroke of luck, Rick was available to take his call right away, having just woken up. Alf was genuinely touched at how happy Rick sounded to hear from him.

"Playing seedy pubs around an old convict settlement is one thing," Alf told him. "But your boys' live album is languishing outside the Top Ten here. It needs some support. You need to bring them back home where they belong. The Albert Hall awaits. And besides, bonny lad, you have some *serious* work to do."

***

The Forgotten North's touring operation, thanks to Rick Armstrong's calm and supremely competent management, was slick, efficient and reliable. Commercial flights, trucks and buses carrying band, crew, equipment and a growing contingent of hangers-on, would arrive in the correct city, and then the correct venue, on time, every time. As Alf had observed, the original schedule had been much more relaxed than the usual breakneck pace of a rock and roll tour, enabling additional shows to be scheduled along the way, time for television and radio appearances, and a good deal of relaxation on the beach in between.

So when Rick made the announcement that he and his family would be returning home early, the troupe, a tight family unit in itself, was collectively sad to see them go, but comfortable in the knowledge that the tour could proceed to its final destination, New Zealand, under the supervision of Rick's assistant road manager. Up until Alf's phone call, Rick had been keen to extend the tour, again and again, expressing more a sense of reluctance to return home than due to any outstanding success. Although initially seeing solid enough crowds and just about breaking even financially, by this point in the tour they were not selling out even modest-sized theatres, and lead singer Freddie Wells's political activism seemed out of place and, for many concertgoers and newspaper reviewers, a turn-off. It was becoming apparent that many of the British expats forming a significant part of the audiences were not as opposed to Mrs Thatcher as Freddie was, and Rick soon discovered that the reason many had come to Australia in the first place was to escape the union dominance and multiculturalism of the old country, both of which Freddie insisted on celebrating loudly between almost every song.

He'd also discovered that much of the Australian music industry appeared to be controlled by a Sunday night television programme called *Countdown*, not dissimilar in format to *Top of the Pops*, hosted by some kind of self-appointed, genial guru named Ian Meldrum, whom everyone called Molly. Rick managed to negotiate a widely coveted appearance on the show, which he was well aware attracted a nationwide audience of up to three million, including in remote and rural areas, and had helped to make stars out of a number of Australian and even international acts, including ABBA and Johnny Cougar.

But when lead singer Freddie Wells flatly refused, on the band's behalf, to lip synch to a backing track rather than play live, there was suddenly no slot available, and a statement was released that, due to a scheduling conflict, the Forgotten North would not be playing *Countdown* after all. Rick farewelled Molly Meldrum with regret, having found him to be a genuine enthusiast, massively influential, and lamented the loss of a great opportunity.

So the continued viability of the latter part of the tour necessitated a series of performances in venues progressively smaller, and to dwindling crowds, along with spasmodic airplay and promotional interviews on local radio. The live album, *Resurgence*, recorded during the band's benefit tour of collieries the previous year, and which was still nudging the Top Ten back home, was released during the tour, but barely made a ripple.

When Rick got off the phone with Alf, and immediately suggested to Sally that it was time for them go home, she at once broke down in tears of gratitude. None of them, she felt, had had any real time to grieve for Rick's mother, and even with the loyal support of their nanny, the burden of a stroppy, perpetually sunburnt teenager and a baby yet to celebrate her first birthday, on tour, in the unrelenting heat of the Australian summer, had become too much to bear. Even the onset of autumn had provided little relief in terms of cooler weather, and nerves and tempers were now frayed beyond any hope of repair.

A raucous farewell party was duly held at the Sebel Townhouse, after which the band and crew would be off to Wollongong and then across the Tasman Sea to New Zealand.

And Rick Armstrong and his family gratefully caught a cab for Kingsford-Smith Airport to be on the next flight home.

CHAPTER THREE

Each night after work, Alf caught the bus to his flat in Pimlico. It was the same modest address to where he and Dolly had moved when they first came south in 1947, when Alf was the Westminster correspondent for a now defunct and long-forgotten Newcastle newspaper, the *Tyne-Tees Ledger*. He was easily recognisable; always carried a battered leather holdall and wore the same, faded beige mac that had become as much a part of his identity as his rumpled suits and untidy, grey moustache. A columnist in the *Daily Mail* recently derided him as having the political judgement of Michael Foot, economic comprehension flailing somewhere between Del-Boy Trotter and Arthur Daly, and the fashion sense of Rumpole of the Bailey. Alf, for his part, actually found all of those comparisons complimentary.

Despite his professional success and the eye-popping remuneration arising from his Donoghue contract, Alf, with Dolly's blessing, had no intention of ever moving to a larger home, buying a car, going abroad on holiday, or visiting a tailor. His idea of a perfect evening was dozing in front of their little gas fire, an episode of the new Thames Television drama, *The Bill*, on their portable colour set, their little terrier, Ernie, curled up on his lap, and Dolly contentedly reading or knitting in the chair opposite.

That night, as they watched the Channel Four news together, just before bedtime, the lead story attracted their attention.

"Home Office Minister, Mr Charles Seymour, has announced today that there will be a full, independent inquiry into a number of incidents involving the police squad, known as Armstrong's Army, and into their conduct more generally during the recent Miners' Strike."

"The Home Secretary and Commissioner of the Metropolitan Police, as well as a number of regional Chief Constables have jointly endorsed this inquiry," Charles Seymour told a gathering of reporters in the cavernous, octagonal central lobby at the Palace of Westminster, "to demonstrate to the country that the police are not above the law, and that any misconduct will be investigated rigorously and dealt with, showing neither fear nor favour." Alf noted that Seymour's statement about the police not being above the law was the same line, almost verbatim, that he had been frequently trotting out during his regular and often coldly confrontational interviews with City Radio's political editor, Roland Moreland.

Mr Seymour was unable to provide any further information as to who might be chairing the enquiry, the proposed terms of reference, nor even its commencement date, and the news quickly moved on to other issues of the day, which included the stunning success of the SDP-Liberal Alliance in recent local government elections. Home Office PPS Janice Best made an appearance, expressing her elation at the fact that Bernie Grant, an immigrant from Guyana, had become the first black leader of a local authority, having been elected to lead the London Labour borough of Haringey.

"This is wonderful news for the Windrush generation, of which my parents were part, and for the immigrant community generally," Janice told the Channel Four reporter. "Britain is now a diverse nation, and this diversity must be represented at all levels of government for ours to be a truly fair society. I may not agree with Mr Grant's politics, but I welcome him to the role as leader of the Haringey Council and I know he will work very hard on behalf of his ratepayers."

Dolly placed her knitting carefully on her lap and looked at her husband. "Doesn't dear Janice always look lovely on the television," she observed. "And she speaks very well too."

"Aye, she's a prodigious talent, no doubt about it," Alf replied. "It can't be easy, being the only woman of Caribbean background in that nest of Tories."

"Will she get into any trouble, do you think, for effectively endorsing a Labour councillor?"

"No chance. She's one of Norman's own. Naebody on the Tory side would dare. There might be a quiet word into Norman's ear, to encourage her to remember whose side she's supposed to be on, but that would be as far as it goes. My assessment is that Norman is quite happy for her to have these little moments of rebellion every so often, as it demonstrates that his Home Office has a more human side. In a funny way, it's good for the Home Secretary's image. But aside from that, she's just a brilliant PPS. Norman is very lucky to have her."

Dolly paused for a few thoughtful moments, recalling another story that had been in the bulletin. "A full independent enquiry into the polis?" she queried. "Is that wise? That doesn't sound like Norman, or even Charles, for that matter. What's going on there?"

"Perhaps there's a conscience at Queen Anne's Gate after all," Alf replied noncommittally.

She eyed her husband with suspicion. "Alf, Pet," she questioned. "What've you been up to?"

***

Alf had been congratulating himself, of late, over his enthusiasm toward embracing all the new technologies, and with the help of his chief cameraman, Jerry Templar, had recently learned how to save his files onto floppy disks which, to his bemusement, weren't floppy at all. What a boon, he thought, as he now had an even more effective hiding place for his more sensitive investigations than the bottom drawer of his desk.

One such sensitive investigation was the one that had occupied the back of his mind for more than thirty years. A lost manuscript by Edwardian author, business tycoon and adventuress, Charlotte Morris, that Alf, along with many others, had always suspected contained highly damaging political revelations that could even have significant ramifications today. He had made little progress over the years, like chasing microscopic dust particles in a shifting ray of light, or floating, fluffy seed pods in a variable breeze. But just last year, he had made a massive breakthrough, although, he recognised, not at all through his own abilities or talents.

It had come about purely by chance, when Alf had been in Sir Norman Armstrong's constituency, gaining an understanding of the political issues that the Home Secretary might be facing toward the next general election. The spectacular, widely admired gardens of an exclusive aged care home, Stonebridge House, were under threat owing to a major property development on a neighbouring site. Alf had been keen to see just how Sir Norman would balance the conflicting needs of his safe constituency, in which there was mounting opposition to the project, with his government's own pro-development policies. The Department of Environment had overridden the local Tory council's veto and allowed the development to go ahead.

His visit to Stonebridge House had afforded him a meeting with a retired seafarer, Commodore James O'Malley, known affectionately to the staff and friends at his care home, as Captain Jim. The two former merchant mariners had become fast friends, and soon discovered that they were fellow seekers of a truth that had eluded Alf, as well as Jim's late and much-missed friend, Major Albert Powell. Alf had in due course discovered the family link with Sir Godfrey Powell, Permanent Secretary at the Home Office; father and son, and in a complicated web of connecting families, strange coincidences and historical intrigue, there remained the heavy presence of two towering figures. Colonel Fforbes Armstrong, and Piers Armstrong MP, the grandfather and great uncle respectively, of Alf's friend Sir Norman, the Home Secretary. With every development, every discovery, the seemingly insurmountable distance separated by decades and generations appeared to shrink just that little bit more. Just who else, Alf often wondered, within the current circle of government, friends and acquaintances, heroes and villains, would find themselves unexpected and unwitting players in this increasingly confusing, convoluted mystery? And how, if at all, would all of these apparently unconnected events, and people, manifest in the modern context?

But now Alf had a real objective that went well beyond the light-hearted satisfaction arising from the exposure of historic scandals amongst the aristocracy, Lords, and the Conservative establishment generally. Things had taken a remarkably personal turn, when Alf had discovered that the late Major Powell's eldest son, Sir Godfrey's brother, had been a high-flying young detective in the early years of the war, had been shanghaied into the Special Operations Executive, and had disappeared on his first secret mission behind enemy lines. Not an uncommon occurrence, Alf would have thought, except that Albert Powell had been convinced that the transfer had been orchestrated for reasons that went well beyond his late son's undoubted talents, and related directly to what young Reg Powell had been working on at the time. A serious investigation that had had the calm and jovial young man unusually apprehensive. The Major, with Captain Jim's support, had spent his final weeks trying so hard to remember, and to tie up countless loose ends. Like mechanical parts of a dismantled chronometer; spread on the table they meant nothing, a demoralisingly impossible puzzle, but connected in the right way, everything made sense.

Having now read and carefully considered what Albert Powell had written, the notes of which were safely in Godfrey's custody, Alf realised that his own long-held theories hadn't been too far from the truth. Perhaps the young Detective Powell had also been getting uncomfortably close to a rather inconvenient truth. And look what happened to him!

Too late to have second thoughts now, bonny lad, Alf told himself, as he settled behind his desk to re-read his transcription of Major Albert Powell's account. He made pencilled notes in the margin as he went along, and underlined a series of names, all of whom were central to a series of seemingly unconnected individuals and events over generations. Charlotte Morris, late Victorian and Edwardian literary identity, unimaginably wealthy; a courtier, business tycoon, adventuress, crusader for human rights. Protested so vehemently against Kitchener's concentration camps in South Africa at the turn of the century that she was fitted up — one of many new expressions Alf was learning from *The Bill* — as a Boer spy. Her life was saved only by intervention from His Majesty, Winston Churchill and, significantly, Colonel Fforbes Armstrong, Sir Norman's grandfather.

Piers Armstrong MP. Sir Norman's great uncle, and as black-hearted, cowardly and evil as his brother, Fforbes, had been kind, courageous and honourable. General Sir John Prentice, decorated soldier and father of the shadowy and malevolent Sir Archie, the head of a government intelligence department so dreaded that even iron men like Sir Norman Armstrong got twitchy when asked about it.

General Prentice and Piers Armstrong had been in South Africa around the time that the retired Fforbes Armstrong had met his death; a fall from his horse while patrolling his farm at night on the hunt for cattle thieves. Coincidence? Major Albert Powell, then serving in the South African Mounted Rifles, certainly hadn't thought so. He had initially suspected Fforbes Armstrong's neighbour, a veteran Boer guerrilla, but soon became convinced of Johannes van Zyl's innocence. Just. An old soldier's instinct for danger, the Major had written, and went on to explain that he had left the army soon afterwards, the mystery still unsolved, having received an offer to work in a bank in Durban, with a future opportunity to work in finance, in the City of London. It was, the Major conceded, an offer he could not refuse.

Once in civilian life, Major Powell had put many of the details of those events out of his mind, only retrieving long-forgotten recollections, in stark detail, in the days and even hours before his death.

Literary luminaries, heroes of Empire, international politics, espionage and war. Even murder? What a combination, Alf considered. A frightening reality even more remarkable than Charlotte Morris's most enduring literary creation; a colonial soldier and amateur sleuth, Captain Richard Fforbes, immortalised in a series of best-selling novels written in the first two decades of the century. The main character was nothing if not a loving tribute to Sir Norman's grandfather, Colonel Fforbes Armstrong himself.

The same Fforbes Armstrong who, to Sir Norman's discomfort, was right up to his neck in it all, just like Sir Norman's great uncle, Piers Armstrong MP. The two brothers; one generation of a dynasty of soldiers and politicians dating back to the English Civil War, and indeed probably long before. Both very complex individuals, but easy to simplify into two camps; the good Armstrong, and the bad. Alf contemplated his friend, Norman, who possessed many of Fforbes's fine qualities. Sir Norman's courage was undeniable; a decorated pilot during the war, a hero of the Battle of Britain, and then a steadfast warrior for the Conservative cause ever since. In spite of his public image, and the terrible things being done in his name, on a personal level the Home Secretary was loyal, kind, a friend in need, and could be wonderfully convivial company. There was a lot of

Fforbes Armstrong in his grandson. But, Alf thought sadly, it was becoming increasingly apparent that there was quite a bit of Piers as well.

And what of the middle generation, Richard? He had still been in the parliament when Alf first started working in Westminster, although they had first met a decade earlier, when Richard had famously defied Stanley Baldwin and his Cabinet to meet with the Jarrow marchers, for whom the teenaged Alf Burton had emerged as unofficial spokesman. Richard Armstrong defied Baldwin again during the Abdication Crisis, and then resurfaced as a quietly powerful figure under Churchill during the war; a man who seemed to be respected, and very well liked, on both sides of the ideological divide.

Where, Alf considered, did Sir Norman's universally admired father fit into the Armstrong doctrine, honed and refined for centuries?

CHAPTER FOUR
CABINET WAR ROOMS
LONDON 1941

"Look here, Winston," Richard Armstrong stated firmly, "I know Dick is not everyone's cup of tea, but he's a hard worker, a great campaigner, and he's loyal. I'd stake my reputation on the fact that he is no traitor." The Prime Minister and his Special Minister without Portfolio were discussing disturbing developments within one of their most critical government departments.

The Ministry of Information, under the irascible command of Minister of State, Dick Billings, was in a condition of seemingly irreparable disarray. Morale was at rock bottom, with fear and paranoia running rampant. A recent initiative had come well and truly undone, leading to recriminations, suspicion, destructive division and the potential looming end of a number of political and administrative careers; and worse. As well as the internal ramifications of this appalling failure, the wider damage to Britain's war effort and nationwide morale was yet to be tested, but could, Armstrong and Churchill agreed, be catastrophic.

The Billings Plan, as it had come to be known, had been a well-intentioned yet ill-fated initiative intended to investigate and test the loyalty of a number of aristocratic families, whose country estates were now being used as military installations. It was common knowledge that a number of upper-class family dynasties had strong historical ties to Germany, the royals themselves being no exception, and Dick, never one to trust anyone of foreign background at the best of times, had been keen to find out if certain families might have retained some of their old loyalties. Britain was fighting for her very survival, and people remained terrified about the ever-present threat of Nazi invasion. Vigilance, Dick reminded the Cabinet, was the price of the nation's survival. Thousands were being killed and injured in air raids on Clydebank, in Belfast, Merseyside, Manchester, Plymouth; it seemed that no part of England, Scotland or Wales was being spared, while London herself was under devastating and sustained attack. Despite the best brave faces, nerves and emotions were being tested to the brink of collapse.

Dick argued that the casual acceptance of Hitler and general denial about any threat Germany had posed during the previous decade should not be forgotten, reminding the War Cabinet that he, along with Richard Armstrong, Winston Churchill, and a growing number of supporters, had fought relentlessly against complacency and Nazi sympathies during the pre-war period of doomed appeasement.

Dick's carefully considered plan was to employ a number of reporters from press baron Paddy Donoghue's stable of newspapers, to travel to the countryside and interview the bluebloods whose family seats were now given over for military purposes. The pretence was that the journalists were putting together a series of articles that would demonstrate that all classes were making sacrifices, pulling together to defeat

Hitler. The archetypal morale-boosting propaganda campaign, a core responsibility of Dick's own Ministry of Information, but with a cleverly concealed main objective. Their real task would be to try to detect any Nazi sympathies, or even any leaking of information to spies and fifth columnists. Transcripts of the interviews, which would hopefully include detailed genealogy and the current spread of relatives in Europe, would be passed on to Intelligence for analysis.

Dick's Cabinet colleagues had applauded the initiative for its cunning originality, and it was approved right away. The timing was particularly opportune, as there were still suspicions about the aerial bombing of Buckingham Palace some months before, during which the King and Queen had narrowly escaped injury, even death. The targeted nature of the attack, the bombs having landed with frightening accuracy and killing one of the palace staff, had suggested some inside knowledge, so the implementation of the Billings Plan was ordered as a top priority. Dick, the perpetual, embittered outsider, was delighted to be warmly embraced by his colleagues for once, and to be in the thick of the action at last. Even the Labour and Liberal members of the Coalition, whom Dick generally despised, offered grudging appreciation of the plan, causing him to, temporarily at least, moderate his naturally belligerent nature. His friend Paddy Donoghue, along with a number of his best investigative reporters, were promptly recruited and put to work.

But things soon took an unexpected turn. Information was definitely leaking to the Germans, it became apparent; not from upper-class British Nazis, but from the very person Dick had recruited to lead the investigation. Paddy Donoghue himself.

"I agree that it's highly unlikely that Dick was complicit," the Prime Minister told Richard Armstrong, as they reflected upon recent events. "But it was Dick's initiative to bring Donoghue in, in the first place. They're old friends."

Richard tried not to cough in the face of a cloud of cigar smoke, which drifted in a shape like a sinister claw between them, under the shaded lightbulbs above the bare conference table. "I spoke up most strongly for the Billings Plan," he replied. "I should be vulnerable to suspicion as well. I've been friends with Paddy for even longer than Dick. We all worked closely together during the Abdication Crisis, and we convinced him to mobilise his papers behind our rearmament campaign. We really needed him because the Beaver really let us down on that one. Look how strongly Paddy called for Chamberlain to go and for you to be PM in his place. I was the liaison between you and Paddy over that whole time. If suspicion by association is going to be applied fairly, I should be in the line of fire as much as Dick is."

"Rubbish, my boy. No one would ever consider you in the same sphere as Dick. Or Paddy. No one questions your loyalty. Or your judgement. Look here, Richard, the best thing for all of us is for this little matter to be dealt with quickly and quietly, and then we can all get on with the war."

"I understand. The first thing we need to do is to get Dick out of the Ministry of Information."

"The wheels are already in motion," the Prime Minister replied. "Brendan Bracken will be a thoroughly reliable replacement."

"What's best to be done with Dick?" Richard asked.

"Let's be honest, he's been even worse than usual since his poor wife was killed last year. He's too much of a loose cannon. Assistant to the PPS at the Department of Economic Warfare, I think, would be just in his line."

"Really?" Richard was sceptical. "They look after SOE. In the wake of this Paddy Donoghue business, do you think that's wise?"

"The department is very well partitioned, and don't forget they also oversee the blockade of German ports," Churchill reminded him, gesturing with his cigar, and dusting some fallen ash off his boiler suit. "Dick can keep himself busy collating statistics and writing reports for the Minister, documenting the economic effect of the blockade. In the meantime, as soon as you can resolve this unpleasantness at the MoI the better. Paddy himself is under close surveillance, of course, as are his people. Can I leave the resolution of this matter in your hands, Richard?"

"Of course."

The Prime Minister stood up, indicating the end of their meeting. "Well, this minor reshuffle of the War Cabinet will at least give me some good news to tell His Majesty at luncheon tomorrow," Churchill said, as they walked toward the door.

"How do you mean?"

"Well, I don't think HM has ever been an admirer of our friend Mr Billings, for all kinds of reasons, I suspect. But he did once say to me, with quite a gleam in his eye, that Minister of Information was the perfect job for Dick, because he could never keep his mouth shut at the best of times."

Richard smiled. He was well aware that the King possessed a full understanding of his limitations as a constitutional monarch, but it hadn't stopped him grilling Winston over a number of his Cabinet appointments. "Do you think His Majesty has really forgiven us for supporting his brother?" Richard asked as the two men made to go their separate ways.

"Oh yes," the Prime Minister replied. "He had a few things to say when I brought Beaverbrook into the Cabinet, of course, and offered a number of perfectly reasonable objections to Billings, but all in all, he's been very gracious. Speaks very highly of you."

A few brief moments of pleasant conversation followed. Richard informed the Prime Minister that his son, Norman, had just been promoted to Flight Lieutenant and was soon to transfer from his fighter squadron, in the service of which he'd won the DFC during the Battle of Britain, to Bomber Command. The Prime Minister offered his congratulations and his regards to Richard's wife, Fiona, then retreated to his private rooms.

Richard eventually reached street level, contemplating that spending so much time working underground meant that you could never tell if it was the middle of the day or the middle of the night. It was dark. He glanced at the sky, observing the distant silhouettes of barrage balloons, like a pod of whales on strings, stranded in mid-air. He contemplated strolling out into Whitehall in the hopeful expectation of finding a cab to take him home to Knightsbridge, but then considered that a walk through the eerie, even ghostly beauty of a blacked-out London, reflecting silkily under an almost full moon, might be a preferable way to clear his anxious mind. Having exchanged some pleasantries with the rather dumbstruck young provost sentry, he set off at a brisk pace along Horse Guards Road, then turned into Birdcage Walk, skirting St James's Park. He remembered with amusement some of the more eccentric safety suggestions to emerge from Dick Billings's old department, regarding how to be seen in the blackout. He had no intention of untucking his shirt and hitching up his jacket so the white shirt tail could be seen from behind. One still had to have some standards of dress. To set the example. He decided he would take his chances in his dark, sober suit, and keep his eyes and ears open.

It wasn't just this mess at the Ministry of Information engulfing his friends, Dick Billings and Paddy Donoghue, or even just how badly the war seemed to be going. He worried constantly about young Norman. Richard himself had flown during the last war, in the RFC, and had lost many of his friends in the skies over the battlefields of France. And now, less than a generation later, they were going through the whole blasted thing again.

Around the time of the Battle of Britain, Norman had invited his father to his squadron for the elder aviator to inspect close up the Spitfires and Hurricanes. Norman and his friend, Perry Walsingham, then invited him to the mess, where he spent a raucous evening with the young pilots, whose faces soon seemed to morph into young men of Richard's own generation; long dead, and missed every day. Richard's natural warmth and friendliness quickly thawed any social barrier arising from the fact that he was well known as the right-hand man of the new Prime Minister, Mr Churchill, as they compared stories of aerial combat, more than two decades apart. How many of those young men were still alive even now, Richard contemplated, as he strode along the darkened streets.

The war in the air had certainly changed in the years between the Sopwith Pup and the Spitfire, Richard understood, but it was just as bloody dangerous. Possibly more so. Norman was a good lad, undoubtedly brave and skilled as a pilot, but he was cocky, overconfident and thought he knew everything. Who doesn't, at his age, Richard ruminated as he walked.

But, Richard thought desolately, he would be very surprised if Norman survived the war. He was an only child, so the dynasty would die out, after hundreds of years of fighting in parliament and on the battlefield, and now, with these two latest generations, in the air. And how Norman's mother would cope when the inevitable finally occurred, Richard mused, didn't bear thinking about. But this was the constant, nagging fear confronting every family, at home, in Europe, and around the world. Richard Armstrong understood better than most that he was just one small insignificant part of an infinitely complicated war machine. No room for any kind of personal feelings, at least for the duration. And he had a job to do.

The following day, back in his private office in the underground labyrinth that formed the government's war rooms, Richard Armstrong perused the latest intelligence reports concerning the rather surprising landing by parachute onto Scottish soil of leading Nazi Rudolf Hess, and the stunning news that a German U-Boat had been captured, with Enigma cryptography machine, and codebooks, intact! Richard was sure that these two momentous developments would have major implications regarding the conduct of the war, and could even mean the difference between defeat and what was appearing to be an increasingly impossible victory. Assuming, that is, that there would be enough of Britain still standing, and anyone left alive, to be able to capitalise on it.

He had on his desk reports on the ongoing surveillance of Paddy Donoghue. He also had the dossier that Donoghue himself had prepared after his most recent visit to an estate in Hampshire, as part of his duties for the Ministry of Information. The family seat being subjected to Paddy's forensic investigation was held by a distantly removed cousin of the Royal Family, and a descendant of the Saxe-Coburg-Gotha line. Richard was impressed by the level of detail that Paddy had managed to glean from his interviews with the current generation, including from Lord Lewis Rutherford of Meon and Solent. Paddy had discovered that the Marquess's real name was, in fact, Louis Ruttenberg, and had been judiciously anglicised even before the assassination of Franz Ferdinand in 1914, over concerns of the nationalistic fervour that seemed to be consuming Germany, and the naval Dreadnought arms race, which Ruttenberg had quite correctly predicted would have only one dire outcome in the end. The large extended Ruttenberg family remained prominent in Germany and boasted current members of the Luftwaffe, the Kriegsmarine and even the SS. Richard noted that Paddy's report had been scant in detail of the Marquess's own loyal service; other reports detailed how he had personally raised an infantry company in 1915, the Petersfield Pals, and went on to command them at Gallipoli, and then for the remainder of the war in the trenches in France, for which he had been personally presented the Military Medal by King George V.

But the security realities in the current context were not to be denied. The family estate, Meondale, was currently requisitioned by the Royal Air Force, and was being used for the training of radar operators and technicians, while the estate grounds were housing hangars and a grass runway where radar and aviation innovations could be tested under realistic conditions, as planes landed and took off, and staged mock attacks. Paddy suggested that one course of action could be to plant some misinformation with the Marquess, monitor his comings and goings and see if that same piece of information made its way to enemy ears.

All very convincing, Richard thought, until he read their own intelligence reports. Paddy, for one reason or another, had come to suspect that he himself was falling under suspicion, and was determined to deflect any blame. A high-ranking aristocrat, directly descended from German nobility and with extended family on the other side, was the perfect basis from which to construct an elaborate and convincing diversion from his own treasonous activities.

Richard closed the folder on his desk and rubbed his tired eyes. It was all so hard to believe. Richard had been friends with Paddy for years, and they had fought a number of political battles together. Political manoeuvrings around the Abdication Crisis, then trying to awaken a sleeping government, and country, to the dangers of Hitler's pre-war ambitions. Against any premature moves toward Indian independence. For recognition of working-class conditions in the North and in Wales. Even the King himself had joined them, having toured Welsh mining villages dying under the burden of mass unemployment, and telling Prime Minister Stanley Baldwin that "something must be done". And finally, against Neville Chamberlain himself, rallying the support of politicians on all sides to support Winston Churchill's move into Number Ten.

The *Daily Focus* and a number of other Donoghue publications had also come out strongly in defence of Richard Armstrong personally as his own career had been under threat;

as Chancellor of the Duchy of Lancaster when he had defied Cabinet collective responsibility and went to meet with the protest marchers from Jarrow in late 1936.

Richard cast his mind back to the small army of proud men he had met in Hyde Park, after their march of almost three hundred miles from a town in which the unemployment rate had reached as high as eighty-five percent. It was as if they had come from a different country. Or a different planet. He remembered a rather dishevelled young man, barely able to walk on his blistered feet and weary legs. He was still a teenager, but the others seemed to look toward him as their spokesman.

The young man explained that the marchers were seeking no special favours; and that a new steel works in their community would provide much needed employment for the despair and disease-ridden town, which was dying, metaphorically and literally. He went on to lay out, politely but firmly, the incidence of malnutrition, the epidemic of TB, and the reality that his home town suffered the highest rate of infant mortality in the country.

Ellen Wilkinson, the local Labour MP who was going to present a petition with twelve thousand signatures to the House of Commons in support of the marchers' cause, also made the most of actually being face to face with an unusually enlightened and influential Tory.

"No one has a job in Jarrow," she told Richard, who reflected that the MP looked as if she was in need of a decent meal herself, "apart from a few railwaymen, local officials, the workers in the co-ops and some who've managed to find at least some work out of the district. The plain fact is that if people have to live and bear and bring up their children in bad housing on too little food, their resistance to disease is lowered and they die before they should."

These facts were hard to argue against, Richard conceded, and after the young man made a remark about the general uncaring nature of Tories, with great respect to present company of course, Richard reminded him that the Baldwin government was actually a coalition. The young man scoffed, labelling it as a Tory government by stealth, and strongly rebutting Baldwin's own claims of one nation, or compassionate Conservatism, which if it existed at all, had completely by-passed the North-east.

Richard remembered the articulate young man's smouldering anger, and the impassioned way he had put his case. What was his name? Alf, was it? That's right. I wonder what ever happened to him, Richard contemplated. He seemed to remember the young man expressing a desire to join the International Brigade in Spain.

"Well, I hope that fine young fellow made it through," he said aloud, and returned his attention to his reports, and to the chilling fact that his old friend, Paddy Donoghue, was a traitor, undermining everything that they were working, and fighting for. Absolutely no doubt about it according to these intelligence reports, and it was now Richard Armstrong himself who would have to order his arrest and inevitable execution.

Why? Richard asked himself, struggling to control a growing sense of anguish. A successful businessman, highly influential, courted by politicians on both sides of the aisle. A beautiful young family. A loyal friend. Why did he do it?

The report mentioned something about Fenian sympathies and anger over British Army activities in Dublin around the

Easter Rising and then after the First World War. The Black and Tans, Richard contemplated. Not the British forces' finest hour, anyone with any sense of right and wrong could recognise that. But why go over to the Nazis? What good would that do? How would the Nazis marching into Ireland make anything better? They might reunite the partitioned land, but at what cost? They'd make the Black and Tans look like your friendly and helpful London bobby, or the cheery Beefeaters that welcomed tourists to the Tower of London.

There was something about this whole mess that made no sense at all, Richard believed. In all the years he had known the newspaper proprietor, not once had he expressed any kind of anti-British sentiment, not even in passing. But what could he do? The Prime Minister needed a quick solution, and for good reason. The situation was precarious; the very future of the country was in the balance. Richard recalled a casual comment the Prime Minister had made to him just after Dunkirk. *We'll all be dead in three months*. The nation's leader had kept his fears private from all but his closest confidants; he knew that the national morale was of paramount importance. Any breach of security, real or imagined, if made public at this high a level, could have devastating effects, and just imagine what the Jerry propaganda machine, especially that snake Lord Haw Haw, would make of it.

The scales would really be tipped in their favour, of course, if the Americans, with their population and industrial might, would join the fight against the Nazis. Richard was aware that covert propaganda efforts were underway to try to undermine isolationist views within the US Congress, including the provision to American Intelligence, via Buenos Aires, of a false account of German ambitions in South America, including a map of redrawn borders under Nazi occupation and proposed Lufthansa routes to major cities of the United States. See how they like it when the Nazis are trying to kick their front door in, as well as ours, Richard thought. It was a comfort that President Roosevelt, re-elected the previous year, was far more sympathetic to Britain's plight than many of his colleagues in government, despite what he had said to the contrary in the heat of the campaign.

And since that arch-isolationist and defeatist Joe Kennedy was no longer ambassador to the Court of St James's, replaced by a much more supportive John Winant, someone with whom Richard was already developing a warm and cooperative working relationship, the propaganda war of attrition against non-intervention was stepping up. But what would it take, in the end, Richard contemplated, to bring the Americans in?

But, back to his more pressing, and deeply personal, issue at hand. "The war effort trumps everything," Richard said out loud, as if to cement his own resolve. He knew that this was not a case where justice could be allowed to take its natural course. There was too much at stake. He placed his hand onto one of the several telephones on his desk. He pictured himself as a masked executioner, gripping the handle of his axe, just before it was raised above his head to be brought down onto an exposed, vulnerable neck. He hesitated, unable to pick up the receiver, just in case there might be a last-minute reprieve. A message or a phone call to say that it had all been a mistake, that Paddy, his friend, was innocent. That he wouldn't have to do what he was duty bound to do. The silence seemed to mock his own hesitancy, told him that there would be no reprieve, and reminded him with icy intensity, that with power, often came uncomfortable, distasteful obligations.

Eventually he picked up the receiver and brought it gingerly to his ear. He noted that his hand was shaking. Just ever so slightly. The switchboard operator answered.

"Sir John Prentice, please." His voice was steady.

CHAPTER FIVE

"Alf. Alf!"

"Why-aye, pet, I wasn't asleep!" Alf sat bolt upright in his chair, spilling the loose pages of his newspaper onto the floor along with Ernie, who tumbled onto the mat with a dull thud, growled in protest and went to sulk in his basket in the corner.

"Didn't you hear the phone?" Dolly asked him. "It's your brother Sidney."

"What's he thinking of, ringing at this time of night?" Alf muttered indignantly.

"It's not even nine o'clock," Dolly told him.

"We haven't missed *The Bill*?" he asked anxiously.

"That's on tomorrow night," she replied calmly.

Alf stood up, tried as best he could to conceal his embarrassment, and walked to the telephone on the little table near the front door of their flat.

"Sid! What fettle, bonny lad?" Alf cried.

"Canny," Sid Burton replied. "Well, actually Alf, I need to ask you something, on the QT. On behalf of the lads, like."

"Aye, of course."

"You probably know they're laying off at the yard here. Austin Wells is back with us at the Fitters and Shipyard Workers Union; thank God he could be spared from the NUM.

We need him, bonny lad. He's working out a plan of attack with me and the other shop stewards. Now, all the lads credit you for saving our bacon in '83, so they're wondering how you see our chances this time."

Alf's role, or lack of it, during the aborted closure of the shipyard almost two years earlier, continued to make him uncomfortable. At that time, Sir Eddie had planned to close the yard entirely and redevelop the site into a luxury riverfront flat complex. But these plans were subsequently shelved following an incomprehensible, once-in-a lifetime series of manoeuvres involving both Rick and Norman Armstrong, as well as Sir Dick Billings, the Secretary of State for Defence and even the Prime Minister; all working together, having been cunningly manipulated by Austin Wells. That unique moment of serendipitous shared political pragmatism had saved more than eight thousand jobs, at least for the moment. Alf had been largely unaware of any of these machinations until Sir Eddie suddenly popped up on BBC Radio Four's *Today* programme, denying the rumours of looming closure and announcing an increased output due to Ministry of Defence contracts. Alf's brother, a fitter of more than forty years' service and a resolute union man, immediately jumped to the conclusion that it had been Alf's intervention that had saved the yard, and had gone on to tell absolutely everyone that, once again, Jarrow's favourite son had delivered the goods for his old home town. Alf was so powerful, Sidney told the lads at a union meeting, that even his boss, billionaire businessman and Tory, Sir Eddie Donoghue, had to do what Alf told him.

"I keep telling you, that had nothing to do with me," Alf told his brother. "That was Eddie's own decision."

"You always were too modest," Sid persisted. "But tell me straight this time, kidda. What are our chances? Not for me, I'm retiring soon as you kna, but I worry for our Nye. He's a smart lad, I couldn't face seeing him on the scrapheap so young. We've seen the effect on our marras for years. Remember when Palmer's closed in '34? It knocked the shite out of everybody. Proud skilled men, you could see the life going out of them as time dragged on. Then Speers ground to a halt and didn't start hiring again 'til the war. Having to go cap in hand to... my God, the Means Test... W' own da' were never the same. Fifty year on, Alf, man, and what has bloody well changed? What've we been fighting for all these years, only to see the same bastard thing happen all over again? I'll not have that for my boy. I won't!"

"I'm afraid the yard has been on borrowed time for years, bonny lad," Alf said. "You know that as well as I do. Austin will do his best for everyone, and I know you will and all, but you won't win this time. The yard will survive, for the moment, but only on vastly reduced manpower. The government has the taste of union blood, they've just beaten the living shite out of Scargill and the pitmen as you've seen. If your lads picket the yard, they'll be facing the same polis that we saw at Orgreave, and anywhere else that lads were getting their heads kicked in. People are going to get hurt, Sid, be careful."

"Bastards!" Sid spat. "Bastards! Bastards! Bastards! If I were twenty year' younger —"

"Forty year' younger more like," Alf observed, and the two brothers laughed in spite of themselves.

"We had some right old rumbles in the old days, didn't we?" Sid remarked wistfully. "Polis, Tories, scabs, Black

Shirts, North Shields lads. We'd fight anyone. The harder the better."

"You were tougher than me," Alf said. "You saved me more than once."

"Bollocks," Sid argued. "You were so good at it you went off to kick the shite out of Franco's fascists once you'd fettled the ones here at home."

From their little kitchenette, Dolly smiled as she listened absently to one side of the conversation. Worlds apart, though less than three hundred miles separated them. Even so, she thought, the brotherly bond remained. Solid as ever.

"So what about young Nye, then?" Sid asked.

"Send him down soon as you like, Sid. I'll put him to work. He can stay with Dolly and me until he gets himself set up."

"Thanks, Alf, I owe you."

"Give over, Sid, man. But take my advice. Sit this one out."

After they had rung off, Sid Burton returned to his modest front room and slumped into his deep chair. He lived so close to the yard that he could hear the works, faintly, throughout the night. It was something he found deeply comforting but, like his brother, he was a realist. Under a Labour government, things might have been different. Even Edward Heath had seen the benefits of keeping people in employment and had stepped in to save Upper Clyde Shipbuilders after the famous work-in led by the legendary Jimmy Reid.

"Wouldn't happen now," Sid muttered, staring at the blank screen of the television set in the corner. "Armstrong's Army would storm the yard, cave a few heads in, break a few arms and legs, and drag everyone out by the scruff of the neck, into the Mariah and off to the nick. Then Thatcher would say something like: 'Of course we regret the loss of jobs in shipbuilding, but you won't get new jobs in shipbuilding by putting up the prices of ships.'" Everything was about money, now. Money and the free market, with community and humanity left in the dust of history.

Things were different in the old days, Sid lamented. He'd been at the forefront of a few industrial actions over the years; safety was an ongoing issue in a yard as old as Speers-Donoghue, and theirs was a constant fight for pay and conditions that would keep up with the cost of living, especially during the recent tumultuous decades when inflation would sometimes spike at twenty-five per cent, and ambitious pay claims could be just as dramatic, sometimes even more. But you could negotiate; sometimes even Sir Eddie Donoghue himself would become involved, and they always seemed to find a way toward a resolution. If both sides were volubly dissatisfied with the result, Sid often thought, it meant that the outcome was probably as fair as it could be.

Relations with the polis was different as well, Sid recalled. None of what Alf revealed in his television documentary about Orgreave — the deliberate, targeted violence and intimidation — went on in the '70s, and before. As a senior shop steward, Sid was often the liaison between the union and the old Sergeant at Hebburn police station. During a dispute, Sid would phone the station each morning, let them know how many pickets were going to be on site, and whether or not any trouble was expected with scab labour or wagons that were due at the yard and might try to cross the line. The polis kept a friendly eye on things, normally a group of about half a dozen would be deployed, who regularly joined the picketers for coffee, and even shared lunches on quiet days. Opposing points of view were respected, and everyone just got on with what they were doing.

The old Sergeant had been retired for quite a few years now; Sid often said how-do and what-fettle on Saturdays as their allotments neighboured one another. But even this younger generation of officers were pleasant enough to get along with, nothing at all like those London hooligans of Armstrong's Army.

On the following Saturday morning, as usual, Sidney woke early, put on his gardening overalls and set off for his allotment. He left his house and stepped right into Charlotte Street; looking to his left he could see the shipyard gantries above the rooves and against the skyline, sitting astride the shipyard's slipways, each one not unlike the framework of the Middlesbrough Transporter Bridge, he often thought. As long as those cranes and gantries are standing, he thought, we're okay. He turned right and walked to the end of his own street, past the corner shop, and around past the pub, where the allotments could be found at the end of the laneway. Adjacent to the allotments and separated by a makeshift fence of scrap timber, was an expanse of long green grass where retired pitmen coursed their whippets and passed the time of day. To his right, and in the middle distance, two large tower blocks rose threateningly from behind the rows of semi-detached houses, and during certain times of the day, cast the coursing green under an ominous shadow. The twin structures dominated the horizon; an angry and uncaring two-fingered salute to a disappearing past.

"Sunlight and steel, streets in the sky, and all that bollocks," Sid muttered. The Ellen Wilkinson Estate. She'd have a few things to say if she was alive to see the damp-ridden, crumbling mess that it had become, he mused. Another great legacy of Donoghue Constructions and a naïve council housing committee desperate to solve their slum housing problems. A number of the lads from the yard lived there and didn't have very many complimentary things to say about it. Constantly malfunctioning lifts, empty flats in disrepair, squatters, gangs of dissatisfied and directionless youths hanging around; drugs and petty crime. And the constant nagging hope that the wheels would still be on your car when you tried to drive it somewhere. His own street had been thus far spared the Donoghue treatment, although occasionally some petty crime and vandalism spilled over from the estate. When he arrived at his allotment, he was happy to see his old friend already there. Sid had brought his thermos, and the two sat down on a pair of old crates, on the narrow pathway between their respective patches, for their usual morning coffee and a convivial smoke.

"What fettle, Sarge?" Sid asked.

"Ee, canny, canny," Sarge replied. "Nae complaints. Who'd listen?"

"There's something I need to ask you."

"Oh aye?"

"I know you keep in touch with a few of the lads at the station. Is there anything unusual going on?"

"Actually, it's funny you say that," Sarge replied, sipping his strong black coffee and savouring a long drag on his cigarette. "I dropped in there during the week, I often do, just to say hello. And this time there was naebody I recognised. They weren't our lads — you could tell that from right away.

Very slovenly turned out, I thought. I wouldn't have put up with it in my day."

"What's happened, do you think?"

"I think we both know what's going on," Sarge replied. "All but a couple of patrol and beat officers have been temporarily reassigned to South Shields Division HQ. Armstrong's Army have set up camp."

"Jesus," Sid muttered.

"And what do you think the desk Constable said when I entered the station?"

"No idea."

Sarge continued indignantly, "Not a polite 'can I help you, sir?', but he said; 'What can I do yer for, *cock*?' His exact words! I thought I'd walked into an episode of *The Sweeney*."

"I preferred *Softly Softly,* myself," Sid replied sadly.

The two men worked side by side for a while, playfully disparaging each other's efforts, and comparing leek sizes with an appropriate amount of nudging and winking, but Sid's heart wasn't in it and he excused himself early and returned home. He went straight upstairs to his son's room, flung open the door and wrenched the covers off the bed, as Aneurin Burton begged to be left alone and allowed to sleep for another few hours, given that it was still, by any normal person's estimation, the middle of the night.

"Time for us to have a bit' craic," Sid ordered, then waited downstairs for his son to emerge in something close to a human state.

CHAPTER SIX
WHITECHAPEL, EAST LONDON
1941

Detective Constable Reg Powell arrived at the corner of Old Cleveland Lane, Whitechapel, following one of the heaviest nights of bombing since the Blitz had begun its relentless rampage twelve months earlier. He unfolded himself from his little black car and walked toward the warden's post.

"Detective Constable Powell, Scotland Yard," he said politely but firmly as a warden attempted to block his path. The elderly warden took a step backwards, having touched the rim of his ARP helmet respectfully.

"Cor blimey," he told his fellow warden manning their little post. "These coppers are getting younger every day. This one looks barely out of short trousers."

The young detective walked along the laneway, closed off to all but essential services. A line of auxiliary fire units, including black cabs with their fire pump trailers, and ambulances extended the length of the laneway itself, while ARP Wardens, uniformed police and women ambulance drivers were milling around. Rubble spilled onto the roadway from several bombed buildings. As Reg approached number twenty-seven, his eyes were drawn to a row of stokes litters lined up on the roadway behind the open back doors of an ambulance. Dusty and bloodstained grey blankets discreetly covered the tragic remains of the night's air raids.

The Sergeant from the local nick approached Reg. They were old friends, the Sergeant having mentored a young, green and fumblingly nervous PC Powell on his first days on the beat, just as the war began. Could it really have been less than two years ago?

"All right, Reg-boy?" the Sergeant asked.

"Hello, Bill," Detective Powell replied with the easy familiarity of old workmates, despite the gulf in age and seniority that separated them. Although still very early in his career, Detective Powell's reputation already afforded him a level of respect and acceptance from the old guard that few other young officers could have dreamed of. "What do we have?"

"The only fatalities on the street were in the knocking shop at number twenty-seven here," Sergeant Harper explained. "Dorrie Foskett's. Four of the, er, ladies, and three punters. Poor Dorrie copped it as well. I thought you might be interested in one in particular."

"Oh yes?"

"Ever heard of Padraig Donoghue?"

"Yes. Owns newspapers all over the place. The *Daily Focus* is the main one, I think. My dad's always complaining about it and writing letters to the editor. They must be well sick of him."

"That's the one." Sergeant Bill Harper showed Detective Powell to the first of the blanket-covered bodies, and lifted the corner to reveal the bruised, bloodied and dusty face of Padraig Donoghue himself.

"Bloody hell," Reg uttered. "And he was in the knocking shop?"

"Certainly was. The wardens pulled him out not one hour ago."

"Well, then," Reg Powell mused. "This is a right kettle of fish, and no mistake."

Reg squatted down and lifted the blanket further, examining Padraig Donoghue's broken and bloodied body. The detective was aware that Donoghue was well known as a politically active newspaper proprietor who had been very vocal in supporting the former King during the Abdication Crisis, some years earlier. He was reputed to be a personal friend of a number of senior and influential Tory politicians, even of the Prime Minister himself. He had put the might of his newspapers well and truly behind the war effort, finally gaining at least grudging approval from Reg's father, and Reg was aware that he currently held a post at the Ministry of Information, working directly for the Minister of State, Mr Dick Billings MP. A very important man, Detective Powell mused. While he ruminated on the implications of a scandal at or near the very top of the government, he looked carefully at Padraig's upper body, clad only in a white vest. He was bruised and battered, and there was a deep cut, more like a slash, on his chest; from a large knife, or even some kind of sword perhaps. It had not been obvious at first glance, hidden as it was beneath congealed blood and caked with cement and brick dust. Powell poked and prodded with his fingers through the jagged tear in Padraig's vest, frowning.

"Anything wrong?" asked Sergeant Harper. "I think the ambulance girls are keen to remove the bodies."

"I'm not sure," Detective Powell replied. "Can you show me where he was found?"

The two men carefully climbed up and over the rubble of Dorrie Foskett's late establishment, carefully stepping between the ARP wardens and other police officers as they searched and dug amongst the collapsed building for any more victims. The Sergeant pointed out the excavations from where Donoghue's body had been dug out.

"What are you looking for?" he asked.

"I don't know," Reg admitted. "Metal reinforcings poking out, jagged pipe ends, long slivers of glass, anything sharp like that."

Both men examined the immediate area carefully. Reg gingerly lay down on the pile of jagged stones and peered into the dark abyss beneath the rubble. There was nothing obvious, although any and all of those potentially lethal items of wreckage were to be found in bombsites generally, as they both well knew.

"Forget it, it's probably nothing," Reg muttered, standing up and slapping at the dust on his trousers and jacket with his hands. "All right, Bill, the bodies can be taken now."

Reg scanned the lane, thinking about Paddy Donoghue's chest wound and how it didn't seem to be consistent with the injuries he would have sustained under the falling bricks. Reg's rocketing professional reputation was built on the fact that he possessed a keen sense of when a crime was being covered up by an air raid, a more frequent state of affairs than a nation buoyed by the unifying spirit of the Blitz would necessarily appreciate. His train of thought was interrupted by the sight of three young men, one slim, another built like a wrestler, the third just simply fat. Their overcoat collars were turned up and cloth caps pulled low over their eyes as they walked briskly along Old Cleveland Lane, stepping over the rubble on either side of the line of emergency vehicles, in brazen defiance of the closure.

The young detective recognised them immediately. Cyril McCann, Harry Barron and Frank *Fatty* O'Farrell. A trio of right young villains, and no error. "Oi, you three! Come here," he called. Sergeant Harper had also recognised them straight away and was briskly but carefully climbing down from the rubble to join his colleague.

"'Allo, Mr Powell, Sergeant Harper!" McCann said chirpily, while Barron and O'Farrell remained sullenly silent.

"It's too warm for those greatcoats," Sergeant Harper ordered. "What are you hiding in there? Turn out your pockets."

"Pardon me?" McCann demurred.

"You 'eard," Sergeant Harper insisted. "You ain't got cloth ears."

"Blimey, Mr Harper, we ain't doin' nothin'," McCann protested, "just taking a shortcut." Despite his complaints, McCann complied, and his friends followed suit.

"What's all this then?" Powell questioned, examining a handful of paper tickets McCann and Barron produced. "*Kiss me Goodnight, Sergeant Major,*" he read. "What's all that about?"

"A night of fun and laughter with the Tweedle Sisters topping the bill, and Elsie and Doris Waters, you know, Gert and Daisy. And Old Mother Riley. A special ladies' night, at the Regal, Bethnal Green," McCann said brightly. "I'll do you a special price. Good seats and all!"

"Do me a favour," Reg scoffed. "I know what your game is. There'd be two hundred seats in that flea-pit music hall, and you've probably forged five hundred extra tickets. And then your unsuspecting punters turn up for the show, having spent their hard-earned money, only to find that they can't get a seat, and you and your little band of villains will be nowhere to be found."

"You can't call it a ladies' night," Sergeant Harper argued. "Everyone knows Old Mother Riley is a geezer dressed up."

"What?" Frankie O'Farrell gasped.

"Look here," Reg ordered. "Unbutton those coats, let's see what you're hiding."

McCann looked indignant. "Straight up, Mr Powell. Harry, Frankie and I are in the entertainment business now. All about morale on the Home Front. We're just doing our bit, like you and Sergeant Harper."

"Doing your bit?" Powell questioned suspiciously.

"It's all legal and above board. You shouldn't think the worst of people all the time, but I suppose you have to in your line of work."

Reg handed the tickets back to McCann and Barron. He noted that O'Farrell's pockets were empty, and a not particularly gentle frisk by Sergeant Harper resulted in nothing else being found beneath or within their coats. "Piss off and stay out of trouble," Detective Powell told them, then returned his attention to the crumbling walls and piled debris of the bombed buildings, and the ambulance personnel as they loaded the stretchers into their vehicles.

Sergeant Harper walked with the young trio until they reached the end of Old Cleveland Lane and past the warden's post and road closure. Just before they continued on their way,

Harper grabbed McCann by the sleeve, looked around and whispered, "How much are those tickets?"

Meanwhile Reg returned to take one last examination of Padraig Donoghue as he was placed into the rear of one of the ambulances.

"Reg!"

The young detective turned around to see his old friend, Tortoise Taunton, lumbering toward him. Reg had joined the Metropolitan Police with Taunton, who undoubtedly would never have passed the entrance examinations if not for the anticipated manpower shortages on the eve of war. Everything about Taunton was slow and awkward; his speech, his ungainly movements, and, according to a number of his less than kind colleagues, his mental faculties.

Unlike Reg, whose potential had been spotted almost straight away and who had been quickly assigned to be trained for CID after the obligatory six months in uniform, it was clear that Tortoise Taunton would be destined to spend his career as a PC on the beat, or behind a station counter, if lucky enough to keep his job at all. But Reg knew that there was more to Taunton than met the eye. He was hardworking, courageous, dogged, methodical and loyal.

"How are you, Tom?" Reg asked as the rear door of an ambulance was slammed shut by a young auburn-haired driver, from whom Reg was having trouble averting his eyes, and who was paying Reg absolutely no attention at all in return.

"Not half bad, ta," Tom replied, then handed the detective a small, shiny silver medallion on a fine chain. "This caught my eye. It was in the rubble not far from Mr Donoghue."

Reg examined it closely, but was unable to recognise the minute, intricate design.

"It's the Stuart coat of arms," Tortoise Taunton said, observing Reg's baffled expression.

Reg stared at his friend, eyebrows raised in surprise. "Blimey, Tom, you've got good eyes, and no mistake." Reg stared again at the tiny piece of jewellery. "The Stuart coat of arms. How did you know?"

"I'm not really sure, to tell you the truth," Taunton drawled. "Some things just seem to stick in my mind. I must have seen a picture in a book, or something."

Both men looked up to see Sergeant Harper returning, clutching a handful of theatre tickets. He noted Reg's bemused expression.

"It's Mrs Harper's birthday," the Sergeant announced, with a sickly smile and a tone of embarrassed defiance. "She loves Florrie and Tilly Tweedle. Thought I'd take the family. It'll be little Dan's first big night out."

Reg smiled. "All right," he said, "I'd better get over to Berkeley Square and give poor Mrs Donoghue the bad news. Well done for spotting this, Tom," he congratulated the PC. "I'm sure Mr Donoghue's family will be pleased to get this back. It probably has some sentimental value."

***

Detective Powell parked right out the front of the elegant Donoghue townhouse in Berkeley Square, next to a temporary A-frame sign on the footpath that ordered 'No Parking During Air Raids'. He ensured his hat was positioned with the necessary precision, double checked that he had managed to slap almost all of the dust off his suit, and that his tie was straight, then mounted the few steps to the door. There were no iron railings to be seen, he noted, all long gone for scrap. He rang the bell, and within a few moments a maid answered the door.

"My name is Detective Powell, of Scotland Yard," he announced formally. "I must see Mrs Donoghue, it's a matter of the utmost importance." The maid appeared stunned, then became lost in a moment of confusion as to the correct form of address for someone as important as a police detective. Eventually she curtsied and invited him into the downstairs drawing room.

While Reg was waiting, a small boy burst into the room with a toy Messerschmitt in one hand and a Spitfire in the other, enthusiastically re-enacting a dogfight from the Battle of Britain. Having run several half-circles around the room accompanied by rowdy impressions of machine guns, he suddenly noticed the intruder, and stopped and stared. By this time Reg had removed his hat and re-flattened his Brylcreemed hair. He smiled kindly at the stunned child.

"What's your name?" he asked.

"Edward," the boy replied. "But my friends call me Eddie."

"Do they indeed?" Reg replied. "May I call you Eddie?"

Eddie needed to think about this for a moment. Eventually he said, "If you like. What should I call you?"

Before this friendship could blossom further, Mrs Donoghue entered, and the boy and his aeroplanes were hastily ushered out by the maid. The door was closed and Detective Powell and Angharad Donoghue, more famously known in the society pages as Angel, were alone.

"I'm very sorry, Mrs Donoghue," Reg began. "Perhaps you should sit down. I'm afraid I have some bad news —"

CHAPTER SEVEN

"And, welcome back to this special Saturday edition of *City Roundup*, with me, Alf Burton, on the City Radio network, right around Great Britain and Northern Ireland. This afternoon, we've been taking an in-depth look at wild confrontations between Wiltshire police, supported by the Home Secretary's own flying squad, Armstrong's Army, and around six hundred new age travellers on their way to the Stonehenge Free Festival. We've been receiving updates from our reporters and sources at the scene, and in just a moment I'll be talking to senior news producer and cameraman, Jerry Templar. But first, for those who might have just tuned in, a little of the political background on today's dramatic events. Plans for banning the annual Stonehenge pilgrimage were underway at the Department of Environment when Sir Dick Billings was Secretary of State. Frequent listeners to *City Roundup* will of course be aware that Sir Dick is now Tory Chief Whip and Party Chairman, and sources close to Sir Dick's old department have told me that our current Environment Secretary has been under unrelenting pressure from both Sir Dick himself as well as the Home Secretary, for the ban to be applied and rigidly enforced. The case for the ban was certainly hardened last year, following what the government claims was damage to local archaeology, and a twenty-thousand-pound clean-up bill from the festivities.

"Around one hundred and forty vehicles decided to make the journey this year anyway but were intercepted well before Stonehenge by a squad of up to thirteen hundred riot police, manning roadblocks. This is sounding depressingly familiar already, isn't it? Once again, we've had reliable eye-witness reports of gratuitous violence by police, against unarmed civilians, including mothers with children. And once again, our Home Secretary, Sir Norman Armstrong is there, taking a very visible and prominent role in the police operation." Alf looked past his panel operator to his producer, at her desk beyond the studio glass wall. She was holding up a piece of paper, on which she'd hastily written in large letters: 'JERRY ON THE BLOWER'.

Alf nodded, then said, "I think Jerry is about to join us now, he's calling in from a telephone box very close to… yes, he's on the line. Jerry, what's the latest?"

"Good afternoon, Alf," Jerry sounded a little breathless, but composed. His news footage of the Orgreave riots the previous year, sold around the world, had cemented his reputation. He was now Alf's top producer, working exclusively for the Burton Investigative Unit. With Alf's blessing, he had decided to hitch a ride to Stonehenge with a couple of Donoghue print journalists who were covering the confrontation for the *Daily Focus*. Jerry considered that another police operation might provide some additional context to the documentary they were currently preparing, a follow up to the previous year's *Strike!* "I can tell you," Jerry continued, reading from his hastily handwritten script, "that coming upon the police roadblock, a number of the travellers' vehicles tried to get away by driving off the road and into a paddock. They became boxed in, and at that point the police went after them on foot. The leading riot squad were members of Armstrong's Army; they had their identity numbers covered and used their truncheons to smash against the sides of the cars, yelling at the people inside to get out, although they didn't allow them any chance to do so. They smashed windscreens and used their truncheons against people who were running away. They then vandalised a number of the vehicles that had been abandoned. A number of the vehicles were set on fire, I don't know by whom. Don't forget that these are the people's homes, not just their means of transport."

"Where was the Home Secretary?" Alf asked.

"He was with the police lines, along with Commander Johnson, the officer in charge of the Armstrong unit. They were coordinating with the senior officer from Wiltshire... Wait a minute... I'm on the phone here, I'm talking to —" Jerry's tone changed suddenly, and the next thing Alf and his nationwide audience heard was the sound of a brief struggle and Jerry's voice receding further and further away from the receiver. "I'm being arrested, Alf!" he cried. "They've taken my camera... all right lads, I'll come quietly, no need to get heavy! Careful with that camera there, boys!"

Alf's rage was intense, and he curled his hands into fists and pressed his nails into his palms until the pain settled his senses. Both his panel operator and producer, brought in on their days off, were stunned. Alf, being the experienced professional broadcaster that he was, recovered within a split second. His two assistants took the lead from him, and re-focused.

"Right, on that dramatic note, we'll take a short break," Alf told his audience. The panel operator cued up the first of a series of commercials, which extolled the virtues of the 1985 Austin-Rover Maestro. "Now we're motoring!" the voiceover announced excitedly.

Alf moved from the studio to the adjoining office, where the regular Saturday announcer, Greg Peters, was reading the paper and drinking coffee, having willingly stood aside so Alf could present his special news programme. He was young, but very accomplished and was working as a general relief, someone who filled in on weekends and worked the graveyard one am to six am shift during the week. But he didn't mind. City Radio was the ultimate independent radio gig; he would have swept up and made the tea for everyone if he had to, and he was looking forward to the day when he would have his very own top rating evening music show on the nation's premier commercial radio network.

"I'll get you to take over now, bonny lad, if that's okay with you. I'll probably come back in from time to time with some updates. I'll do a quick handover after the ad break. Thanks for being so accommodating."

"Works for me," the DJ said cheerfully. As they walked into the studio together, he said, "Jesus, Mr Burton, no wonder everyone says you're the best in the business. I was listening to Jerry getting arrested. Live on air! There'll be a gold gong from the Radio Academy for this." Alf's mind was more focused on ensuring that Jerry could be bailed straight away and would emerge from the police station uninjured, but he considered Greg's assertion, nonetheless. There was always room for another award on Alf's crowded trophy shelf.

The young DJ handled his own panel, as well as taking calls himself, so required no producer or panel operator. Alf sent his loyal little crew home, with thanks for their commitment in turning up at very short notice on a weekend.

Alf sat at his usual seat while Greg half-disappeared behind the panel. The commercials ended, and Alf said, "Thanks for your company this afternoon, we're returning you to your normal Saturday programming, but keep listening to City Radio for all the latest. Tirra for now." He nodded across the desk.

"Well, thanks Alf, dramatic stuff. Let's just hope that Jerry's situation is resolved quickly. This is Greg Peters back with you, broadcasting from London, and on your local City Radio station. Coming up we've got the Thompson Twins, Jean-Michel Jarre, Rod Stewart, Ultravox, Dire Straits, Nick Lowe and Style Council, as well as Creedence Clearwater's John Fogerty; his first album in ten years, *Centerfield*, is doing very well, listen out for the title track. But now, here's the Forgotten North and their new single, *Industrial Canal-side Blues.*"

Despite his anxiety over Jerry's plight, Alf admired Greg's traditionally deep radio voice, his rapid-fire delivery, but mostly his mastery of the mixing desk, something that Alf himself had never been able to operate competently, and still couldn't, even after eight years working for the Donoghue commercial radio network.

A permanent operator had been assigned to Alf quite early in his radio career, after he had accidentally allowed the words "smug upper-class gobshite", his own words in fact, to be broadcast following a frustrating interview with Lord Peter Carrington, then Leader of the Conservative Opposition in the

117

House of Lords. This in turn led to a strongly worded letter of complaint from the Opposition Leader, Mrs Thatcher, straight to Eddie Donoghue. Alf often reflected that although Eddie steadfastly resisted calls for Alf to be sacked or at least suspended, it had been Chief Opposition Whip Norman Armstrong who had spoken up for him and smoothed ruffled feathers in the end.

Alf left Greg to his afternoon music programme and hurried downstairs to his office on the executive floor. Alf knew that he was one of only a small handful of people to have direct access to Sir Eddie Donoghue, and it was something he never took for granted. Or abused. He phoned through to the duty switchboard operator, who advised Alf where Sir Eddie could be reached.

Having filled his boss in with what had happened, the next phone call he made was to Gwynne Fielding.

Jerry was back at work by Monday morning, and received a hero's welcome as he arrived at the Burton Unit offices on the executive floor. Despite the early hour, Terry Cox joined them and laid on some bottles of champagne from the PR office conference room wine bar. There was still no sign of Rick, even though it was almost certain that he and his family were back home again.

Sir Eddie himself was on hand to make sure Jerry was none the worse for wear, and to offer his personal congratulations for Jerry's commitment and professionalism. When Jerry cheekily asked Sir Eddie whether or not he would get his overtime extended to cover the several hours he was banged up, Eddie responded by telling him that the old Speers Shipping policy would apply. In the good old days, a merchant seaman's pay was stopped the moment the ship disappeared beneath the waves and out from under him. The moment Jerry was arrested, Eddie asserted, was the metaphorical equivalent. Everybody laughed, but Alf knew, despite the Donoghue group's innumerable and often terrible faults, stiffing their more valued employees was not one of them, and that Jerry would be backed one hundred percent, financially and legally. Mind you, Alf reflected, this loyalty to staff was something that might not be quite so evident to thousands of shipyard workers at the present time.

"It wasn't so bad," Jerry told them. "In fact, it was all worth the grief in the end, just to see the custody Sergeant at the Salisbury Road nick shit in his nice uniform pants when Gwynne Fielding arrived, accompanied by Valerie Smedley QC."

The charges of hindering and obstructing police were never going to fly, Valerie robustly informed the Sergeant as soon as she had reviewed the police case, and were certainly not supported by any of the rather vague evidence the arresting officers were able to provide. And she further informed him, in a not impolite yet nevertheless intimidating and sustained tirade, that the only sensible course that would avoid embarrassment to his force would be to think carefully about the consequences of proceeding with the charges, which would undoubtedly, in due course, lead to a civil action for wrongful arrest and any number of other dramatic consequences. The final result, she asserted, would probably see the custody Sergeant directing traffic and issuing parking tickets on the Salisbury Road for the remainder of his sorry career.

After a very short period of consideration, the custody Sergeant told Valerie that, on reflection, he considered a stern caution would more than suffice, given the circumstances.

However, he went on to explain, it appeared that an unfortunate accident had occurred on the way back to the police station. Somehow Jerry's broadcast quality Betacam camera had been damaged, and the video cartridge, containing footage easily as dramatic and damning as had been caught at Orgreave, was smashed beyond any recovery. The duty Inspector, called in to support the Sergeant in the face of Valerie and Gwynne's intimidating presence, was faintly apologetic, but Gwynne and Valerie assured Alf and Jerry that they would be raising the matter directly with the Home Office to ensure appropriate compensation was paid for a very expensive piece of professional equipment.

When Jerry and Alf were alone, Jerry confided, "Those coppers that collared me were also at Orgreave. I recognised them."

"Did they recognise you?" Alf asked.

"Ooh yes. No doubt about that."

"How do you know?"

"Well, it was possibly due to the fact that one of them said, and I quote: 'We've got you this time, you little bastard. Good luck putting this on the fucking television, you dipshit. Time for you to be taught a lesson you'll never forget.' No, 'that you'll never *fucking well* forget'. It seems to be Armstrong's Army policy that at least one profanity must be present in each and every sentence uttered."

"Did they get rough?"

"Rough yes, but not actually violent as such. I'd imagine the fact that I work for you and Sir Eddie made them think twice. I didn't get a belting, got called a few names, that's about it. No worse than what you'd cop from a schoolyard bully. One of them, you know there's always the good cop and the bad cop, well the quiet one was another face I recognised. Remember the one that was going to belt us with his baton in the street at Orgreave? You stood in front of us and calmed him down. You gave him your card and told him to get in touch, on the quiet." Alf nodded. Thus far no contact had been made, so it appeared that, in spite of Alf's prediction, the young officer hadn't been pricked by a nagging conscience after all. Mind you, Alf thought, who could really blame him? Officers who broke ranks always got one hell of a time from their colleagues. God knows how Honest Ron Coburn managed it for so many years.

As usual, Sir Norman Armstrong's highly visible role in active police operations garnered wide coverage, polarised between the fawning adulation of the leading tabloids — "Our Home Secretary Hero" — and the criticism of the *Guardian* and the vitriol of the *Militant Voice*, whose photographer had managed to capture the Home Secretary issuing instructions to Commander Johnson, while gesturing in such a way that, on the right angle, could have been mistaken for a Nazi salute. It wasn't clear whether or not the dark area visible directly beneath the Home Secretary's nose was an unfortunate consequence of a shadow, or whether there had been some creativity at play in the darkroom prior to publication. Either way, the implication was obvious. The Donoghue *Daily Focus* group of papers took a generally measured stance, although Alf's own column, *Westminster Watch*, took a very critical line, as did Roland Moreland's television reports.

***

"A full independent inquiry! I wouldn't mind so much if someone had the courtesy to let me know. I found out about it from the news, for God's sake!" Metropolitan Police Commissioner Ron Coburn was in the office of Charles Seymour, Special Minister of State at the Home Office. Having once been Deputy Chief Whip, Seymour was much more used to dishing out tirades, but, on this occasion, he found himself on the receiving end. Being well aware that Honest Ron and the Home Secretary were old friends and RAF comrades, Charles thought it prudent to take it. Up to a point.

The Commissioner had been at the Home Office for a good part of the afternoon, briefing the Minister on a number of matters, including two recent football-related tragedies. A fire at Bradford City stadium had killed fifty-six people and injured between two and three hundred. The cause, although yet to be confirmed, was thought to be a burning cigarette dropped in a styrene cup and then discarded amongst accumulated rubbish beneath the antiquated wooden stand. There had been a number of acts of conspicuous bravery on the part of local police and the spectators themselves. The Commissioner, having consulted with the local West Yorkshire Chief Constable, had collated a list of names for consideration for bravery awards. The Commissioner then solemnly updated the Minister on facts surrounding the death of a young fan in Birmingham, tragically killed amid rioting between Leeds and Birmingham City supporters that had resulted in a further twenty injuries and a trail of destruction in and around the stadium itself.

The politically thorny issue of football hooliganism had now spread across the North Sea to Brussels, where thirty-nine people had died and six hundred had been injured at the

European Cup final at Heysel Stadium, between Liverpool and Juventus. The deaths and injuries had occurred as a crowd surge crushed people against a wall which subsequently collapsed, and although blame was being laid primarily at the door of the Liverpool supporters, Commissioner Coburn suggested that they should wait for all of the facts before rushing to judgement, and should at all costs avoid making any kind of inflammatory comments. His sources in the Brussels police were suggesting that there may have been other factors in play, including questions over the condition of the stadium itself.

"Too late," Charles replied, looking at his watch. "Sir Norman is at Number Ten now and is about to do a press conference with Mrs Thatcher. It should be on the radio; we can have a listen."

They tuned in just in time to hear the BBC announcer say: "...the Football Association has taken the dramatic and controversial step of banning English clubs from playing in Europe. We now cross to Downing Street, where the Prime Minister and Home Secretary are briefing reporters, along with senior officials of the Football Association."

The FA Chairman explained that the travel ban was a pre-emptive move as it appeared that European football administrators were set to impose their own sanctions, and that it was important that the governing body of British football took the lead. "It's now up to English Football to put its house in order," he concluded, causing Charles Seymour to roll his eyes and mutter something about the bleeding obvious.

"We have to get the game cleaned up from this hooliganism at home and then perhaps we shall be able to go overseas again," the Prime Minister said, the FA officials having been unceremoniously shunted aside.

Sir Norman, in a somewhat rare appearance at any media event, congratulated the FA on its decisive stance, and urged the judiciary to apply the toughest sentences possible when adjudicating on cases of football-related violence. He also provocatively mentioned Neil Kinnock's opposition to the ban, mocking the Opposition Leader's assertion that "any ban of English teams would only benefit those who caused the murderous riot in Belgium", and then went on to accuse Labour of being too soft and therefore untrustworthy; not only on football hooliganism, but on any other law and order issue as well.

"So, nothing provocative then," the Commissioner muttered, then returned to his notes to complete his briefing. Once the football-related matters were dealt with, he turned to the recently announced independent inquiry, his anger about which had been festering in the time between the announcement and his scheduled briefing at the Home Office.

"Look, I'm sorry that you weren't advised straight away," Charles Seymour countered politely, while not sounding at all apologetic. "It was an oversight, on my part. There was no disrespect intended."

"No disrespect, are you serious?" Ron spluttered. "I should have been *consulted,* not summarily advised! And what I mean is, I should have been *consulted* by the Home Office beforehand, not told by the bloody press afterwards! I've spent my life dealing with corrupt and generally misbehaving police officers. Given the latitude, I could have sorted out that mess unfortunately known as Armstrong's Army, in five minutes flat. I've been trying to get Norman to address issues with the

124

unclear chain of command since Orgreave. Give me the latitude, I'll bring 'em in hand."

"I thought that's what Commander Ray Johnson was supposed to do," Charles argued slyly. "He was your own appointee, seconded from Thames Valley. The Home Secretary approved his appointment, on your own recommendation as I understand it, with the intention of, to use your own words, putting in place a strong leader to take them in hand."

Ron had to grudgingly back down. Just a little. "Well, he hasn't quite done what I expected," he acknowledged, a little sheepishly.

"You mean he went native."

"Yes. Completely housetrained almost straight away."

"So maybe in light of this, the time is right for a good look, from someone genuinely impartial. A full independent inquiry, just as we've announced. I would have thought that you would be right behind it, given your hard-won reputation."

"Well, Channel Four said I'm right behind it, so it must be true," Ron grumbled.

Charles Seymour allowed his own tone to become more conciliatory. "Well, best laid plans... It's not your fault that Johnson wasn't up to it. Although the Home Secretary holds him in high regard, operationally speaking."

"Charles, Armstrong's Army needs to be *disbanded*," Ron stated firmly. "That's the only solution."

"I'm afraid that's not going to happen."

"Why? The strike's over. They've done enough damage, surely to God. None of us are going to come out of this unscathed. You only have to see what's happening in Sheffield, at the trials of the Orgreave defendants. Those lawyers, Fielding and Smedley, are chewing us up and spitting us out without even trying. The best thing we can do is to put that whole episode behind us, as much as we can. Not that it's going to be easy to do that. I warned Norman about all this nearly a year ago. Did you know that Alf Burton is working on another documentary, this time focusing on the social and legal aftermath of the strike? He and Fielding are working closely together, God knows what's going to come out. It's going to make his first programme look like a repeat of *Dixon of Dock Green*. All of us are vulnerable, Charles. Your office politically, and a number of forces and constabularies, legally."

"The unit is not going to be disbanded, Ron, that's all there is to it. The best we can do is go through the pain of this enquiry, root out the bad apples and then get on with it."

"Why?"

"Why what?"

"Why is the unit not going to be disbanded?" Ron persisted. "As far as I can see there's no longer any operational need for their existence. And we can't afford the damage to continue."

"You've seen the news about the Speers-Donoghue shipyard, I take it?"

"Yes, they're going to shed thousands of... Oh my God! The Home Secretary is going to deploy them to Tyneside. Don't tell me we're going to have to go through all this again? When is this all happening?"

"The advance unit is there already. They've taken over a good part of the Hebburn nick."

"Bloody hell, Charles," Ron spat, "it was bad enough Archie Prentice trying to go behind my back all the time, roping my boys to do his dirty work without me knowing. I stamped all of that out, and our departments are now working cooperatively. The ongoing investigations into the Brighton bombing are a case in point — an example of what can be achieved with genuine cooperation, communication and trust between separate departments. I thought the days of me being embarrassed by people that should know better were over. But now this! Not only have I been ambushed by the public announcement of this bloody enquiry, but now I'm the last to know about this latest deployment of the flying squad. I'd expected better from this office. I thought we were all friends, as well as colleagues."

"Well, yes, of course we are, Ron," Charles reassured him. "The Tyneside deployment was discussed at Cabinet level and by the Civil Contingencies Unit, after which this office liaised directly with Ray Johnson, the *operational* commander. As to the enquiry, I gather a decision was taken jointly by Sir Godfrey and Sir Norman. It took us all by surprise to be honest, and it was up to me to do the publicity. I made the assumption that you, as Met Commissioner, were in on it, along with some of the regional Chief Constables, which is why I announced it the way I did. I made a mistake in my assumptions, but at least saved you any public embarrassment. As far as the great British public knows, this is partly your idea, with input from the Chief Constables. In terms of the announcement, I think I did you all a favour. But there's still a lot of work to be done, Ron, who's going to chair it, terms of reference, the usual bumflufferies. There's no doubt that you were always going to be called in to help at some stage."

"Well. Good," the Commissioner grunted sarcastically, then slumped in his chair, deflated. "Sorry, Charles. I'm sorry for letting you have it. It's not your fault. How is Norman, by the way? I don't think I've had any more than a few words with him since, you know. I saw him briefly at the VE Day fortieth anniversary commemorations at Westminster Abbey but didn't get much of a chance to say anything more than hello and goodbye. He arrived at the last minute, then left immediately after the service."

"On the surface, he's just the same," Charles remarked. "As for what's going on underneath, who can say? I guess he'll deal with it in his own way. We're there for him if he needs us, I'm sure he knows that."

"Is his son home yet, do you know?"

"From what I hear Alf Burton got on the phone to Sydney and convinced Rick to come home earlier than planned. He may even be back already, although I don't believe he's called. Sir Norman certainly hasn't said anything."

Ron knew better than to ask how Charles knew about what had obviously been a private phone call. They chatted companionably for a few moments, then Ron said his farewells, excused himself and left. On his way out, he was waylaid by a civil servant.

"Excuse me, Commissioner," the man said. "But Sir Godfrey Powell sends his compliments, and wonders if you might be able to spare him a few moments. He won't keep you long."

The Permanent Secretary, that's torn it, Ron berated himself. Earwigging undersecretaries had obviously overhead his confrontation with Charles Seymour and had run straight to their boss. You can't come into the Home Office and start yelling at Her Majesty's elected representatives without some consequences. And you certainly didn't want to end up on the wrong side of someone as powerful, upwardly mobile and as well liked as Sir Godfrey Powell. The next Cabinet Secretary, Sir Norman Armstrong had assured him, and a good man to have on your side.

As soon as an uncharacteristically nervous Commissioner Coburn was ushered into the Permanent Secretary's office, he began his apologies, but Sir Godfrey quickly cut him off.

"Oh, I wouldn't worry about that at all," he said, to Coburn's wide-eyed surprise. "Charles has roughed up plenty of people over his career. It'll do him the world of good to get some of it back, from time to time."

"Ah," was all the Commissioner could say.

"Would you like a coffee?" Godfrey asked him. "Or something a little more medicinal? I think the sun is close enough to the yardarm."

"Coffee, please," Ron said, just starting to relax as Godfrey ushered him toward a pair of comfortable chairs and buzzed for refreshments. They made pleasant, inconsequential conversation while they waited for their coffees to arrive. Once they were alone again, Godfrey got to the point.

"Did you know that my brother was a policeman? In the war?"

"I didn't know that," Ron answered, genuinely surprised for the second time.

"He was a detective working out of Scotland Yard. In 1941 he went into the Special Operations Executive, the SOE. Unfortunately, he went missing during his first mission, early the following year. He was no doubt captured, tortured, and killed by the Nazis."

"I'm very sorry to hear that, sir," Ron replied. "I lost my own brother. He was a sapper with the BEF, working on the railways in France. Ended up on the *Lancastria* when they were evacuated in 1940. Dunkirk. We only found out the truth about it much later; they kept it quiet at the time. My parents never really recovered, I don't think."

"Mine were the same," Godfrey replied. "My mother died later in the war. Pneumonia. My father battled on, largely for my sake, I think. He just passed away last year."

Ron wasn't quite sure what to say, or where this was even going. He was relieved when Godfrey continued.

"My father was always fascinated by my brother's work. I was too, of course. I was a few years younger than him, I just made it into the Home Guard. My brother helped me get there; got me in several months short of my sixteenth birthday. Actually, an awful lot of months. I certainly can't pretend to compare with your record, in the RAF of course... But I was wondering, and this is purely a *personal* favour you understand, if you might be able to provide me with some information about my brother."

"What kind of information?"

"Well, anything really. I curse myself that I didn't do this while my father was alive. He was becoming more and more interested in Reg's career, especially towards the end. Anything to do with SOE is going to be very hard, if not impossible, to find out in our lifetimes, I would think, so Reggie's police service is therefore the only part of his war activities that we'll ever know anything about. Anything for the family records would be very greatly appreciated."

"Yes, of course. I'd be very happy to be of help."

"Given my position —" Godfrey began.

"Don't worry," Ron reassured him. "I'll be discreet."

As Ron made his way to the street where his car and driver waited, he thought about Sir Godfrey's request. He was of course very happy to be of assistance, but thought that someone with Godfrey's security clearance could have easily found out just about anything, no matter how classified. Ron smiled. He probably didn't want to ask Archie Prentice for a favour, and who could blame him for that? Ron's old CO, a tricky customer as he had so often said, was someone you stayed well away from unless there was absolutely no alternative, and you certainly didn't want to be in his debt under any circumstances. But from Ron's own perspective, a favour done for the Permanent Secretary of the Home Office would be quite a handy little line of credit to keep in your pocket for a rainy day, especially the way the current ominous winds were blowing. But aside from that, Sir Godfrey was a thorough gentleman in every sense, and someone with whom Ron shared the common grief of a brother lost way too young, and someone Ron would have happily helped out in any case, with no strings attached.

The Commissioner's driver, a white-haired, elderly PC, had been waiting patiently, and Ron offered his apologies as soon as he climbed into the passenger seat.

"Sorry, Tom. The meetings just dragged on."

"Back to the Yard, sir?"

"No, straight home now. Bright and early in the morning, though."

As the driver determinedly negotiated the afternoon traffic in the unmarked, black Ford Consul, the Commissioner glanced at the piece of paper in his hand. After a few moments he turned to his driver.

"Tom, when did you join exactly?"

"Spring of '39, sir," he replied. "A few months before war was declared, it was."

"This is a long shot. You don't happen to remember a lad named Reggie Powell, by any chance? He joined about the same time as you. Went to CID almost straight away."

Tortoise Taunton was silent for so long that Ron wondered if he'd even been listening. Finally, he said. "I remember him. Along with you and old Bill Harper, he was one of the few real friends I've had in this job. And they fucken well murdered him, the bastards."

CHAPTER EIGHT

As Detective Powell was ushered into the drawing room, he noted that pictures had been removed from the walls, ornaments from the mantelpiece above the fireplace had gone, and the elegant furniture was mostly hidden under white sheets. He was soon joined by Mrs Donoghue, and they sat on comfortable chairs either side of a low baroque coffee table.

"Thank you so very much for coming back, Mr Powell," she said.

"No bother, I'm sure," Reg replied, and placed his hat on his knees. He looked around the room. "Are you leaving?"

"Yes. I'm taking young Edward... away. It's too dangerous here. God only knows what's going to happen."

Reg was about to make a vague comment about the dangers of defeatism, but changed his mind. "I see," Reg replied instead. "What about your late husband's business?"

"Oh, that's in very good shape. The board of directors have everything in hand. I intend for my son to still be alive to take his rightful place, when he comes of age. Regardless of any other external factors."

Like whether it's under a British or German regime, he thought bitterly. Then Reg remembered the endearingly boisterous little boy he had first met in that very room, careering around with his toy aeroplanes. "That's still a few years away," Reg observed. "How old is young Eddie now?"

"Only five, but you cannot plan too far ahead when one's family is concerned, Detective. My husband was very clear on that. I intend to honour his wishes."

"Very, ah, admirable, Mrs Donoghue."

"There's no need to be patronising, Detective Powell," she said sharply. "I can see what you're really thinking. You probably have very good reasons for your own patriotism, and your well-known dedication to the job that you do. My sole loyalty has always been to my family, and I intend to keep what little I have left, intact. If you consider this defeatist, or even treasonous, then that is your own business."

The fact that his thoughts had been read with such ease made Reg intensely uncomfortable. "I'm very sorry, Mrs Donoghue, I meant no discourtesy."

She smiled. "It doesn't matter. But I want to talk to you about my husband's death."

"What about, exactly?" Reg asked, now even more discomfited. He had been deliberately vague about where the body had been found when he had first broken the news, and to his relief, Mrs Donoghue had not asked too many questions. But it soon became clear that she knew a lot more than Reg might have given her credit for.

"There's no need to be embarrassed. I know where my husband was found, and I know why he was there. My husband had many powerful and influential friends. *Loyal* friends. I still have access to certain avenues of information."

"I don't understand what you're trying to tell me," Reg said.

"I believe my husband was murdered," Angel Donoghue said with enviable composure. "I believe he was dead before he was... placed in the establishment in which his body was found."

Reg remembered his own concerns about Paddy Donoghue's chest wound, and now deeply regretted having not made further investigations at the time. "Why would you think that?" he asked.

"Because he knew about... something."

"You mean, military secrets? The war effort?"

"I've been told that if I make trouble, certain people are going to feed rival newspapers a story that my husband was not only a frequent customer of, what's the word? Tarts, but that he was spying for the Germans."

"Who do you mean by 'certain people'?" Reg asked.

"You know who I mean."

Reg wasn't sure that he actually did. "Perhaps you would care to tell me," he encouraged.

"Things are not always as they seem," she replied. "And people rarely are."

Reg emphatically disagreed. In his mind matters were clearer than ever. Things were exactly as they seemed. The honourable British and her brave allies, led by Mr Churchill, were fighting against the evil, jackbooted, murderous Nazi regime. And Reg was going to do everything possible to help, and do his bit toward victory, as unlikely as that seemed under the current bombardment and in the wake of Norway and Dunkirk. Things could not have been clearer, or more straightforward.

"Perhaps, Mrs Donoghue," he ventured, "is it not possible, just playing devil's advocate, you understand, that Mr

Donoghue, with great respect, was at Dorrie, that is, Mrs Foskett's, um, disorderly house, for a perfectly obvious reason? As you yourself said, things are rarely what they seem. And why would people, whoever they might be, accuse him of spying, if he was not?"

"Don't be so naïve, Detective Powell. It does you no credit."

Reg felt that his professional façade was being systematically undone by Angel Donoghue's assured, even calculatingly cool, manner. It wasn't helping Reg's composure that she was intimidatingly beautiful as well, and Reg understood that he himself was no sophisticate like Ronald Colman or Jack Buchanan, both of whom could have easily matched wits with Mrs Donoghue. But Reg, if nothing else, was confident in his abilities as a policeman, and decided to assert his authority. He stood up and walked to the mantelpiece, on which stood the last remaining photograph, yet to be packed, of the Donoghue family. As was.

"I've had my own suspicions, Mrs Donoghue," he said firmly, looking carefully at the photograph, and the happy faces of wife, husband and son. "But if I'm going to take things further, I need specific information, rather than what appears to be little more than women's intuition. You said that if you made trouble, there would be unfortunate revelations in the press. Made trouble about what?"

"About this." Mrs Donoghue herself stood up, and produced a large and thick envelope, which she handed to Reg. She was now close enough for him to smell her perfume, and observe her flawless, blonde beauty, and her nearness did nothing toward his regaining of any sense of authority. She reminded him of slightly younger Anna Neagle, whom he had recently seen at the pictures in a film about Edith Cavell, the heroic nurse from the Great War. He read the handwritten notation on the envelope. "In case."

"In case of what?" he asked, puzzled.

"In case something like this happened to him."

"Do you mean this is his will? I really don't need to see —"

"It's not his will, Detective." She returned to her seat and took a cigarette from a gold case. She offered one to Reg, but he declined. She lit her own with matching gold lighter, and inhaled heavily, as if steeling herself for what was to come next. "It's a record of nearly five years of investigation into — I won't say any more. It's all there, in my husband's papers. I believe that the information inside is the real reason that he was killed. Nothing to do with his work for Mr Billings at the Ministry, and nothing to do with *allegedly* frequenting houses of ill-repute during air raids. And I assure you, Mr Powell, my husband was no spy."

Reg remained silent. He was aware that Padraig Donoghue was Irish, and the attitude of that country toward the Nazis, in Reg's eyes, left a lot to be desired. He was aware that a number of his colleagues were keeping a close eye on several London-Irish, whose sympathies were known to be republican. And imagine remaining neutral, and even, if stories are to be believed, actually helping the Germans. They must have had a shock when Nazi bombs actually fell upon Dublin several months earlier. Reg might have allowed himself to be convinced that the late Mr Donoghue, the most famous and successful of all of the London-Irish, was not a frequenter of Dorrie Foskett's, but on the spying issue, his mind would remain well and truly open.

Mrs Donoghue continued. "From what I understand, you are very well regarded in your profession. An honest man. Perhaps you might be able to get to the truth."

He examined the envelope again. "The truth of what?"

"Be careful, Detective. Beware the enemy within."

"The enemy within?" Reg replied, unable to hide his general bewilderment. "You mean, like fifth columnists?" Spies like your husband, he thought.

"You must leave now, Detective. I have to catch my train, and I still have a lot to do."

"Perhaps you will be kind enough to let me know where you can be reached."

"I think not. I have no wish ever to see you, or this benighted and doomed country ever again, Mr Powell." She extended her hand. "I wish you the very best." As he took her hand, carefully avoiding what appeared to be razor-sharp diamonds on her abundance of rings, Reg thought, with some confusion, that her tone was no longer coldly defiant.

She bid him farewell in a way that was almost apologetic.

***

"Powell!" The parade ground voice of Superintendent Sunderland Havill echoed around the cluttered Scotland Yard CID offices, as Detective Powell himself appeared from behind a filing cabinet.

"Sir?" he answered, as a number of his colleagues suddenly found great interest in the papers on their desks and looked determinedly downwards.

"My office!" Havill commanded tersely, and Reg complied, unconsciously rolling down his shirtsleeves and straightening his tie as he walked through the lingering cigarette smoke.

As soon as Reg was seated, Havill consulted some typewritten papers on his desk.

"Even by your standards," he said, in a tone of resigned exasperation, "this is quite, quite unbelievable. If I've understood your report correctly, you want to reopen investigations into the circumstances surrounding the death of Padraig Donoghue at Dorrie Foskett's. Not only have you asked to question, *question*, one of the most prominent members of His Majesty's Government, the former Minister of Information, but also to seek permission to dig up the corpse! Have you gone raving mad?"

"It's all there, sir," Reg replied, gesturing at his own typewritten submission on the desk in front of them.

"Yes, so I've read. If you were so concerned about Donoghue's injuries, why didn't you do something more about it at the time? You could've come to me then."

"I should have, sir, and I'm awfully sorry. I made a mistake by not following things through. But in my defence, there was nothing conclusive at the time, and I didn't come by certain other information until afterwards."

"Ah yes, this Donoghue dossier you allude to," Havill replied. "All a lot of unsubstantiated rumour, innuendo and the adding of two and two to make five, if you ask me." Havill leaned back in his chair and regarded Reg carefully. "You really are a monumental pain in the arse, Powell."

"Thank you very much, sir," the young detective replied impassively.

A few moments passed, during which the young man was subjected to a stare that was excruciating in its intensity and duration. It was quite a relief for Reg when Superintendent Havill finally spoke. "I wouldn't bloody well do this for anyone else," he barked. "First of all, keep this under your hat. Especially this blasted dossier, not a word to a living soul. I'll ask the Commissioner to speak to Mr Morrison, the Home Secretary, and see if I can clear the way for you to speak to Mr Billings, *informally,* at this stage. Then, and only then, will we make a decision about whether to proceed further and, if so, how. In the meantime, bring me everything you have. Best any sensitive papers are not left lying around. I'll take care of them myself."

"Thank you, sir," Reg replied, and observed a brief, friendly smile on the Superintendent's face.

"Now get out," Havill ordered harshly, pointing at his office door with his pencil and returning his attention to his papers. As Reg was about to close the office door behind him, Havill called, "How is your father, by the way?"

"He's very well, thank you for asking, sir."

"Good. Pass on my regards, won't you."

CHAPTER NINE

"Order. Brothers, order!"

The stop work meeting was being held in the old and draughty shed that, until the previous year, had housed the museum of Speers shipping history, with particular emphasis on the line's most notable peacetime tragedy — the sinking of the RMS *Lady Georgiana* in 1919. Plans for a state-of-the-art film studio and production facility in the now disused corner of the shipyard had collapsed, in part due to the impracticalities of the site, its proximity to the constant noise of manufacture, but in the end mainly because Sir Dick Billings had been well and truly shouted down by his colleagues over the matter of a government subsidy. He had initially tried to divert funds from the National Film Finance Corporation, then from the fund provided by the Eady levy, all to no avail. His desperate attempts to empty the dwindling coffers of the doomed Arts Council then met with surprisingly strong opposition from Stuart Farquhar MP. The Minister for the Arts had, unsurprisingly, been reluctant to do any kind of favour for the man who had bullied and tormented him for the vast majority of his career. If not for the influence of the most senior moderate, Northern Ireland Secretary Stanley Smee, Farquhar would have remained trapped and powerless in the depressing and unsatisfying wilderness of remote backbench irrelevance, and a damp and windowless office in the most inaccessible corner of the parliamentary buildings.

The sudden apparent political impotence of Sir Dick Billings had not gone unnoticed by a number of observers. In this instance not even his most powerful friend, Sir Norman Armstrong, could shore up his influence. The implications for the Chief Whip and Party Chairman personally, and the Tory Party as a whole, were being discussed in whispers all over Westminster and in much of the political press.

"Brothers!" Sidney Burton's bellow brought the large rank and file gathering to a semblance of order. A makeshift stage and long table had been erected against the shed's riverfront wall, and shop stewards and union officials were holding court. Behind the stage there was the unfurled banner of the Amalgamated Fitters and General Shipyard Workers Union. For the members, especially the older ones, the banner held the sacred significance of regimental colours during the red-coated days of the British Army, and had seen a few desperate battles of its own over the years. It was faded and frayed, even torn in places, but still standing.

"Order *please!* I'm now going to introduce Mr Austin Wells."

There were cheers and whistles as Austin Wells stood up and smiled in acknowledgement. The workers all fell silent for one of the union heroes of the recent Miners' Strike.

"Thank you, Brother Sidney," Austin said. "Now brothers, we find ourselves once again on the front line, in the fight against unemployment, and the fight for our rights as British citizens to have meaningful employment, for the betterment of ourselves, our families, to sustain and nurture our own communities; and for the good of the nation as a whole. Employment should not be a privilege, but a fundamental human right, as it has been for nearly forty years, when Mr Attlee, Mr Bevan, Mr Cripps, Miss Wilkinson and the Labour Party, with unstinting support from their union brothers, rescued this country from Tory greed, war profiteering and laissez faire neglect. But I warn you, brothers, the battlelines have changed. This Thatcherite country is very different than it was even one year ago. Even now, Armstrong's Army has mobilised against us, we'll see them here at the yard soon, make no mistake —" There were loud jeers at the mention of the Home Secretary and his now notorious special squad of police. "We've seen their tactics at Orgreave, and at Babbington, and Cresswell, and all over Scotland and Wales. Even pitted against unarmed, innocent travellers at Stonehenge. Using the police as a weapon of a corrupt state to destroy the working class, and the vulnerable, of this country once and for all. You must consider this, brothers, you must take into account all of the consequences, as you consider what course to take. It's up to you; there must be a decision that is taken by ballot, and democratically —"

One man in the front row looked to his neighbour. "What's all this bollocks?" he muttered. "Wells is conceding defeat before we even begin the fight, the gutless gobshite." He took one pace forward, and loudly interrupted. "What I want to kna is, where is Austin Wells?"

"Don't be so bloody daft, Clackers," Sid Burton said from behind the long table. "What're you talking about? He's standing right in front of you, man!"

"You kna what I mean," Clarence Bolton replied, and Austin gave way. "Where is the same Austin Wells that we

143

saw last year, on stage, at Headleyton, Nottingham, in Wales and everywhere, talking victory, defiance, talking solidarity and unity? We heard him on the radio and on the television, standing up to the Home Secretary, to the Prime Minister, to the government —"

He got seven shades of shit kicked out of him, that's what happened, Austin reflected, but his expression remained benign.

"A man who through his speeches and practical actions, bravely supported our brothers in the NUM. He was the man that everyone looked to, even more than Mr Scargill I would say, on the front line at least. Now here he is, back with the Amalgamated Fitters and Shipyard Union, and for w', he's already talking concessions, and defeat, before we've even begun!"

"Sit down, Clarrie," Sid Burton ordered. "Brother Austin isn't saying any such thing —"

"Well then, let him come out for w', with the same strength that he did for w' brothers from the pits —"

By now the momentum was with Clarence Bolton, a veteran fitter, union man and self-proclaimed proud communist. His contribution was cheered as thousands of accusing eyes glared at Austin, contemplating if he really was a gutless gobshite and class traitor. The mass of shipyard workers seemed to surge forward half a step in a wall of frustrated determination. But Austin Wells had faced down tough crowds before, and he was not going to be intimidated or allow his own opinion to be silenced; battered, bruised and emotionally broken as he was from the Miners' Strike. As Sid Burton quietly planned how they might safely bundle Austin out of the shed if things got out of hand, Austin Wells himself seemed to expand in size as he took a step forward. He was about to open his mouth when Clarrie continued.

"Now from what I hear, management have been making secret offers to certain fitters and other skilled workers, the younger men mainly, to stay under a new contract of employment and with reduced pay and conditions. How many have already broken ranks and signed? What does the union have to say about that, Brother Austin? Are you really w' brother? When this is all over, you'll still be paid, will still have your cushy TUC job, paid for by the workers out of their hard-earned wages! Maybe your Tory marras will give you QANGO to keep you quiet! Enjoy spending your thirty pieces of silver —"

The group reaction was mixed. A number shouted in support of Clarrie, but it appeared that the majority felt he had gone too far. Murmurs of "belt up, Clackers, you daft bastard" and "at least let him say his piece" could be heard amongst the general rumblings. There were also one or two hesitant queries about what a QANGO might have been, and answers to the effect that it was some kind of tropical fruit, something like a pineapple, didn't seem to make much sense in the context of Red Clarrie's accusation.

"Brother Clarrie has the right to speak his mind," Austin said, raising both hands. "That is democracy. Just as I have the right to demonstrate that he is completely wrong, as I'm about to do. If anyone here can point to someone that has fought harder for union members' rights and benefits than I have, then let him name that person right now. You may not agree with me, brothers, but I have the right to be heard. If anyone can give an example of when I've ever let down the lads, in negotiations, or in public, or even in private, speak now."

Even Clarrie grudgingly remained silent. "You and Sid's brother Alf saved our bacon in '83, Austin," emerged a voice from deep within the audience. "You can do it again."

Austin acknowledged the support with a brief nod and smile, choosing not to correct the perpetual mythology of Alf's involvement. "All I'm saying is that we are in negotiations with management, and I just ask for a little time."

"Negotiating bollocks!" Clarrie spat. "Did Armstrong's Army negotiate at Orgreave? Or at Stonehenge? Did Thatcher negotiate with anyone before she decided to murder the union movement and the pit villages? I say the time for polite negotiation is over. It's time for us to rise up in solidarity against the —"

Sid Burton stood up. "This meeting is adjourned. We'll reconvene one week from today."

"Adjourned?" Clarrie bellowed incredulously. "Now just wait a minute —"

"And now, we have a little surprise for you," Sid continued, not allowing so much as a breath in which Clarrie could try to seize control of proceedings once and for all. "A great hero of the labour movement, just returned from a successful tour of Australia and New Zealand, and a man who worked hard for our NUM brothers last year, helping to raise thousands of pounds for miners' relief, and also promoting our cause to his millions of fans around the world. He is the real Local Hero. Please show your appreciation for Freddie Wells!"

With his acoustic guitar, Freddie mounted the stage, slapped his brother Austin playfully on the shoulder, then faced the workers.

"This song," he told them, "was written in 1931, thousands of miles away, but the enemy is the same. And the fight goes on. *"Which side are you on, brothers, which side are you on?"* Freddie sang, strumming heavily on his guitar, with the entire shed soon picking up the words and singing along. *"Will you be a scab, brothers, or will you be a man?"*

Freddie then led the gathering in a rendition of his own acoustic shuffle *Canny Fettle*, which despite Rick Armstrong's opposition had been released as the Forgotten North's third single the previous year and had become their biggest hit to date. *"The sun shines on the shipyard, whippets run free on the green —"*

The first line of the chorus, *"The fitters' union has got w' backs,"* garnered a cheer as enthusiastic as any of those to be heard during a Forgotten North concert.

Freddie's brief turn was concluded by a singalong of *The Red Flag*, and at the meeting's conclusion he made himself available for autographs and to chat with his large contingent of fans amongst the shipyard's workforce.

Once the seemingly endless line of autograph seekers had finally been satisfied, the Wells brothers left the shipyard together in Freddie's somewhat battered and rusty Riley Elf, the neck of his guitar poking out the back window and Austin's overnight bag on the back seat.

"When are you heading back down south?" Freddie asked.

"Tomorrow."

"Champion," Freddie replied with genuine delight. "Sharon will be dead pleased to see you. I can't wait to show you the new place."

"That'll be nice. I think you might have saved me from being torn to shreds in there, by the way."

"Bollocks, you would've won 'em back. Tempers are running high, they're shitting themselves, man. And who can blame them?"

"I was very happy to see you, nonetheless."

"So how's it looking, genius?"

"Not good at all. I'll tell you why. The last major dispute over pay and conditions at the yard was in '78. Donoghue crumbled because the printers' unions went out in support, and then the TV studio technicians and building workers threatened to do the same. The whole Donoghue conglomerate was grinding to a halt. It was around the time of the Winter of Discontent, don't forget, so things were already becoming impossible for any business that relied on transport in any form. Eddie had to back down, he had no choice. The yard has always had a reputation for being militant, from what I hear the government were happy to be shot of it when it was privatised in '63 or '64. Generally speaking, Sir Eddie has pretty much caved in every time there was a demand. As a result, the yard is grossly overmanned, inefficient, and unprofitable. We only just managed to save it in '83, when it was going to be closed down and the site re-developed. But things have changed. The secondary picketing ban means the lads are on their own this time, and the government will do anything to further weaken the union movement as a whole. Even if the MoD contracts are disrupted, they'll stay loyal to Eddie. And to make things more complicated, Sir Eddie has personally offered a very generous re-deployment package for a large number of workers, with attractive opportunities to work in his other businesses. Building, shipping, road transport, hospitality, even some media internships. Not for everyone of course, but for a significant number. But if, and

148

only if, major industrial action is avoided. If the members dig in, the offer will be withdrawn."

"That's just so bollocking typical of the Thatcherite doctrine," Freddie said angrily. "They drive reasonable people into extreme action, then say, oh yes, cock, we'll negotiate with you, just abandon any kind of protest first. Surrender on our terms, *then* we'll listen to what you've got to say, but we won't have to do anything about it because you've already given up." There was a brief moment of silence; then Freddie asked, "So where do you go from here?"

"I'm fucked if I know," Austin replied. "On the one hand, I can call *everybody out*, and wind everyone up to a big fight that we simply can't win. I'll go down in history as the last doomed leader of the union movement, and thousands of people will lose their jobs with no hope of any redeployment or retraining. On the other hand, I do everything I can to smooth the way towards the inevitable, promote compromise and see that the maximum number of workers are given new opportunities, and the damage will still be devastating, but not as bad. If I do that, I'll be widely seen as a gutless bastard and working-class traitor who caved in to management and allowed Thatcherism's final victory."

Freddie genuinely felt for his brother. It was easy spouting your opinions from the stage, but the level of responsibility on his brother's shoulders was something he knew he could never sustain. He deeply regretted how much his brother seemed to have aged over the preceding year, and knew just how deeply he felt his sense of responsibility to the working men and women he represented.

Austin Wells had been subjected to a vicious, personal campaign from the Conservative press, had been spied on by the government, and had narrowly avoided prison for contempt of court. He had seen his miners crucified by not only the government, but even the BBC, which had selectively edited footage of the Orgreave riot to make it appear that the miners were the real aggressors and Armstrong's Army had been acting in self-defence. It was incredible that Austin was still upright at all, his brother thought admiringly. "Sorry, Austin, belting out *Which Side Are You On* probably didn't help you back at the meeting," he acknowledged. "Is there anything I can do to help?"

"Just keep being yourself," Austin reassured him. "This one I have to navigate on my own. I'll be about as popular as Ernie Bevin at a Communist Party meeting."

"Did the Commies hate Ernie Bevin?"

"Some did. They thought he sold out the miners and the working class by negotiating an end to the General Strike. Sound familiar? People have long memories."

"Do you think there might be some of your genuine old school reds amongst the Fitters and Shipyard Workers?" Freddie asked.

"I wouldn't be at all surprised. I think our Clackers might have those tendencies, don't you? And you could see he had a lot of support amongst the rank and file."

"Well, better you than me, genius. You'll do what's best, I have nae doubt. But please let me know if I can help."

"You can help by keeping the red flag flying. Speaking of which, when're you getting off your great big hairy arse and going back to work?"

"We have a show at Albert Hall in a few weeks, nearly sold out already, so Rick told me earlier today. We're launching the new album soon, *Industrial Canal-Side Blues.*

150

The title track is already out as a single, you might've heard it on the radio. I'm doing a bit more writing, and Rick's always got us doing promotional stuff; you know, interviews and appearances at record shops, that kind of thing. Then we'll be off on a long tour again, around the country and then Europe, extending over winter and well into the New Year.

"Albert Hall," Austin marvelled, grinning with brotherly pride. "I take it you'll be on your best behaviour there," he added mischievously.

"Oh aye, Rick has already laid down the law. But in return for me being all respectable and dignified beneath the royal architecture, he's booked us in at the Brixton Academy for a one-off nostalgia gig. We're going to dig into the vault and from the '70s punk days."

Freddie was happy to see Austin's lined and weary face crease into a broad smile. "You mean, *Fuck You, You Fascist C—*?"

"Most definitely, kidda!" Freddie interrupted excitedly. "And *Die Tory Scum*. All the old favourites."

"What did Rick say when you told him what your set list would be?"

"He said we've earned the chance to blow off a little steam. A kind of remission for good behaviour and hard work."

"How is he, since his mother —?"

"Just the same as ever. It hasn't been an easy time. The Australian tour didn't really go all that well, to be honest with you, despite all the press reports to the contrary. It was hot as fuck, man, tempers frayed, and our records tanked in the charts. We still broke even, made a little money, more thanks to Rick's management than our own abilities. We skived off quite a bit, at the beach mostly, we all ended up looking like lobsters. I had a big argument with the country's top music promoter who then wouldn't put us on his TV show."

"That's hardly surprising," Austin commented, grinning.

"I got revenge though."

"Do I really want to know how?" Austin asked with a slightly apprehensive smile.

"We were at the ABC studios, it's like the equivalent of the BBC over there. Anyway, while Rick was trying to negotiate a compromise with the producer of the show, I went to the studio where they film the performances. The show's called *Countdown* by the way, and there was a lighting rig behind the stage, that lit up with the name of the show, one letter at a time."

"What did you do?"

"I disconnected the letter O. Imagine mum and dad's surprise when they sat down on Sunday night with the kids, and watched, in six-foot letters, the word —"

"Yes, I get the message." Austin couldn't help but laugh.

"Unfortunately, the rest of the tour wasn't quite as much fun," Freddie continued as the shared laughter subsided. "After a canny start, in decent-sized theatres and arenas, we ended up playing a series of rough pubs around Sydney and in country New South Wales. I started to feel like Johnny Rotten must have, when McLaren booked the Sex Pistols into all those Honkytonk joints in the American South. It was my fault, mainly. Too much politics, I can't help myself. We fared a little better in New Zealand. But Rick held us all together as usual. I don't think Sally had a very nice time, with the baby. But with Rick, I don't know, it's like he won't let anyone in.

It's hard to say how he's going. We're all worried about him, but don't kna what we can do to help."

"I met his mother," Austin recalled. "Lady Armstrong, at the funeral of the cab driver that was killed at the Headleyton Flyover last year. She seemed to be a very warm, nice lady."

"Aye, she was that. She came to our show at Thames Television last year, when we recorded the live special. It was the night of some big government reception for the G7, with the US President and everything. From what Rick told me, his old man wasn't best pleased, but she chose to support Rick, and us, instead." Freddie became thoughtful as he struggled with the gears, making a grinding sound that set Austin's teeth on edge, and accidentally jerking the clutch with such violence that Austin thought he might have suffered some minor whiplash. "It makes you wonder, how someone like that could be married to a Thatcherite bastard like Armstrong for all those years and put up with him. You've met him. What do you make of him? Hang about, it's time for the news." Freddie turned on the car radio and rotated the knob as the signal became clearer, his eyes leaving the road long enough for Austin to have to loudly warn him as the little Riley was veering ominously toward a parked car at the kerb.

"Here is the news, from City Radio Northeast. After forty-eight days of proceedings, fifteen miners from Orgreave have been acquitted of the charge of riot, and a further eighty have had their charges dropped. Senior investigative correspondent, Alf Burton, reports."

"Ha'way, the lads!" the two brothers cried in unison, elated over the acquittals, and that their own much-loved friend was there to report on it.

"After forty-eight harrowing days for the defendants and their families," Alf's gruff but measured voice emerged from the radio, "today at Sheffield Crown Court, all fifteen miners on trial have been acquitted. Gwynne Fielding and Valerie Smedley QC were part of a team of lawyers defending the miners, and they are with me now. Miss Fielding, you've been highly critical of the behaviour of the police, and indeed the conduct of the Home Secretary, Sir Norman Armstrong, throughout the strike and beyond. Are you feeling vindicated today?"

"Vindicated, of course," Gwynne stated, her voice reflecting her sense of exhausted euphoria. "But we must ask ourselves, at what cost? Trust in the police has completely broken down, even in the most law-abiding of communities. And the actions of the police themselves, and their commanders — and I'm including the Home Secretary in this — must come under intense scrutiny. There was a concerted, organised plan by the police to terrorise not only miners exercising their lawful right to strike, in effect the criminalisation of the act of picketing, but also the calculated terrorising of wider communities, to bully them into submission."

"She knows what she's on about," Freddie said, and Austin nodded in agreement.

"Now, there's been two levels of this behaviour," Gwynne continued. "There's been the physical injuries, they've been well documented, but I would say that this entire process, the legal process, has been government-sanctioned terrorism in itself. Working men have been put on trial in such a way and on such terms that they were paralysed by fear, in that whatever the strength of their defence might have been,

154

whatever the merits, or lack thereof, of the prosecution case, they were well aware that they could have gone to prison for the rest of their lives. And, as I've previously mentioned, this was reinforced by the Home Secretary boasting in the press incessantly, about the charge of riot carrying life imprisonment."

"Miss Smedley," Alf said, "if I can ask you, how do you respond to the police claims about violence from the pickets? A number of injuries to the police have also been well documented. Would you concede that there was violence on both sides and the police, as well as the miners, had a right to defend themselves?"

"Bollocks! Whose side are you on, Alf?" Freddie's outrage was palpable as he yelled straight at the radio, and Austin had to once again remind him, robustly, to keep his eyes on the road as he drifted nerve-janglingly close to the centre dividing line, and a constant stream of oncoming afternoon traffic as they entered Newcastle itself. "What sort of question is that?"

"Alf knows what he's doing," Austin consoled him. "He has to allow both sides of the argument. People will make up their own minds."

"Well, mebbes," Freddie muttered sceptically, as Valerie Smedley QC took up the commentary, neatly avoiding the specifics of Alf's question.

"The evidence of a concerted and organised campaign is right before our eyes," she said. "The passage of the Police and Criminal Evidence Act through parliament is a case in point, increasing police powers in terms of stop and search, and also in terms of creating the roadblocks which were a key factor in preventing flying pickets from reaching their destinations. A similar tactic as applied recently at Stonehenge."

Alf concluded his live cross, and informed listeners that there would be a special edition of his programme *City Roundup* the following Friday during which the implications of the verdicts would be discussed at length, and Home Office Special Minister of State, Charles Seymour, and NUM spokesman Austin Wells, would be his headline studio guests.

"That'll be worth a listen," Freddie said. "I'll tune in."

"You'd better," Austin replied.

The two brothers listened to the remaining bulletin in silence; then the conversation carried on from where they had left off.

"Face to face, Armstrong's not as big a prick as you might think," Austin replied.

"That just makes him all the more dangerous," Freddie remarked.

Freddie had recently moved into a new home on the outskirts of Newcastle, and Austin admired the mock Tudor style as Freddie steered the car, trailing a cloud of white smoke like a bridal train, into the gates and along the gravel driveway, which skirted a manicured lawn, rose garden and precision hedgerows. The doors to the four-car garage were already open, and Austin couldn't help but laugh as Freddie parked the careworn little Riley next to his black Range Rover, which was parked next to his red Porsche, which was in turn parked next to his vintage Rolls Royce Silver Ghost.

***

"Commissioner Coburn is on the line, Sir Archie."

"Thank you, my dear." Sir Archie Prentice waited a brief moment, then heard the call transferred. "Ah, Young Ronnie, how are you?"

Commissioner Coburn was in such a good mood that not even smouldering decades-long annoyance at being called "Young Ronnie" by his old RAF commanding officer, could subdue his elation. "Some good news at last, Archie. A joint operation between Special Branch, the Strathclyde and Sussex Police Forces and Norman's lads, has resulted in an arrest in Glasgow. An IRA member. They believe him to be behind the bombing at Brighton."

There was a moment's silence, as Sir Archie gripped the phone and closed his eyes tightly.

"Are you still there, Archie?" Ron asked.

"Yes, sorry, go on."

"I thought you might like to give the good news to the relevant people, before the public announcement."

"Yes, I would very much like that. I'll advise the Cabinet Secretary and the Prime Minister first, then the Prime Minister can inform those of our friends and colleagues most affected." There was a further brief moment of silence. "Ron, perhaps you'd like to tell Norman. He'd appreciate it, coming from a friend; from one of us."

Archie's totally unexpected act of selfless consideration took Ron completely by surprise. "Thank you, Archie, I'll do it right away."

The Commissioner immediately phoned through to Roger Davenport, Sir Norman Armstrong's Principal Private Secretary. He was relieved to find out that Sir Norman was going to be working in his office all that afternoon, and asked

Roger to advise the Home Secretary that he would be there as soon as possible for an urgent briefing.

Before he left his office, he called for his driver, and picked up a folder containing copies of some typed and handwritten pages retrieved from a dusty old personnel file.

Once in the car, he said to his driver, "A while ago we were talking about your friend, Reg Powell. You said that they murdered him. Who did you mean exactly?"

"Them Nazis of course, sir. We never knew what really happened. It was something hush hush. He just disappeared from the job, and we heard later that he'd been on a secret mission somewhere in Europe, and went missing. He was smart though, he would've given them Jerries a run for their money."

"I see. Might you have any idea about the types of cases he was working on, when he was transferred?"

"I don't rightly know, sir. The last time I saw him, we were at a bomb site in Whitechapel. It was in the summer of '41. Old Cleveland Lane. A knocking shop had copped it, Dorrie Foskett's. One of the punters was someone high up in government. No, not in government, but working *for* the government. He was a newspaper owner, that's right, Padraig Donoghue. It was all hushed up, like everything else that went wrong in those days. No mention in the Sunday papers of him being found at Dorrie's. It would've been a big scandal."

"Sir Eddie Donoghue's father," Ron said thoughtfully.

"If you don't mind me asking, why are you suddenly interested in Reg?"

"I'm doing a little favour for his brother, Godfrey. Sir Godfrey, I should say. He's the Permanent Secretary at the Home Office."

"Is that high up, sir?"

Ron smiled. "As high as you can go."

Tom nodded with satisfaction. "Reg would've loved that. I remember he had a younger brother, now you come to mention it. Reg got Bill Harper to help get the young lad into the Home Guard. He was too young, but apparently, he'd been driving his family mad about doing his bit. Bill fixed it somehow."

Ron remembered Bill Harper fondly. He had been Ron's Sergeant when he first walked the beat, with PC Taunton, down the East End, just after the war. The Commissioner later worked with Harper's son, Dan, who as his Detective Sergeant, had been a loyal support during his long anti-corruption crusade. Ron had been pleased to finally give Commander Dan Harper the promotion he deserved, to Deputy Assistant Commissioner, when Coburn himself had been appointed to the top job nearly two years previously.

"Your memory's never let us down, Tom."

As they pulled up at the Home Office, Tortoise Taunton said, "You can tell Sir Godfrey, if I might be so bold, that his brother was dead proud of him."

"Always be as bold as you like, Tom," Commissioner Coburn said.

***

Sir Norman Armstrong was fulsome in his thanks that Ron had taken the trouble to tell him the news personally, before the Prime Minister's official briefing scheduled for later that afternoon. Behind the heavy door of the Home Secretary's private office, the two old friends spent some emotional minutes together, at the end of which, to Ron's intense surprise, Norman embraced him and held him tightly for several moments.

Soon afterwards, Ron was welcomed into the office of Sir Godfrey Powell, who already knew about the arrest and warmly congratulated the Commissioner. They briefly discussed their ongoing concern for Norman, but agreed that this news would be a welcome contribution toward his recovery, as it would for all of their friends and colleagues who had sustained injuries and lost loved ones.

"I have a little information regarding your brother, from his personnel file," Ron explained. "It's a little light, to be frank, but I've copied his service record for you, along with a number of his commendations. His Superintendent was Sunderland Havill, who you can see held Reg in very high regard."

"Old Sunny Havill, eh?" Godfrey commented. "Commissioner in the '60s, we remember him, don't we? He was the one that shut off your direct access to the Home Office right after the '64 election. Norman had barely time to clear his desk before the new broom arrived. I was much lower on the totem pole in those days, of course. I got shifted from assisting liaison with your squad, to passports and immigration. Norman wasn't the only one whose career was in the doldrums for a while."

"It certainly set us back," Ron recalled. "But we all got there in the end, didn't we?"

"We certainly did."

"Oh, here's an interesting little coincidence. My driver is a chap named Tom Taunton. He's been in the job since 1939, joined around the same time as your Reg. He told me how some strings were pulled to get you into the Home Guard."

Godfrey laughed. "My goodness me, he must have a good memory. That's true. I was driving my father, and my brother, mad, wanting to have some kind of proper way to be involved. It seemed like everyone was in uniform or doing some kind of war-related job. Even my mother was involved with coordinating evacuees and working with the Red Cross. I was a year or so too young, but my dad asked Reg to see if there was anything that could be done. I was the real-life Private Pike, which is funny in itself because I ended up in the same unit as Jimmy Perry, who wrote *Dad's Army* all those years later. My dad and I always laughed when we used to watch it, because Mrs Pike reminded us so much of my own mother, who used to steam in... Sorry, Ron, you didn't come here for a trip down memory lane."

"Tom said a couple of things you might find interesting," Ron continued, smiling at the thought of a young Godfrey Powell, parading in a line of veteran warriors and being told off about the scarf that his mother would have no doubt insisted that he kept wound tightly around his neck. "First of all, he remembered how proud of you your brother was." Godfrey smiled, his eyes sad. "He also said that he recalls the last time he saw your brother, they were down the East End. A knocking shop had been blitzed, and one of the deceased punters was Padraig Donoghue."

"As in —" Godfrey began.

"Apparently so. The circumstances were all hushed up."

"Thank you, Ron. I can't tell you what a help you've been. Perhaps one day I might have the pleasure of talking to your driver. It would be nice to speak to someone with such a direct link."

"I'm sure that can be arranged."

Once he was alone, Godfrey thought carefully. He sat down behind his desk and wrote a brief note, then sealed it within an envelope. He then ascertained that Sir Norman's driver would not be required for at least one hour, at which time he would be conveying Sir Norman to Number Ten.

Within a few moments, Eric Baker reported to the Permanent Secretary's office, his cap held under his arm in the military fashion.

"I have a brief job for you, Eric," Sir Godfrey said. "You'll be back in plenty of time to take Sir Norman to Number Ten." Eric nodded. The former Royal Marine and black cab driver had been recruited personally by the Home Secretary in the autumn of 1983 and was now an indispensable part of the Home Office.

"Can you take this envelope over to Padraig Donoghue House, please? It's for Alf Burton. Private and confidential."

"Yes, sir." As Eric left, he shed at least a part of his façade of formality. "Great news about that Irishman they locked up," he commented. "That'll do the Guv'nor a power of good."

Eric was a familiar face at Padraig Donoghue House, having often delivered Home Office ministers for studio interviews, so he was immediately allowed past reception and to the executive floor, where the Burton Unit had its offices.

Eric was surprised to be greeted by a young man, immaculately attired, but with a striking resemblance to Alf himself, although much slimmer and infinitely better groomed.

162

The young man immediately extended his hand. "My name's Aneurin Burton," he said. "Please call me Nye. I'm Alf's new personal assistant, and general slave." He noticed Eric's bemused expression, "He's my uncle. My da', Sid, is Alf's brother. A lot of people talk about the resemblance."

"You certainly have a better tailor," Eric chuckled. "And hairdresser."

"A lot of people say that too."

"Is he around?"

"I'm afraid he's tied up in the studio upstairs. He's pre-recording an interview with someone from the Labour Shadow Cabinet about something or other."

Eric glanced at his watch. "I don't have much time. I need to give him this envelope, it's private. From Sir Godfrey Powell."

"Of course. I'll take care of it myself, and make sure he gets it as soon as he's finished upstairs." Eric hesitated for the briefest of moments, but then thought if Alf trusted his nephew as his closest assistant, then that was good enough for him.

"My name's El, by the way," he said as he handed Nye the envelope.

"Oh aye, I know. My uncle speaks very highly of you." The Rottweiler, Nye thought privately.

Later that afternoon, armed with Godfrey's note, Alf made his way downstairs to the morgue, where past issues of the papers were stored. He took a large file and opened it on a sturdy, sloping desk, feeling like a Dickensian clerk labouring under the flickering candle in some dank office. It didn't take him long to find the relevant issue of the *Daily Focus*, from forty-four years earlier. The death of their own proprietor had naturally dominated the front page.

NOTED NEWSPAPER MAGNATE KILLED

It is with deep regret that we report that Mr Padraig Donoghue, publisher of the *Daily Focus* and numerous other newspapers across Great Britain, was killed in a recent air raid. Mr Donoghue was in London's East End, investigating conditions and morale, for a series of articles planned for a future Sunday edition feature.

Mr Donoghue was also recently on secondment to the Ministry of Information, acting as liaison between the government and the nation's popular press, ensuring that vital news and information could reach the general public in the timeliest manner.

Minister of Information, Mr Dick Billings MP, described Mr Donoghue as a patriot and a keen supporter of the war effort. "I am speaking on behalf of His Majesty's Government when I say this. Mr Donoghue had unhesitatingly placed the might of his newspaper empire at the nation's disposal, in the interests of our efforts to defeat Hitler," Mr Billings said. "This is a great loss to our nation, but we will follow his example, and keep fighting, as he would have wanted. As our Prime Minister said: we shall never surrender."

Mr Billings also expressed the nation's condolences to Mr Donoghue's widow and young son. Meanwhile, Editor-in-Chief of the *Daily Focus*, Mr Horace Trimble, said that Mr Donoghue's work would be carried on by his loyal staff, and that he will be greatly missed.

Warm tributes have also been received from the Prime Minister and senior members of the Cabinet, as well as fellow newspaper proprietors, Their Lordships Beaverbrook and Rothermere...

Alf re-read Sir Godfrey's note. He vaguely wondered if Eddie knew the real truth of where his father had apparently met his end. It certainly wasn't going to be a subject that Alf would raise with him. So, here it was. Reg Powell had been looking into the death of a prominent, senior associate of the government. The circumstances of his demise were potentially embarrassing, so there was a cover up. Not the first, or the last time, Alf knew from long experience. Then, coincidentally, Reg disappears into SOE and is never seen again. Reg's father had seen much more than a coincidence. Sir Godfrey had his suspicions as well.

And there was Dick Billings, in the thick of it, as ever. Alf was aware that Billings was replaced as Minister of Information very shortly after, by Brendan Bracken, then disappeared into an administrative backwater and really wasn't seen again until his famous fights with Nye Bevan during the post-war Labour government. Coincidence? Alf wondered. Or was there a reason that Dick had been quickly shuffled out of the way? So who else might have been at the heart of things? Norman's father, Richard Armstrong, of course. Mr Churchill's fixer-in-chief.

Alf had come to know Richard Armstrong very well in the last years of the post-war Labour government, when Alf had been a young and militant Labour-supporting correspondent. Unlike Dick Billings, Sir Norman's popular father had remained on friendly terms with virtually all of the members of the coalition War Cabinet, including Prime Minister Clement Attlee himself, and he remained influential, widely admired and respected, even from Opposition.

When, as a new lobby correspondent, Alf had approached him for comment on the finances of the fledgling National Health Service, his support of the British Nationalities Act, and his thoughts on Foreign Secretary Ernie Bevin's push for nuclear armament, Richard immediately remembered Alf from their first encounter a decade earlier in Hyde Park.

When Richard Armstrong announced his retirement leading up to the 1950 general election, he was the one Tory that Alf was quite sad to see bowing out. Even Aneurin Bevan, the Minister of Health and Housing, and no fan of bipartisanship under any circumstances, had been kind about Richard Armstrong. In particular, his strong support for the NHS and a number of other Welfare State initiatives; and the fact that he had remained solid even when the budgets had blown out beyond anyone's wildest fears.

Alf smiled, as he recalled the last time they'd spoken, on the eve of the election that would all but annihilate the Labour Party's majority and shatter any remaining hopes of decades of socialist government. "I don't know why," Richard told him, "but I have a feeling that you and my son might get on quite well. You're on the opposite extremes ideologically, but, if you can put up with each other, you might encourage one another toward a more sensible middle ground. It would do you both some good, personally and professionally. He's a good chap, Alf, as you are. And at some stage he's going to come to the realisation that he's not right all the blasted time. You might even come to the same realisation about yourself. Make the effort." Alf took the retiring MP's advice, and here they were, a little battered and bruised, but still standing, more than thirty years later.

Alf returned to his office to find his desk unusually tidy, and his mac hanging on his coat hook rather than slung over his chair. He smiled. Young Aneurin was proving to be very useful, although this new sense of order was taking a bit of getting used to. Alf's production manager, Jerry Templar, was reporting that Nye was a hard worker, could write copy surprisingly well, and was working diligently as an assistant researcher on the new television documentary they were preparing, on the court sequel to the Orgreave riots and the real, human consequences of pit closures. Alf soon became completely lost in his own thoughts; about fathers and sons, dark family secrets, murder and intrigue, and whether or not *The Enemy Within* would be an appropriate title for his new documentary.

He was jolted back to reality as Nye strode breathlessly into his office. "Roland is about to record his report on the Brighton bombing arrest. He thought you might like to be there."

"Let's go," Alf replied immediately, and they went upstairs to the studio floor. They entered the control room, from where they could see Roland seated at the news desk in front of two cameras which, to Nye, resembled robotic monsters out of an episode of *Doctor Who*. Each camera was controlled by a headphone-wearing operator standing behind it. A makeup technician was dabbing Roland's forehead as he shuffled his notes. Alf explained to Nye that the reports would form part of the local ITV news services, wherever Donoghue Publishing and Broadcasting controlled the local broadcast franchise. Other independent stations also bought coverage, particularly political news and analysis, as the operation Roland had inherited from Alf when he assumed the role of national political editor was, Alf pointed out proudly, the best informed and most respected in the country.

"Ready when you are, Roland," the director said into the intercom. He was seated at the control desk with the video editor. A bank of screens showed the view of the cameras on the studio floor.

"OK," Roland replied; the makeup person silently disappeared while an assistant walked in front of the camera and thrust forward a chalk board, detailing a production code number and date of recording, with a built-in, saucer-sized stopwatch which would count down thirty seconds.

"Very quiet, studio, now please. The Moreland Report, part one, take one." The clock counted down until zero, the assistant disappeared off camera, then dramatic orchestral theme music followed, overdubbed with the pre-recorded announcement by one of City Radio's smoothest voices. "From Padraig Donoghue House, London, broadcasting to D-ITV regions throughout Great Britain and her islands. This is the Moreland Report. And now, here is national political editor, Roland Moreland."

"I never had my own theme tune when I was political editor," Alf grumbled good-naturedly, eliciting a chuckle from Roland's director. "And I had to flipping well announce myself!" he added.

"Good evening," Roland said, gazing confidently into the camera. "Tonight, we bring you the news that an arrest has been made in connection with the bombing of the Conservative Party conference in Brighton last October. In an exhaustive investigation involving a number of police forces, including Sussex and Strathclyde Constabularies, backed up by special units from the security services and the Metropolitan Police, eight hundred guests from fifty countries who had stayed at the Grand Hotel in the weeks leading up to the attack were progressively eliminated from police enquiries. Only one guest could not be accounted for, and it became apparent that this guest had stayed in the hotel under a false identity. Fingerprints on his registration card were matched with those of a known operative for the provisional IRA, who was arrested last night in an IRA safe house in Glasgow. It is understood that the man in custody was planning further attacks with IRA accomplices.

"Metropolitan Police Commissioner, Mr Ron Coburn, today lauded the arrest, stating that it was as a result of tireless work and interdepartmental cooperation between a number of police forces and government agencies, and hoped that this would now bring some comfort to those most deeply affected. The Home Secretary, Sir Norman Armstrong, was unavailable for comment. However, Home Office spokeswoman, Janice Best, made a statement just moments ago from the House of Commons —"

"Right," the director interjected over the intercom. "We just need to do the intro for the PM's comments. Then you'll be just in time for your radio spot after the news. Then back here to record your interview with Mr Smee."

Roland nodded.

"We'll leave you to it, lads," Alf told the director. He leaned forward and pressed the intercom. "Thanks, bonny lad," he called. Roland looked up to the control room glass and smiled.

Alf and his nephew left the control room and walked down the carpeted corridor past the radio studios. They met up with Secretary of State for Northern Ireland, Stanley Smee, as he was ushered into the green room for pre-interview hospitality, the lavishness of which made the Donoghue studios a popular destination for politicians. It also helped to compensate for the fact that the interviewees often felt like they'd done several rounds with Joe Bugner after having been grilled by either Alf himself or Roland Moreland.

"Hello, Alf," Stanley said, and the two men shook hands. Smee was a regular guest on Alf's weekly radio programme, *City Roundup*, and despite the robust nature of their on-air encounters, they remained on friendly terms. Nye noted the minister's bodyguards, who remained discreetly close by, ever watchful despite the comfortable and evidently safe surroundings.

"What fettle, bonny lad?" Alf asked. "Have you met my nephew Nye? He's working with me now."

Stanley shook hands with the younger Burton. "Very pleased to meet you," he said. "I hope, in time, you'll be a lot nicer to me than your uncle is."

Nye didn't quite know how to respond. From working in the antiquated, remote drafting office in a rundown corner of the Speers-Donoghue shipyard, to consorting with Cabinet ministers and celebrities as they passed through the Donoghue studios, was still taking some getting used to. He opened his mouth to reply, but nothing came out. He flushed with relief when Alf rescued him.

"I see you've appointed a new PPS, young Mr Warbeck. A little dickybird also told me that you were instrumental in bringing Stuart Farquhar out of the wilderness as well, despite the best efforts of the Dries to defund his department. Are we seeing a new resurgence of the Awkward Squad? The rise of the moderates? I'm thinking that could be the theme of my next *Westminster Watch* column."

The Awkward Squad had been the name given to a dissident group of moderate backbenchers, that had also once included Sir Norman's Parliamentary Private Secretary, Janice Best, and had been informally led by Stanley Smee himself when still a backbencher. The name had been one coined out of frustration by then Chief Whip Norman Armstrong, as the rebellious group came out against a number of Thatcherite reforms. With the help of Sir Dick Billings, Norman had waged a relentless campaign against them, and had finally defeated them through a combination of bullying, intimidation, blackmail, and one or two strategic promotions. Sir Dick, Norman's successor at the Whips Office was, if anything, even more aggressive in his fight against any weakening of the Thatcherite defences. As a result, moderate voices had been predominately silent during recent times — a sad state of affairs, in Alf's opinion. "How's this for a headline," Alf continued. "Thatcherites! Beware of Rising Damp!"

Stanley Smee chuckled. "Nothing so dramatic, Alf. Appointments in the Conservative Party are made on their merit. Our people are individuals, unlike the automatons of the other side. No union patronage, or warring factions, here."

"Nice one," Alf replied. "Can I quote you?"

"Of course."

"Would Friday week suit, for the show?" Alf asked.

"I'll be in Belfast. You have a studio there, don't you?"

"Yes, but I prefer face to face, wherever possible, if that's all right with you. The Friday after?"

"Fine. As they say in Hollywood, get your people to talk to my people."

"I'll call your private secretary now and set it up." Never one to miss any kind of opportunity, Alf kept going. "Changing the subject, what's this I hear about an Anglo-Irish agreement, which is set to turn the long adhered-to policy of Ulsterisation on its head? What was it the Prime Minister once said? 'The government of Northern Ireland is a matter for Northern Ireland and for the British government, and no one else.'"

"How much do you know?" Stanley asked, and thought that he wouldn't be at all surprised if Alf knew just as much, if not more, than he did.

"Off the record, I understand that you are supporting negotiations between the Prime Minister and Mr Fitzgerald, the Taoiseach, in what my sources have described as the most significant development in relations with the republic since 1922. Now, correct me if I'm wrong, but the agreement will be in the form of a cooperative plan that falls into a number of general areas. The proposed pillars of the agreement will be matters of politics, security, the administration of justice, and law; and agreeing to enhance cross-border cooperation between governments and agencies. Not everyone is in favour. I'm aware that your own personal relationships with all sides of the Irish situation are smoothing the process for the Prime Minister, and will be key to achieving a final agreement. I also understand that the Prime Minister hopes to be able to make a joint announcement before the end of the year."

As Alf was talking, Stanley Smee was looking increasingly nervous. "Alf, off the record, you're not too wide of the mark, but we've still got some considerable way to go, and you're right, there is some opposition emerging even from within the Cabinet. I'd hate anything to come out publicly and derail —"

"You know I don't work like that," Alf reassured him. "I want a peaceful solution in Northern Ireland as much as anyone, and I think this is a positive step. But if I were you, I'd be more worried about the Unionists; from what I hear they're deeply unhappy, as is Mr Gow at the Treasury. It looks like we might be seeing ideological divisions re-emerge." The other likely troublemaker, Alf considered, would be Sir Norman Armstrong, but he kept that assumption to himself. The Home Secretary had never been a fan of any kind of compromise regarding Northern Ireland, and Alf wondered if the ultimate Thatcherite loyalist might even join Mr Ian Gow in opposing the agreement.

"I think that's being overly pessimistic," Stanley Smee told him. "Discussions are ongoing, and are at a sensitive stage, so the less said publicly, the better at this stage."

"I understand. All I ask is that you give me a frank, in-depth interview as close as you can to the announcement. That's all. And give me the names of the Cabinet members who oppose it."

"Nice try, Alf, you know I won't break Cabinet confidentiality. But as for the interview, you're on!"

"Done," Alf replied. Nye stared in wide-eyed surprise as both Stanley and Alf pretended to spit on their own hands and slapped each other's palms.

"Can you come to the studio now please, Mr Smee?" a young assistant interrupted, and the Secretary of State went off for his discussion with Roland Moreland, his bemused security men in tow.

Nye was still staring at Alf in something between hero worship and disbelief.

"What's a Tea-shock?" he asked eventually.

***

"And you're with us this afternoon for a special edition of *City Roundup*, broadcasting from London right around Great Britain and Northern Ireland, and we're joined this afternoon by Special Minister of State at the Home Office, Charles Seymour MP. Mr Seymour, a very warm welcome to the programme."

"Thank you, Alf, as ever, it is good to be with you."

"Can I ask, why you are here this afternoon and not the Home Secretary himself? What is he hiding from?"

"Really, Alf, I think you're channelling Roland Moreland. I'd expect greater measure from you. He's not hiding from anything, or anyone. As you well know, I am the Home Office spokesman for matters relating to the Miners' Strike, now mercifully over."

"Well, that didn't stop the Home Secretary from speaking throughout the strike itself, talking up the riot charges, very unwisely, and generally expressing his opinion."

"Sir Norman is the Home Secretary, as you rightly point out. He is therefore perfectly entitled to speak on behalf of his own department."

"So, in light of what's happened at the trial, do you think his ongoing commentary on the riot charges was wise?"

"I'm certainly not going to presume to speak on behalf of the Home Secretary."

"Let me bring to your attention something that Mr Michael Mansfield QC has said, following the collapse of the trials. He says that the Orgreave prosecutions used the courts and the criminal law for political purposes, and that the arrests of nearly eleven thousand miners last year, mass arrests on a scale never before seen, were for political reasons. The result of those arrests, he asserts, has been political trials. If I might go on, then I'll give you time to respond; I'm paraphrasing here, the only conceivable explanation, for the fact that thousands of law abiding citizens, entire communities, could suddenly and collectively commit criminal offences, Mr Mansfield says, is that large numbers of police have been prepared to fabricate evidence. How do you respond, Mr Seymour?"

"Well, as far as I can see, that is just a lawyer advocating strongly on behalf of his clients."

"Strongly and successfully, wouldn't you say? His own clients, and those of Valerie Smedley QC, and Gwynne Fielding all got off, and, even more embarrassingly for your department, the remaining eighty had their charges dropped."

"I wouldn't describe it as embarrassing. That is justice taking its course. If anything, it validates the existence of an independent judiciary, despite what conspiracy theorists might say. We all must accept the court's ruling."

"Let me read you a quote from Gwynne Fielding. 'It became obvious, as the line of police witnesses entered and exited the courtroom, that many officers had had large parts of their statements dictated to them, and that many of them had

175

lied in their statements, and then compounded those lies by committing perjury. They claimed to have seen incidents and actions that they could not have seen, or that they had personally arrested someone they had not, because other more reliable documentation, such as police vehicle logs, showed that they were somewhere else at the time. One statement with a signature that we knew was forged by a police officer, miraculously disappeared from the courtroom over lunchtime, and was never seen, or even referred to, again. Even the prosecutors were looking embarrassed and had no option but to drop the remaining charges.' Any comment, Mr Seymour? You have an opportunity here and now, to apologise on behalf of your government, for the egregious injustices that have been revealed."

"Any comment from me on these matters would be premature. And don't forget the Home Secretary announced, with the full support of Commissioner Coburn of the Metropolitan Police along with a number of Chief Constables, a full independent inquiry into the policing of the strike. No doubt all of these matters will be looked into rigorously."

"An inquiry that is yet even to convene. We don't know who'll be chairing it, or the terms of reference. We had the announcement, and now, nothing. In light of the events at the trial, I put it to you that the miners and communities affected deserve answers more than ever."

"Well, these things take time."

Alf looked carefully past the microphones and across the desk to Charles Seymour, whom he had known since the days in which Charles had been an assistant, then Deputy Whip under Norman Armstrong, in both opposition and government.

For the first time, Seymour's aura of smug superiority seemed to be crumbling.

He doesn't believe any of this bollocks any more than we do, Alf contemplated, as he continued to observe Seymour's expression; not unlike a garrison commander under siege, knowing it was only a matter of time before the enemy would be battering in the gates, and everyone within doomed to be either killed or taken prisoner.

Beyond the studio glass, Austin Wells observed quietly. Awaiting his turn.

***

The Home Secretary's Parliamentary Private Secretary, Janice Best, met Sir Godfrey Powell at the door to the Home Secretary's private office, having just completed taking instructions that she would in turn pass on to the backbenchers, to ensure every member was fully briefed on the latest Home Office policy. Sir Godfrey was due for his own meeting at any moment.

"How is he?" Sir Godfrey asked.

"Seems to be in good form, considering," Janice replied. "But it's hard to really tell, isn't it? He's really encouraging my police reform initiatives, which I'm grateful for. If we could just come to some face-saving way to quietly disband Armstrong's Army, I think we could be making real progress. I dread to think what's going to happen at the shipyard dispute. Oh, by the way, he told me that Mr Justice Wigham will be hearing the Garry Parker murder trial."

"Wigham?" Sir Godfrey answered thoughtfully. "He's certainly been earning his money lately."

"Indeed," Janice replied. "As you know, Sir Norman and the entire Cabinet were delighted when he ruled that the strike was illegal, due to the absence of the national ballot, and stopped the union from disciplining the Headleyton miners who wanted to cross the picket lines and go back to work. Mind you," she added sadly, "it was all to no avail. Headleyton Colliery is about to cease operations, the first of many. And our poor detective —"

"I was going to say something about breaking eggs in the cause of making an omelette," Sir Godfrey replied, "but it seems rather trite and flippant in the circumstances."

"Do you know much about him, the Honourable Mr Justice Wigham?" Janice asked, wishing to avoid any kind of philosophical discussion with the Permanent Secretary about the political and personal implications of the strike. Her own opinions were now diverging so dramatically from the government line that she didn't want to place Sir Godfrey in any kind of awkward position, yet she sensed that he too was a lot more sympathetic to the government's ideological enemies than he could afford to let on.

"Old Wiggie Wigham. I know *of* him, yes. When Sir Norman was Home Secretary under Douglas-Home back in '64, the department was much involved with investigating institutionalised corruption and police links with West End villains, particularly one named Cyril McCann. I think he's what my father might have called a 'rum cove'."

"McCann?"

"Well, yes, but I was thinking more of Wiggie Wigham in this case. I remember his name came up in connection with some of the enquiries that Mr Coburn was making at that time, nothing ever stuck though. Wigham seems to be a bit of a mixed bag. He's been known to take an unexpectedly activist stance, but he's also a Tory through and through, and an old friend of a number of very senior people in the government. Including our own lord and master."

"I wonder what that means for the trial, then." Janice mused aloud. "Good news or bad news?"

"Good for some, not quite so good for others."

"Yes, but which way around?"

"I beg your pardon, Sir Godfrey," Roger Davenport poked his head anxiously around the half-opened door. "But the Home Secretary is quite anxious to see you."

Godfrey smiled. That was Roger's polite and subordinate way of begging Godfrey to move his backside on the double, because Sir Norman was getting very impatient.

"Thank you, Roger, I'll be right in."

Janice returned to her own office and reflected once again upon her own conflicted feelings over how the wheels of justice were currently rotating. Although she was quietly pleased that the defendants at the Orgreave trials had been acquitted, and a large number of others had had their charges dropped, she also felt a degree of loyalty to Sir Norman, and the Home Office at large, although much of the time, she felt personally at odds with its operations and objectives. It was causing her no end of problems within her own South London constituency, and she was aware that one of her strongest supporters, local activist Quentin Quiggin, had now abandoned her and was planning to run as the SDP-Liberal Alliance candidate at the next election. Janice's own election agent was telling her that she was increasingly unlikely to retain her seat. Her senior role at the Home Office and political friendship with Sir Norman and the even more unpopular

Charles Seymour, were undermining her efforts in the community, despite slow but steady progress toward her most sacred wish: genuine root and branch reform of the police.

She hadn't been all that surprised when Valerie Smedley QC had exposed egregious dishonesty and procedural malpractices during the Orgreave trials, and wondered just how those same police, members of the Home Office's own unit, Armstrong's Army, would fare during the trial of Mr Parker. Once again Janice was conflicted. She wanted to see justice done, of course, but the undercover police officer killed in the minicab had been a valued member of the Home Office security detail before returning to undercover duties. Janice had liked him very much, and all of the senior Home Office staff missed his quiet, dependably reassuring presence; his long red hair in a ponytail discreetly tucked behind his collar.

And now, of course, Armstrong's Army was going to be right at the heart of everything again, at the increasingly tense Speers-Donoghue shipyard dispute, which threatened to erupt into violence at any moment, and derail once and for all Austin Wells's delicate negotiations. Janice now really felt for Alf Burton. He too was caught in the middle of two warring factions, with loyalties divided, and no end to the conflict in sight.

Perhaps, next time she was at Donoghue House for a studio interview, she might quietly ask him just how he did it.

CHAPTER TEN

Despite the frustrations of living at home with his lovingly protective parents, along with his extremely annoying younger brother Godfrey, Reg Powell enjoyed spending evenings with his father, as they chatted about his work, the progress of the war, and what to do about Godfrey's constant complaining that the war would be over before he was old enough to play his part.

Reg considered his father a genuine hero and remained fascinated by his tales of life in the former colony of Natal, during the days he commanded a detachment of the South African Mounted Rifles, based in Pietermaritzburg. Like most men of his generation, the retired Major tended to be less forthcoming about his experiences on the Western Front, where he had served as a Captain in the Natal Rangers, under his much-revered Colonel and mentor, Fforbes Armstrong. Now that the nation was at war, as His Majesty had said, "for the second time in the lives of most of us", Reg's father was as frustrated as young Godfrey at his inability to make what he considered a significant contribution; although he was out most nights as an ARP Warden, a job which Reg knew was far more difficult and dangerous than widely appreciated. He also worked in the City, where he had taken a vital role in the Lend

Lease negotiations with the US, and remained heavily involved in the financing of manufacturing, importations and other essential building blocks of the overall war effort. And besides, in Reg's eyes at least, he had more than done his bit in the last lot, and had paid a terrible price, although only a very small number of people knew the real truth. War wounds were not always visible to the naked eye. Reg had come to understand that very well, and he loved and respected his father all the more for the shared intimacy of comprehension.

As they sat opposite each other in easy chairs in their front room, smoking companionably before the elder Powell was due to leave for duty at his warden's post, Reg chose this moment to ask a question that had been nagging at him with increasing intensity as his investigations into the death of Padraig Donoghue progressed. "Dad, did you ever have a situation that you thought wasn't quite right, and you perhaps weren't quite sure why even, but you didn't know just how far to push it?"

"Well, that's an interesting question," Albert Powell replied. "Are we speaking hypothetically, or is there something in particular that's troubling you?"

"Hypothetically," Reg replied.

"Nothing that immediately springs to mind. Actually, here's one. Not long before we left South Africa, Sar-Major MacNair and I were investigating —" Major Powell stopped himself. He was about to recount his suspicions and investigations surrounding the death of his dear old friend and former commanding officer, Fforbes Armstrong, whom Reg had known as a rather eccentric avuncular figure, and at whose farm they had spent many happy hours as a young family before they came to England a decade and a half earlier.

Albert could hear the old Colonel's warnings, as clearly as if the old boy was sitting right there in the comfortable front room with them: "Look, I won't say too much. For your own sake. Suffice to say, my brother Piers is this generation's member, my family's contribution, along with God knows who else from the ranks of the so-called upper class. The Most Worshipful Order of Liege Knights of Charles the First. The Banqueting Club. You never hear of them, but they're pulling the strings, you mark my words. But they have no honour, and they're dangerous." The old Colonel had been adamant about something else as well: "And if you do get back to England eventually, don't take any chances. Stay well away from my family."

So what of the old Colonel's warnings, the need for secrecy? The potential danger. What about his own rather suspicious death, thrown from his horse? Fforbes Armstrong had deeply distrusted his brother, by then a retired MP. Then there was Piers Armstrong's associate General Sir John Prentice, Coldstream Guards. Both of these men were in the old province of what had once been the colony of Natal around the time of Fforbes Armstrong's death. Coincidence? Most probably.

But what of the present? Piers Armstrong, Albert Powell was aware, had been dead for some years. But Sir John Prentice? And what to make of the Right Honourable Richard Armstrong MP? A very powerful man, Churchill's closest advisor in the War Cabinet, so everyone says. "I hope my son gives that lot a wide berth," the Colonel had told Albert all those years ago. But had Richard Armstrong heeded his father's warnings? Did he even know of his father's true feelings, as they had been separated by continents for most of

Richard's life? Even now, thousands of miles and many years away, the old Colonel's warning seemed to be just as stark, just as pertinent.

"Suffice to say," Albert Powell continued finally, thinking that the less his son was burdened by his own secrets, the better, "that you won't always get your man. There are times that circumstances conspire against you, and there's nothing you can do, no matter how hard you try, or what is at stake. There are times you have to pick your battles. The most important thing is to live to fight another day." Albert noted that his son was unusually preoccupied. "Is everything all right, Reggie?"

"I probably shouldn't say too much. It's just that, something I'm working on is... not quite as it seems. I'm not completely sure just how to go about it from here."

"Have you spoken to Sunny Havill? What does he advise?"

"Oh, he sends his regards, by the way. He told me to be sure of my facts, and to tread carefully."

"I'm sure that's good advice."

At that moment, it appeared that the room was being consumed by a tornado, as Godfrey, arms and legs flailing, flew through the air and knocked his brother out of his chair and onto the carpet. After a brief struggle, Godfrey's dominant position was reversed and he found himself lying flat on his face, his arm bending to what was feeling like an impossible angle behind him, and with Reg applying just enough pressure to cause a series of involuntary whimpers to emerge from between Godfrey's clenched teeth.

Albert Powell regarded his two boys. "Reggie, is there something you can do about getting this little menace into the

Home Guard? At this rate Hitler won't get a chance to destroy our home, Godfrey would have seen to it already."

"I'll be down the East End tomorrow," Reg replied, slowly releasing his grip. "I'll talk to Bill Harper. See if he can pull some strings."

CHAPTER ELEVEN

"I've just found out who the presiding judge is going to be at Garry's trial," Gwynne Fielding told Alf Burton. Both had now become so blasé over the fact that their phone calls were very likely being tapped, they used the opportunity to have a little fun, and to strategically show Sir Archie, and whoever else might be listening, that they knew they were being surveilled, and didn't give a fig. They had been particularly emboldened since Gwynne and Valerie's overwhelming victory at the Orgreave trials. Alf had even taken to ending his phone calls with: "Tirra, Archie!"

"Tell me, bonny lass," Alf replied.

"Justice Wigham. Just as we thought, it's a fix. He's already taken a strong anti-NUM stance, as you know. I'm sure it's no coincidence that he's going to be hearing Garry's case. They need a safe pair of hands who will try everything to minimise the damage from forged police signatures and perjured statements."

"Wiggie Wigham is quite an enigma," Alf observed. "You never quite know which way he's going to jump."

"How much do you know about him?" Gwynne asked.

"Not a great deal. His name came up in connection with the West End corruption enquiries in the '60s. Nothing ever stuck though. There were rumours that a prominent villain, Cyril McCann, had something on him, but no one ever knew for sure. Wigham used to frequent McCann's most prestigious club, it was called the Top 'n Tail, in a little courtyard just off Great Windmill Street in Soho. He wasn't alone there; it was very fashionable in those days to be seen in clubs run by villains. Politicians, pop stars, football players, actors and celebrities all gravitated there. No one gave it a second thought. But I do remember that when McCann came up for trial in, I think around '74 or '75, Wigham was all set to preside, but recused himself, on the grounds of exhaustion and ill health. How do you think this will affect Garry's prospects?"

"Hard to say," Gwynne acknowledged. "Wigham is famous for having a breathtaking ignorance of the law; I think that was clear to anyone from the comments he made about the Headleyton miners' case. Austin Wells soon put him in his place, and just ignored him, you might recall."

"That's right. What did Austin say? Something about an unelected judge interfering without cause into union affairs?"

"Yes, and got slapped for contempt of court and a massive fine for the NUM. But here's the thing. Mr Justice Wigham has always been keenly attuned to public opinion. He adjudicates by the tenor of the press coverage. He reads the *Times*, the *Sun* and the *Daily Mail* religiously. I'm afraid your paper doesn't get a look in, Alf. Yours is way too even handed. Law students have written volumes about it, over the years."

"How does he get away with that?" Alf scoffed. "I can't believe you could be a circuit court judge for decades without knowing your business."

"Don't be so sure. The press loves him because his sentences for the most part reflect their own editorial opinions. I'd go as far as to say that some editors actually plant little hints for him in their coverage. He also has a lot of political support, from none other than our old friend Sir Norman. I also understand he's quite friendly with the Conservative Party Chairman."

"Is he?" Alf considered this rather fascinating alliance. He was aware that Wigham and Sir Norman were at school together, but the notorious Sir Dick Billings and a Lord Justice with a few apparent closeted skeletons was a situation that bore further investigation. Alf was aware that Billings was also a frequent visitor to McCann's establishments in the good old days. Was that where they first met? What did they get up to? Alf made a brief note on his desk blotter.

"And," Gwynne continued, "if anyone ever asks him a legal question, for instance at a function, or a journalist perhaps if he couldn't avoid them; whatever question they ask, he always answers like this." Gwynne affected her best mocking upper-class tone. "Ah yes, my dear fellow. That's all very well, but we must carefully consider the case law."

Alf laughed. "You mean, every question, whatever it is?"

"Every question, the same answer. The person he's talking to obviously doesn't want to appear ignorant, so they invariably just nod and agree with him."

"But if he's disregarding evidence and law, he must be getting overturned on appeal consistently," Alf countered, not sure if Gwynne was joking or not. "The Lord Chief Justice must have something to say about that."

"His appeal rate is no higher than anyone else's."

After Alf had rung off, he sent for his new personal assistant.

"Nye, I want you to do a little something for me, kidda. Talk to Roland. See what you can find out about a judge: the Honourable Mr Justice St John Wigham."

Nye wrote the name in his notepad. "Wait, how do you spell Sinjin?" he asked.

"Like Saint John."

"Why is it pronounced Sinjin then?"

"You know, like Marjoriebanks is pronounced Marshbanks, Cholmondeley is pronounced Chumley, that kind of thing. Some people say Powell like pole."

"What? That's weird. Is that a London thing?"

"Look, just try not to think about it too much. Anything we have in the news archives on Wigham; newspaper, audio tapes from the radio, and video. I'd be interested in any public comments he's made over the past few years. And also a look at his sentencing habits, and how they might reflect the tone of public opinion at the time."

***

"I've found what you were after about Mr Justice, The Honourable *Sinjin* Wigham," Nye Burton told his uncle. "There's been a lot written about him, but there are very few recorded public comments; in fact, I could only find one. The general tone of editorial opinion around him seems positive. The Conservative papers seem to congratulate him for sentencing that reflects community standards —"

"Whose community, I wonder," Alf contemplated aloud.

"The left-leaning ones hint that he's a little harsh, although not with any real venom. He seems to have developed a reputation as something of an activist around the issue of freedom of speech, and has been loathe in the past to pass heavy sentences for breaches of the Obscene Publications Act, or over matters of street offences involving prostitution, and also matters that fell under the old Sexual Offences Act. He's quite a fan of *Lady Chatterley's Lover.*"

Perhaps he was working for Cyril McCann all along, Alf thought. But then, who wasn't in those days?

"What was his public comment?" he asked.

"Well, in 1979, before the election, the legal affairs reporter of the *Daily Focus* managed to corner him as he was leaving the Ritz Hotel following one of Sir Eddie's Tory Party fundraisers. He asked Wigham for his comments on whether or not forensic evidence tendered by the Crown should always be trusted, even if it conflicts with credible witness accounts given under oath."

"What did he say?"

"He said, and I quote, 'In these instances, my dear fellow, one can do no better than give careful consideration to the case law.'"

***

"Morning, Alf!" Roland had taken the one flight of stairs from his own floor to Alf's office, and was all but bursting to pass on some news. "How are you?" he asked breathlessly.

"Not bad for a Monday," Alf replied. "Your overall coverage of the Brighton arrests was very well done, by the way. Comprehensive, factual, and sensitive. Nice work."

"Oh, thanks. Coming from you, that means a lot. What are you working on at the moment?"

"A few little projects bubbling away. The main thing is our documentary on the aftermath of the strike, the sequel to last year's instalment. But I've just received funding approval from Sir Eddie to commission a ten-part series on poverty and inequality around the country. I've been so preoccupied over Orgreave and the strike for the past year, I've really failed to appreciate the growing crisis in homelessness. More people are sleeping rough than ever, yet you rarely hear anything about it. I take my share of the blame for that. It's time to tell a few home truths to the great British public. I'm not sure that the longer-term implications of the sell-off of council houses have really been considered either, despite the rosy assurances of the Thatcherite propaganda machine."

"Can't wait to see that," Roland replied. "And by the way, just warn me before the broadcast of your second Miners' Strike feature, so I can book my holidays and be out of the country when it goes to air." They both laughed, although the fightback from the government following the airing of the first instalment had been so sustained and violent, it had nearly driven poor Sir Eddie to a nervous breakdown, and there had been real threats of government sanctions that would have sunk the entire Donoghue group of companies. Mind you, Alf realised, there would be more chance of Arthur Scargill being invited to a friendly weekend house party at Chequers with the Thatchers than of Roland running away from any kind of fight against the government. His famous on-air confrontations with the Prime Minster over the sinking of the *Belgrano*, and what he considered her willingness to casually accept unprecedented levels of unemployment, were just two examples of his constant urge to get under the ruling party's skin.

"Now then, guess where I was on Saturday morning?" Roland asked, anxious to get to the point of his visit.

"No idea, but I feel you're about to tell me."

"I was in Harrods."

"That's nice. I don't think I'd pass the dress code to get into Harrods. Luckily, Dolly and I can always find everything we need in Gupta's Mini-Mart, which is very conveniently close to our little flat in Pimlico."

"Another fine establishment, I have no doubt. Guess who I saw there? At Harrods, I mean."

"Tell me."

"One Eric Baker, aka the Rottweiler."

Alf thought that Harrods would have been the last place Sir Norman's driver would have likely frequented, but you could never really tell. Being one of the most senior government chauffeurs was probably quite lucrative after all, and he probably had a few quid tucked away from his years driving his black cab. Perhaps the old Peckham boy was getting a taste for the finer things. It was all very interesting, but Alf couldn't see why Roland had felt the need to come up and tell him personally.

"Guess who else was there?" Roland went on.

"Surprise me," Alf replied, not wanting to hasten the conversation, as Roland appeared to be enjoying himself so much.

"I'll give you a clue. Wherever go-eth the Home Secretary's Rottweiler, there go-eth the Home Secretary. No wait, I think that should be the other way round."

Alf thought it was nice that Sir Norman was finally feeling like getting out of his Knightsbridge townhouse, a dark and depressing Victorian museum, as Dolly had once described it, for a reason that wasn't directly related to work. Perhaps he was feeling a little better generally, which was a nice thought.

"I saw another couple of interesting people there, too," Roland continued. "All enjoying a late breakfast, or early lunch."

"Really?" Alf said.

"The Conservative Party Chairman, for one."

"Sir Norman and old Dickie have been friends for years," Alf observed. "It's hardly surprising they'd be out together. Perhaps Norman was there to offer Dick some moral support while he grovelled to the Fayed brothers after that leak of what he said to the 1922 committee, when their purchase of Harrods was made public. I understand that other senior Tory figures were very upset, after all you don't want to make enemies of anyone who nonchalantly waves half a billion quid around in one go. Not when there's an election to be fought in the next couple of years."

Roland chuckled. The most fascinating thing for Roland and Alf, and indeed for most of the chattering class of political commentators, was that a Tory backbencher had had the courage to leak against their Chief Whip and Party Chairman in the first place. It was perhaps another indication of Sir Dick Billings's dwindling power and influence. The headline writers had enjoyed themselves; Alf's favourite was from their own *Daily Focus*:

TORY DICK EXPOSED IN RACISM ROW — AGAIN!

Much of the media coverage had been in general, rather than in specific terms as regards to Dick's actual comments, but a cartoon in *Private Eye* showing Sir Dick as Lawrence of Arabia, locked in an affectionate clinch with a camel, left their readers in no illusions as to what Sir Dick had been implying, as he had let forth a typically Billings-esque tirade to his appalled colleagues.

"That's what I figured at first," Roland mused. "So, in light of the emergence of the Fayeds, Sir Eddie might no longer be the number one golden pet billionaire, then?"

"As the Chinese say with appropriate dread, we live in interesting times."

Roland laughed. "Still, compared to Dickie's 'be British or bugger off' kerfuffle from a couple of years ago, this latest little faux pas barely created a ripple."

Towards the end of 1983, Sir Dick had created a tumultuous national uproar when, on Alf's own radio programme, he had blamed increasing crime and urban civil disobedience on "your inferior foreign culture", and had less than politely encouraged immigrants to embrace British values or hastily depart back whence they came. It had been another in a long and distinguished line of racially charged, vulgar public gaffes from the accident prone, enduringly Teflon, yet in some ways unaccountably likeable, octogenarian MP.

"Perhaps not in the wider community this time," Alf acknowledged, "but it certainly set a few government choppers gnashing."

"Anyway," Roland continued, keen to eke out his story to the greatest dramatic effect. "Then I laid eyes on the third person at their little tête-à-tête brunch."

"Go on," Alf sighed.

Roland allowed a moment to heighten the suspense. "None other than… His Honour, Mr Justice Wigham!"

Alf gasped.

"I thought that might attract your attention. I wouldn't have given it a second thought, if Nye hadn't been down our office collating some information about Wigham for you last week. I understand that he's presiding over the Garry Parker trial."

"He is. Oh, nice work, Roland. Did they clock you at all?"

"I don't think so."

"What about Eric?"

"He gave no indication of it."

"Right, bonny lad. When are you talking to the Chuckler again?" The increasingly grim and determined countenance of the Home Office Special Minister of State, Charles Seymour, as he struggled to remain polite under relentless interrogation from Roland during their regular interviews, had afforded him the ironic nickname of "Chuckling Charlie".

"Probably later this week. I'm just waiting on confirmation from the Home Office press liaison."

"This Home Office has form on blatant meddling in the legal process," Alf commented. "Norman spouted numerous bone-headed prejudicial public comments about the Orgreave defendants, right up to their trials. I warned Godfrey, they'll never learn —"

"Bloody hell, Alf!" Roland interrupted, his already intense admiration for his predecessor as national political editor having taken another step higher. "You have direct access to the *Permanent Secretary?*"

Alf cursed his own lack of discretion. This was the second time he had let slip an arrangement that, for both Godfrey and Alf's sakes, needed to remain completely confidential. He swiftly moved on. "It should be interesting to hear Mr

Seymour's views on the value of an independent, apolitical judiciary, in light of this. See where it takes you; if nothing else it'll make it clear to them that they're not as clever as they think they are, and we know what they're up to."

"I'll stick it to him," Roland promised, and cheerfully departed back to his own office. It wasn't often that he knew something Alf didn't, and it was an exquisitely satisfying feeling.

As soon as he was alone, Alf jumped straight onto the phone.

"Gwynne Fielding, please," he requested as soon as the phone was answered. "It's Alf Burton." There was a brief pause, before Gwynne came on the line. "Why-aye, bonny lass," he cried. "Guess who was having egg and chips in the caff at H.A. Rod's at the weekend!"

But the conversation soon took a wholly unexpected turn. When Alf delightedly suggested that they might now have some serious grounds to question Mr Justice Wigham's assignment to Garry's case, Gwynne surprisingly begged Alf not to make any trouble. Things were at a critical phase, she explained. Garry himself had lost his bottle and was now desperate to plead guilty to just about anything up to and including regicide, just to put an end to his ordeal and to provide some certainty. Gwynne told Alf that this was not uncommon for prisoners living with the uncertainty of extended remand. The daily prison routine made them such creatures of habit that any kind of inevitability became desperately yearned for. She explained that even the toughest of hard men were known to fall to pieces over something as seemingly benign as a move to another cell, a change in regime conditions, or a new cellmate, no matter how convivial. In the seemingly endless months of Garry's remand, he had fallen into the prisoners' day to day routine and was well placed within the hierarchy of his wing. Anything out of the ordinary, no matter how inconsequential, could tip the balance from calm acceptance to an almost hysterical sense of panic. These breakdowns often led to fights with either the officers, or other prisoners, or both, and a term in either solitary confinement or the prison infirmary. Garry was, thus far at least, putting on the face of stoic acceptance, but Gwynne could see that it was only a matter of time before he unravelled in spectacular, and possibly tragic, fashion.

"But surely," Alf said, now having misgivings over his own general belief that Garry had been guilty all along. "He's seen the results with the Orgreave lads. All yours acquitted and the rest with their charges dropped. That must have given him some hope."

"He's well beyond that," Gwynne replied. "He sees his own case as different. Anyone with even a barely functioning brain has sympathy for the Orgreave victims, but Garry recognises that killing an innocent cab driver and an undercover member of Special Branch, whether accidental or not, is in another universe altogether."

"Is he going to consider naming names, to help himself? Can he not see that the real culprits should be brought to justice?"

"He won't under any circumstances; says he won't be lumped in with the grasses and the nonces. Apart from his own pride, he says his life wouldn't be worth living."

"His wife? Can't his family talk sense into him?"

"This is the problem, Alf, he won't even take visitors any-more. He says it disrupts his routine and saying goodbye each time is just too hard. He's communicating by phone and letter only, and even then, it's all about the television shows he's been watching, and the funny things that the other prisoners say and do. Look Alf, I've tried everything. I even had Austin Wells try to visit, but Garry wouldn't even see him, wouldn't leave the wing. Mr Scargill has offered his support. Austin's brother has also offered, but despite being a big Forgotten North fan, Garry won't even accept Freddie Wells's visit. All we can do now is go with his instructions, and hope that the CPS, and Justice Wigham, are in a conciliatory mood."

Gwynne went on to explain that plea negotiations were now underway with the Crown Prosecution Service, and the feeling was that Garry's guilty plea to either manslaughter or riot may keep his term below ten years. Gwynne was anxious that nothing happen to upset the current state of diplomatic relations, and she all but begged Alf to not make any trouble. At least for the moment.

"I understand, Gwynne lass. The only person who knows is Roland. He's a good lad, he won't want to do anything to harm Garry's chances for a just outcome. Such as they are."

Having had what in hindsight was quite a harrowing phone call with Gwynne, Alf reflected on what, if anything, he could do. When Norman Armstrong had been Chief Whip, the two of them often met up at a seedy pub in south London, The King's Head, apparently established in 1650, and having undergone only the bare minimum of rebuilding or maintenance since. It was far enough away from Westminster gossipers to remain a tightly controlled secret, and the meetings involved the exchange of information; leaks for Alf from the Chief Whip, and the odd tipoff from Alf whenever he sensed political problems or backbench unrest looming. It had been a mutually beneficial routine that ensured Alf remained the best-informed lobby correspondent in the country, and Norman's own pipeline of information was all encompassing. Their success in their individual, and polar opposite roles, was very much dependant on the other, and each had always recognised it, although grudgingly at times.

But even the previous year, that Godawful bastard year of 1984 when, just as you thought things couldn't get any worse, they invariably did, there was still an unspoken understanding and trust between them. They still looked out for each other, as much, and as inconspicuously, as they could.

But since Brighton, Norman was unreachable, and dangerously unpredictable. In ordinary circumstances, the apparently casual and friendly but carefully constructed conversation over Garry Parker's situation might have gone something like this.

"Listen, bonny lad," Alf would have said. "You were spotted with Dickie Billings and Wiggie Wigham, having an intimate lunch at that little corner store down the street from your house in Knightsbridge."

Sir Norman would have gone through the motions of obfuscation but would have instantly understood Alf's message. "A man is entitled to have a bite to eat with a couple of old chums, on the weekend, without it becoming common gossip in that rag of a newspaper you write for, or as part of your weekly screechings on the radio." Norman would have thrown in some good-natured ideological warfare as well. "In our Party, we have free choice, we can speak to whom we wish, unlike your Labour and union *marras* under the state control of your Stalinist regime, who have to ask permission to so much as buy a newspaper that's not the *Socialist Worker*, or have any kind of conversation with anyone to the right of Tony Benn or Michael Foot. Which, by the way, is ninety-nine percent of the country."

The sparring would have continued. Alf would have invited him to come on his radio programme, in answer to which Norman would have said something like: "Some of us have to run the country, you know, I can't fritter away my time debating the meaning of life on some pointless discussion programme on the wireless." Alf would have replied along the lines of: "Bollocks to your pompous, ignorant elitism", and the following Friday, Sir Norman would have arrived at the studio, right on time, and given Alf an eventful, intense and unrelenting on-air debate that would have made great listening. In the meantime, Norman would have got the message about interfering with the course of justice, or at least being caught out doing so, would have grudgingly, and privately, conceded he was in error, and set about quietly putting things right. Norman was a good man, Alf reflected, despite being a Thatcherite and standing for just about everything that Alf personally reviled. There were just times he needed to be reined in, for his own good, as Alf had done on a number of occasions throughout what would have been their thirty-five-year friendship, this year. Alf recognised that he himself needed some wise words of restraint from time to time as well, and his own career and credibility had been saved through Sir Norman's interventions on more than one occasion. In spite of their own individual faults and failings, between them they managed to find some semblance of a middle ground, keeping each other on the straight and narrow, and making them better men as a result. Professionally and personally.

"I do miss my old marra," Alf said out loud, with wistful sentimentality. He wondered if Norman felt the same way, in moments of quiet reflection.

But what to do now. Alf felt he couldn't risk a phone call to Norman like in the old days, and they certainly couldn't meet without Norman's entourage of private secretaries and bodyguards coming along for the ride. Since Brighton, the Winged Mafia — Sir Norman, Cabinet Secretary Sir Peregrine Walsingham, intelligence chief Sir Archie Prentice, and Commissioner Ron Coburn as the junior member, had closed ranks. Alf knew that, aside from members of the Home Secretary's own department, his old friend Sir Dick Billings and senior members of the Cabinet, Sir Norman was maintaining an aloof, often icy distance from everyone else. Alf was pleased, if perhaps a little jealous, that Norman was finding some comfort in his close friends and immediate colleagues, and felt that they were all fundamentally decent in their own often misguided ways. Except for Archie Prentice, who had no scruples and had elevated deviousness and generally amoral behaviour to the level of a disciplined martial art. He bugged and earwigged anyone he wanted to, on spurious reasoning and without accountability. And worse.

Alf knew that even Norman had his reservations about Archie, ever since they had been in the RAF during the war, but their little cabal of old marras, the Winged Mafia, was now more solid than ever. Alf also knew that he needed to tread carefully where Archie was concerned, knowing that the former RAF Group Captain would cheerfully order your execution and make you disappear without a trace, and without it disrupting his breakfast. And without a second thought. As Alf had very nearly discovered for himself, in fact. If not for

Norman Armstrong's intervention when Alf had been snatched by Special Branch over the Charlotte Morris papers, Alf reflected with an involuntary shiver, his scattered, piecemeal remains could very well be fertilising a Cornish field, or feeding fish in the English Channel somewhere off Rame Head, at that very moment.

What to do, what to do. After an afternoon of indecision as to whether or not a phone call to Sir Norman would be worth the risk after all, Alf came to the conclusion that the chance of making things worse was a real possibility. Eventually, he settled on a far more subtle approach, and invited Roland Moreland for a private briefing in his office before his interview with Charles Seymour.

At the appointed time, Home Office Special Minister of State Charles Seymour was delivered to Padraig Donoghue House by Eric Baker, who took up his usual position with the producer outside the studio, as Charles entered and took his seat in front of the microphone. As he was making his adjustments, Roland briefly excused himself.

"Sorry, Mr Seymour," he said, "I just need to tell my producer something. I'll be right back."

Charles nodded agreeably. Roland walked out of the studio to where Eric was chatting amiably with Nye Burton, who had come to observe the interview.

"Hello, Eric," Roland said cheerily. "All right?"

"Wotcha, Roly," Eric replied. "Battling on. No rest for the wicked. And you?"

"Never better. By the way, it was nice to see you in Harrods the Saturday before last. Sorry I didn't get a chance to say hello."

Eric smiled brightly. "That's all right, it doesn't matter —"

Roland darted quickly back into the studio before Eric finished talking, while the realisation that his boss had been rumbled briefing Wiggie Wigham struck the Home Secretary's driver in the manner of Monty Python's famous fish dance.

"Oh shit," he muttered, gripping his chauffeur's cap in his hands and thinking that it was going to be a tense, silent trip back to Queen Anne's Gate, contemplating what they were going to say to Sir Norman.

***

To say that Terry Cox was relieved to see Rick Armstrong's return would have been a dramatic understatement. Armstrong and Cox Public Relations, housed on the executive floor of Padraig Donoghue House and almost entirely devoted to promoting the interests of the Donoghue Group, was a financial and highly visible success; a living embodiment of the "Who Dares Wins" culture of the Britain of the ever more exciting 1980s. Their events and promotions frequently dominated the gossip and social pages of the national press and provided glossy spreads for any number of celebrity and fashion magazines. As Rick had been away on tour for more than six months, there was much to be brought up to date, and the two business partners sequestered themselves away in Rick's office to go over what had been happening while Rick had been away. They had spoken spasmodically on the phone, and Rick had offered some half-hearted advice, but Terry had been feeling increasingly out of his depth, especially as the situation at Speers-Donoghue remained on a knife edge and threatened to erupt into all-out war at any moment.

"Oh, before I forget," Terry said. "Bob Geldof has been on the blower, several times."

"What did he want?"

"He's trying to rustle up a few bands for a charity concert. A follow-up to the song for Africa they recorded last year. Doesn't sound too promising, if you ask me."

"I think our lads are doing enough of that kind of thing," Rick replied with unhidden disinterest. "I'll give him a call later, if I remember."

They turned their attention to Erin Airways, a matter of personal interest for Rick as he had sunk a large amount of his own money into the struggling airline, which was still to see any black ink on its balance sheet. There had been an additional shock recently, when one of Donoghue Publishing and Broadcasting's own travel magazines had labelled the airline the worst in Europe, in terms of customer service and reliability, and had urged its readers to avoid flying Erin Airways at all costs. Rick understood that Sir Eddie was leaning on Sir Dick Billings to do all he could to expedite the privatisation of British Airways, to try to level the playing field and make things easier for the Donoghue owned airline to access coveted slots at Heathrow, and rights to fly across the Atlantic to east coast cities in the US. Little progress was being made, prompting Rick to wonder whether or not the old Tory warrior was losing his touch. No doubt his father would be brought as general fixer at some point, Rick thought with a mixture of pride laced with a newly felt bitterness.

"The advertising campaign is going well," Terry observed. "'Anywhere with Erin Air' seems to be sticking in people's minds, and we are doing saturation coverage. Billboards, TV, radio, and mags. Ticket sales are solid, but not really taking off. Taking off —" Terry felt quite satisfied by his witticism, although it passed clean over Rick's head.

"I'm not surprised things are not doing better," Rick grumbled. "What that ad should say, is anywhere, provided you want to fly out of a city where it rains three hundred and sixty-four and a half days a year —"

"I think that's Manchester, not Birmingham," Terry offered with a smile, which quickly evaporated as Rick continued.

"—to a sunny resort that may or may not be finished when you get there. And because there's a better than even chance that your flight will be delayed or cancelled, don't rely on making it to your holiday resort until most of your bank holiday weekend off is already over. In fact, you'd do much better by renting a copy of *Carry On Abroad* from your local video shop, staying in and just getting hammered in front of the telly."

"I don't think things are quite as bad as that," Terry ventured.

"Experience foreign cultures," Rick continued, "provided your interpretation of foreign culture is fat, sweaty and sunburnt geezers from the suburbs with knotted handkerchiefs tied around their heads, carrying old copies of the *Sun* or the *News of the World* which flew out on the same plane that he did; and eating sausage, eggs, beans and chips at the local British-themed caff." Terry half-smiled again, but with overwhelming discomfort. This commentary was vintage Rick Armstrong; the master of amiable sarcasm, always ready with a joke or a light-hearted rant to keep spirits high when things were grim. But his tone had changed, and there was an undercurrent of dissatisfaction, even resentment, in his demeanour that Terry found a little off-putting, and perhaps even a little frightening.

"And to make things worse, while everyone is madly tossing off the tame Tory Billings, to try and speed up the British Airways privatisation, to give us a better chance at some Heathrow slots for the Atlantic routes. What happens?"

"Um —" Terry wasn't sure.

"Branson starts flying transatlantic and beats us to it. From where? Fucking Gatwick! And who names a fucking airline Virgin, for —" Rick struggled to think of another profanity but failed, "—fuck's sake!" he concluded.

Terry sat in stunned compliance, while Rick went on, having shuffled some papers on his desk and selected one in particular. "Now, to the pay-tv proposal. Whose genius idea was it to call the twenty-four-hour news channel the FNC, the Focus News Channel?"

"Actually," Terry corrected. "It's FNN, Focus News Network. Sir Eddie thought it would be brilliant cross-branding with the newspapers, which have been known as the *Daily Focus*, and not forgetting the *Sunday Focus*, since 1905, when it was changed from the *City Pictorial* —"

"Yes, I can do without the history lesson. Eddie plans to have a strong editorial line on this channel, as far as I understand. Hard news during the day, strong unashamedly one-sided conservative commentary after seven pm. A prime-time Thatcher propaganda channel, in fact."

"Yes, there's already been support from big sponsors, and the government are right behind it. It's going to be a lucrative —"

"Oh yes, I have no doubt. But did anyone think that the initials might not be the best idea?"

"It was Eddie's idea."

"If you focused your mind — no pun intended — on matters outside of your underpants, or away from that white powdered shit that you're shoving up your nostrils five times a day, and thought about business once in a while, you might have spotted the obvious marketing flaw."

"Marketing flaw?"

"What do you think people are going to call a right-wing Tory propaganda platform with the initials FNN?"

"Um —" Terry had been so taken aback by Rick's totally uncharacteristic barb, and the intensity of his barely supressed anger, that he was now flustered almost beyond coherence and unable to answer.

Rick continued. "Congratulations one and all, as we celebrate the launch of the *Fascist* News Network. That will be the name that sticks. Every time someone like the Prime Minister, Lawson, Heseltine, Seymour or my dad is on there, spouting their Thatcherite drivel, anytime there's a controversy, it'll be eternally known as the Fascist News Network. And, as you've pointed out, it would be sharing branding with one of the most respected, and widely read, national newspapers in the country; a masthead that's currently appreciated across all demographics for its fearless *objectivity*. As Eddie says, they stick it to both sides equally and the punters love it. But FNN will drag the whole group down into the fucking shit. The Daily Fascist, the Sunday Fascist. There's a massive working-class readership of the *Focus*; not that there is much of a working class any more — they've all been dumped on the scrapheap. And a few more when the shipyard starts laying off. If we're not careful how we handle this, anyone not a rusted-on Thatcherite wouldn't be seen dead with a copy of the *Focus* under their arm. And what about the political coverage on radio and TV? Labour, the unions, the Militant Trots, everyone will line up against us. Not everyone in this country's a Thatcherite, sometimes people in the Westminster bubble, or the second to top floor of a Fleet Street media headquarters, might forget it."

"I didn't think of that," Terry murmured, having slouched into his chair, defeated.

"Well, this is why Eddie pays us an ongoing fee that makes a telephone number look like it represents small change. We are here to advise him on exactly this kind of thing, and to lay out the potential consequences for him, to help him come to a final decision. We're here to protect him from himself. I'll put together a report and come up with some alternatives. When does a final decision have to be made?"

"Final decision?" Terry questioned, with mounting panic. "It's all done, the legal registrations, government reporting, logos and station identifications, everything is done. It's virtually ready to go; I'm just waiting for Erin to give me the nod as to when it's going live, then we can start planning the launch —" Terry suddenly wondered whether or not he should make a break for the door, as Rick was giving every impression that he was about to stand up, upend his desk and throw his telephone against the wall. After a brief, if terrifying moment, Rick visibly calmed down and Terry uttered an undisguised gasp of relief.

"Sorry, Terry, that was out of order. You've had a lot to deal with while I've been hiding away on the other side of the world. It's not your fault, I'm sure I'm over-reacting. We'll sort it, one way or the other, between us. Just like we've always done. It's not even twenty years, and look where we are. All this, from that little record shop just off Carnaby Street."

They smiled at each other. They had been friends since school, and had remained loyal to each other, above all else, since. If only to be back in their crumbling little single-roomed shop selling the latest Jimi Hendrix, Janis Joplin and The Who records; Amen Corner, Herd, Move, Faces and Mott the Hoople; posters, eight-tracks and cassettes. Every time it rained, they had to gather up all their wares, frantically stack them in a corner and cover them with tarpaulins as the virtually condemned building leaked like a rebellious government minister.

"Speaking of the shipyard," Terry continued after a few brief moments of shared camaraderie. "Erin says —"

"No amount of smiling and sunshine can make the loss of thousands of jobs look any better," Rick replied sadly. "We're not miracle workers."

"But that's our problem," Terry replied solemnly. "Everyone thinks you are."

CHAPTER TWELVE

So it came to pass that over seventy-two thousand people in Wembley Stadium, an entire nation glued to either their television sets or listening to the stereo simulcast on radio, along with a global audience of just under two billion, watched Live Aid, the charity concert that Terry Cox had dismissed as not sounding too promising.

Rick had been so preoccupied with his backlog of work that he had completely forgotten to return Bob Geldof's calls. The slot originally planned for the Forgotten North right after the opening; the band of the Coldstream Guards followed by a brief set by the hastily, and temporarily, reformed Status Quo, was filled by Style Council.

The following week, Freddie Wells led his band onto the stage at Brixton Academy, where a crowd of just under three thousand gave a rousing cheer. As usual, Rick was keeping watch backstage, and was still mentally flaying himself alive, despite Freddie's entreaties to the effect that the band didn't give a shit. Freddie asserted that Bob Geldof was a twat, and that the lads probably would have ended up in a backstage fist fight with Bono and those smug U2 fuckers anyway, so, all in all, it was probably for the best that they weren't there at all.

Freddie's general negativity to the concept of Live Aid had resulted from his involvement in the recording of the charity single, several months previously. Just before they had left on their extended tour of Australia, Freddie had grudgingly turned up for the recording of *Do They Know It's Christmas*, really only to keep Rick happy.

Having initially been offered the line "tonight thank God it's them", it had soon become apparent that Freddie did not possess anywhere near the vocal range required for that climactic line, and after some mutterings and whispered complaints, he had been ushered to the back row of the chorus where his only contribution was singing "feed the world" over and over again. Having loudly expressed his opinion that the song itself was a load of white colonialist middle-class patronising shite, he stormed out of the studio before the recording was even complete, and never expected to be invited back for the live show anyway. As it turned out, his voice, and even his presence, went totally unnoticed in the final mix and accompanying video.

But now, on stage at the Brixton Academy, the real Freddie Wells let fly. With a theatre full of ageing punks; a raging sea of spiked hair, torn denim, union flag T shirts and safety pins; pogo-dancing in short bursts only as their shins and knees weren't quite rising to their mid-seventies peak, the Forgotten North opened with their sped up version of *Jailhouse Rock*, a song featuring on their current live album, *Resurgence*, recorded during their colliery benefit tour the previous year. He dedicated the song to the miners, shipyard workers and minorities suffering under the fascist rule of Thatcher's not-so-secret police. It was a very neat segue into their second tune, and one that Rick knew they had been dying to play for ages. A succession of A chords was strummed with string-breaking heaviness, and drum skins pounded with as much power as could be mustered, then the opening line: *"Fuck You, You Fascist Cunt —"*

Freddie introduced the third song by describing Thatcherism as a cancer on society and conjured the spirit of Aneurin Bevan: "He had the Tories' measure," Freddie shouted, his voice distorting through the speakers. "Lower than vermin, he called them." The audience erupted. "And I dedicate this next song to the chief racist money-grubbing rat in the Tory shite-hole. *Sir* Dick Fucking Billings!" With strings of saliva flying, *Die Tory Scum* had the audience boisterously screaming along.

About ten minutes into the show, it became clear that the vast majority of the audience were completely spent. The pogoing had stopped, people were staggering and being held upright by their friends, and even Freddie was so puffed and hoarse that he could barely make a sound. The remainder of the band appeared similarly stunned and exhausted. Being a punk icon was clearly a much younger man's game. He looked off stage to Rick, who gave him an encouraging thumbs up. He shrugged and changed to an acoustic guitar, while a roadie strode onto the stage with stools for the three guitarists.

"Back to reality," he told the audience. "This next one is off our last studio album, *Winter of Discontent*. Feel free to sing along. And if anyone's brought their kids, I'm sorry about the swearing earlier."

Canny Fettle shuffled along in its predictably relaxed way, and in due course Freddie began to feel that he wasn't breathing air laced with rusty razorblades. He and the band recovered sufficiently to try their new single and a couple of tracks from the yet to be released new album, *Industrial Canal-Side Blues*, as well as further selections from their first album, some more memories of their punk days, although much more sedately performed, along with a number of Chuck Berry, Animals and Rolling Stones' covers.

After just under an hour, around half their usual time on stage, the band took their bows and departed without an encore. The audience seemed just as relieved as they were. Concerned that their performance had somewhat short-changed their fans, most of whom had been invited as members of the official fan club, now known as the Flat Cap Army, the group joined the throng in the foyer and on the footpath, to sign autographs and have their photos taken. Rick observed that it seemed more like a warm farewell liturgy to their collective, rebellious youth, now receding into the half-forgotten distance under the desperate struggle to make their way in the 1980s Britain of Thatcher, Lawson, Tebbit, Billings and Armstrong.

To his surprise, Rick found that he too was something of a folk hero, having so publicly taken on the police, and indeed his own father, over Armstrong's Army's harassment of Freddie Wells during the Miners' Strike, and was subjected to a tidal wave of sympathy over the very well-publicised death of his mother.

They eventually departed the Academy in an ageing and rattly chartered coach, well past its best days, courtesy of one the many largely forgotten and neglected Donoghue subsidiaries, Chamrock Charabancs. Freddie sat opposite Rick on the high-backed, worn, yet still quite comfortable seats which faced each other with a table in between them, upon which was a selection of refreshments.

"Well, that's it," Freddie lamented as he hammered his way into a Watney's Party Seven. "The old days have been farewelled, and it's time to be all respectable."

Rick laughed. "I'll believe that when I see it."

"Well, perhaps not *all* respectable. But no more yelling at everyone, it doesn't do any fucking good anyway. Sharon doesn't like me swearing on stage; she says it will be a bad example for our kids, when we have them. Especially now that we're going to be there forever, on video. Not sure that they're a good idea anyway. Who's going to want to come out for a show, when they can whack in a video cassette and watch us at home, sitting on the couch and getting mortal?" Freddie sighed, and looked out the windows as the coach negotiated the Brixton Road. "We've lost, Rick," he said eventually. "Anyone can see that. Even Austin is trying to talk peace with Donoghue, trying to avert war at the shipyard, and stopping the lads from getting their heads kicked in. If Austin has given up, it means it's really all over."

Rick noticed that Freddie was having trouble pouring beer from the oversized can. "You've forgotten to hammer the other little hole to let the air in," he told him.

"Oh, yes. Thanks. The Watney's Seven is another part of our golden years that's disappearing," Freddie lamented, while Rick considered the Watney's beer undrinkable. Rick wasn't even sure it was still available, but Freddie knew someone with a lockup full of unsold cans, and the temptation of a bulk purchase had been too great to resist.

"Austin's miners got off," Rick observed. "The first lot were acquitted, then the rest had their charges dropped. Alf's friend Gwynne Fielding was representing them, along with that QC, Valerie somebody. There are some powerful allies, it's not all doom and gloom. Kinnock seems to be gaining ground. Who knows what'll happen before the next election?"

"Quo is gone," Freddie continued sadly. "We saw the last of them at Live Aid; they won't be back again, scattered across the world like a broken family. It's like everything good is coming to an end. There's no future."

Rick couldn't disagree. Since Brighton, he'd stopped obsessively planning months, even years ahead, confining his ambitions to getting through the week as agreeably as possible. Whatever future there was would have to take care of itself. If not for his family; Sally, his irritating but ultimately lovable teenaged son James, and their beautiful little ray of sunshine Ellie, along with his corporate responsibilities; he would have stayed in Australia, lying on the beach until his skin blistered and all the pain and the anger had been seared completely away, leaving little more than a charred skeleton. Which was about how he felt anyway.

"Well, can't mope around," Freddie stated, brightening up a little. "It's going to be up to us, now, to carry on the tradition. Might as well just settle into our looming middle age, hit the road again and play some uncomplicated rock and roll. I'm going to write some songs about tits and shagging just like everyone else. No more Jarrow March, Miners' Strike, shoeless kids and Fuck the Fascists. And make a few more quid along the way."

"You've earned it, Freddie," Rick told him.

"I think we all have," Freddie replied. "Look, Rick, tell me to mind my own business, but have you seen your da' since you got home?"

"Not exactly," Rick confessed.

"Have you even spoken to him?"

Rick didn't answer.

"Now he's the last person I would ever have any sympathy for, well, the second to last. Actually, third if I count Denis along with... anyway, you should go and see him. Life's too short, man. Naebody lives for ever. Your mother taken... I looked at my brother when I made my little appearance at Speers-Donoghue. He looks about a hundred years old, for Christ's sake, and he's only two years older than me! All this shite isn't doing us any good at all. The stress, the constant anger, the fighting and confrontations, we're all going to be dead before we hit fifty at this rate. Austin told me that your da' is not as big a prick as he looks. His exact words, more or less. Fucking well go and see him and make right whatever's gone wrong between you." Freddie paused, as if summoning up some courage. "It wasn't your da's fault," he added finally, "what happened at Brighton."

Rick remained silent, as Freddie continued. "Our da' was pitman in his day, the black shite fucked his lungs and he can barely leave the house now. Has an oxygen tank, and tubes stuck up his nose, and looks like a living skeleton. He told Austin and me years ago, that if he saw us anywhere near the pit, he'd have the skin off our backs, man. He told us to go our own way. In his life he's loved my mother, Austin and me, his marras at the pit, the union, and his pigeons and whippets. That's his whole life, man! That's what he has to show for it. He won't even move out of his little council house; fuck knows I've tried to buy them a nice bungalow. You won't have your da' forever, Rick. Make the most of him."

There ensued a few moments of brooding, and not altogether comfortable silence. Eventually Rick said, "It mightn't be such a bad thing that Status Quo have disappeared into the sunset."

"There's nothing good about that," Freddie replied sullenly, relieved, at least in part, that the subject had been changed.

"It's just that I was playing the new album last night at home, and —"

"And what?"

"Well, now that Quo are off the road, it might not be quite so apparent to everyone that the track you've nominated as the second single, *Hold the Line*, is quite similar to *Hold You Back*."

"What do you mean quite similar?" Freddie asked, his forehead furrowed.

"Well, aside from the words, it's pretty much exactly the same. Same key, same chord changes. I played the tracks back to back. It's obvious."

Freddie drummed the table and nodded in time as he silently played and sang the tune in his head, his face dropping as the realisation struck. "Ah bollocks, man!" he cried. "I thought it sounded familiar when we were recording it, but I thought I'd just dreamed it!"

CHAPTER THIRTEEN

"Close the door."

"Sir?"

"I've had an answer from the Commissioner's office."

"Already?"

Superintendent Havill handed a slip of paper across the desk. "If you call this number, you can make an appointment to see Mr Richard Armstrong MP."

"Not Billings then?"

"Look, Reg, I don't think you understand the significance of this. Billings is a nobody. Hardly anyone in government can stand him, and he made such a pig's ear out of running the MoI that he's now shuffling papers in some out of the way administrative office. Armstrong, on the other hand, is one of the top members of the War Cabinet, a close personal friend and colleague of Mr Churchill himself. The only way you could get closer to the Old Man, would be to sit on his knee and light his cigar."

"Blimey."

"Exactly. See what you've bloody well started? Now listen, Reg. You didn't get to be staring at a Sergeant's exam after such a very short time in the job without being very good at what you do. But don't get cocky. The fact that they've wheeled Armstrong out means that they think you might be onto something, and they're taking it very seriously. They might even be worried. Remember what I said. Tread very carefully. Be one hundred percent sure of your facts, and don't forget that when it all comes down to it, we're all on the same side. It's not a gentleman's game at this level, my boy."

"I don't really understand what you're getting at, sir."

"Just be careful, and keep me informed."

***

Reg Powell parked his car, double checked the house number, then walked up the few steps to the front door. Within a few moments an elegant and expensively dressed lady on the brink of an enchanting middle age answered, her expression immediately welcoming and warm.

"Can I help you?" she asked.

Reg whipped off his hat with record speed. "My name is Detective Constable Powell, from Scotland Yard. I have an appointment with Mr Armstrong."

"Oh, of course. My husband is working in his library. I'll show you the way."

"I beg your pardon, Mrs Armstrong," Reg said as he followed her up one flight of stairs and then another, under the gaze of a number of portraits; generations of Armstrong statesmen and warriors. "I didn't actually expect you to answer the door yourself."

"Oh, we're not at all grand here," Fiona Armstrong replied. "I suppose you were expecting a butler, rather like Jeeves, to answer the door."

"Well, yes actually," Reg confessed. They had reached the library.

"My dear," Mrs Armstrong called through the half-opened door. "Mr Powell is here."

"Thank you." Richard stood immediately from behind his desk, upon which were stacked a number of official ministerial red boxes, and walked forward to shake the young police officer's hand. "Please take a seat," he offered, and the two men walked to a small corral of easy chairs in front of an empty fireplace.

"Can I offer you anything, Mr Powell?" Fiona Armstrong asked. "Have you eaten? Tea perhaps?"

Reg was half-way to sitting down when Mrs Armstrong spoke, and he stood up straight again as if the chair was on fire. "No, but thank you all the same."

"Well, I'll be downstairs in the drawing room if you need anything. Goodnight, Mr Powell. Very nice to have met you."

What a charming lady, Reg thought as he made his second attempt at sitting down. At that moment a young man appeared in the doorway, in the uniform of a RAF Flight Lieutenant. Reg immediately noted the purple and white ribbon on the young officer's chest. The Distinguished Flying Cross.

"Oh, sorry, Dad," the young man said, "I didn't realise you had someone with you."

"No bother, Norman," Richard replied. "Are you off out?"

"Yes. Perry Walsingham and I are having dinner at the Savoy, then we might go on somewhere. The Astor perhaps, in Mayfair."

"Perry's on the mend, then?"

"Oh yes. In cracking form."

"Good news. Pass on my best. But be careful, don't get carried away, and listen out for the siren. Remember what happened at the Café de Paris."

"We'll be careful, Dad." Norman Armstrong hovered for a moment, then realised an introduction to his father's guest was not about to be forthcoming. He nodded politely at Reg, who offered the same in return, feeling slightly jealous of the dashing figure the younger Armstrong cut in his tailored uniform. Reg was convinced that his own endlessly frustrating lack of success with what the lads at the station termed "crumpet" was wholly due to the fact that he was one of the very few young men to be seen in the street not wearing uniform. At least one of Reg's colleagues had even been presented with a white feather, the thought of which filled Reg with dread. Boy Scouts probably have more success with women, he sighed inwardly, as he looked admiringly at Norman Armstrong, suspecting that a decorated pilot would have absolutely no difficulties in that department.

Armstrong bade good night to his son, admonished him again to be sure to take cover in the event of a raid, and sat opposite Reg in one of the easy chairs. "Are you sure you wouldn't like a drink?" he asked.

"Yes, thank you," Reg replied. "I must say, sir, that it's very good of you to see me at home."

"Best all round, I think. Look here, I'm sorry about not introducing you to my son. In the circumstances —"

"I understand, sir," Reg replied, and pulled his notebook and pencil from his inside pocket.

"Now," Richard said. "I understand you have some concerns regarding the recent death of Padraig Donoghue."

"Well, yes."

"You can speak freely," Richard assured him. "I'm here to help."

"Well," Reg decided to lay all his cards on the table; sometimes the biggest risks reaped the most dramatic rewards. "I had some concerns at the time when his body was pulled from the rubble of Dorrie... Oh, I do apologise; that sounded insensitive. I understand that you and he were friends."

"We were, but I'm also a realist. I was in the RFC in the last lot. Paddy isn't the first friend I've lost to war, and I fear he won't be the last. We deal with it, and move on."

"At the time," Reg continued, "I thought there might have been something not quite consistent about his injuries. I still have my suspicions."

"Suspicions? I obviously don't understand the procedures as well as you, but a medical examination would have confirmed this one way or the other, would it not? An inquest?"

"Well, this was my error, Mr Armstrong. The body was dealt with through the normal procedures surrounding a routine death by enemy action. The superficial injuries were taken at face value during the examination. I didn't express my concerns at the time, but I've since received some information that has given more weight to my suspicions. Mr Donoghue's injuries were severe, as you would expect, but there was a particular wound that could have been caused by another action. I should have been more diligent at the time. I made a terrible mistake, and I'm trying to put it right."

"I see," Richard replied. "That was admirably forthright. So where does that leave your investigations now? I take it you believe there was some foul play surrounding Mr Donoghue's death."

"I certainly can't rule it out," Reg replied carefully. "It's not uncommon to see crimes that have been hidden amongst air raids. The wound I referred to could have been caused by a large knife, even a sword. But of course, that is speculation."

"I see," Richard repeated. "A sword wound, I'd have thought, would be highly unlikely in this day and age. Are your investigations leading you in any particular direction?"

"I'm exploring a number of lines of enquiry," Reg replied. It was a standard obfuscation, and one that an experienced political operator like Richard Armstrong would see through immediately. The detective tried to relax, and decided to become much more transparent, increasingly comfortable with the warmth of their developing rapport.

"I was hoping to have the opportunity to talk to Mr Billings," Reg went on. "I wanted to ask him about Mr Donoghue's role at the Ministry of Information, and whether or not there might have been something that he was working on that could have put him in some personal danger."

"I can answer that question. Even though Mr Billings was Minister of State, he was very much under my supervision. I don't mention that to imply that I'm in any way more competent than or superior to Mr Billings, but to illustrate to you that I'm perfectly qualified, and well enough informed, to answer your questions comprehensively. Padraig Donoghue's role at the Ministry was to act as a liaison between the department and the mass circulation press, of which his own newspapers formed a considerable part. This role was also by virtue of his prominent role within the Newspaper Proprietors Association. It was all about efficiently disseminating information to the public, about air raid precautions, careless talk, food and nutrition. About questioning whether or not one's journey is really necessary, about how to immobilise one's vehicle when there's an invasion alert, about rations and digging for victory. Of keeping calm and carrying on. Morale boosting and safety propaganda. All very important as part of the war effort, but nothing that would have placed him in any danger. And nothing that would have granted him access to any sensitive matters."

Reg was making hurried notes as Richard spoke. He reached into his pocket and pulled out the small Stuart Coat of Arms on its little chain. He leaned across and showed it to the MP.

"Do you recognise that, by any chance, sir?" he asked.

Richard took it and examined it carefully, the first icicles of anxiety constricting his stomach.

"It's the Stuart coat of arms," Reg prompted.

"Yes, so it is," Richard replied noncommittally.

"It was found in the rubble near Mr Donoghue. I've established that it wasn't his, and I've also managed to confirm, with a degree of certainty, that it didn't belong to any of the other, er, customers, or the ladies that were on the premises at the time."

Richard handed it back. "I'm afraid it means nothing to me."

"Was Mr Donoghue spying for the Nazis?" Reg asked.

Richard was taken aback. He was aware that he hadn't been able to disguise his surprise, but he recovered quickly. "Why would you think that?"

"The suggestion came up in my enquiries. I'd rather not say from whom."

"I see." Richard replied. "Officially, it's something I can neither confirm nor deny."

"Unofficially?" Reg asked hopefully.

Richard thought carefully. "Unofficially, I suppose we must all keep an open mind," was his carefully constructed reply.

"Can I also ask, sir, if you have ever heard of something called the Most Worshipful Knights, no wait sorry, I have it written down, the Most Worshipful Order of Liege Knights of Charles the First? Perhaps more commonly known as The Banqueting Club?"

By now it was taking all of Richard's two decades of experience as a politician and statesman to avoid telegraphing his deep sense of alarm. "I can't say I have," he replied calmly, "although I've always given the gentleman's clubs of London, assuming that's what it is, a wide berth. I'm a member of a couple but I never go. My uncle Piers, who was my predecessor in my constituency, was much more inclined in that direction. If I want to hear boring old men talking incessantly, I can go and sit in the House of Commons for an afternoon."

Reg laughed at the MP's own mischievous chuckle. "Sorry to ask this, but were you surprised when you learned that Mr Donoghue had been found in an, um, in a disorderly house, if I can put it that way?"

"Frankly, no," Richard replied, relieved that the questioning appeared to be veering in a different, although he conceded, probably just as awkward a direction. "I'm afraid his private life was... complicated. If there are any suspicious circumstances surrounding his death, I would suggest that they may have related more to matters surrounding his personal life and, ah, arrangements, than any work that he was doing for our government, or any rumours surrounding other... activities."

"I'm very sorry, Mr Armstrong, but I'm going to have to initiate proceedings to have Mr Donoghue's body exhumed. That way I can have it examined thoroughly by the police surgeon, and we can establish for certain one way or the other, whether or not his injuries were consistent with the bombing."

"And you firmly believe this is necessary?"

"I do."

"I see."

"Would I have your blessing, Mr Armstrong?"

"You need neither my blessing, nor my authority. You have your job to do, and you must do it as you see fit."

"It's presumptuous I know, but would be very helpful to me, if I could say that I had your support. I'm sure you would be keen to get the bottom of your friend's death as well. I only regret that my negligence earlier on has led us to taking this action."

"Well, I don't believe you have been negligent, and I admire your conscientiousness. I'm sorry I didn't introduce you to my son. I think you two would get on rather well. Perhaps another time."

"Yes, I would like that very much."

"Now, as to my support, you have it, of course. Anything I can do to help. What was Mrs Donoghue's reaction, when you told her what must be done? That couldn't have been an easy conversation."

Reg felt suddenly conflicted. Richard Armstrong had been so unexpectedly helpful and courteous; a large part of him wanted to discuss aspects of the late Mr Donoghue's Banqueting Club file with him and get his reaction. Mrs Donoghue had hinted that she still had very influential and well-informed friends. Was Mr Armstrong one of them? But then, if that was really the case, why did she entrust her husband's work, the very reason she suspected for which he had been killed in the first place, to a lowly Detective Constable? Why, if she *really* had friends at the top? Things are rarely what they seem, she had told him. Perhaps she was right. Suddenly life didn't seem so straightforward at all, and Reg began to wonder just where this was all going to end. Tread carefully, and be sure of your facts, Superintendent Havill had cautioned him on more than one occasion. Reg likened the feeling that was coming over him to that exquisite terror-excitement just after the siren had gone; that expectant silence, when you knew that it would only be a matter of time before the bombs started falling.

"Well, thank you very much for seeing me, Mr Armstrong," Reg said, closing his notebook. "And thank you for being so obliging. It's been a great honour to meet you, but I've taken up way too much of your most valuable time." As he stood up, his eyes were drawn to the large portrait dominating the wall adjacent to the door. The subject was a soldier, standing proud and tall in his red tunic and white helmet. A ceremonial sword hung from his belt, and Reg noticed that the determined, sharp-featured face beneath the helmet could have easily been Richard Armstrong himself. And the face was very familiar, although Reg suddenly realised that his own unique memory was of a much older man. The name of Armstrong hadn't registered at first, but now it all seemed to make sense. He knew very well who the man was in the picture, but he asked anyway. "Who is that, sir, if I may ask?"

"That's my father, Colonel Fforbes Armstrong. It was painted in 1894, when both he and my mother were staying here in London. It was when I was born, as a matter of fact. His uniform in the picture there is from the Queen's Own Natal Rifles, but he later went on to lead the Natal Rangers at the Somme, at the grand old age of sixty-five."

"I knew him," Reg replied, unable to take his eyes from the almost life-sized image on the wall and feeling an almost disturbingly intimate connection with the warm and friendly eyes beneath the sharp peak of his white helmet.

"You knew him?" Richard questioned, sceptically but with his stomach now feeling like it was doing somersaults within. "How could that be?"

"When I was a small boy," Reg told him, unable to take his eyes from the picture and smiling with the warmth of cherished childhood memories. "My dad used to take us, my mother and me, out to Colonel Armstrong's farm, not far from Pietermaritzburg. It was run like a military camp; I remember the sentry box, the saluting of the flag at sunset. All his old soldiers worked on the farm, they used to take me riding, and we'd run around and play on the veld. I remember some of his men, they were so nice to me. Private Stringham, he had most of his face shot away at the Somme. Private Willis, an ancient veteran of the Zulu Wars. The Colour Sergeant, Benson, and the Colonel's Zulu batman, Corporal Black. Those two were always arguing with each other, it was very funny." Reg was smiling longingly at his memories of an idyllic early childhood, and much-loved friends, thousands of miles and many years away.

Richard, for his part, was comprehensively wrong-footed by this surprising familial link. He thought carefully. "My goodness me! Powell! Of course, why didn't I realise? You must be Captain Powell's son." Richard's tone was convincingly joyous, but his real feelings were those of an intense, debilitating dread.

"That's right, Mr Armstrong," Reg said excitedly. "My father transferred to the South African Mounted Rifles after the war and was made up to Major. He was sort of a policeman himself, in and around what had been the old colony of Natal."

"I met your father," Richard said. "We were both visiting my father in hospital as he was convalescing from his wounds." Richard also remembered that Captain Albert Powell had just been released from Craiglockhart, a hospital for shell-shocked officers, but kept that to himself. "My God, your father, and his Sergeant; MacNair, I think his name was, saved my father's life. They found him in a shell crater after the first day on the Somme. If not for his rather harebrained decision to wear his old QONR red tunic that day, they might never have stumbled across him,"

"My father told me all about it," Reg said. "I can't wait to tell him that I've met you today." Suddenly Reg wasn't the serious and mature police detective, but a boy captivated by colonial adventures long past, and the intense pride he felt in his own father's battlefield bravery.

"I'm sorry, Detective Powell," Richard said, "I would love nothing more than seeing your father again in the future, but I'm afraid you won't be able to tell anyone about our meeting today. Not even him. The Official Secrets Act applies, I'm afraid."

Reg immediately agreed, although wondered why, if Padraig Donoghue's war work related solely to propaganda and essential yet ultimately harmless information. But he was hardly going to argue with someone as senior and powerful as the Right Honourable Richard Armstrong MP. He inwardly cursed himself for his momentary lack of professionalism, but noted that the MP didn't seem to mind, and appeared as captivated by their shared nostalgia as he was.

The two men exchanged a warm farewell, and Richard assured Reg he would provide whatever help and support he could toward Reg's investigations. He also promised that as soon as circumstances allowed, he would make every effort to reacquaint himself with the man who had saved his father's life, all those years ago. In that other war.

He escorted Reg to the front door, told him to mind himself in the blackout, and watched the young man as he walked to his car. Having noted through the half-open door to the drawing room that Fiona was reading contentedly and listening to *In Town Tonight* on the wireless, he went back upstairs to the library, and closed the door. The anxiety-induced pain in his stomach was so intense it caused him to almost double over. He clutched at his midriff, struggled to his desk and collapsed onto his chair.

I've been a politician too long, he thought. The lies just come so easily, and totally convincingly. There was as much chance of Paddy Donoghue voluntarily going to Dorrie Foskett's establishment in the East End as there was of Winston Churchill surrendering to Hitler that very night. Paddy held to the same obsessive family values as did Richard, and his father before him. He would never have disrespected his wife, or his son, in that fashion. Richard Armstrong wasn't even convinced that Paddy was a traitor at all. So why was he really killed? If that young detective but knew it, he was dangerously close to the truth. Richard knew in his heart that the road leading to Paddy Donoghue's death lay in what that tiny medallion symbolised, and to a night in that very room, at the height of the Abdication Crisis, when Dick Billings had, true to form, been too talkative for his own good.

But, Richard Armstrong reminded himself, the national interest. The war effort. Everything else must come second. He was compelled to believe that his old friend Padraig Donoghue was working for the Nazis, due to his Irish Republican sympathies. The official line. Had Richard known then what he knew now, would he have still made that phone call to Sir John Prentice, knowing full well what the inevitable outcome would be?

Of course he would have, he told himself. He had no choice then, as he had no choice now. It was in his own interests, as much as the nation's. There would be no future for Norman, if he survived the war, nor for any future generations, without the mythical glory of the well-preserved myth of the Armstrong family history remaining intact.

The cramps in Richard's stomach intensified. He reached for his father's decanter and poured a much larger than usual measure of Scotch. His hand was shaking as he brought the crystal glass to his lips. He picked up the receiver of his telephone. The executioner donning his mask. Again.

CHAPTER FOURTEEN

"Thank you for joining us this afternoon on *City Roundup* with me, Alf Burton, right around the nation and Northern Ireland, on the City Radio network. Now, a change of pace first up this afternoon, and a real treat for me. I'm delighted to say that activist and lead singer of one of the hottest groups around at the moment, the Forgotten North, Freddie Wells, has joined me in the studio. Freddie, a very warm welcome to the programme."

"Thank you, Alf, I appreciated the invitation."

"First of all, congratulations on your latest album, *Industrial Canal-side Blues*. It's already racing up the charts, so our music department tells me."

"Our fans are very loyal, Alf, we appreciate it, that's why we always try to do our best for them."

"You've been very vocal, not only in your music, about your distaste for the current government, and you've strongly supported the miners over the past year or more. Now that the strike is well and truly over, and the unions by any objective evaluation have lost, how do you see the current state of the country?"

Despite his own general feelings of hopelessness, Freddie knew that his fans expected him to be combative, and he wasn't going to disappoint. "The battle may have been lost, but not the war. Don't forget we have another fight on Tyneside. Thousands of people standing up for their right to work. People will rise up all over the country and vote this corrupt, right-wing, uncaring government out, and they'll be out for a generation. Who will ever trust the Tories again, after what they did to the miners, what they're doing to the shipyard workers, and how they corrupted the police to their own political ends? Bring on the next election, when we'll take back the country once and for all."

"The opinion polls don't necessarily bear that out. Mr Kinnock may well lead Labour to victory whenever the next election may be but, but it's far from a certainty. Like it or not, the Thatcher Government has strong support in the country, and a massive majority in the House."

"Who believes polls? They're all rigged anyway."

"Even the ones that say Labour's ahead?" Alf asked cheekily. Friend and fan he might be, but he had a job to do, and no one got a free ride on Alf's radio programme, or in his newspaper columns.

"You have to treat these polls with caution, and speak to the actual voters in the street," Freddie replied, seemingly relishing the prospect of a debate. "It's the only way to gauge public opinion and, by the way, if one or two Tories condescended to step out of their ministerial limousines, or their Knightsbri… or their luxury flats and mix it with some real punters once in a while, they might actually appreciate that it's not all champagne and caviar in the real world, and most people are struggling to get by. To keep a roof over their heads, their children fed. The fundamental essentials of life, things that should be a basic human right, are out of reach of many people. Living in Thatcher's Britain is an uphill battle for your average punter, hardly any of whom actually have a job these days. And don't forget, this is a world where legitimate protesting like maintaining a picket line has effectively been criminalised."

"You clearly feel passionately about this, have you thought of standing as a candidate yourself?"

"Bollocks to that, oh, can I say bollocks on the radio? Shite, sorry. Um —" Alf sighed with resignation, at the thought of the thousands of letters of complaint that would be flooding in, probably the most since Dick Billings had advised troublesome immigrants to "bugger off" a couple of years previously.

"So I take it a run at the next election is out of the question?"

"For me, definitely. But if my brother chooses to stand, I'll be supporting him one hundred percent. He's the real talented one in the family, Alf, I'm just a broken-down old guitar player."

The interview continued as Alf, a rock fan himself and devoted admirer of the old masters, asked a few questions about Freddie's music, his own favourite artists, and what inspired his lyrics. Freddie took the opportunity to urge Neil Kinnock to start fighting harder, and suggested that Derek Hatton was leading the way on Merseyside, and that a significant move toward embracing the Militant philosophy would be just what the country was demanding from their Labour movement, not a moderating pivot to the right. He channelled the spirit of Nye Bevan, reminding listeners of his famous assertion that people gravitating toward the middle of the road tended to get run down. He also had a number of complimentary things to say about Quentin Quiggin, the probable SDP-Liberal candidate for Streatham and Vauxhall, and expressed his appreciation for Quentin's efforts as a member of Police Watch, and at the forefront of Gays and Lesbians Support the Miners.

Alf gave a good plug for the Forgotten North's upcoming tour, preceded by the anxiously awaited Albert Hall show, which was also going to be broadcast live to a nationwide audience on the City Radio network. As Alf was about to signal his panel operator to cue up the current number one single and title track from *Industrial Canal-side Blues*, Freddie said, "If I could just make one more point, please, Alf."

"Of course."

"If certain people think they can intimidate us into not playing at Albert Hall, purely for political reasons, I say to them that we will not be bullied. We won't be silenced."

This was fascinating! If political pressure was being applied to the Albert Hall administrators, this was going to be a big story. Government censorship of the arts for political purposes. Alf recalled that a Frank Zappa concert had been pre-emptively cancelled in the early seventies, but his impression was that it had been more about the potential vulgarity of the concert rather than for any political or protest reasons.

"Who's trying to stop you?" Alf asked excitedly.

"Best I say no more."

As the song played, both men removed their headphones and shook hands across the desk.

"Thanks, Freddie," Alf said. "That was champion. Now that we're off air and off the record, tell me who's trying to censor you."

"Naebody, as far as I know."

"But you said people were intimidating —"

"I didn't. I said that *if* people were... I don't know if they are or they aren't."

Alf laughed. "Ha'way, bonny lad. You *should* run for parliament."

"It was Rick's idea. The show hasn't quite sold out, he figured a little controversy might just shift the last few tickets."

As the song ran into a commercial break, Alf made a quick internal phone call to his office. His nephew entered the studio with a couple of minutes to spare, just before the end of the programme at six pm.

"Just came through," he told Alf and handed him the statement.

"Nice work, kidda," Alf said as he prepared to throw to City Radio's evening music schedule.

"And that's just about it for us, for another week. After the six pm news, Greg Peters is on deck filling in on the dial-a-disc programme, so listen out for the number and be ready to phone in your request. I'll be calling in requesting a track from *Industrial Canal-side Blues*, called *Hold the Line*. There's something vaguely familiar about it, I can't put my finger on it. But it's a great piece of rock and roll, and hopefully Greg will have time to fit it into tonight's playlist. Now, speaking of the Forgotten North, since our interview earlier this afternoon with Freddie Wells, we've been in contact with Number Ten Downing Street, the Home Office, the Department of Environment and also the office of the Chancellor of the Duchy of Lancaster, and no one was prepared to comment. But I can tell you that in the last few moments, we've just heard directly from Stuart Farquhar MP, Minister for the Arts, who has stated that, *to his knowledge*, no one from the government has made any attempt to prevent the Forgotten North from playing at the Albert Hall. Thanks for joining us on the programme everyone, tirra, and have a canny weekend."

Listening in his office, Rick Armstrong smiled with satisfaction, while Alf, not for the first, time, reflected on what a sad loss to politics the younger Armstrong was proving to be.

The following morning over breakfast, Rick was delighted to read, on page two of the Saturday edition of the *Daily Focus*, that the non-story about the government trying to gag Freddie Wells was getting a decent run:

FORGOTTEN NORTH CONTROVERSY; GOVT DENIES CENSORSHIP CLAIM

There was just enough momentum in other media to result in a last-minute rush and the sale of all of the remaining tickets, allowing the Forgotten North, the controversial, angry and rebellious working-class heroes, to claim that they had crashed their way through to establishment legitimacy on their own terms. And had sold out the Royal Albert Hall.

***

Having edited down countless hours of interviews from miners and their families which had not been used in the 1984 documentary, *Strike!*, Alf decided that the former pit village of Headleyton would be the main focus of their second instalment.

Alf's upcoming visit to the town was highly anticipated, with many warm memories of the Forgotten North benefit concert at the Headleyton FC pitch, at which Alf had made a memorable speech, and then had actually joined the band on stage for a singalong of the community's unofficial anthem, *Canny Fettle.*

Alf and his production team, including Jerry Templar, their video editor known to everyone simply as Slug, and someone who rarely saw natural light outside his editing booth, a couple of young researchers and Alf's nephew Nye, walked the length and breadth of Headleyton, knocking on doors and assembling a diverse collection of voices and opinions. Alf was saddened but not surprised to find a community rent by divisions and festering bitterness. In the pubs, the working men's club and on the street, people were willingly talkative in blaming the Coal Board, each other, Arthur Scargill, scabs, union rebels that had taken the NUM to court and won, Austin Wells, the Home Secretary and Mrs Thatcher. And not necessarily in that order.

"It's just typical Tory bastardry," one unemployed pitman told Alf from his barstool. "Divide and conquer. Well, you can see for yourself."

Headleyton had been torn apart like frayed fabric; families, workmates and friends fighting each other on the picket lines, in the pubs, on the footpaths and on their front doorsteps. Houses had been egged, windows broken, cars vandalised, and threats uttered. People had shivered their way through last winter and had gone hungry for the sake of their children. The next one, looming ever closer, was looking like being even worse.

The courtroom battle had driven a further wedge through the ragged shreds of unity and sense of common purpose, when a group of dissident NUM members had broken away to fight for their right to go back to work free of NUM sanctions, at which point Mr Justice St John Wigham found that the absence of the national ballot rendered the Headleyton picket line illegal. Justice Wigham also ruled that the union must not apply any punitive measures to the rebel miners, and said in his summing up that the Headleyton division of the union had run roughshod over the rights of its members, and that, "It should be plain for everyone to see that, without a national ballot, the strike in Headleyton is unlawful, and contravenes the union's own protocols."

Austin Wells, who had been present at the hearing, spoke to reporters outside the Headleyton Borough Crown Court buildings, assuring the wider NUM membership that the verdict was over a local technicality only, and could not be seen to have implications for the national strike as a whole. He called on the national membership to ignore Justice Wigham's ruling, and when interviewed by Roland Moreland on the steps of the courthouse, went even further.

"What we have here, Mr Moreland," he said, "is just another example of a Tory judge, hopelessly compromised by his own politics. Who elected him to make these ill-founded demands on our membership? Where is the democracy? This is exactly what Mr Scargill is referring to when he calls out the 'anti working class sentiment' that has been the order of the day throughout this industrial dispute, and I further agree with Mr Scargill's observation that this is just another attempt by an unelected judge to interfere in the union's affairs."

Austin's provocative comments, which also extended to referring to Mr Justice Wigham as a "corrupt old fool", might have made great entertainment when later repackaged for nationwide broadcast, but did no favours for Austin himself, Arthur Scargill, nor their union. He and Mr Scargill were subsequently cited for contempt of court, and the union fined two hundred thousand pounds. When this went unpaid, an increasingly annoyed Justice Wigham ordered sequestration of NUM assets, leading to some very uncomfortable, yet self-inflicted, moments for the Cabinet Secretary and other senior members of the government.

The fate of Garry Parker was very much a part of the welter of opinion and anger that was swirling through the community like a swarm of irate bees seeking a target. A close friend of the cab driver killed bitterly referred to Garry as a murdering bastard and expressed the hope that he rotted in prison for the rest of his days. But there were also mutterings about his innocence, and Alf got the impression from some that Garry was protecting a couple of headstrong and naïvely stupid young lads, who had wanted to disrupt the flow of scab lorries to the pit, but had got more than they bargained for and had never intended for anyone to get hurt. Alf remained sceptical that the intention had ever been that benign, and was still not wholly convinced of Garry's innocence, but kept his thoughts to himself in the hope that some clues might be forthcoming as to the identity of the real culprits, if, in fact, they existed at all. He put the word about that he would speak to anyone, off the record, and with guarantees of anonymity, but no response was forthcoming.

Alf and Jerry Templar also visited the old Headleyton Flyover beneath which the killings had taken place. The road beneath was the bypass, known locally as the Ring Road, and a turnoff about half a mile north of the flyover led to the access road to the now defunct Headleyton Colliery. Alf and Jerry leaned over the safety rail, watched the traffic passing beneath, and also observed the weeds sprouting between the concrete kerbing and the bitumen of the bridge carriageway itself.

"Don't tread too heavily, bonny lad," Alf warned Jerry. "We'll end up falling right through."

"Why was it closed?" Jerry asked, stepping more gingerly as he took some general background shots, panning around with his camera on his shoulder.

"Cracks in the pylons, apparently," Alf replied. "Another great crumbling concrete monument, financed by the ratepayers, and brought to you by Donoghue Constructions."

When Jerry was satisfied that he had enough footage, he lowered the camera. "I like and admire our boss as much as anyone, Alf," he said. "But how does Sir Eddie keep getting away with it?"

"Friends in high places," Alf replied. "And deep pockets." Alf had been carefully scanning the flyover and the road on either side, along which you could see for hundreds of yards in each direction before the road disappeared in gentle curves and was lost in the trees and a scattering of homes behind high hedges. A key aspect of the police case was that Garry had supposedly been right where Alf and Jerry were standing at that moment and had been clearly recognised by police officers. Yet those same officers had offered only limited observations of the others on the bridge, and where had they been to get such a clear view? Garry had emphatically stated that there were no police anywhere near. It's unlikely that anyone driving along the Ring Road at fifty miles an hour could have made such a decisive identification. And as Garry said, if there were police around, why didn't they go straight to the embankment to help, and then call for the ambulance from their portable radios? Alf was aware that an ambulance hadn't been called for several minutes, the time it had taken for a passing motorist to reach a telephone box on the outskirts of Headleyton itself. According to statements in Gwynne's brief, the first on scene had been a lorry driver, very probably the poor sod for whom the concrete block had been intended, and yet his own statement had been lacking in any kind of detail, other than his shock at being confronted by the overturned minicab and the two dead bodies on the grass embankment. Understandable, Alf thought. And yet —

Jerry noticed his boss in deep contemplation. "Everything all right?" he asked.

"There's something funny about this, Jerry, man," Alf replied.

Later that afternoon, Alf was welcomed at a reception at the town hall, where a special surprise had been planned for him. In the ballroom, at one end in the corner was a Miners' Federation of Great Britain banner, dating back to the General Strike, and also something that took Alf's breath away. Hanging on the wall, beneath the dark wood and gold leaf of the Great War roll of honour, extending from one side of the room to the other, was a large hand-painted banner, faded and frayed, but still clearly legible.

HEADLEYTON WELCOMES THE JARROW MARCHERS

Alf touched the fraying cloth and was momentarily so overcome that Jerry placed a supportive hand on his shoulder.

The reception was very well attended, and Alf spent considerable time signing autographs and copies of his books that people had brought from home. The leader of the borough council, Betty Watson, introduced Alf to an elderly lady, seated on one side of the room, wearing a headscarf and thick-rimmed glasses with wings like an old American car. As if she'd just walked off the set of the *Coronation Street* of twenty years earlier, Alf thought as he was introduced.

"Alf, this is Mrs Bickerstaff," Councillor Watson told him. "She's been anxious to meet you. She has something very important to tell you."

Alf leaned down and shook hands with Mrs Bickerstaff. "Delighted to meet you, bonny lass," he said.

"Now, Mr Burton, do you remember me?" she asked.

"I'm afraid I don't."

"Well, you know my brother very well. Jack Seaton. He served with you on the freighters on the Atlantic and Murmansk runs during the war. In those overloaded and leaky old Speers coffin ships. A miracle either of you made it through."

"We had a few narrow scrapes, I admit," Alf replied. "I saw Jack last year; we were doing some work at the Lady Georgiana Museum. How is he?"

"Ee, he's champion. But I actually remember you from the Jarrow March, nearly fifty year' ago now. I was helping me mam make sandwiches for all you lovely boys as you passed through. You kna', Mr Burton, you'd remember this, some wouldn't even take the food, even though anyone could see they were hungry. They asked us to wrap the meat from the sandwiches so it could be sent home for their bairns. I'll never forget that. You walked nearly three hundred flipping miles, and it made not a hap'orth of difference in the end, did it?"

"Well, I agree with you to a point," Alf replied, "but in the longer term I think it helped to at least lay the foundations for the Labour victory in '45. I think the march had more effect on the people than on the politicians —"

243

"Excuse me, Alf, but the band is about to begin." Councillor Watson was hovering anxiously as the Headleyton Colliery Brass Band, surviving beyond the death of the pit thanks to a generous donation from Freddie Wells and the Forgotten North, were limbering up on the cramped stage for a performance in honour of their VIP guest. Alf took Mrs Bickerstaff's hand in his. "Tirra, bonny lass, it's been wonderful to meet you. Again. Send my best to Jack."

"I certainly will. I listen to you on the wireless most Fridays."

"That's nice," Alf replied as he straightened up, feeling the twinges of age in his back. "Do you enjoy it?"

"Rarely," she admitted. "Too many adverts, you're way too nice to those Tories you always have on, especially that rotten Seymour, and that music you play from time to time is just *awful!* I like Roland Moreland. He's on our local news on the television here as well. You could learn a few things from him, Pet."

***

In his office at Conservative Party headquarters, Smith Square, Party Chairman and Chief Whip Sir Dick Billings was perusing confidential seat-by-seat polling that he had commissioned. In his assessment, the next election wasn't going to be the bloodbath that a number of so-called experts were predicting. There might be a small swing against the government, but with a majority of one hundred and forty-four that was only to be expected. He was also casting around for someone expendable, at Sir Norman Armstrong's request, and he thought he had found just the man. In the neighbouring constituency to Norman's own, in actual fact.

The Home Secretary was as aware as everyone else that the constant waves of controversy crashing up against the Home Office were causing career-ending damage to Janice Best in her south London constituency of Streatham and Vauxhall. Sir Norman, as ever loyal to his own beyond any call of duty, had asked Dick to find a worthless seat-warmer, preferably from the damp side of the party, kick them off the ticket, and parachute in Janice Best. She would be a local MP any constituency would welcome with outstretched arms, as she had proven time and again to be highly competent, selfless, hard-working and wholly committed to her community. Sir Dick, for his part, felt that Janice would be far better served to accept defeat, then become a candidate for Labour or the SDP-Liberals where she'd probably feel much more appreciated and at home. But in this, as in almost all cases, the Party Chairman was happy to defer to the judgement of his old friend, and couldn't deny Janice's work ethic or her abilities, even though, had she been a man, he would probably have referred to her as a bleeding heart limp-dick. Politically, Sir Norman was almost never wrong. In any case, he had a rather clever way of phrasing an order as a polite request. Parliamentary colleagues defied the Home Secretary at their peril, and Sir Dick valued his friendship with Sir Norman very highly and would never have done anything to jeopardise a political and personal friendship that had underpinned each of their careers for decades.

The polling made interesting reading. Should an election be held then and there, Sir Dick was in line to maintain his own majority in Uxbridge-Ruislip which, in percentage terms, had remained consistent since he had first been elected in 1934. Charles Seymour, although deeply unpopular due to his high national profile as principal Home Office spokesman, looked as if he would hold on with only the slightest of dents in his own enviable majority. Northern Ireland Secretary Stanley Smee, who was as respected in the country as Charles Seymour was despised, would actually increase his majority yet again, as would Arts Minister Stuart Farquhar, and other former members of the Awkward Squad including Stanley Smee's new PPS, Perkin Warbeck.

"Funny old world," Sir Dick muttered, reminding himself that they were still at least a couple of years away from a general election, and anything could happen in the meantime. He allowed his thoughts to return to his oldest friend. Sir Norman Armstrong was a good speaker and campaigner as well, Dick reflected. One of the best, in fact. He never took his safe seat for granted, which brought Dick to study the latest numbers from the Home Secretary's constituency of Stonebridge South-east.

This constituency had always been held by the Armstrong family, and had been gold-plated safe Tory for as long as anyone could remember. Dick's knowledge of the constituency's history extended back to the early nineteenth century, and the first of the modern Tories, James Armstrong; a veteran of the Peninsular Wars and finally Waterloo, where he had been a staff officer to the Duke of Wellington himself. The seat had been reliably handed down thenceforth, with each man holding power for a generation or more. Arthur Armstrong, who achieved the rank of Major like his father, took on the seat on his return from Crimea, then it was a toss-up as to which of his sons, Fforbes or Piers, would follow in his parliamentary footsteps. The decision was made for him, Dick was aware, with Fforbes choosing a military career in the colonial armies. Meanwhile his brother Piers made his name as a politician, served as First Lord of the Admiralty and Secretary of State for the Colonies, and famously attested that all British foreign and colonial policy should be about the furtherance of British control of the Suez Canal; and that nothing, and nobody else, really mattered. His singular devotion to this cause had afforded him the not always respectfully applied sobriquet of "The Suez Pier". He was also heavily involved in campaigns against Home Rule for Ireland, was widely reported to have been one of the architects of the disastrous Jamieson Raid into the Transvaal, and had then become an enthusiastic champion of Britain's hard-line suppression of Boers, both combatants and civilians, through the pioneering use of concentration camps, which killed thousands upon thousands of Boer and native African non-combatants. Including little children, whose deaths Piers Armstrong notoriously blamed entirely on the "filthy Boer habits" of their neglectful mothers.

After finding himself on a militant suffragette assassination list, along with Liberal Prime Minister Asquith, Piers Armstrong offered unqualified support to Liberal Home Secretary, Winston Churchill, and encouraged relentless and violent suppression of the suffragette movement, culminating in the deployment of a special squad of tough East End policemen to aggressively deal with protestors, culminating in the violence of 1910's Black Friday. He remained opposed to any extension of the existing franchise, and unsuccessfully lobbied against the Representation of the People Act in 1918.

There followed a slight adjustment in the family line. Piers Armstrong was a confirmed bachelor and had no children, so the next generation in power proved to be the son of Colonel Fforbes Armstrong, Richard, who served from 1920 right up until his retirement at the General Election of 1950, at which time Richard's son Norman emerged as the latest MP of the family line.

Dick reflected on the previous generations of Armstrongs. He had never met the Colonel, who by most accounts went mad after the Somme and became a recluse in South Africa, but he had known both Piers and Richard Armstrong, professionally and personally. Richard Armstrong, Dick thought, was a genuinely great man. A statesman and a gentleman, to whom Dick knew well that he owed his entire career. And possibly even his life. As for Piers, even Dick's much envied and often used encyclopaedia of profanities and insults possessed no word that could do justice to that amoral Savile Row suit full of shit.

But, for better or worse, all the Armstrongs were long-serving, powerful men who had done more than their fair share to shape the country and her empire over the past one hundred and sixty-five years. And for generations beforehand as well.

Norman's unmatched abilities as a local MP had resulted in his already insurmountable constituency majority growing at each election, until it was now the safest constituency of any persuasion in the country, by a large margin. The constituency borders had been adjusted sometime before the war, with Richard, and then Norman, retaining the blue-ribbon Tory-voting leafy suburbs; the middle-class, white-collar commuter heartland now known as Stonebridge South-east.

But this time, things might be a little different, Dick pondered. A new generation was coming of age and would be voting by the next election. The major development, which was now known as Stonebridge City Centre, had been opposed vocally by the local Conservative council. But the Department of Environment had overridden the council's veto and the project had gone ahead, in the face of bitter local opposition. A borough councillor, Marjorie Spratt, had been causing trouble all over the place, particularly indignant that the expansive construction was going to heavily impact the gardens surrounding the exclusive aged care home, Stonebridge House. Not even Dick Billings, as Conservative Chairman, could shut her up. Norman's own role in the approval process, or to be more accurate, his steadfast refusal to become involved, had done him significant damage locally. It could be a difficult balancing act, when government policy and the national interest intruded on local constituency matters. And now, with Norman heavily committed with his Home Office responsibilities, he could no longer be the active and highly engaged local member his constituents demanded. And of course, with the unfortunate fact that the widely loved, enormously popular Lady Eileen was no longer around to support him locally, things looked to be taking an unprecedented turn. There was no danger that the seat could be lost, Dick considered, but the majority could be as much as halved.

Dick ruminated on the grief that only a husband could know. He opened his drawer and gazed at a black and white photograph, which could easily have been of a beautiful 1930s star of the stage or of the cinema. It was his own wife, Celia, killed early in the Blitz, and someone Sir Dick was increasingly anxious to join.

"Not long now, my love," he murmured. He slammed the drawer shut angrily. "I've been fucking well saying that since 1940," he growled, returning his focus to his papers.

What to do about Janice Best? Would she even accept another constituency if offered? Dick suspected not. She was one of that increasingly rare breed of politician that was really in it for her community rather than for careerism, ego and personal or financial gain.

"There's not many of us left," Dick said out loud. There was around half of the term still to play out, and two years or more was an eternity in politics, so anything could happen. But on these current figures, it was looking very unlikely that she would hold on.

"That treasonous ungrateful pervert Quiggin," Dick spluttered. "If I had my way he'd be strung up by the bollocks —" Quentin Quiggin was the troublesome community activist who had supported Janice in 1979 and then again in 1983, for her personal integrity and commitment rather than her political allegiance. Quentin was also a member of Police Watch, had been vocally critical of the conduct of the police in Brixton over a number of years, and then around the time of Orgreave during the Miners' Strike, and was at the forefront of the highly effective fundraising and political movement, Gays and Lesbians Support the Miners.

Pinko-poof-prick-wanker, Dick mused, and now the little shit had deserted Janice and run off to the SDP-Liberals and was probably going to run in his own right next time. Pinko-poof-*opportunist*-prick-wanker, Dick added inwardly.

He closed his file and checked his watch. Time to head off to the Commons for Prime Minister's Questions. That'll do his spirits the world of good, watching Margaret make mincemeat out of Kinnock and his band of limp-dick losers and their predictable juvenile questions. Mind you, Kinnock was a vast improvement on his predecessor. That ghastly bearded little comedian was right when he urged members at the 1983 Tory Party Conference to kick Foot's walking stick out from under him. Dick involuntarily rubbed his eye, remembering his own experience at that eventful conference in Blackpool. Susan Smee, wife of the Secretary of State for Northern Ireland, had blackened his eye and knocked him unconscious after he had drunkenly, and loudly, speculated why it was that Stanley, then brand new to the portfolio, hadn't yet been assassinated. But now Dick considered, with unusually prescient self-awareness, that it hadn't at all been a clever or funny thing to say, especially so considering what happened the following year at Brighton.

CHAPTER FIFTEEN

As the working day drew to a close, Alf returned to his office from the studio floor and slumped in his chair, his mind fully occupied by Major Albert Powell and his deathbed memoir. Norman Armstrong had often accused him of latching onto any kind of conspiracy theory, no matter how implausible, while Alf, for his part, had always maintained that a good dose of intrigue made the world of investigative journalism go around. If ever there was a time to let one's imagination run unfettered to see just where it ended up, this was it. Alf reached for his transcript of Major Powell's writings and laid the pages out on his desk. If he combined what he had learned from Major Powell's recollections, with what his own long investigations had unearthed, he could see that things were falling into place. Piece by agonisingly intricate piece.

But, on the side of the devil's advocate, the late Major had been an old man, and even Godfrey had lovingly admitted his grasp on reality generally was varying day to day. Whose wouldn't be at the age of ninety-two?

What if the long years of grief and unhappiness had planted a false trail in the depths of Albert Powell's troubled mind, and had led him in a totally misguided direction — lost and tormented in a complicated maze of enduring grief, uncertainty and false recollections from which the only escape would be his eventual death? Just for the sake of the exercise, if nothing else, where did Albert's theories lead?

Alf reached for some more paper and began scribbling in pencil. Then more paper, then names, and arrows linking names. Years also linked by arrows. Some sheets screwed up and immediately discarded, others contemplated at length, and additional notes made.

So... Charlotte Morris. Late Victorian and Edwardian author, royal courtier and heiress to the massive Speers fortune. No, much more than an heiress, a formidable executive who was able to sway the cigar smoking good-old-chaps of the Speers board to embark on a humanitarian programme to try to make amends for the havoc they had unleashed, as they murdered, invaded, cheated and stole to increase the company's global domination. A novelist and historian, and war correspondent, who had so angered Kitchener over her stance on the Boer War concentration camps that he, or people on his behalf, had concocted evidence that she had been feeding sensitive information to the Germans, to be relayed in turn back to the Boer guerrillas. She and her secretary, Dorothy Keppel, were arrested and held under guard, awaiting a military tribunal. While under house arrest, she wrote an account of a certain secret society, the origins of which dated back to the English Civil War. How did she know about them? Most probably through her family and royal connections. The Most Worshipful Order of Liege Knights of Charles the First. The Banqueting Club. Dangerous and without honour was how Fforbes Armstrong had described them to Major Powell. Membership was secret, and was handed down through aristocratic, political and military families. Alf was now convinced that one of those families was the Armstrongs. Another, allowing his speculative theories their full uninhibited freedom, was almost certainly the Prentices. Sir John, and now Sir Archie. That made perfect sense; Archie was the shadowy keeper of the nation's secrets. Unaccountable, unmanageable and widely feared, even dreaded. Who knew what he really got up to, with everything cloaked under a dark and heavy blanket of secrecy?

But, back to Charlotte Morris, under house arrest with her secretary, and probably lover, Dorothy Keppel. Here enters Colonel Fforbes Armstrong, Norman's grandfather, who was able to use his friendship with former war correspondent Winston Churchill, and in turn the Palace, leading to a judicious royal intervention from the new King; Charlotte and Dorothy were saved. But, just one of many paradoxes. If Colonel Fforbes Armstrong was a club member, so to speak, why was he so keen to assist in saving the lives of the two adventuresses? The answer was very clearly set out in Major Powell's recollections.

Nearly twenty years later, Charlotte died; the influenza, just weeks after the Armistice. Her will was subsequently read, the stenographer's notes of which Alf had secured some years previously when the firm of Twilley and Company, Solicitors at Law, had been wound up, the last remaining Twilley having departed to the great courtroom upstairs. Or downstairs, Alf reflected. Present at the reading of the will was Charlotte's personal physician, Doctor Sir Cedric Knollys, also Physician in Ordinary to Queen Alexandra. And Piers Armstrong MP. The minutes recorded a sealed envelope being passed to Dorothy. The terms of the will also gifted Trafalgar Hall, the Speers family estate, to the Admiralty. What was it now? Alf knew from personal experience it was being used as a refuge and safe house for Archie Prentice's unnamed intelligence department, because Alf himself had spent some time there in the tender care of Special Branch two years earlier, following his ultimately mistaken claim that he had secured a copy of the long lost Morris papers.

But then, the inconsistencies again. Like his grandfather's own intervention eighty-two years earlier, it was Norman Armstrong who had saved Alf's life, he was sure of it, and had foiled whatever diabolical plans Sir Archie was concocting for him. Just when you began to think that the Armstrong dynasty made the Borgias look like the epitome of kindness and morality, they appeared in a wholly different light; displaying integrity and courage. Thanks to two men, generations apart.

Within months of the reading of Charlotte Morris's will, Dorothy Keppel travelled alone to South Africa, where, by chance, she met a Major in the Mounted Rifles, Albert Powell. Godfrey's father. They then, together, visited the now retired Colonel Fforbes Armstrong's farm, where Dorothy Keppel took custody of Charlotte's secret manuscript, hitherto in the care of Colonel Armstrong himself. More contradictions. Alf reached for additional sheets, and scrawled names and arrows until his desk virtually disappeared under an increasingly precarious pile of paper; a snowy mountain on the brink of avalanche.

And who was one of the few survivors when the *RMS Lady Georgiana* foundered on her final voyage? Alf's new friend Commodore Jim O'Malley, now approaching the end of his ninth decade and living in a blissful married state with the redoubtable legend of the old music halls, Florrie Tweedle, in the Stonebridge House care home. And a man who, for a split second at least, held in his hand the envelope of papers that would have answered any and all of these frustrating questions. And, if legend was to be believed, potentially brought down everyone from Tory MPs and lords, and possibly even 'er indoors at Buckingham Palace. But despite Jim's heroic efforts as a young Third Officer, neither Dorothy Keppel nor the envelope were ever seen again, lost with the *Georgiana* on that terrifying, stormy day in 1919, on the outer reaches of the Bay of Biscay. Yet the fear, or the excitement depending on which side of politics you were on, of those documents ever being found had cast a shadow that remained even now. Why? All ancient history. Or was it?

Now. To the real, dangerous, unpalatable and very personal truths. Fforbes Armstrong, the fine old Colonel and eccentric recluse, living on his farm with many of his old regimental friends and comrades, died in 1924, a fall from his horse. Major Powell and his ever-reliable Sar-major, MacNair, investigated but found no evidence that his fall was anything other than an accident. Despite the fact that both Piers Armstrong, the Colonel's brother, and General Sir John Prentice, father of Sir Archie, were in the former province of Natal when the Colonel died. Alf had seen the records from the shipping line himself. Major Powell recalled that Fforbes Armstrong did not trust his brother and had apparently made a rather curious statement to Major Powell when he had been at the Armstrong farm with Dorothy Keppel. "If ever you get back to England," Colonel Armstrong had warned, "Stay well away from my family."

Forward to 1941. The Powells were living in London, the retired Major an influential merchant banker. His son, Reg, joined the Special Operations Executive, and disappeared on his first mission several months later. Tragic coincidence? Very likely, yet Major Powell didn't think so, and although he had no idea what his son was working on immediately before his transfer from Scotland Yard, he was convinced there was a link. Not just with what he was working on at that time, but with the lost manuscript, and with events in South Africa all those years before. He had no evidence, just, as he had written, the fact that his old soldier's instinct for danger rarely let him down.

Alf had managed to progress just a little further than had the late Major. He now knew, thanks to Sir Godfrey's enquiries with Commissioner Coburn, that Detective Powell had been investigating the death of Padraig Donoghue, killed in an air raid, and apparently in a house of dubious repute down the East End. So, a mere sex scandal was hardly likely to lead to such a thorough investigation by one of Scotland Yard's finest, so it had to be something more. What if Padraig Donoghue's death *was* suspicious? What if Reg was getting close to the truth? But what truth? If only Alf could look at it through the old Major's eyes.

Alf shook his head. It was all becoming fanciful, but then he reminded himself that this little personal exercise was all about letting any kind of wild theory room to run, to chase it wherever it went. How could Reg's death have been in any way connected with events in South Africa and, by default, with the lost Morris manuscript? Piers Armstrong was dead by 1941, but what about Sir John Prentice? What did Padraig Donoghue know, and what was Detective Powell about to find out, that could have led, directly or indirectly, to the deaths of both?

Alf tipped a handful of papers onto the floor and rummaged around until he found some space on one sheet. He wrote General Prentice in big letters, circled it and wrote a question mark.

What about the royal doctor, Sir Cedric Knollys? Physician in Ordinary to old Queen Alexandra, attended Charlotte Morris in her last hours, during which, Alf believed, the existence of the manuscript was revealed for the first time. Alf scattered papers about until he found a loose page almost black with tightly spaced notes, circles and arrows. Knollys, pronounced Knowles. Alf chuckled. Young Nye would have something to say about that. Died within a few days of Queen Alexandra herself. He was certainly no spring chicken, probably just coincidence. Again.

These theories were all very well, but Alf's journalistic instincts told him that there had to be a current angle. What were the implications? A murderous gang of amoral political manipulators running rampant for hundreds of years, lurking in the sewers and the seedy alleys of politics and government. The Prentices. The Armstrongs; well, some of them. Who else? But more importantly, who might have been trying to stop them? Who was threatening their existence? Padraig Donoghue perhaps? In the course of his investigations, had the brilliant young detective stumbled upon —

"My God, what am I doing?" Alf cried, as the images of Norman, Rick, Sally and the new generation of Armstrongs, James and little Ellie, appeared in front of him, and whose smiling faces suddenly contorted with fear and pain as they were trampled and bloodied under the rampaging feet of Alf's unfettered imagination. He suddenly felt like a cynical seducer who steams into someone's happy family, has a good deal of mischievous, obligation-free fun, then departs unscathed, having left an incriminating note. Homewrecker, he muttered accusingly. Is this what it's come to? Descending to the depths of a scandal rag gossip columnist, concocting disgrace for the sake of... But what about Godfrey? Could Alf go anywhere toward uncovering the truth of his brother's death without dragging the people he knew and loved into the mess? What if the investigation into this one possibly totally, tragically innocent death during wartime, opened the floodgates and unleashed an unstoppable torrent of revelations that would rapaciously and mercilessly destroy almost everyone around him? Truth then became an irrelevant passenger, one who didn't pay his fare and was unceremoniously thrown from the fast-moving train and quickly forgotten.

Plots and counterplots. Paranoia. The last time he had felt so conflicted had been following the resignation of Harold Wilson in 1976, when he and a pair of young BBC reporters had been invited to the home of the former Prime Minister, who had laid out his firm belief that his political demise had been the result of scheming by the intelligence services, and a threatened military-style coup.

Alf had felt sufficiently enthused, and palpably outraged about the old school tie brigade's alleged conspiracy to bring undone the jumped-up working-class, *northern* usurper, that he raised the matter with Norman Armstrong during one of their regular dinners at the Burton flat in Pimlico. Eileen was, of course, absent, choosing to live in their constituency home rather than the unrelenting intensity of Westminster and London.

Alf was well aware that Norman himself was no stranger to scheming and backroom manoeuvrings, having recently done everything in his power to dislodge Edward Heath from the Tory leadership, and install Mrs Thatcher as the new Conservative Opposition Leader.

Alf had had his own thoughts on Mrs Thatcher during the leadership spill and had expressed them to Norman in typically robust fashion: "I tell you, bonny lad. You're backing the wrong horse. Everyone knows it's going to be Willie Whitelaw. I know you think Margaret walks on water, but she'll get a handful of votes at best. The Tories will never elect a woman leader, you're crackers if you think she even has a chance."

From then on, Norman never hesitated to cheerfully remind his old friend of his comments, and that even the stalwarts of the Labour Party, Shirley Williams and Barbara Castle, had stated that the country was ready for a female PM, and that Mrs Thatcher shouldn't be underestimated. Alf, in spite of himself, was pleased that Norman had dug himself well and truly out of the political wilderness as the Chief Tory Whip and one of their top strategists. Despite the fact that it was clear that the Tories were going to lurch further to the right than they ever had under Heath, and would therefore never beat Callaghan, and the Labour Party would, thankfully, be in power until beyond the next century.

The evenings together at Pimlico meant more to the pair of unlikely friends than they would ever admit publicly, or even to themselves. Things usually began with Norman ranting good naturedly about Rick, who with his mother's blessing, had stepped right away from the Armstrong family tradition of military service followed by a career in politics. The theme of Norman's dissatisfaction was that Rick, although turning thirty, still had hair down to his shoulders, wore torn jeans, T-shirts — beads! — and ludicrous great hairy jackets. His working life was spent with a disreputable young scruff named Terry Cox, and they toiled away above a south London betting shop in damp and peeling conditions that would have been about as healthy as working down the pit. As to what they did? Something to do with promoting equally disreputable singers and other young people of questionable talent and morals. But, Norman had to grudgingly concede, Rick had never asked his parents for any money — in fact had rejected a number of offers of financial support — and, according to Eileen, who knew much more about these matters than Norman, was doing very well in his own right. He had just bought a home in Holland Park, into which he was about to move with his beautiful girlfriend, Sally, and their fast-growing son. That was another thing, Norman complained. Why doesn't Rick just do the decent thing and marry her like normal respectable people would? Imagine having a six-year-old son and not even being married! It wasn't natural.

"It's a different generation, old marra. It's not like it was when we were growing up. Old farts like us have to move with the times."

"Yes, that's what Eileen says," Norman conceded. "So, what was it you wanted to ask me about tonight, on the quiet?" Norman and Alf, along with Dolly, were crowded around the small table in the dinette of the Burton flat, having just finished dinner.

"I'll clear away, then go to the other room," Dolly said, standing up. "I'll leave you to it."

"Don't be silly," Norman replied. "I know Alf tells you everything anyway. Stay, it will only save Alf going over it all again later." Dolly cleared the plates, then served coffee and re-joined them.

"Off the record," Alf said, "I've had a couple of meetings with our former Prime Minister. Myself and a couple of lads from the BBC were invited to his home, and he had a few interesting things to say."

"Such as?"

"Tell me about Archie Prentice."

"That name doesn't ring a bell."

"Really?" Alf arched an eyebrow. "Who's in that photo then?"

"What photo?"

"You showed it to me last time I was in your office at the Commons, man! You'd just got it framed, the one that was taken on VE Day. And an impressive band of future achievers too. Let me remind you who's in it, all looking very dapper and Brylcreemed in the essential RAF fashion. Sir Peregrine Walsingham, by then already demobbed and in the Civil Service, now Permanent Secretary at the Treasury. Our mutual friend Commander Honest Ron Coburn of the Metropolitan Police, now set to climb the ladder further thanks to his part in the recent demise of Cyril McCann and Harry Barron, and the police corruption rackets. And one other person apart from your good self: then Group Captain Prentice, your CO. Now Sir Archie. Who is he?"

"Oh him," Norman waved his hand dismissively. "Senior administrative civil servant, something to do with economic statistics, I think."

"MI5 or MI6?" Alf asked mischievously.

Norman sighed with frustration. He knew Alf wouldn't be deterred, but there was sufficient trust between them for

Norman to confide. At least a little. "As you well know, we don't acknowledge the existence of MI6. And your photographic — no pun intended — memory is going to get you into big trouble one day, and no doubt I'll have to be the one to bail you out, just like I always do."

"I know you'll be there for me, bonny lad. So, who is he? MI5 or MI6?"

"Well, neither, if you must know. His department is one that we *really* don't acknowledge, if you get my meaning. Why do you ask? How did you hear about him?"

"Let's just say his name came up in conversations with Mr Wilson."

"Really? I'm surprised Mr Wilson had heard of him."

"Mr Wilson seems to think that he was under surveillance while he was PM, and Prentice's department was digging dirt to try and discredit him, as well as his personal staff and close colleagues."

"Are you referring in particular to the redoubtable Mrs Williams?"

"Oh aye. Baroness Falkender now, don't forget. He suggested also that there might have been some meddling from the South African secret service, to do with attempting to nobble opponents of apartheid."

Norman scoffed. "You've always been too fond of any old conspiracy theory, and ready to embrace it uncritically. These are the meanderings of an old fool who's lost his mind. I would have thought even you could see that, through your pink-tinted glasses."

"He's only two years older than me!" Alf retorted. "But it gets much better. He hinted at a coup plot."

"A what?"

"A coup, orchestrated by Sir Archie Prentice, along with some senior military figures, to remove him from office."

"You can't be serious," Norman replied, genuinely dumbfounded. "This is Great Britain, not some Godawful central African banana republic. And for what purpose?"

"Mr Wilson was *very* serious," Alf assured his friend, "and there could be any number of reasons. The fact that he was too far to the left, that he was way too powerful for a working-class lad from the north — the *not one of us* syndrome."

"I've never heard anything so ridiculous. Are you going to run with it?"

"I haven't made up my mind yet."

"I'd leave it well alone, if I were you. The problem with lobby correspondents, present company excluded, to a point, is that they all want to be like those two meddling reporters, their names escape me, at the *Washington Post* who exposed Watergate. Paranoia and blind ambition running mad in the interests of a desperate desire for fame."

"You may very well be right. It's just that —"

"Just that what?"

"The two lads from the BBC took what they had to their superiors, and the next minute they were locked out of their offices, and their contracts terminated. Just like that."

"I'm not surprised, falling for a load of old rubbish like this."

"Possibly at the behest, or at least the encouragement, of someone high up in the political… sphere. Acting on behalf of Sir Archie. Any thoughts as to who might have been roped in to nobble 'Auntie' over this?"

"I can't think," Norman replied. "I don't know why you'd be asking me anyway. We're in opposition, don't forget. By the way, why had both you and a BBC crew been invited? Sounds like a funny kind of arrangement."

"Well," Alf conceded, "I think Mr Wilson had forgotten he'd asked me first."

"Well, that to me speaks volumes."

"So, what do you make of it?" Alf asked.

Norman now spoke in his on-the-record voice. "You were right to have listened to Mr Wilson's concerns, and showed sound judgement when you decided that further investigations were unwarranted, based on the fact that Mr Wilson's memory isn't perhaps quite what it once was. It does you great credit that you chose not to embarrass our former Prime Minister in this way. He may have been on the other side, but even I can't criticise his misguided integrity. And the dignity of the office itself is of prime importance, and I for one am pleased that Mr Wilson has been spared the humiliation."

Alf's meandering thoughts morphed back to the here-and-now, as he stared at the precarious stack of papers on his desk, and those that had cascaded onto the floor. A temporary, relative sense of calm had descended as he recalled happier days with his old friend, but as his eyes darted back and forth across the papers in front of him, reading and considering his scribblings, lines between years and people, exclamation marks, circles around key aspects, question marks and doodles, he felt the tension rising again. He felt pressure behind his ears and a tightening of his chest. His heart was beating like mad; he could feel it, and he grabbed his steel-wool, unruly hair with both hands and pulled until it hurt.

The quest was really no longer about a mysterious manuscript that may or may not be at the bottom of the Bay of Biscay in the wreck of an unseaworthy ocean liner. Also the resting place for more than a thousand souls, including Dorothy Keppel. A long-held dream of the destruction of the Tory party was a nice comforting ambition to carry in the back of your mind year after year, Alf reflected, but the real issue at hand was the death of SOE operative Reg Powell. Major Powell had believed that there was a direct connection, and now Godfrey deserved to know the truth. Piers Armstrong MP. Sir John Prentice. Richard Armstrong. The Most Worshipful Order of Liege Knights of Charles the First. The Banqueting Club. Sir Archie Prentice. Sir Norman Armstrong.

Alf sat quietly for an interminable time, staring straight ahead and tapping his teeth with his pencil. "It's all bollocks!" he cried suddenly. "Bollocks! A military and Civil Service uprising against an elected Prime Minister? In this country? Never. Bollocks, bollocks, bollocks!" He swept his desk with his arm, sending the remaining piles of his scribble-covered papers cascading onto the floor. "Just like all this Banqueting Club is bollocks. All shite! Norman was right all those years ago. Rampant paranoia and ambition distorting any kind of rational, clear thinking. None of it's true. None of it is true. More than thirty years spent chasing nothing at all!"

"Alf! Alf!"

Alf suddenly looked up to see his nephew framed in the doorway, his sudden arrival such a shock that Alf very nearly tumbled backwards out of his chair.

"You scared the shite out of me, kidda," Alf told him, breathless and a little embarrassed. He felt the general pain and tightness in his head and chest subside. He stared down at the floor surrounding his desk, hidden under the remnants of his frenzied writing and doodling, and covered with pens, pencils, a stapler and countless paperclips from a coffee cup which he

266

had upended when he sent the majority of his work onto the carpet.

"What in God's name are you doing?" Nye asked, staring in bewilderment at Alf's chaos, and at Alf himself, who had a wild-eyed look of unchecked hysteria about him. The unruly wire brush of his hair was in even more disarray that usual, Nye observed, as if he had been literally attempting to pull it out. Nye wondered for a fleeting moment if his uncle had been having some kind of mental breakdown, and whether or not he should call a doctor.

"Auntie Dolly's been on the phone, she's worried sick,' he said, noting with relief that Alf seemed to be calming down in front of his eyes. "Thinking you've been kidnapped by the IRA again. The switchboard says they've been trying to ring you. No answer. Jesus, Alf, what's going on? And who were you talking to, by the way? Is anyone else here?" Nye looked into the darkness of Alf's office, the shadows surrounding the desert island of yellow light from his desk lamp. Alf suddenly realised it was dark outside. How long had he been there?

"It wasn't the IRA, bonny lad," he explained, recovering quickly, and trying to divert attention from his disarray. "It was the Irish Revolutionary —"

"I don't think that matters at the moment, do you?" Nye scolded impatiently. "It's late, you need to call home and tell Dolly you're okay. She's in a right state. She's probably already been on the phone to Commissioner Coburn, and the Home Secretary, demanding they mobilise the entire Met to go and look for you. Ring her now, then I'll drive you straight home." Nye eyed the papers on the floor, his natural curiosity aroused. "What are you working on, by the way?"

"Nothing. Nothing at all." Alf looked at his nephew with loving pride, and a sudden interest in a future beyond his own lifetime. The Armstrongs and the Donoghues weren't the only ones with dynasties to be nurtured, he mused, as he lifted the telephone receiver and prepared to grovel.

***

With the eastern gardens now hidden behind a high fence and the noise of heavy construction intruding, relaxing outdoors at Stonebridge House wasn't the same as it used to be. Sir Godfrey Powell contemplated how much his father would have disliked the clouds of dust floating above their heads; the noise of engines as lorries plied to and fro, the rowdy conversations of the unseen bricklayers and labourers above the rattling of the cement mixers. But Jim and Florrie O'Malley, still basking in the glow of newly found connubial bliss, were determined not to be discouraged from enjoying the late summer in the gardens of their home, and they invited Alf and Godfrey to join them for tea on the lawn. Alf considered this a sensible precaution, although he conceded not even Archie Prentice would stoop to bugging an old folks' care home. Would he?

"So, what have you found out?" Florrie asked excitedly, as soon as the bustling nurse had delivered their tea and cakes on a tray and had departed back inside. There were no secrets between the newlyweds, and Jim had explained much of what Major Powell had suspected, and how Jim's own remarkable life had come to be indelibly linked with that of Albert Powell, unbeknownst to each other at the time, for just a few weeks in

1919. And then fleetingly once again in 1926, on the original *RMS Calcutta Queen*, pride of the Speers Line.

"Well," Alf began. "I'm not sure that I've really got any closer to the truth, other than having expanded upon Major Powell's theories, somewhat, that is —" Alf began floundering, and noted Jim's suspicious look. "Ha'way," Alf uttered, prompting a fit of giggling from Florrie.

"Ooh, I *do* love the way you talk," she purred. "We still listen to you every Friday on the wireless, don't we, Jim? 'A very warm welcome to the programme'," she said in a creditable, husky imitation, and all four burst into the laughter of relief as seemingly unshakeable tension had been relieved.

"What's this new introduction, theme tune and announcer all about? That's getting rather grand," Jim observed.

Although very comfortable in his imperfect skin, Alf acknowledged that he could be prone to the odd bout of professional jealously, and he wasn't going to allow Roland Moreland to have the upper hand. If Roland had his own theme tune, Alf was going to have a better one. And not just screeching violins lifted from the shelf of the City Radio music library, but an original instrumental theme penned by one of Britain's top rock stars and voiced by one of City Radio's best young announcers. Both Freddie Wells and Greg Peters had been delighted to lend their talents, and Alf had been thrilled with the result. He couldn't think of how best to explain this without looking like a self-important twat in front of his friends, but thankfully Florrie came to the rescue.

"Oh no," Florrie told her husband. "If you're the headline act, it's all about the dramatic entrance. When Tilly and I were topping the bill during the war and in the years afterwards, Mr McCann always insisted that we were announced with the appropriate grandeur. Frankie O'Farrell used to do it; he had such a rich, deep voice. He was enormous; they used to call him Frankie 'The Fatman' O'Farrell when he grew up. As a lad, it was just Fatty. He died young; it was very sad."

Both Alf and Godfrey stared, political and family intrigues suddenly, if temporarily, forgotten.

"Sorry, Florrie, Mr McCann did you say?" Alf asked.

"Oh yes, Cyril was our manager right up until the late fifties. Our style was falling out of favour by then, of course, everything was getting very sophisticated in the clubs, and people just stayed home and watched the television. Not much room for a pair of ageing music hall variety girls like us. There was quite a bit of snobbishness about variety performers, you know. Tilly managed to pick up a couple of small roles on the television, but radio was really more our style, like with dear Tommy Handley on ITMA. *Workers' Playtime,* then later with Frankie Howerd on *Variety Bandbox.* Wasn't he naughty in *Up Pompeii?* He has done well." Florrie became lost in melancholic, even slightly bitter, nostalgia. "How many of those so-called serious actors that looked down on us, how many of those could have filled the halls like Tilly and I used to... In fact, when Tilly became ill and could no longer perform, Cyril used to give me some work at his clubs, a little light music and comedy, the audiences were small, but kind. And his dancing girls were all so sweet to me. It helped to pay the bills. In fact, I must tell you, if not for Cyril I certainly wouldn't be here at Stonebridge House." She glared in the direction of the high wall and the building site. "Or what's left of it. After Tilly died, he paid for my room here, and continues to support me, his cheques arrive regular as clockwork. Without him God knows where I would have ended up. And of course," she added, looking lovingly at her husband. "I'd never have met my darling Jimmy." Commodore O'Malley's lined face creased into a faintly embarrassed smile.

Cyril McCann, Alf mused. The Sultan of Soho. Notorious West End gangster and colossal, systematic corruptor of police officers. Commissioner Coburn's career had been built on fighting corruption and bringing down crime kingpins like McCann. Coburn had ultimately triumphed over both, dismantled the corrupt cabals of police, sent McCann to prison for several years along with chief enforcer and bagman, Harry Barron, and, thanks to Alf's glowing coverage in the newspapers at the time, would be ever after known as "Honest Ron".

"Some terrible things have been written and said about poor Cyril over the years," Florrie commented. "Not least by your good self, Alfie dear, if I recall correctly. You were very unkind about him in the papers when he was sent to prison ten years ago." Alf suddenly didn't quite know what to say, or where to look. It was true; he had taken a very strong line against police corruption and the cancerous influence of organised crime upon society, in particular how it seemed to be sanitised and glamorised in the press, and the brutal, fundamentally disgusting reality ignored. Cyril McCann had been widely known as Y-Fronts, as it had been strongly rumoured that, following a dispute within his organisation, he had personally strangled Frankie O'Farrell with the Fatman's own voluminous underpants. Alf could never quite understand the logistics of such a manoeuvre but, fair or not, the sobriquet had stuck. How much, if any of that, did Florrie know, he wondered? Alf was about to offer a hesitant defence, but Florrie continued. "But it's a long time ago, and I'm sure it wasn't personal. Cyril is not a man to bear a grudge, he always said nice things about Mr Coburn too, despite the fact that he was the man who chased him mercilessly for over ten years and finally sent him and Harry to prison. Well, I guess Cyril and Harry weren't saints, but they were always very nice to Tilly and me. And they're both in Spain now, relaxing in the sun with a few old friends, I shouldn't wonder. Good luck to them." Florrie raised her teacup and invited the others to do the same. "To Cyril and Harry. And, of course, dear Frankie O'Farrell," she said. "God bless them." As Godfrey raised his own cup, he wondered what Sir Norman, or Commissioner Coburn, might think of the permanent head of the Home Office toasting one the most notorious London villains of the twentieth century. In due course the conversation returned to the reason they were there on that late summer's day, while the first whispers of autumn hovered expectantly on the afternoon breeze.

Alf told them. "I drove myself mad, one night in my office, making frenzied notes and drawing diagrams, lines between seemingly unconnected events and people." Jim O'Malley nodded knowingly. His own joint efforts with Major Powell had made their rooms look more like a military operations centre, with books, photographs and maps, charting the course of several lives, across two continents and the seas in between; of triumph, happiness, sadness and disaster.

Alf continued, "I began to see sinister overtones, dark interpretations almost everywhere. My nephew found me in my office, late at night, drowning under a sea of papers, notes, and scribbles, mildly hysterical. He said I reminded him of Worzel Gummidge. But, having recovered my senses somewhat, I understand how, magnified by unrelenting grief, the Major became so obsessive and focused on seeing what, I'm sorry to say, was simply not there."

There was stunned silence. Even Godfrey's practised self-discipline seemed to crumble for a split second, as he stared at Alf in complete surprise. Jim was similarly dumbstruck, while Florrie looked between the three of them, puzzled.

"I believe," Alf continued, "that Major Powell, Godfrey's father and Jim, your dear friend, was a great man. As was Fforbes Armstrong, his friend, and grandfather of our Home Secretary. I believe Fforbes Armstrong fell from his horse while chasing what he believed to be cattle thieves on his farm. A tragic accident. I think that Reg, Godfrey's much-loved and missed elder brother, and the source of so much pride for both Godfrey and the Major, was a fine young man, and an extremely talented detective. These talents were recognised early, and he was recruited into the Special Operations Executive because of those abilities, and because of those abilities alone. He died in the service of his country. Jim, how many shipmates did we lose during the war? How many unnecessary deaths? As brutal as it is, in war, these things happen. Reg was a brave policeman, and an even braver secret agent lost, we must assume, behind enemy lines.

"As for the so-called Banqueting Club, the Most Venerable Order of, no I mean the Most Worshipful Order of Liege Knights of Charles the First. Of course, they exist, they always have, and they always will. Every country has them, in one form or another. In dictatorships they're at the forefront. In democracies like ours, or like in the US or other places, they have to work in the shadows. It's a fact of life. Godfrey understands this, I know." Godfrey nodded his confirmation. "So, Major Powell was certainly right to have his suspicions, but... I think he was wrong. I'm sorry that he didn't find the peace that he so deserved in his last days."

"That's all very well, but what about —" Jim began, but Florrie placed a restraining hand on his arm, and he fell silent.

"Well, I'm satisfied," Godfrey pronounced, to Alf's gratitude cutting off any further questioning from Jim. "Thank you, Alf. It's a load off all of our minds."

An hour or so later, having bid affectionate farewells, Godfrey and Alf walked to the car park. Godfrey had driven out in his vintage MG, as the day offered little or no chance of rain, while Alf had booked a cab for the brief ride to the railway station.

"Are you sure you don't want a lift?" Godfrey asked, then wondered if Alf would actually fit into the narrow passenger well. And if he did, could he ever get out?

"Best I don't, bonny lad," Alf replied as the cab pulled into the car park. "For any number of reasons."

"You're probably right." Godfrey looked up at the wide first floor window, from where his father would wave madly every time Godfrey left from his weekly visit. "Dad would be very happy to think that Jim and Florrie have his old room. It's actually the best one in the entire building, I made sure of that."

Alf could see that Godfrey was becoming a little emotional, especially now that Florrie and Jim appeared in the same window that had once framed Godfrey's father's frail form. The newlyweds were waving like a pair of honeymooners on a ship departing the quay for a wedding cruise. Both Alf and Godfrey waved back.

"He couldn't have hoped for a better son, Godfrey," Alf said quietly. "He was lucky to have you."

A few moments of silence ensued; then Godfrey suddenly turned to Alf and extended his hand. Alf took it. "Thanks, Alf," he said, eyes glistening. "For everything."

"I haven't done much," Alf replied.

"Oh, I think you have," Godfrey assured him, as the two men went their separate ways.

***

"Alf. Alf, pet!" Dolly was used to her husband nodding off in his favourite chair in front of the television, snoring loudly, while Ernie, their little terrier, curled up on his knee as pages of his newspaper spilled onto the mat. Invariably Alf would sit bolt upright as soon as Dolly placed her hand on his shoulder, or quietly ask if he was awake, and indignantly deny that he had been asleep in the first place. But tonight, Alf didn't make a sound, and for a split second his eyes opened wide and Dolly could see the private terror deep within. She knew instinctively what was wrong. A dream; a spectre from the war. It was the first one he had had in a while, and it usually meant that he was worried about something. Or someone.

"Are you all right, pet?" she asked quietly, placing her palm lovingly on his cheek. He covered her hand with his own, knowing that she always understood. "Oh aye. I was back on the old *Lady Dorothy*; she was going down off Finisterre. Torpedoed. The captain had just given me our position. Funny thing, it was Jim O'Malley, although he never served on freighters like me. He commanded the liner, *Calcutta Queen*, *CQ2*, right through the war. But here Jim was on the old *Dorothy*. I had to transmit our position, but for some reason I couldn't remember how to operate the RT set."

"Gwynne is on the phone," Dolly said quietly. "Do you feel up to talking to her?"

"Aye, definitely. It's Garry's pre-sentencing hearing tomorrow. She might want to meet up before court."

Alf gently placed the protesting Ernie onto the floor, then walked to their little telephone table by the front door of the flat.

"Why-aye, Gwynne lass!"

Gwynne's voice was subdued. Alf thought she sounded utterly defeated. "Sorry to bother you at home, Alf. I've just had word from Governor Barrett. Earlier this evening Garry hanged himself in his cell."

Alf was stunned. "I'm sorry, bonny lass," he said quietly, then didn't quite know what to say after that.

"Can I ask you something, Alf?" Gwynne went on.

"Of course. Anything."

"Did you say anything about Garry's case to any of your friends? I mean your high up friends?" Gwynne was suddenly cautious about who might be listening.

"No, not a word, just like I promised. Why?"

"It's just that something strange happened today. I had a call from Valerie. The CPS told her that, having reviewed the evidence again, they might be able to more favourably consider a dramatic downgrade of the charges and a humane sentencing recommendation. Apparently, Commissioner Coburn intervened personally, and wrote a detailed report expressing doubts on certain aspects of the evidence, and even naming individual officers as unreliable. There was suddenly a very real chance that Garry would be — would have been — home again on bail within days."

"I didn't say a word," Alf told her, "other than to ask Roland not to raise it during his interview with Seymour."

After Gwynne had rung off, Alf sat on the stool next to the telephone table, considering the implications. Had Honest Ron finally had enough, and made a dramatic last-minute intervention, or had there been a quiet instruction from even further up? It wouldn't be the first time Sir Norman had felt an eleventh-hour pang of conscience and acted, albeit quietly, following a cryptic message from Alf.

"Not that it matters now," he sighed, and stared dejectedly for a moment at the telephone. After several seconds, he picked up the receiver and began dialling. He waited quite some time for an answer but was relieved when he heard that unmistakable voice. "Sorry to call so late… actually I don't know what time it is, I'll look, ha'way man it is late, it's nearly nine. Sorry. Actually, I just wanted to make sure you were all right, like. For no reason, really."

Retired Commodore Jim O'Malley was no stranger to the perils of the sea, and the nightmares that invariably followed. When Dolly tiptoed off to bed an hour later, Alf and Jim were still on the phone.

CHAPTER SIXTEEN

Reg Powell arrived with customary punctuality at Warrior House, the head office of Speers Colonial Holdings, on Threadneedle Street, in the City of London. A uniformed commissionaire greeted him as he entered a carpeted, high-ceilinged reception hall. The décor was dark timber and seemed to represent a period long past. It gave the appearance of the heart of a fading empire; traditional, stolid, and stifling. A large portrait dominated the entry hall from the far wall; a Post Captain in Nelson's Navy. The founder, Sir Charles Speers himself. Above the portrait was the company coat of arms, which told its own concise story of the company's long history. It was a billowing mainsail, set behind a cross consisting of a rifle and a spear.

"Can I help you, sir?" asked the commissionaire.

"Yes. I'm Detective Constable Powell, Scotland Yard. I have an appointment with Sir John Prentice."

"Very good, sir. You'll be wanting the top floor. I'll phone up to Sir John's secretary and let her know you're on the way up. I'm afraid the lift is out of order, but I'd imagine a young chap like you will have no trouble with the stairs."

"Thank you," Reg smiled, and observed the doorman as he limped toward his desk and his telephone. "Last war, was it?"

"Yes, sir, kind of you to notice, sir. Copped it at a place called Kut."

"My father was at the Somme," Reg replied. "One of his friends was out in the Middle East. He told my dad that the locals said that when God invented Hell, he realised it wasn't horrible enough, so he came up with Mesopotamia —"

"And added flies!" the two concluded the sentence together. The older man was delighted that his largely forgotten experience in the desert, where sunstroke and dysentery were easily as murderous an enemy as was the relentlessly brutal Johnny Turk, was actually appreciated after all. The phone call to the upstairs inner sanctum was made, and Reg was shown to the foot of the stairs with a big smile.

"Sir John will be with you directly," a secretary said as soon as Reg reached the top floor. "Please make yourself comfortable. I'll bring in some tea."

"Thank you," Reg replied as he was shown into the boardroom, the paned windows of which looked out over Threadneedle Street and were, like so many around London, taped up in neat crosses against a potential blast. I wonder just how much good that would really do, Reg contemplated, once the force of an explosion sent jagged splinters of glass flying. He examined in turn the paintings and portraits that together formed a comprehensive historical gallery of the Speers Colonial leviathan. It was clear that the company history was a very important part of its present culture. There were three generations of Speers memorialised in portraiture: Captain Charles Speers himself, his son Horatio and grandson Nelson, all of whom had helmed the global business through its generational growth. The row of elaborately framed portraits, fittingly positioned on the wall behind the head of the long table, also showed three formidable women. Lady Georgiana Speers, née Wellesley, the much younger wife of Sir Charles and matriarch of the empire, and her granddaughter, Charlotte Morris (née Speers). Who was Dorothy Keppel? He wondered. Her portrait, a black and white photograph, slightly smaller and rather less grandly framed than the paintings, hung next to Charlotte Morris. Reg noted that Charlotte's married surname on the plaque beneath her portrait was in much smaller and in distinctly finer print than her family surname. The poor husband obviously hadn't rated much of a mention, Reg thought. Couldn't have been easy marrying into a dynasty like this.

There was something familiar about that name. Charlotte Morris. Of course, she was an author. His father had a couple of her historical works in his bookshelf. A history of the Queen's Own Natal Rifles, and a biography of Kitchener that had outraged Major Powell so much that he had almost covered the pages with his pencilled corrections at what he considered her very loose adherence to the facts and misplaced vitriol. Reg also recalled that there had been an entire shelf dedicated to her works in the Armstrong library. Funny how there always seemed to be a connection, wherever you went.

"Detective Constable Powell, I'm sorry to have kept you waiting," Sir John Prentice hurried in and immediately shook the young man's hand. He was slim, white haired, and with a neatly trimmed moustache. "Ah, I see you're enjoying our little potted history of the Speers Companies."

"Fascinating," Reg commented.

"Let me fill you in, while we wait for our tea. The gentlemen there, Captain Speers, a man who proudly belonged to Nelson's Band of Brothers, founded our great enterprise. His old ship, *HMS Warrior*, was damaged almost beyond repair at Trafalgar. Captain Speers purchased the ship rather than see her placed in ordinary, or become some prison hulk somewhere, and within a couple of years she became our first passenger and cargo ship, sailing regularly to the West Indies. From that one ship, the Speers operations grew, along with the British Empire herself. At one stage we had our own armed vessels to protect our shipping, and our own private army. Our militia provided invaluable support to Cecil Rhodes as he opened up southern Africa for us, and Captain Speers himself was a visionary, a man before his time, having championed the cause of the Suez Canal for decades. Sadly, he never lived to see his dream realised, but his legacy remains. Even now we are a company upon which the sun never sets. Our shipping line became the most prestigious way to travel to Africa and the East, and we pioneered ranching, plantations, finance and engineering all over the world. We're all tied up with the war now, of course. Now, this fine lady, Georgiana Speers, née Wellesley, second cousin of the Duke of Wellington himself. Captain Speers first laid eyes on her at the Duchess of Richmond's Ball, the night before the days of battle that would come to be known as Waterloo. They were married within weeks, and the dynasty was born."

"At Waterloo, did you say, sir?" Reg queried, thinking just how much his father, a keen student of history, would enjoy this journey through the golden age of Empire. "What was a naval Captain doing at Waterloo?"

"Oh, he had as good as left the navy by then. He was still a half-pay officer, on the beach, but had spent the decade following Trafalgar building up his business interests. He was friends with Uxbridge, the commander of Wellington's heavy cavalry, and managed to get himself attached to the Duke's personal staff. Just for the sheer adventure of it. Captain Speers also held the honorary rank of Colonel of the Royal Marines, so he was able to mix it with the most senior of army officers. Speaking of which, this chap over here is Major James Armstrong, who was also on the Duke's staff at Waterloo. He and Captain Speers became firm friends, and when he retired from the army, Major Armstrong, on Captain Speers's invitation, became a much-valued member of our board of directors. He was an experienced battlefield commander, of course, and trained our private militia. His influence as an MP was also invaluable to the progress of the company."

They turned their attention to the side wall of the boardroom, showing a collection of pictures of ships, illustrating the evolution of the Speers shipping line from sail to steam.

"This is the *Calcutta Queen II*," Sir John said proudly. "Just launched from our own Tyneside shipyard last year, and now in service as a troopship, under the command of our foremost officer, Commodore James O'Malley who, I should mention, is directly descended from this gentleman here," Sir John pointed to another portrait. "Sean O'Malley. Captain Speers's sailing master at Trafalgar, and the Speers Line's first Captain and Commodore. A very influential man in the formative years of the company, and a great and loyal friend to our founding father. Now that brings me to this rather stunning account of the Battle of Trafalgar." Sir John gestured to the wall past the foot of the table, which was dominated by a large and detailed picture of a Nelsonian naval battle. "Here you see two French ships of the line, stern on, and in the background to the left, you can just make out the *Victory*, Nelson's flagship as I'm sure you're aware, almost hidden by the smoke of battle. Here in the foreground, just about to slip between the two French ships, is the *Warrior*, under the command of Captain Speers. You can see that she was dwarfed by the two French ships, and outgunned."

They were now standing right in front of the picture. Reg leaned forward to read the inscription on a small plaque attached to the gilded frame. "Lay us between them two big buggers, Mr O'Malley," he read aloud.

"That was the famous command that has resonated through naval history."

"What happened?"

"The objective, which was to protect the *Victory*, was achieved, but at a terrible price. The *Warrior* was dis-masted, and holed very badly. More than half of her crew were killed. It was said that blood could be seen coursing from the jagged wreckage of the gunports like waterfalls. By a miracle, both Captain Speers and Master O'Malley survived, although O'Malley lost an eye and walked with a severe limp for the rest of his days. The *Warrior* made it home, under tow. Captain Speers subsequently declined a command on the North American Station, and the rest, as we say, is history."

"I'm surprised you haven't moved some of these treasures to a safer location outside London," Reg remarked.

"This building, and indeed this boardroom, has been the centre of our world since around the time of Waterloo. During that time, we've been attacked by Radicals, Chartists, Fenians, anarchists, militant abolitionists, home-grown Marxist revolutionaries, suffragettes, and in the last the twenty-five years by the Germans twice. By Zeppelin in the last lot, and by bomber this time. Ah, I nearly forgot a peaceful but nevertheless inconvenient sit-in by people protesting our involvement in India. We're not going to start running away now."

Their attention returned to the paintings and photographs of the ships. "Now here is the *RMS Lady Georgiana*, in her prime, one of the three famous Speers Ladies, as they were known. There was no more prestigious a way to travel to a Civil Service posting in India, or a diplomatic or military assignment in Africa, in late Victorian and Edwardian times, than on the Speers Ladies. The *Lady Georgiana*, the *Lady Emily*, and the *Lady Charlotte*. Only the *Lady Georgiana* survived service in the Great War, but then tragically collided with a drifting mine in 1919, on her way home from South Africa. Terrible loss of life. In peacetime, too. It's not something you expect. It was on board the *Georgiana* that Miss Dorothy Keppel," Prentice pointed at the wall of portraits, "was lost, having been in South Africa on company and literary business. Let me take you back to the other wall to the portraits —"

"I believe, Sir John, I can claim a small family link with the Speers Line."

"Really?" Sir John was suddenly wary. "How so?"

"My family came to England on the original *Calcutta Queen*, in 1926. I remember it very well. I was about to turn eight years old."

"Well, that is fascinating," Sir John replied, relieved. "Ah, our refreshments have arrived."

284

They took a seat at the table, while Sir John's secretary poured their teas and proffered cream cakes sprinkled liberally with icing sugar, a luxury that Reg had not enjoyed since before the war. Sensing Reg's reaction, Sir John put his hands up and said, jokingly, "All above board, Detective. We save our limited rations for special meetings and occasions. Our chef works wonders. Please tuck in."

Reg wanted so much to appear aloof and mildly uninterested, but his will failed and it finally took a supreme effort of restraint to stop himself reaching for a third jam and cream-filled pastry.

"How long have you been with the company, Sir John?" he asked, spraying icing sugar in a small cloud over the dark polished tabletop.

"Since 1924," Sir John replied. "I had the honour of being elected chairman in 1935."

"Now," Reg said, feeling that it was time to re-establish an appropriate sense of professionalism. He took his notepad and pencil from his pocket. "I understand you wanted to talk to me about concerns regarding the infiltration of fifth columnists and pacifists into the unions that represent your workers, both here in London and in your shipyard on Tyneside."

"Actually, I did not," Sir John replied. "Our own internal policing measures, supported by military intelligence, ensure that we have no trouble of that nature."

"But Superintendent Havill said —"

"Yes, I'm afraid Sunny Havill was a fellow conspirator in on my little deception."

"Deception?"

"Do you enjoy your work, Detective?"

That's a funny question, and no mistake, Reg thought. "Well, er, yes, I suppose, but I don't see what that has to do with anything, with great respect, sir. Why am I here, exactly?"

"But you've wanted to do more, for the war effort. I see that you've tried to join the RAF on more than one occasion, and you've also made application to join the military police. But the nature of your work meant that you couldn't be spared from Scotland Yard."

"Yes, that's true." How did he know that? Reg wondered, and what was this all about?

"I'm now going to make you an offer. I must say to you that anything we say, from now on, is subject to the Official Secrets Act, regardless of the outcome of our discussion."

I'm getting used to that, Reg was about to say, but checked himself just in time. "I understand."

"I may be Chairman of Speers now that I'm in my dotage, but my main career was in the army. Coldstream Guards. I'm still involved in some aspects of the military, in what you might call an advisory capacity. Have you ever heard of the SOE? The Special Operations Executive?"

"No," Reg replied.

"Good, I would've worried if you had. It's very new. It's going to be critical to the war effort, and it needs good men. You've come very highly recommended indeed."

"Have I?" Reg asked.

"Most definitely. From your superiors, as well as from someone *very* high up in government. Don't worry, Detective, I'm well aware of your meeting with Mr Armstrong. I'm at liberty to say that you impressed him a great deal."

"Did I?" Reg asked.

"Oh yes. You're just the kind of chap this new organisation needs."

"Am I?" Reg asked, then gathered his thoughts. "What kind of, I mean what —?"

"What will your role in SOE be? I can't say specifically, but I suspect there will be some activities in Europe."

Behind enemy lines! Reg thought with a potent mixture of excitement, fear and dread. No more oily spivs with their little pencil moustaches and shiny suits, forged ration books, enemy aliens, drunken fights between army and navy, blackout violations and black-market contraband. No more counting the corpses of women and children as they're dragged out of bombed houses, schools and shops. Real war work at last, in the thick of it. He couldn't quite believe it. *And they want me!* He thought with barely contained pride.

"The SOE needs you, Detective. It might be something of a clichéd line, but it's the truth."

"Of course, the answer is yes, but I'm just working on something —"

General Sir John Prentice observed the young man's turmoil. "You've been selected for something specific," he interrupted. "In order to meet a critical deadline, you'll need to report to SOE by tomorrow night. They've taken up a good part of a great house in Cornwall. Trafalgar Hall. Have you heard of it?"

"No."

"I've taken the liberty of having your papers prepared. You'll need to be on the train first thing tomorrow morning. I need your answer now."

"But, my cases. There's one in particular that I would very much like to see through to the end. I need to correct a mistake that I made —"

"Superintendent Havill told me of your famous zeal and conscientiousness, Detective Powell. It does you great credit. Your role with SOE will form an essential part of efforts to support the growth of organised resistance in... No, I won't say any more. I understand that Mr Havill is already reassigning your work, anticipating that you would jump at the chance to serve your country in this way. I hope he was right."

"Of course," Reg replied.

On his way out, Reg observed a portrait that he hadn't noticed earlier. The face was very familiar, yet the eyes were cold, distant. The subject seemed to be what his father might have called a "cold fish".

Observing Reg's interest, Sir John said, "That's the late Piers Armstrong, MP, and another distinguished board member. You see over here, his father, who was the son of James Armstrong, whom we discussed earlier."

That's the resemblance, Reg thought. Had to be related to Richard Armstrong. An uncle perhaps, or cousin. Colonel Fforbes Armstrong's brother, perhaps? He looked about the right age, but there was something truly discomfiting about the general air of... cold determination... portrayed. Richard Armstrong was warm and kind, and with a natural, reassuring sense of authority. From what he remembered of Fforbes Armstrong, brother of Piers and father to Richard, there was a similar sense of reassurance in his strength and loving kindness.

Not with this one though, Reg contemplated, as he found himself momentarily unable to move from the gaze of Piers

Armstrong's frigid, grey eyes that seemed to stare back at him in calculating triumph.

***

"Right, this little problem of ours is solved. Our young friend is now at Trafalgar Hall, and any breath of scandal within the government over a leaky ministry has been nipped in the bud. Dick Billings is well out of the way. I don't believe we'll have any problems from Mrs Donoghue, although she is being a little stubborn."

The evening following the meeting with keen young detective Reg Powell, General Sir John Prentice was still at Warrior House, in the boardroom, and in intense conversation with a young man in the uniform of a newly promoted RAF Group Captain.

"Stubborn?" the young man queried.

"She won't sell. Says that our late and lamented friend Paddy spent his life building something for the benefit of his son. A board of directors is in place, and the Daily Focus Proprietary is going to be renamed Donoghue Publishing, and will be all ship shape for young Eddie when he comes of age."

"When will that be?"

"He'll turn twenty-one in 1957."

"Won't have to worry about him sticking his oar into things that don't concern him for a while then. And, by the way, I don't understand where Richard Armstrong fits in. Is he one of us, or not?"

"*Mr* Armstrong to you, boy," Sir John replied. "And he's one of us all right. He just doesn't always realise it."

"Funny kind of arrangement, I must say," the younger man muttered.

"Oh, I nearly forgot." Sir John produced a small item of jewellery and slid it across the table toward his son. "Lost something, have you?"

Group Captain Archie Prentice turned pale and picked up his society coat of arms. "Where was this?" he asked.

Sir John slapped the table in sudden anger. "Some eagle-eyed Bobby found it in the rubble near where you dumped Donoghue's body. Careless, boy, careless. How many times have I told you?"

CHAPTER SEVENTEEN

Sir Dick Billings joined the throng of MPs in the Members' Lobby, as they crowded through the Churchill Arch and into to the Commons chamber, under the watchful eye of Mr Churchill himself, and David Lloyd George. He rolled his eyes as he observed a number of his Conservative colleagues briefly touching the left foot of Mr Churchill's imposing statue as they passed.

"Superstitious twattery," he muttered scornfully, then noticed Janice Best off to one side, chatting with the Parliamentary Private Secretary at Stanley Smee's Northern Ireland Office, Perkin Warbeck.

"Piss off, Warbeck," Dick growled as he approached them, now wearing the sinister cloak of Chief Whip. "I want to talk to Miss Best." As Warbeck disappeared, Janice speculated that being accosted by the Chief Whip was something that would have scared her half to death a couple of years before. But not now. Being part of the Armstrong Home Office, while creating no end of trouble politically, had its advantages. Sir Norman was fiercely protective of his staff, and other MPs crossed the invisible wall of protection at their dire peril. But Janice also knew that Sir Dick and Sir Norman were factional allies and old friends, so she would have had no concerns at any rate.

Dick grasped Janice by the elbow and propelled her to a corner away from the throng. He looked around to ensure they weren't being overheard and leaned closer to Janice, who tried hard not to recoil as his breath, she surmised with watering eyes, could probably strip paint.

"How are things in the constituency?" he asked.

Janice was immediately wary. "Not easy at the moment," she confessed.

"That would be an understatement, I shouldn't wonder," Sir Dick acknowledged. "It's time to think about yourself. This parliament needs you, and if you stay where you are, we're going to lose you at the next general election."

"We're only halfway through the term," Janice replied defiantly. "I've got plenty of time to turn things around. I'll work hard —"

"Look, Janice," Dick interrupted. "I've been in this fuck-awful game for fifty-one years, God help me. I know most people hate my guts, but even those people who do, recognise that I know what I'm talking about. You won't turn this around, no one could. Things have gone too far. The fact that you gave us two terms in that constituency is a miracle, an aberration. An accident of history."

Now Janice was feeling genuinely ill, and only just succeeded in stemming tears of hopeless frustration. "What are you saying? That you want me deselected for the next election?"

Dick looked around. Things were much quieter now as the Commons had almost filled for another Prime Minister's questions. "I'm not saying that at all," he replied. "I've been looking around and I think I've found just the place for you. Stonebridge Central and North West, it neighbours the Home Secretary's own constituency. He calls it Stonebridge Leftovers; used to be part of his own constituency years ago, until the boundaries were re-drawn in his father's time. It's safe, nowhere near as watertight as Sir Norman's seat, but where is? But there's a comfortable majority. You'll see out a long career there. That braindead pinko Burton isn't right very often, but I think he hit the button right on the hammer when he wrote that you have the strength and the talent to go all the way to Number Ten, given the right opportunities. Not in my lifetime of course, but sometime in the distant future. But it'll never happen if you stay in Streatham and Vauxhall."

Janice didn't quite know how to respond.

Sir Dick continued. "Stonebridge Leftovers is a good constituency. I understand there are even dark... black... that is, there's a growing number of ethnically multi-racialist people moving in. You should fit in well. Actually, I didn't mean that the way it sounded. I'm trying to say that it's not your traditional white middle-class stuck-up —"

"But what about Dudley Bayliss?" Janice interrupted before Dick could dig himself further into trouble. "He's held that seat since 1964."

"Old Bayliss is going to be retiring at the next election," Dick replied.

"Is he?" Janice asked, surprised. "He didn't mention it when I saw him earlier. In fact, he was talking about how the polls are improving and that he might even increase his majority if things keep going as they are."

"Bayliss won't stand next time. He just doesn't realise it yet." Dick reflected on the weaponisation of the Chief Whip's dirt book, meticulously expanded in Norman Armstrong's time and now even more comprehensive under the harsh, unforgiving regime of Sir Dick Billings. If the great British public were privy to what Sir Dick knew about a number of MPs, of all persuasions, the Raving Loony Party would be the only one left that people might feel inclined to vote for. As for Bayliss, Sir Dick was sure he would see the sense of a discreet and quiet retirement.

"Is he going to be kicked out for me?" Janice asked.

"No, there are plenty of reasons to put him out to pasture. The local election agent will be delighted. She's done wonders with that limp-dick, imagine what could be achieved with someone of real talent, like you."

"Does Sir Norman know you're talking to me about this?"

"Of course."

Janice contemplated matters for a few brief seconds. A genuinely safe seat, a constituency for life if circumstances remained favourable, and a steady rise through the ranks to something in Cabinet, and then maybe even the biggest job of all... Imagine what could be achieved! Janice considered the many social and personal causes that informed her day-to-day working life. Imagine having real power to make genuine change for the better. A genuinely new Britain. "I couldn't do that," she said eventually. "I couldn't leave my constituency."

"Norman said you'd be bloody-minded about it," Dick grumbled. "Well, we'll do everything we can to support you, of course. But if I were you, I'd be thinking about another job."

Sir Dick got the surprise of his life when Janice leaned forward and kissed him tenderly on the cheek. "Thank you, I mean it. I'll admit that I often feel like my loyalties are torn, but I'll not walk away from my community, or Sir Norman.

I'll do my best, and take the consequences, whatever they may be."

Dick was still standing, dumbfounded, his fingers lightly touching his gnarled cheek where he could still feel the light, sweet touch of Janice's lips, and smell the residual cloud of her perfume. He was lamenting that he wasn't half a century younger, when he became aware of the Prime Minister sailing past toward the chamber, a small flotilla of assistants and secretaries in tow, like tenders following the royal yacht.

"How are things in the party, Dick?" she asked as she strode past without slowing.

"Everyone's right behind you, Prime Minister," Dick called, as she swept into the House of Commons.

"I'm bored with all this," Dick muttered, and instead of entering the chamber behind his Prime Minister, he strode off into a high-ceilinged corridor. Annie's Bar seemed a more appealing option than Prime Minister's Questions.

As he walked, he suddenly had the feeling that someone was walking very closely behind him. He stopped suddenly and turned around. There was nobody there. He glanced at a recessed arch in which was displayed the bust of Piers Armstrong MP.

"See you in Hell, you bastard," he muttered, and then walked on.

***

Sir Archie Prentice, in a state of unaccustomed agitation, had asked for an urgent and highly confidential meeting with the Cabinet Secretary. The outdoor gathering between Godfrey, Alf, the old sea captain and Florrie Tweedle at Stonebridge

House had finally split the last length of fraying twine holding Archie's nerves from almost total collapse. And to make things worse, they were unable to pick up the conversation, despite having one of Archie's agents lurking in the bushes, bumbling around with a receiver that resembled a speaking trumpet, like a real-life Inspector Clouseau. Not knowing what was said had caused Sir Archie sleepless nights, extreme anxiety and even some rather worrying, intermittent chest pains. Any number of revelations could have been made that could not only bring down the government, the monarchy, perhaps even western civilisation. But, most worryingly in that litany of potential disasters, also Sir Archie Prentice himself.

Archie had been in such a state of agitation that he had begged Sir Peregrine to meet him on his own, secure ground; not his usual modern headquarters, but a nondescript building on Threadneedle Street, on a long-term lease from Speers-Donoghue and, to all intents and purposes, an office and archive staffed by a number of government clerks and statisticians.

Sir Peregrine was delivered to the front door by the Home Secretary's driver, Eric Baker, who, when duties permitted, was often given jobs where a particular degree of discretion was required. With Sir Peregrine's own long-serving driver on sick leave, the Cabinet Secretary wasn't inclined to trust the discretion of someone from the relief pool, so had phoned his old friend Norman Armstrong, and asked a favour.

Eric eyed the old stone building with suspicion; he could just make out some carved lettering above the door. Warrior House. "Are you sure this is the place?" he asked.

"Yes, thank you, Eric," Sir Peregrine said. "I shouldn't be much longer than an hour."

"Very good, Cabinet Secretary, sir." Eric was well aware that he frequently got away with an unusual level of familiarity with many senior members of the government, but even he recognised that "righto guv" wouldn't be quite the thing with the Prime Minister's closest confidant, and head of the entire home Civil Service.

Sir Peregrine pressed an intercom outside the heavy front door and was admitted within a few seconds. He regarded the portrait of Captain Sir Charles Speers that took up most of the wall opposite the doorway, then took the lift to the boardroom on the top floor.

Having opened the car door for Sir Peregrine, Eric returned to the driver's seat, observing with satisfaction that he was parked on a double yellow line, and hoped that a meddling traffic warden would come by, so he could explain in flowery detail just who the hapless parasite would be writing a ticket for. He settled back behind the wheel and reached for the book Sir Norman had loaned him: the Home Secretary's own signed copy of Alf Burton's *Working-Class Heroes*. It was one of Alf's first major literary successes and explored the humble backgrounds of three of the most influential people in post-war politics: US President Harry Truman, British Health and Housing Minister, and father of the NHS, Nye Bevan, and Labour Foreign Secretary Ernie Bevin. It was heavy reading, with much intricate detail about the complex post-war world; the birth of the United Nations, Truman's own domestic problems with McCarthy and industrial disharmony, as well as troubles closer to home as the Attlee Government battled to enact its ambitious manifesto, in spite of having no money of its own, facing a backlash over ongoing rationing and shortages, and being obliged to actively reinforce democracy in Europe and Asia against the threat of Communism as well.

Eric was particularly enjoying Alf's school-boyish preoccupation with the constant flow of insults that had been hurled back and forth between Aneurin Bevan and his arch-enemy Dick Billings, then serving as Shadow Spokesman on the progress of EFM pre-fab housing.

Eric chuckled as he read of one of Dick Billings's frequent rants, "I've heard that Mr Bevan has been described as his own worst enemy. Well, let me tell, you, not while I'm around he ain't!" And another. "Mr Churchill may well have described Mr Bevan as a squalid nuisance and a merchant of discourtesy, but I would go further. I would describe Mr Bevan as a right royal pain in the — and the rudest — I've ever met."

A case of pot and kettle if ever there was one, Eric thought. Obviously, the sensibilities of publishing in the late fifties precluded the use of certain profanities, so some imagination was called for. Right royal pain in the arse? Obvious. Eric contemplated the latter. He spoke aloud. "Rudest bastard? Rudest fucker? Rudest prick? Rudest twat?" Dick Billings had been known to use any and all of those epithets in the course of normal conversation. "Rudest knob? Rudest dickhead?" Too mild. "No, it had to be rudest cu—" The solution to Eric's question remained unspoken, as he observed a traffic warden striding toward him with ticket book and pen already in hand. As a black cab driver Eric had waged a constant war against the unwanted intrusions of the black rats into his working days, who, he contended to anyone who would listen, had persecuted him without cause and made his life a misery for years.

"Let's be having you," he muttered, got out of the car and met the black-uniformed officer with dreaded yellow band around her cap, as she approached the car. Arguing with the authorities was exhilarating if it was one working person to another, but Eric suddenly remembered that he was working for the most powerful people in the country, and the thought of berating someone doing a thankless and awful job, just to put food on their family table, from the position of such privilege, suddenly seemed deeply contemptible. He simply couldn't abide bullies under any circumstances. He smiled, introduced himself, and began to politely explain.

When Sir Peregrine Walsingham entered the top floor boardroom it was dim, the heavy curtains were drawn, and Sir Archie Prentice was seated at the head of the polished table, on one of the many high-backed, heavy, and not particularly comfortable chairs. The Cabinet Secretary admired the portraits on the panelled walls and marvelled at the enormous painting that seemed to tell the entire dramatic story of the Battle of Trafalgar within its gilded frame. A discreet assistant served tea and coffee, then left them alone.

"Is everything all right, Archie?" Peregrine asked. Pressure had been growing from senior politicians, including Sir Norman Armstrong, and even from one of the Cabinet Secretary's own senior colleagues, in the form of Permanent Secretary at the Home Office, Sir Godfrey Powell, to rein in the increasingly aggressive intrusions of Archie's department. Sir Peregrine had been waiting for the right moment, and some considerable time had passed, but having been asked to Warrior House by an unusually rattled intelligence chief, Sir Peregrine was grateful that the perfect opportunity now presented itself.

"No, it bloody well isn't," Sir Archie cried. "Godfrey has been asking questions about the circumstances of his brother's death. After all these years, I ask you! I knew as soon as Burton started sniffing around Stonebridge House it was more than just looking into Norman's constituency political problems. He's been talking to that old sea captain, O'Malley."

"Are you quite well, Archie?" Sir Peregrine questioned, his eyebrows raised. "What's all this about an old sea captain?"

"The old boy was friends with Godfrey's father!" Archie cried. "By coincidence they ended up in the same old folks' home, what were the chances of that?"

Sir Archie's air of galloping panic was obvious, but the Cabinet Secretary remained completely bewildered. "What in God's name are you talking about?" he asked. "What has Godfrey's father got to do with anything? And, by the way, he's dead. I went to his funeral last year."

"Yes, that's something at least." Archie noticed his old friend's shocked expression. "No, I didn't mean it quite like... But O'Malley was the Third Officer on the old *Georgiana* when she went down," Sir Archie persisted. "You know, when the Morris papers were supposedly lost. Godfrey's father was in the South African Mounted Rifles, was friends with Norman's grandfather, Fforbes Armstrong. So many connections. So many loose ends."

"You're making no sense at all. I'm none the wiser," Sir Peregrine told him, his bewilderment and exasperation now patently obvious.

"Godfrey's had Young Ronnie poking around personnel files at Scotland Yard; he and Burton seem to be in it together. It's all getting out of hand! Now they've all met up, the sea captain and some blasted old woman who's appeared from nowhere and is now part of it. They were all together, at Stonebridge House! God knows what's going to come out!"

"Archie, calm down," the Cabinet Secretary said, thinking it was about time to stem the tide of chaos. Archie's face was red, bordering on purple, and Sir Peregrine was having serious concerns that he might just keel over from the strain. "I still haven't the faintest idea what you're on about."

"And, have you heard? Some boffin has found the *Titanic*, at the bottom of the Atlantic!"

"The *Titanic*?"

"Yes! Just how long do you think it's going to be before someone has the bright idea of searching for the old *Georgiana* and snooping around —?"

"For God's sake, listen to yourself. You're not making any sense. You need to take a deep breath and calm yourself."

Archie took his friend's advice. When he spoke again, he was much more composed. "Let's just say, Perry, that it would be in the national interest, a matter of the utmost national security even, for certain matters, historical matters, and certain people's involvement in such matters, hypothetically speaking, not to be revealed under any circumstances. Even now. It could ruin everything. Everything we've fought and worked for, all because —"

"Archie, stop!" Sir Peregrine ordered, and the normally icily composed intelligence chief fell silent. To Sir Peregrine's relief, Archie's face seemed to be regaining some of its usual pallor.

The Cabinet Secretary regarded him for what seemed like excruciating minutes but was, Archie soon realised, only a matter of seconds. Eventually Peregrine said, "Listen to me. Pull yourself together. We've been friends for more than forty years. They laughingly call us the Winged Mafia, you and I, Norman and Ron, but it's deeper than a trite and amusing adjective. We've had our disagreements over the years, but we've always stuck by one another. And we've all survived, and prospered. And the country has been safer because of us. Millions of our fellow Britons rely on us. I'm telling you, if you panic, if you decide to go rogue on us, embark on any kind of reckless lone action, for whatever ill-founded reason; and if you go anywhere near Godfrey, or even Burton, or, God forbid, any of Norman's elderly constituents, you and I will fall out." Archie gasped, and found himself unable to breathe. Sir Peregrine continued, his tone now a little softer. "Think rationally for a moment. Now, I don't know exactly what you're alluding to here; I don't want to know. But do you really think that Godfrey would embark on any course of action that might hurt the government, or the nation? He's going to be the next Cabinet Secretary, when I retire. You, or most likely your successor, will answer to him. This department, the one that you've spent your life nurturing, and your father before you, will survive, or be abolished, at his discretion alone, so, my advice is, don't make him your enemy. Whatever Godfrey discovers, he'll deal with it in his own way. I trust him, and so should you."

"Yes, all right, I see that," Archie said, his breathing returning to normal. "That's all very well, but what about Burton?"

"I suggest that it's time to take a more measured approach, generally." Sir Peregrine's suggestion was his uniquely polite way of issuing an order. "We've won. It's time to cut back your widespread surveillance on the NUM, particularly on Scargill and Austin Wells, and also on Alf Burton and his staff for a start. Alf is this government's authorised chronicler. He has more friends, even on the Right, than you might think. We've had a bit of a family argument over the miners, things have been a bit frosty, but these wounds will heal. And we all know what happened last time you tried some funny business with Alf. If anything like that was to happen again, I don't think Norman would be quite so forgiving, do you?" Then the Cabinet Secretary added with quiet menace, "Mark my words, Archie, none of us is indispensable."

Sir Archibald Prentice looked like he'd been punched in the stomach, and then suffered an uppercut to the face as he doubled over. After a few more moments of excruciating silence, Sir Peregrine stood up. "I've changed my mind about that drink." He walked to the sideboard and picked up a crystal goblet, eyeing the portrait of General Sir John Prentice. Where would we be without people to do our dirty work for us? He mused, so we can go home at nights with clean hands. And clear consciences. He returned to the table, where Archie was staring catatonically into his empty glass. Peregrine reached for the decanter and filled his own.

"Listen, Archie," he said finally. "We've got enough on our plates without dropping our bundle about things that might never happen, or spending our lives seeing red spies wherever we look, or damaging manuscripts at the bottom of the sea. Let's turn our attention to a real red who, from what Norman has told me, is about to make a name for himself on Tyneside."

Gradually, Archie sat up straight as he recovered his wits, and offered his old friend a brief expression of pure gratitude, before any trace of despair disappeared like scraps being wiped from a dinner plate. He pressed a button hidden beneath the table, and within seconds a suited assistant appeared. "Can you bring me the file on Clarence Bolton and the rebel ship workers, please?" The assistant disappeared without a word.

Peregrine took a sip from his goblet, wrinkled his nose and pursed his lips. "What's this?" he asked.

"Madeira," Archie replied. "It's a tradition dating back to old Captain Speers himself. We're still working through his own supply, in fact. What we're drinking here is around one hundred and fifty years old."

Peregrine gingerly took another sip. "When do you retire, by the way?" he asked.

"If we give due consideration to Civil Service rules, I'm afraid that horse bolted some time ago," Sir Archie replied. "Yourself?"

"The stable door is well and truly open."

"What are you going to do?"

"Close it again. The Prime Minister, and the country needs me. Needs us."

Archie raised his glass. "To the Honourable Company," he said.

"The Honourable Company," Peregrine repeated. "And the Winged Mafia."

"The Winged Mafia," Archie replied, smiling, as their glasses touched with a reassuring clink.

***

Eric Baker had lost track of time, having been engrossed in Alf's book, so he was surprised when Sir Peregrine Walsingham let himself into the passenger seat without Eric having even noticed him emerging from the building. The

Cabinet Secretary was effusive in his apologies about the time he had been gone.

"No problem, sir," Eric said, as he started the engine and moved off into the traffic.

Sir Peregrine noticed the parking ticket Eric had tossed onto the dashboard. "Did you have a little bother?" he asked.

"I had a little discussion with a traffic warden," Eric replied. "I was about to explain why we were here, but then I remembered we're on a hush-hush job, so I just told her that I was driving for a government departmental secretary.

"What was the response?"

"She said that she didn't care whose secretary I was driving around; a double yellow line is a double yellow line and rules are rules."

"Well, I guess we of all people can't argue about that," the Cabinet Secretary replied with a smile. "But I think we'll be able to resolve it easily enough. After all, we know the Home Secretary, don't we?" They both laughed. Sir Peregrine continued. "How is Norman, by the way?"

"Much improved, I think, Sir Peregrine. He's back in business. Well and truly."

"What makes you say that?"

"Next week I'm driving him to Donoghue House. He and Alf Burton are going to have what Mr Burton described as 'a nice bit' craic' on the radio."

"That's good news," Sir Peregrine replied, genuinely pleased. "We can only hope that nothing else goes wrong between now and then, and that Alf gives him an easy run, first time back in the saddle, as it were."

***

The Party Chairman remained preoccupied with precarious poll numbers, and the problems facing Janice Best in Streatham and Vauxhall. From the Whips' Office at Twelve Downing Street, he contemplated whether or not, given time, she might be able to appreciate more fully just what losing her seat might mean, and reconsider her refusal to be parachuted into Stonebridge Leftovers. Sir Norman was certainly doing all he could to encourage her and had even promised her a more senior role in the Home Office as an inducement, or even to find her a junior ministry in another department. But Janice remained true to her principles, and so far, her chosen course was Home Office PPS; and Streatham and Vauxhall, or bust.

But all might not be lost, Dick conceded. He'd recently commissioned a more detailed breakdown of the actual situation in Janice's constituency. The latest numbers were showing a slight improvement in her prospects; her constant public crusade on police reform and the equally public cooperation from Commissioner Coburn, were helping to at least stabilise her approval ratings, and stem the stampede of supporters deserting her like the proverbial rodents off a foundering ship. Current projections suggested that she was in line to lose by a large margin, but she remained confident that she could turn the tide. At least that's what she kept saying. And Dick reminded himself again that there was still plenty of time. Perhaps there was cause for some optimism after all.

"I've been wrong before, I suppose," Dick mused out loud. "Can't think of any occasions specifically, though," he added.

But civil unrest and policing remained uncomfortably front and centre in the public consciousness; every day there seemed to be reports of another pocket of racial unrest, or incidence of police violence; Molotov cocktails, injuries and violent deaths as a result of public disorder. Unspeakably tragic consequences of police carelessness with firearms, most recently in the Birmingham suburb of Handsworth. Sir Dick Billings, normally outspoken, provocative and even tactless on issues relating to immigration, race and inner-city behaviour generally, was currently remaining tight-lipped in the interests of not inflaming tensions further. This was a stance noted with admiration and surprise by Alf Burton and appreciated by Janice Best and a number of her moderate colleagues. But unfortunately an old friend, Enoch Powell, now in the parliament as Ulster Unionist MP for South Down, reminded the nation of his "Rivers of Blood" speech from seventeen years earlier, with an unmistakable tone of "I told you so", resulting in a blistering rebuke from Janice Best, more public discussion in the press about government disunity, and calls for calm on all sides by the Home Secretary himself.

It would be extremely helpful, not only for Janice, Dick thought, but for the government as well, if Armstrong's Army and the rest of the nation's police would stop regularly shooting and otherwise generally knocking the living shit out of the voters. Just for a little while. Or if they insisted on continuing, to do it *quietly.*

It was time for the news. Dick reached for his radio and switched it on.

"Good afternoon, this is City Radio London News. We are receiving reports of mounting unrest in the south London district of Brixton, following the apparent accidental shooting of an unarmed woman in her home, by officers of the Metropolitan Police —"

"Fuck me sideways, not again!" Dick moaned. The newsreader described the increasing tension on the streets, as Dick imagined the inevitable images that would soon be broadcast into lounge rooms across the nation and probably internationally. Police behind helmets and riot shields pitted against angry local youths. Petrol bombs, stones, bottles and other missiles flying through the air; upended and burning cars, buildings alight and looted shopfronts with shattered glass covering the footpaths like jagged hailstones. And the Home Secretary, in his own version of police riot equipment, at the vanguard of the police lines, offering suggestions to the field commanders. Like it or not, Dick mused, this was Thatcher's Britain. Or perhaps this part of it was Armstrong's Britain.

Dick glanced once again at the report he had commissioned on the political future of Janice Best. He slowly and deliberately tore it into pieces, dropped each shred into his wastepaper basket, and rested his head in his hands.

CHAPTER EIGHTEEN

Reg Powell had enjoyed the three-and-a-half mile walk from Trafalgar Hall to the village, and although the late winter sky of watery grey had remained threatening, any rain had obligingly stayed away. He admired the cottages, the little shops and the pub, the spired church, the welcoming railway station, and imagined this was just the kind of place that would present the idealised image on a recruiting poster. "This is what we're fighting for, lad," would be the message, and anyone not possessing a heart of stone, or the soul of a traitor, would be rushing to the local barracks to join up. Reg contemplated recent events in the Pacific and the Far East; the attack on Pearl Harbour, the fall of Singapore. At least America was in now; in fact, the US Eighth Airforce had just arrived in England, so he'd been told. And that had to be cause for some optimism, he considered.

He walked to the village green, an expanse of grass within a circle of cottages, neatly pruned hedgerows and one or two shops, the centrepiece of which was a tall marble pillar, a memorial to the fallen of the Great War. There was an inordinately long list of names for such a small community, Reg thought, and reflected with a shiver just how seamlessly his father's name could have fitted between Pierce and

Preston. A separate plaque at the bottom of the obelisk attracted his attention.

In Memory of
Charlotte Morris (Née Speers)
Taken by the influenza in 1919
And also

of

Miss Dorothy Keppel,
Lost in the *RMS Lady Georgiana* disaster, 1919;

Late of Trafalgar Hall

And from whose generosity this fine memorial became possible.

Reg noted the names with interest, remembering the boardroom at Warrior House. Connections and coincidences. Or were they coincidences? What did it all mean? Probably nothing.

"Aren't there a terrible lot of names for such a small village?" Reg turned, startled to see a girl standing beside him. She was about his own age, had red hair, was tall, her perfume was intoxicating, and Reg found himself almost breathless at her proximity as he stared at her lightly freckled face. He couldn't remember the last time he'd actually walked out with someone. The last time he'd been to the pictures was months ago, with Tom Taunton, when they had shared a rare afternoon off, watching the Marx Brothers in a matinée double feature at the Odeon, Leicester Square. And that *certainly* didn't count.

"Yes," he replied shakily.

"Are you new around here?' she asked. "I haven't seen you. I live in the village. It's very boring. And lonely. I'm here working on a farm. Everyone I know lives miles away." She stood very close, and gazed directly, intently, into Reg's eyes in a way that made him actually feel some weakness in his knees.

"I'm just passing through," Reg replied carefully, his voice barely steady.

"I thought you might be billeted at Trafalgar Hall. There's all kinds of military business going on there. I think some secret things. It sounds all very exciting. More exciting than riding around on a tractor or picking vegetables, that's how I spend my days. I'm sure I don't know what I'd do, if I met someone from there, face to face, just like we are now. I might just swoon, with the excitement."

"Actually, I —" Reg began. Then he said, "I'd be interested to know what's going on there as well. But picking vegetables is valuable. The country has to be fed. Digging for victory, and all that."

"Why aren't you in uniform?" She moved away suddenly, her tone decidedly frostier.

Again! Reg moaned inwardly. If only he could just spend one day in an actual real military uniform. If only he could cut a figure like the young Battle of Britain hero Norman Armstrong, whom he'd briefly encountered during his interview with Norman's father. He was probably Reg's own age or even a little younger. Tailored RAF blues, purple and white ribbon of the Distinguished Flying Cross. Off out to a very sophisticated London restaurant, then a nightclub, where no doubt hordes of glamorous women would be —

"I'm a Quaker," Reg said suddenly, as that was all he could think of, regretting the sudden lack of proximity with this beautiful apparition, and desperately wanting her standing close to him again.

"What does that mean?" she replied suspiciously. "Do you quake with fear if you're in danger?"

"No," he said. "It's a religion. "They, that is we, don't believe in war."

"You mean you don't hate Hitler?" she asked, eyebrows raised in surprise.

"Well, um —"

"Would you like to buy me a cup of tea?" She asked suddenly, her voice once again inviting. "The Daffodil Tearooms are just past the green. You can see it from here, look. They do lovely cakes, whenever they can. My favourite drink is their orangeade, wonderful on a summer's day when you've been working in the fields. It's a bit cold today, isn't it? A nice cup of tea would make me feel all warm inside."

It became clear that no for an answer was not going to be taken, but at that point Reg knew that he had completely abandoned free will and that he would have followed her just about anywhere. She linked her arm around his, tightly, and he began to feel a little light headed as they walked together across the green to the little tearooms, as the late afternoon sun found its way through the grey for a brief moment, before retreating from the evening shadows.

As dawn broke the following morning, Reg was ordered from his bed, having only just crawled in and having fallen into a deep, exhausted slumber. He was escorted to some rooms on the upper floor, in a wing of Trafalgar Hall to where he had thus far not been. He was shown into a large room, nondescript, although the lavish design of the large fireplace gave some indication of the grandeur of the room in its glory years. There was a doorway dividing this room and the one adjacent, and Reg was able to see a large four-poster bed in the centre of the next room, and a large paned window beyond. To his eye, the bed's timberwork looked like it had been roughly hewn out of railway sleepers, and hardly befitting of such a grand house as this. Nevertheless, he thought, it certainly looked comfortable enough. Someone was having quite a nice war.

"Right then, Powell." An unnamed Lieutenant was sitting at a desk, in front of a wall in which the rows of books could easily have been bricks holding up the high ceiling. He had a folder open in front of him and was reading from some carbon-copied typewritten pages. "You've been a bit of a naughty boy, I see. Wasting the afternoon in some sad old tearooms, then out till all hours, drinking at the village pub, chattering away without a care in the world. And after that —" The officer looked at Reg with lowered eyebrows and lips pursed with distaste. At that moment, as if on cue, Reg's fantasy redhead from the previous night entered, and at least had the good grace to look apologetic. Reg's own expression remained impassive.

"This is Miss Gibbons," the officer announced triumphantly. "Does she look familiar?"

"I'm very sorry, Reg," Miss Gibbons said. "It was nothing personal. All part of the training, I'm afraid."

"Right," the Lieutenant said. "Pack your bags, Powell. You're leaving. You've failed the —"

At that moment the Colonel in charge entered from the adjoining room, muttering apologies for being late. The Lieutenant shot out of the Colonel's chair as if it was spring loaded.

"What's going on?" the Colonel asked as he took his seat. "Ah, young Powell. Training all but complete, I see. You've done damned well. Jolly good, jolly good."

"Really, sir?" Reg queried. "It felt to me like I was about to get the sack."

"What?" The Colonel looked up at the Lieutenant in surprise. "Explain," he commanded.

"Powell spent a good deal of last night with Miss Gibbons," the young Lieutenant told him. "I'm afraid he fell for it completely. And her," he added slyly.

"Oh, dear me," the Colonel sounded surprised. "Let's look at Miss Gibbons's report, then, shall we?"

"They spent the night in Miss Gibbons's upstairs room at the Spanish Lady public house in the village," the Lieutenant went on, a little disappointed that Reg wasn't looking anywhere near contrite enough. "There were complaints about the noise. Went on 'til all hours. Sounded like a Roman orgy, according to the landlady. All kinds of calling out, yelling and moaning. Shocked, she was. Shocked!"

The Lieutenant pointed over the Colonel's shoulder at some notes in the file, then stood back. He continued to regard Reg with a superior and patronising disdain. By now Reg's composure was beginning to crumble somewhat, and his face turned noticeably red as he tried to hide his embarrassment. It was true, Miss Gibbons had been loudly enthusiastic, making Reg forget, at least for a little while, that she was so obviously a plant; a test for Reg's resolve and his ability to keep secrets.

314

"Oh, damn and blast it, Powell, you have been talkative," the Colonel glared at Reg, his tone genuinely aggrieved. "I thought that you of all people would understand the need for discretion. How many times must we tell you that that any personal information given out could be used against you, your colleagues, or the people you love? And against your country. Careless talk, careless talk. It's not just a propaganda motto for gossiping women in a fish queue, young man. Careless talk really does cost lives. I've seen it before and will doubtless see it happen again and again. You're no use to us if you start running off at the mouth every time you lay eyes on a pretty girl."

"It wasn't only his eyes that he laid on —"

"Oh, do belt up!" The Colonel scolded his Lieutenant. "This is serious. Life and death. We've lost far too many talented recruits in this way. They do well in their training, no doubts about their courage or abilities, then fall at the last hurdle when they find themselves walking out with Miss Gibbons, or with one of her equally charming colleagues."

"Sorry, sir, it all just slipped out," Powell said sheepishly.

"Slipped *in*, more like," the young Lieutenant sneered, but then became impassive as the Colonel turned suddenly in his chair and glared up at him.

"Miss Gibbons was very persuasive," Reg ventured apologetically.

"That's one word for it," the Colonel grunted. "Oh, dear me, this is all very distasteful." The Colonel suddenly turned his attention once again to his Lieutenant, who seemed to be treating the looming end of Reg's short career in intelligence as a personal victory. "Lieutenant, you're an arse of the first rank. Get out of my sight."

The young officer stood, stunned. "I-I don't understand, sir," he stammered.

"You've both been played, you idiot. Now bugger off." He was far more polite to Miss Gibbons. "Thank you, Miss Gibbons, you're dismissed. For the moment."

The Lieutenant beat an embarrassed retreat, while Miss Gibbons looked decidedly relieved that she hadn't vamped poor Reg toward the destruction of his career. Although, she reflected sadly as she closed the door behind her, had she been more successful at her task, that very nice — and generously affectionate — young man would undoubtedly have had a much better chance at a long life.

Once the Colonel and Reg were alone, the Colonel continued reading from Miss Gibbons's neatly typed and detailed account of their hours together. "Now, let me see. So grateful in your homesickness and loneliness to have someone like Miss Gibbons to confide in, eh? Touching, Powell, touching. I could shed a tear myself. From a family of pacifists, are you, Powell? From Solihull? Your father a socialist and conscientious objector in the last war? Sent to prison for it, was he by God? Well, I wonder what the distinguished Major Albert Powell, formerly of the legendary Natal Rangers and hero of the Somme, and of Amiens, and now one of our most indispensable City financiers, would have to say about that. Oh, I see there's more. In your disgrace, your mother had to become a Windmill Girl to save the family from the poorhouse? Oh, the shame of it! And you have a brother who recently auditioned for ENSA, on the strength of his ability to do a credible impersonation of Tilly Tweedle, but failed because he couldn't find anyone to play Florrie convincingly enough." The Colonel closed the file, threw his spectacles down on top of it and rolled his eyes. Reg remained impassive.

Finally, and to Reg's intense relief, the Colonel smiled. "Yes, yes, it's all very well playing games, but it's time to get down to some serious business. We have a little something lined up for you, as I believe you're aware." With the prospect of an actual mission, Reg's embarrassment evaporated, and his face brightened considerably. The elderly Colonel looked across his desk at the eager young man with a deep sadness. The poor chap had no idea, he thought.

The Colonel sighed. How many more like Reg was he going to face across his desk in the ensuing months? Or years. It was a cruel irony that the best young people were selected for the toughest, most complex and ultimately dangerous missions, and almost invariably did not return. Once Reg had come and gone, there would be a conga line of equally patriotic, keen young men — and women — to take his place. Perhaps the last war was for nothing after all, if less than a generation later, the same factory conveyor belt of fine young people was being fed into the —

"Are you all right, sir?" Reg asked.

"Yes, yes, ghosts from the past. Nothing to be concerned about. Now, we've been very pleased with your progress, young man. You came to us highly recommended, even by Sir John Prentice himself, and he's not an easy man to please. And you haven't let us down. It's time for you to put some of this training to good use. But let me say this to you, beware of overconfidence. Not everyone is as gullible as my young adjutant. If you talk too much, you'll trip yourself up, it's inevitable. And the people you'll be confronting are not London villains, black marketeers and spivs. The Nazis have far less enjoyable ways of extracting information than our obliging and fragrant Miss Gibbons."

"I promise I'd never talk, sir, under interrogation," Reg said earnestly, and with a naïve sincerity that the Colonel actually found quite touching. And heartbreaking.

"Don't be such a bloody fool, Powell," he replied sadly. "Everybody talks. Eventually."

CHAPTER NINETEEN

On a Friday afternoon, not long after four pm, Alf looked past his panel operator through the glass wall of the studio and saw Sir Norman Armstrong approaching at his usual brisk pace, flanked by his two minders and his ever-present and loyal personal driver, Eric Baker. The Rottweiler. Alf smiled and waved to Eric, who answered with a cheery thumbs up.

The Home Secretary entered the studio just in time to begin their interview. Alf had hoped that he might have arrived a little earlier, a chance for some reassuring words between old friends, or even just some trivial small talk to help to bridge the gulf that had opened between them. But the fact that he was here at all was a major step forward, and Alf was going to make the most of it.

The Home Secretary donned his headphones, while Alf's producer helped him to position his microphone, before returning to her own little control centre beyond the studio glass. The commercial ended, microphones were switched on and the ON AIR light glowed above the studio door.

"Welcome to *City Roundup*, with me, Alf Burton, right around the nation, on the Donoghue City Radio network. My first guest this afternoon is the Home Secretary, Sir Norman

Armstrong. Sir Norman, a very warm welcome to the programme."

"Thank you, Alf, it's always nice to be with you, and your listeners."

"Sir Norman, what do you see as the principal challenges for the Home Office as we head towards 1986?"

The Home Secretary made a practised case for vigilance against terrorism and lawlessness and talked generally about how computers and technology were taking an increasing role in the fight against crime. It was a gift of a question, and one that gave the Home Secretary latitude to speak at self-serving length.

Sorry, bonny lad, Alf thought, as Norman completed his rather long-winded free advertisement, extolling the benefits of the Home Office and its value to Britain in uncertain times. I'm afraid it's not going to be quite so friendly from now on.

"So, Home Secretary," Alf began. "Despite advice from your colleagues, including the Commissioner of the Metropolitan Police, and many others, your elite police unit Armstrong's Army has not been disbanded. We've seen their tactics discredited in court cases, their truthfulness questioned, and their culture of dishonesty and thuggishness exposed. An independent enquiry has been announced but is yet to convene. They have very strong critics from within the ranks of the nation's senior police, including the Chief Constables of a number of regional forces, who blame them for laying waste the relationship between police and communities, particularly in industrial and mining areas which are now suffering in the wake of pit closures and the imminent loss of thousands of shipyard jobs. We saw more violent confrontations near Stonehenge, further urban unrest in south London and in the

Midlands, and once again credible allegations of police heavy-handedness, and carelessness with firearms, have been made. It doesn't get much heavier handed than shooting a poor woman in her pyjamas, still in bed.

"And once again we've seen you personally on the front line, at Stonehenge, and in Brixton, directly overseeing operations. We hear reports of undercover officers infiltrating the CND and Greenham Common, and phone tapping and general spying. Your department, Home Secretary, with respect, is unaccountable and out of control. What can you possibly say to atone for such political weakness, in failing to control this politicised rogue unit of government mercenaries, terrorising honest, working citizens, including unarmed ladies in bed, with scant regard for justice or due process, in your own name?"

The aggression of Alf's follow-up question caught everyone by surprise; even Alf's producer wondered if the Home Secretary would abruptly walk out. Eric Baker, listening outside the studio, silently mouthed the word "blimey", and the Home Secretary's colleagues at the Home Office, crowded around their office radio, waiting in nervous anticipation of what was going to follow.

At Scotland Yard, Commissioner Coburn was listening with DAC Harper and Tortoise Taunton.

"Oh, dear oh lor', that was a bit rough," Taunton drawled.

In his office at Padraig Donoghue House, Rick Armstrong sat in stunned silence, while in the neighbouring suite where Sir Eddie Donoghue worked, the tycoon sighed and bemoaned another probable rift in his long but occasionally rocky friendship with Sir Norman. Dick Billings, working in his office at Twelve Downing Street, muttered, "predictable bolshie twat." Roland Moreland, writing an opinion piece for the following day's *Daily Focus*, listened with admiration and considered that even he might have gone a little easier with the opening questions.

From the Cabinet Office, where Sirs Archie Prentice and Peregrine Walsingham were contemplating matters of national security, particularly as pertaining to one Clarence "Clackers" Bolton, communist agitator now leading a militant splinter of the Amalgamated Fitters and General Shipyard Workers Union, Prentice commented, "I've warned Norman, time and again about Burton. When is he ever going to learn? You should have let me see to that red troublemaker once and for all when I had the chance."

In the studio, Sir Norman timed his silence just to the point of exquisite discomfort, looking Alf directly in the eye. "Was that a sermon, or a question?" he asked finally. "Because if you intend to spend the afternoon just spouting your own biased and ill-informed opinions, I might as well just leave you to it."

Norman's tone was icy, but Alf noticed Norman's ever so slightly cocked eyebrow, and while his expression remained steadfastly serious, the smile shining in his eyes was unmistakable. The broadcaster felt like leaping for joy. He muted his microphone.

"Welcome back, old marra," he said. Sir Norman allowed himself a smile and nodded at his old friend.

Then, almost as soon as it had begun, the brief truce was over, the microphone was back on, and the battle recommenced.

…The long-awaited public inquiry into Armstrong's Army finally convened, headed by recently retired judge, the Honourable Mr Justice St John Wigham. After taking evidence over several weeks, much of it in camera despite the Home Secretary's assurances of transparency, Mr Justice Wigham found that there was no evidence of organised violence, or of a policy aimed at the orchestrated intimidation of the miners themselves, nor of their wider communities. The much-speculated-upon existence of a secret policing operations manual was denied under oath by the most senior officer of Armstrong's Army, Commander Ray Johnson.

Instead, Wigham found that individual officers had acted in a manner that exceeded their authority and recommended disciplinary action against a number of officers from the Metropolitan Police, South Yorkshire, and Merseyside forces, but declined to name them publicly. Commander Ray Johnson himself was singled out for specific criticism, for his failure to supervise and control rogue elements within the unit, and he subsequently took a reduction in rank and returned to non-operational duties with his own force, the Thames Valley Police. Bizarrely, Mr Justice Wigham heaped praise upon the Home Secretary Sir Norman Armstrong, and Special Minister of State Charles Seymour, for their "tireless and courageous commitment toward exposing the truth". Quentin Quiggin, who in 1984-85 was a convenor of Police Watch and a pivotal figure in Gays and Lesbians Support the Miners, and who subsequently served one term as MP (SDP-Liberal Alliance) for Streatham and Vauxhall (1987-92), described the Wigham Commission as "a farce" and "rigged from the start".

Finally, in 1989, following intense lobbying from Orgreave defence lawyer, Gwynne Fielding, Valerie Smedley QC and a number of Labour politicians, including former NUM spokesman and now member for Stonebridge Central and Northwest, Austin Wells MP, the Home Office agreed to pay nearly half a million pounds in compensation to a number of the Orgreave defendants. In spite of this, both South Yorkshire Police and Armstrong's Army have maintained their strong denials of any wrongdoing.

Gwynne Fielding, also a vocal critic of the Wigham Commission's findings, welcomed the compensation but qualified her praise by pointing out that it was much, much too little, and far, far too late. She was deeply unhappy about the refusal to concede any wrongdoing on the part of the police. When interviewed for this volume in 1993, her rage was unabated. She said, "It's beyond belief that the police can be exonerated from systematic wrongdoing. The trials for the Orgreave defendants were a case in point. I've never seen organised perjury on that scale. The fight for justice for the victims of Orgreave will continue. We won't give up, even if it takes another thirty years or more. We are cautiously heartened by the attitude of Sir Norman Armstrong's successor as Home Secretary, Charles Seymour. We hope, in time, that his actions will match his wholly unexpected conciliatory attitude."

But as 1985 drew to a close, problems for the Thatcher government were mounting. Police were once again under heavy criticism following widespread race rioting, and civilian deaths and injuries from police firearms incidents. The Anglo-Irish Agreement was ratified in November, angering Unionists and even Thatcher loyalists Sir Norman Armstrong and Ian Gow, who said the terms of the agreement would "prolong, rather than diminish, the agony of Ulster". In the New Year, the Westland Affair would claim senior scalps, disrupt Cabinet and further test old loyalties. Sir Norman Armstrong would remain under intense criticism following the Brixton riots, come into personal conflict with the Prime Minister over the Anglo-Irish Agreement, and a depleted, yet just as aggressive, Armstrong's Army would be back on the frontline of industrial warfare, as a bitter dispute at the Speers-Donoghue shipyard simmered perpetually on the brink of violence.

From:

A New Britain — Thatcher and the end of Consensus (Volume III) by Alf Burton

© 1994 Donoghue Publishing and Broadcasting

EPILOGUE
WEST LONDON
Summer 1965

"Well, Norman old cock, I think we can safely say, that we're both well and truly fucked."

Sir Dick Billings drained the last of his brandy and brought his glass down heavily onto the bar, a signal the landlord knew very well, and he was almost immediately on hand to offer a refill. "Still, you're still young, you have plenty of time. And they can never take my 'K' away from me. It could be worse."

"I can't believe Maudling declined the second ballot," Norman Armstrong replied, his tone desolate. "I might've had half a chance under him, if not staying on as Shadow Home Secretary, at least something in the Shadow Cabinet."

"I understand your frustration, Norman," Dick consoled him. "In ordinary circumstances, it would have been you, everyone knows that. Democracy leaves a lot to be desired, especially when it's applied to internal party matters. Mind you, imagine how poor Enoch is feeling. Did anyone at all vote for him?"

Both men stared desolately into their brandy glasses. Norman had lost count of how many Dick had swallowed, while he had barely touched his first. Folded open on the bar in front of them was the latest edition of *Westminster Scene*, a widely read weekly magazine full of all the latest gossip and news from in and around the Houses of Parliament. An article by Norman's friend, top freelance lobby correspondent Alf Burton, wasn't making optimistic reading for either Norman or Sir Dick. As their brooding silence lengthened, Norman once again absently cast his eyes over the text.

In historical terms, Edward Heath is an unlikely Conservative leader, having neither an aristocratic background nor a large personal or family fortune. Under reforms initiated by his predecessor, Alec Douglas-Home, Mr Heath is the first to have actually been elected leader by the parliamentary party, rather than being quietly anointed, or "informally emerging", as in the past.

Prior to his rise to the leadership, Mr Heath served in a number of senior government posts including Chief Whip, Minister of Labour and Lord Privy Seal, and was at the forefront of failed negotiations promoting Britain's entry into the European Economic Community. The French veto of two years ago resulted, at least in part, from the Nassau Agreement, an alliance between Harold Macmillan's Government and the US Kennedy administration, that allowed British submarines to be equipped with American nuclear warheads. French President, Charles de Gaulle, fearing too much American influence in European affairs, led the opposition against Britain's attempt to join the EEC. Sources close to the negotiations believe that Mr Heath's efforts were actually thwarted at the eleventh hour by an unfortunate contribution by then Transport and Maritime Affairs Secretary, Dick Billings. Critics of the veto might have noted that France wasn't so hesitant to allow American involvement when it had achieved its own liberation from the Nazis, a point which Mr Billings, as he then was, rather pointedly made to the French President, during what appalled witnesses described as "an aggressive, sustained and vulgar, unprecedented personal attack".

In the leadership ballot, Heath defeated Reginald Maudling and, more surprisingly, Norman Armstrong in a tight contest, leaving Enoch Powell, not quite so surprisingly, a distant fourth.

So, where does this leave two of the Conservative Party's most tireless warriors, Norman Armstrong and the always entertaining Sir Dick Billings? It's hard to see Sir Dick returning to any senior role, certainly under Mr Heath, and one must consider his age, now over sixty. It would be fair to assume that he will serve out this term on the back bench and then coast into retirement. It is well known that he enjoys a close relationship with at least one prominent businessman in London. Perhaps he might choose the world of private commerce for the last gasp of his rather colourful career.

Norman Armstrong is a different matter altogether. In his mid-forties, he is widely liked and respected, and was appointed to the critical post of Home Secretary under the brief administration of Alec Douglas-Home. Mr Armstrong's commitment to reform and anti-corruption initiatives impressed many, and no doubt worried a few as well, but sources close to the Opposition Leader suggest that Mr Heath is no fan of the former Home Secretary, and it is unlikely that we'll see him in a senior role in the Tory Opposition in the near future...

"Why-aye, bonny lads!" Alf Burton suddenly appeared as if from nowhere and sat heavily on a stool next to Dick Billings, then leaned forward and nodded a polite greeting to Norman. As usual, Alf presented quite a contrast to the fashionable elegance of both Dick and Norman's tailored suits, wearing his usual rumpled jacket, frayed collar and loosened tie. His beige mac was folded over his arm, and he rested it on the bar next to him. He noted with satisfaction the copy of *Westminster Scene* on the bar, with his own article on the open page. "Nice to see you broadening your minds," he observed.

"Haven't you got somewhere to be?" Dick muttered. "Like the Kremlin?"

Unperturbed by the coolness of his welcome, Alf asked, "So how do we feel about our new Leader of the Opposition, then?"

"No comment," Dick growled. "Now fuck off, you conceited bolshie twat before I kick your well-padded arse all the way to Traitor's Gate."

"No comment?" Alf was incredulous. "Now, let me predict the tone of my column for tomorrow's *Tyne-Tees Ledger*, to be expanded in next week's *Westminster Scene*, and any number of other fine publications around the country. I think it might go something like this. Just hours after Mr Heath was democratically elected as Conservative Party leader, two of the Tory Party's most prominent and influential members declined to offer their congratulations, signalling that, just months into opposition, there are already deep divisions —"

"All right, all right, shut up and let me think for a moment," Dick grumbled.

"Of course, we're delighted for Mr Heath," Norman interjected. "He is the right man to lead our party to the next election, and he has our wholehearted support."

"That's right," Dick continued. "Couldn't have put it better myself." He jabbed his finger down hard onto the magazine. "And I have no intention of retiring, so you can write that in your northern rag, then wrap your cod and chips in it. Or wipe your arse with it. And not, by the way, necessarily in that order. Now take that as a comment and fuck off!" Alf waved a cheery goodnight and departed.

"I've said it before, and I'll say it again. How you can be friends with that red agitator is beyond me, Norman," Dick muttered.

"He's not as bad as all that," Norman replied. "His work appears in a number of papers and magazines apart from this one, and not just in out of the way places either. And his books always sell very well. Don't underestimate his influence, he's a better friend than enemy, just ask Enoch. Alf's nowhere near as pink as he used to be, anyway."

"You mean he's nowhere near as red. He's still quite a bright shade of pink, if you ask me. He's been fucking well insufferable since his *old marra* Wilson was elected. Another northern twat we have to put up with. The working-class lunatics really have taken over the asylum."

"I think you should make the effort with Alf. He can be useful. What do they say about politics and strange bedfellows?"

"A fact to which our old friend and associate Johnny Profumo could testify," Dick chuckled, then muttered, "Lucky bastard. Ah well, I suppose I have no excuse not to go and visit my constituency more often now."

"I'm surprised you can remember where it is," Norman replied, only half joking.

"It's all right for you, Norman. I don't know how you do it, all that local handshaking and smiling at... *people*." Dick's pronunciation of the word "'people" indicated the intensity of his contempt. "Mind you, I suppose that's why your majority has more zeros than my bank balance."

"Come on, Dick. Everyone knows you've always been one of the best campaigners in the country."

"Maybe, up to a point, but your father, God rest him, was the best of all. And I know you remember this, Norman, in those days you had to build your audience through force of personality, in community halls, and on street corners. You had to walk the streets of your constituency until your feet swelled and blistered and you could barely stand up, in all weathers, knocking on doors and shaking hands. Streets and factories and offices during the day; pubs, clubs and community events at night. It was unrelenting, hard graft. This next generation coming through now have no idea. All you have to do now is park yourself in front of a microphone for the Home Service, or a television camera, and you're away. I'd love to see how long the current crop of flash twats would last campaigning the way we used to." He looked at his watch. "Bollocks, is that the time? I'm due over at Berkeley Square for dinner. Listen, why don't you come too? Eddie and Sarah would love to see you. Little Erin is growing up faster than you can imagine. She's a real terror already."

"No, I really should get back to Knightsbridge, thanks all the same."

"Why, Norman, for God's sake? You have no red boxes to work through. You'll phone Eileen, that'll take half an hour, then all you'll do is sit in that depressing old Victorian tomb you call a library and watch that little telly of yours, crying into your Scotch as you grieve over your lost career. Come with me, we'll make a night of it. You can find out what Eddie's plans are for BSMI, now that it's been privatised."

"That little operation has disaster written all over it," Norman scoffed. "Eddie knows nothing about shipping and shipbuilding. He owns a building company, some newspapers and magazines, and an ITV region in an area so remote that it has about ten viewers. What could have possessed him to spend good money on an old shipyard on the Tyne, which everyone knows is outdated and unsalvageable? It's inevitable that it'll go the same way as Palmer's did thirty years ago, with all the dire consequences. British Speers Maritime Industries was, and is, a basket case. It has been since the thirties, when it was Chas R Speers and Co. If not for the war, it would never have reopened at all after they mothballed it. There's no doubt you did the government a favour by pushing so hard for its privatisation. But why Eddie parted with a penny of his own money is a mystery; it will drain all his other businesses until he's in the poorhouse, mark my words. We should have paid him to take it off our hands."

"Funny you say that." Sir Dick was about to explain some of the intricacies of the privatisation deal that he had masterminded, but then considered that the fewer people in the know about the real financial arrangements that went on over the BSMI privatisation, the better. Norman was a fine politician and a very smart man but could be naïvely straight-laced. There were some financial and political realities that he could never grasp.

A major factor in the ownership transition had been the towering hull of the *Calcutta Queen III*, a state-of-the-art luxury liner on the brink of completion and dominating the yard's number one slipway. The progress of the liner might have been misunderstood by the Treasury officials overseeing the complicated costings, thanks in no small part to Dick's own report, which had implied that construction was a long way behind schedule, with myriad faults and examples of poor workmanship to rectify. He argued that the seemingly endless drain on the taxpayer should be brought to an abrupt end; and the sooner someone else was paying for what was bound to be a white elephant, the better. There was no future in cruising the ocean, and only five percent of the transatlantic passenger trade remained with the shipping lines. Everyone knew that the Boeing 707 was the future. And besides, if a patriotic, wealthy businessman like Eddie Donoghue, who unstintingly supported the Tories, had such a ship in his fleet, she would be immediately made available to the government should the mass transportation of troops become an urgent necessity. Another auxiliary troopship in these most dangerous times, Dick argued in Cabinet, would ensure that Britain retained her military dominance, and would give the red menace something to cry about. For good measure, Dick reminded anyone who'd listen of the contribution of her predecessor, known as *CQ2*, which, under the command of the Speers Line's renowned Commodore, Jim O'Malley, had ferried thousands upon thousands of troops to every theatre of the war over two decades earlier, and had made an indispensable contribution to the defeat of the Axis Powers. Even Mr Churchill himself had celebrated the role of the great liners in the nation's final victory, making specific mention of *CQ2* and her formidable commander.

As a result, Eddie Donoghue, up and coming City businessman and strong Tory supporter, picked up a powerful, spanking new ocean liner that was all but complete, save for the final fitting out, for virtually nothing. Secretary of State for Transport and Maritime Affairs, Dick Billings, was congratulated for his efforts in undoing another costly nationalisation fiasco set in motion under the post-war Attlee Government, and received his reward at the subsequent Queen's Birthday Honours; for services furthering government-private industry cooperation. Meanwhile, in due course, the newly incorporated Speers-Donoghue shipyard presented its affiliated shipping line with a golden opportunity to compete in the growing leisure cruise market during the Northern Hemisphere winter, when the ship would be taken off the barely viable Atlantic run to New York, and would carry thousands of ecstatic holidaymakers off in search of sunnier climes.

"Mind you," Norman ventured, gingerly sipping his brandy, "Wilson will probably want to buy the whole thing back now."

"Don't even think about that," Sir Dick grumbled. "But you underestimate Eddie, and his determination and ambition. Look at what he's achieved in less than ten years since he took control of his family company. It's now almost unrecognisable from the middling newspaper chain we remember from his father's time. Shipping and transport will only be a part of what is going to be a massive and diverse group of companies. Independent television is the future, Norman, and Eddie has big plans to expand there as well. And consider this. Independent radio. That'll be next."

"He'll never compete," Norman observed sceptically. "The BBC does everything already. Home and World Services, the Light Programme. Why even bother? He might as well just anchor a boat with a transmitter offshore and broadcast like the rest of the pirates."

"Speaking of the BBC," Dick said brightly, "did you hear that Harold tried to have *Steptoe and Son* taken off air on election night, because he was worried that his working-class constituents might have stayed home instead of going out to vote? I'm talking about Wilson, of course, not Harold Steptoe, although we might just as well have elected him, for all the use Wilson is likely to be."

"I quite like *Steptoe and Son*," Norman replied sullenly, staring into his glass.

Dick looked at his friend, whom he could see was becoming increasingly morose. "Oh, for Christ's sake, stop being such a wet blanket," he scolded. "Listen, Eddie's also investing in property, in a big way, and look at his building company. Donoghue Constructions is now the favoured builder for many councils around the nation. Slum clearances, and council housing estates. Tower blocks. Streets in the Sky, sunlight and glass. Solid, dependable, and clean. Affordable, safe housing for generations to come. All these old two-up, two-down piles, cold-water shitholes, literally. Damp and disease-ridden overpopulated slums being razed to the ground in favour of modern, clean, high-rise flats. And the building methods are modern. These flats will be standing, long after we've all gone, Norman. Britain is being transformed in front of our eyes, even your champion-of-the-working-class-pinkochum Burton must see the benefits. What local authority housing committee can look at these proposals and say no? Eddie Donoghue will do more to house the poor and working class in this country than that sanctimonious shit, Comrade Bevan, ever did. And, Norman, there's a pension plan in there for us as well, if we're smart enough to hang on tight to Eddie's coattails. And perhaps do him one or two little favours along the way."

"Well," Norman replied, "As you know, I'm all for whatever's in the national interest."

***

Sir Dick ended up at Berkeley Square for dinner at the Donoghue household without his friend. Ever a creature of habit, Norman was adamant that he needed to phone Eileen at the usual time, and that he wanted to be alone to consider his political future. Or lack thereof.

After a celebratory dinner, during which little Erin was a boisterous and welcome presence, Dick took a cab to Soho, where he was looking forward to visiting one of the newest clubs. As Dick stepped out of the cab, two other men, wearing dark suits, narrow ties and trilby style hats, were approaching on foot.

"Recognise him?" Detective Chief Inspector Ron Coburn asked.

"Can't say I do," replied newly promoted Detective Sergeant Dan Harper, walking beside his boss as they approached the pink and purple neon sign that announced the presence of the Top 'n Tail Club, tucked away in a courtyard just off Great Windmill Street. Coburn also observed the pristine white Mark II Jaguar parked nearby, a sure sign that the proprietor was in.

"Sir Dick Billings. Tory Politician. Used to be Transport and Maritime Affairs Secretary under Macmillan and Douglas-Home. There are all sorts of funny rumours about him."

"Sex or money?" Dan Harper asked.

"Money, mainly," Coburn replied, "As far as we know."

Dick was allowed instant access past the doorman, who immediately moved to block the path of DCI Coburn and his Sergeant.

"Members only," the doorman growled, while DS Harper thought he must be the fattest man that he had ever laid eyes on.

Before Ron could present his credentials, another man approached. He too was big, but unmistakably well-muscled. "It's all right, Frankie," he told the doorman. "Let them in." Frankie grudgingly stood aside, as the other man greeted them politely.

"Evening, Mr Coburn. Welcome to the Top 'n Tail. Who's your friend?"

"Evening, Harry," DCI Coburn replied coolly. "This is Detective Sergeant Harper. You'll be seeing quite a bit of him."

"Any friend of yours, as they say, Mr Coburn. Can I show you to a table?"

"No thanks, we're not staying."

The two police officers walked through the reception lobby and into the club itself. The lights were low, and the lingering smoke from cigarettes, pipes and cigars caught in their throats and made their eyes water. A bar was off to one side, and tables crowded the floor in front of the stage, almost all of which were full. A slow blues riff, Dan thought it might have been *Little Red Rooster*, emanated from a number of speakers around the room, and there was a lone dancer on stage, systematically removing items of her already minimal attire as she writhed a slow, steamy bump-and-grind to the beat of the music. The girls serving behind the bar and attending the tables wore fishnet stockings, lace bodices, undersized top hats, and had rabbit tails attached to their thongs.

Ron pointed at a middle-aged man seated alone at one of the front tables, his attention wholly riveted on what was happening on stage.

"Over there, second table from the left, the sweaty geezer playing pocket billiards," Ron said into Dan's ear. "Wiggie Wigham. Old Bailey judge." He gestured to another part of the room. "Dick Billings, of course, you saw him as we came in. A couple of the lads from the local nick enjoying the hospitality over there. Sitting slightly apart in the corner there, is Dudley Bayliss. Another Conservative MP. Backbencher. Behind the bar over there is Cyril McCann himself."

McCann instinctively peered through the smoky half-light of the room, and recognised DCI Coburn. He waved and smiled. Coburn offered a discreet nod in return.

"Ah, Young Ronnie! Surprised to see you here. Business or pleasure?"

"Working tonight, Archie," Ron replied, shaking hands with a man who had suddenly appeared out of the gloom.

"Jolly good, don't let me stop you." The man disappeared into the haze on the way toward the restrooms.

"Who's that?" Dan asked.

"Archie Prentice. Sir Archie now. Senior civil servant. Something to do with economic statistics."

"Doesn't sound like much fun."

"I'm sure he finds his own little ways of making things more interesting," Ron observed ruefully.

Detecting that further information wasn't about to be forthcoming, Dan asked, "What was 'Young Ronnie' all about?"

"Archie was my CO during the war, when I was with Bomber Command. He's called me 'Young Ronnie' ever since. Drives me mad, to tell you the truth."

"You flew with Norman Armstrong, the former Home Secretary as well, didn't you?"

"I did. I was his bomb aimer. Perry Walsingham was our navigator."

"Who's Perry Walsingham?"

"Just been appointed Permanent Secretary at the Treasury."

"Is that high up?"

"Oh yes. He'll be Cabinet Secretary one day, I expect."

Dan wasn't quite sure what a Cabinet Secretary was, but DCI Coburn's implication was that it was a very senior position. "Nice to have powerful friends," Dan said, eyeing his new boss with even greater admiration.

"Not quite so powerful now than Norman is no longer Home Secretary."

In due course the music finished, and a short man in a loud checked suit and bright bow tie emerged onto the stage and stood behind a microphone stand. The lighting was turned up and it reflected off his largely bald pate, covered by a sparse comb-over.

"I used to be a waiter," he said, while the audience made no secret of their lack of interest as they waited for the next dancer. "I brought a meal over to a diner, very upper-class he was, very superior, and he says to me... no, no, listen... he says to me, 'My good man, you have your thumb on my steak.' And I said, I said, 'I'm very sorry sir,' I said, 'but I didn't want to drop it. *Again.*'" He chuckled loudly and observed the complete lack of reaction from the audience. "Drop it... *again*... come on, this is class! Oh, please yourselves. Now, my mother-in-law, is so fat, so fat she is —"

The routine struggled through its excruciating course, the comedian bravely battling through the audience's initially benign indifference which soon assumed the feeling of quiet hostility. He decided to abandon his usually foolproof routine about the family of West Indians that had just moved in next door, and instead nodded to an invisible stagehand. A glittering curtain was pulled back to reveal an upright piano on the edge of the stage, the seated pianist hastily arranging his sheet music.

"And now, for your listening pleasure," the comedian announced, not even troubling to hide his sense of relief that his act was over, "the wonderful, Soho Flo!"

A lady of late middle age, heavily made up and wearing a sequined dress that was way too tight for her ample frame, walked onto the stage to a smattering of half-hearted applause.

She stood behind the microphone and after a brief piano introduction, began to sing, in an uncertain and raspy, yet strangely pleasant voice, *"Why am I wearing these beautiful clothes, what is the matter with me-ee... I've been a bridesmaid for twenty-two brides, this one'll make twenty-three-ee—"*

"Get off!" a voice emerged from one of the front tables.

Then a second voice. "Either get off or *get 'em off!*"

"Oh God, no," a third voice contributed. "Bring the girls back on, we don't want this old bag!"

Even from the back of the room and with their view filtered by the clouds of cigarette, pipe and cigar smoke, both Ron and Dan could see the intense hurt on the singer's face, her voice faltering as she struggled to complete her old music hall number, while fighting back tears.

At that moment the fatter of the doormen strode past both policemen to the front, brushed past Wiggie Wigham hunched and alone at his table, and joined Cyril McCann himself just in front of the stage. There was a brief struggle, the sound of glass breaking, and a couple of muffled protests that quickly fell silent. Dan was about to move to the front to intervene, but DCI Coburn gently held him back, as the three rowdies were propelled toward the side of the room and disappeared through a door. There was a loud, sickening crack as someone's head struck the doorframe with terrifying force on the way through. Soho Flo finished her song, then embarked on something a little brighter, while what remained of the audience now knew, on pain of a similar fate, to afford her the appropriate respect. They clapped along. *"Will you let me hold your hand tonight, as we stroll along the Strand tonight —"*

"Let's go," Ron said, and the two police officers walked out into the street as Soho Flo fought courageously on. *"I'll be seeing yoo-oo, at the end of the pier —"*

Harry Barron was still standing sentry at the door, offered the two officers a cheerful goodnight, and urged them not to be strangers, as they were always welcome at the Top 'n Tail, where all kinds of enjoyable hospitality awaited their pleasure.

"So that's the old Windmill Theatre," Dan commented, as they emerged from the courtyard and onto Great Windmill Street. "My dad used to talk about that."

"Yes. Now, I'll help you put some names to faces. The doorman who helped Cyril McCann throw those idiots out, was Frankie *Fatman* O'Farrell," Ron explained. "I'm keeping a close eye on him at the moment. I have it on good authority that he's been meeting with certain East End businessmen with a view to a coup against McCann. Problem is, if I know, then I'm sure McCann knows as well, and is just waiting for the right moment. I have a feeling poor Frankie-boy isn't going to live to be an old man."

"Bloody hell," Dan muttered. This was starting to get serious. People could get hurt. And worse.

"The other one —" Ron continued.

"Harry?"

"That's right. Harry Barron, known as the Boltcutter, you can probably guess why. He's all smiles on the surface, but be very careful around him. He's vicious, and very smart. He'd happily cut you into little pieces and feed you to his tropical fish without a second thought. Never, ever get close enough to him that he can hand you anything or slip something into your pocket. Never shake his hand. He's the chief bagman." DS Harper nodded, then Ron continued. "Look Dan, you know that I'm not very popular around the place. I watch my back all the time, in fact sometimes I feel safer with villains like Barron and McCann than I do with our own people. It's going to be even tougher now that Norman Armstrong is no longer Home Secretary. We're on our own again. If you come and work on my squad, there'll be no going back. You'll lose friends, your career will probably stall, and you'll be in danger, as much from our own as from the villains. But I'm not going to give up. If it takes me ten years, I'm going to fight until I've cleaned this cesspool up. And my little team are right with me."

"You remember my old man, don't you, sir?"

"Of course. He was my Sergeant when I first walked the beat down the East End in '46. I miss him as well."

"He'd turn in his grave if he saw what the job had become. I'm in. One hundred percent. I'm doing it for him."

They walked along the street beneath the coloured signs and lights from the bars and clubs; the Panama, the Nosh Bar, and countless other entertainment, dining and drinking venues of varying condition and repute.

"Where does all this end, sir? Do you think?"

"Hard to say. You saw the calibre of members in the club."

"The Commissioner?"

"Old Sunny Havill? I doubt it, to tell you the truth. I think he's naïve, and too willing to take advice, or at least believe assurances from his inner circle. But I don't think he condones this. He's just blissfully ignorant. I think he just comes from a generation that, you know, when one of your chaps slapped you on the back and said everything was tickety-boo, you just took the chap's word for it. He's close to retirement now; I think even he recognises that he's past it. The new man is going to be the key to everything."

"Why do they call him Sunny, by the way? Certainly nothing to do with his disposition."

"His name. Sunderland. Sunderland Havill."

"Poor sod," Sergeant Harper replied.

"Speaking of your father, there was someone in the club that he would have remembered very well. The singer."

"Soho Flo?" Dan asked.

"Her name is Florrie Tweedle. In the war, she had a double act with her sister, Tilly, around the music halls. Comedy, singing and dancing. They were hugely popular, even travelled overseas — the Far East — on tours with Vera Lynn, to entertain the troops."

"I have a vague memory, from when I was small," Dan said thoughtfully. "I think Dad might have taken us to see them during the war. An old run-down theatre in Bethnal Green, long gone now, I expect."

The two detectives walked on in comfortable silence. It wasn't all doom and gloom, Ron reflected. Even though his friend Norman Armstrong was out of office, the former Home Secretary still had some influence, even from Opposition, and he remained a steadfast and unswervingly loyal friend. And there was Archie Prentice, of course; newly knighted and the head of a government secret organisation, known euphemistically as the Honourable Company, for reasons Ron couldn't comprehend and was smart enough not to ask. And Perry Walsingham, one day he'll be the most senior civil servant of all, of that there was no doubt. In many ways more individually powerful than even the Prime Minister. And they were all his friends, since he had first joined the RAF as a naïve teenager in 1943, driving everyone mad with his frequently articulated dreams of joining any constabulary that would have him. There was something deeply comforting about their little comradely network, as they all made their own way, and strove for their own successes. They all knew instinctively that if one was in any kind of danger, the others would close ranks in an impenetrable, protective circle. The bond was still there, unbreakable, even twenty years on.

And thanks to an initial introduction by Norman Armstrong, DCI Coburn had, from time to time, been quietly meeting up with a very affable, if rather poorly turned out, reporter named Alf Burton. Ron was aware that he wrote primarily about politics for a number of newspapers and magazines, as well as having written several successful books about working-class history. He was a very good friend of Norman Armstrong, for reasons Ron couldn't even begin to understand, as they seemed complete opposites. But nevertheless, having first been briefed about Ron's work by Norman Armstrong when he was Home Secretary, Alf was keenly maintaining his professional interest in Ron's campaign, and was compiling notes for a series of articles for future publication, about a crusading detective he insisted on naming "Honest Ron". Ron suddenly realised that they weren't on their own at all. Far from it.

"Not only are we going to survive," Ron exclaimed suddenly, and unexpectedly slapped DS Harper hard on the shoulder. "But we're going to win as well!"

"Beg pardon?" Dan asked, having been rudely shocked out of quiet contemplation, and a deep sense of sadness as he considered what his father would have made of poor Florrie Tweedle, eking out her twilight career as Soho Flo.

"Anything and everything is possible," DCI Coburn replied cheerfully, imagining just how easily DCS — Detective Chief Superintendent — Coburn rattled off the tongue.

They arrived back at their unmarked black Zephyr. Ron slid into the passenger seat while Dan, the junior man, sat in the back. Their driver, a grey-haired, middle-aged PC, also in plain clothes, was waiting patiently.

"Back to the Yard, sir?" Tortoise Taunton asked.

***

Norman Armstrong chose a brisk walk home rather than a short ride by cab, and soon arrived at his terraced townhouse in Knightsbridge. He went straight upstairs to his library, which had changed little since it had been decorated by his grandfather in late Victorian times. He poured a single measure of Scotch from his grandfather's decanter and raised his glass to the large portrait. Colonel Fforbes Armstrong returned his gaze from beneath the pointed peak of his white helmet. Norman studied the picture closely; the military bearing, immaculate red tunic, and ceremonial sword. The Queen's Own Natal Rifles, and then the Natal Rangers. Norman wondered if that was the very helmet and tunic that the eccentric, elderly Colonel insisted on wearing when he led his regiment over the parapet on that first day on the Somme.

"I wonder what ever happened to that sword?" he said aloud. Ever the creature of habit, he checked his watch and walked over to the ornate desk that faced away from the front windows. It was time to phone Eileen.

They chatted lovingly for nearly half an hour. Eileen was outwardly sympathetic over Norman's stalled career, but secretly delighted at the prospect of having her husband spending much more time at their home in the constituency. He might even have some time to work on healing what appeared to be a growing rift between father and son. Rick had turned nineteen this year and was resisting all of Norman's urgings to embark on a military career as a grounding for his inevitable entry into politics, for when Norman himself chose

346

to retire. Eileen was firm in their son's defence, saying that the little record shop just off Carnaby Street that Rick had just opened with his old school friend, Terry Cox, was doing quite well, and if Rick couldn't go his own way in this day and age, what had been the bloody point of fighting two world wars in the cause of freedom? Norman couldn't quite see the connection, but he decided on less futile argument and in lieu, a campaign of quiet, subtle persuasion. Military and politics had been the destiny of the Armstrong family for hundreds of years, and Norman wasn't going to preside over the wholly unnecessary and premature demise of a dynasty that had shaped history for generations, just because his son insisted on growing his hair like a mop, selecting his wardrobe from charity shops, and consorting with all kinds of equally ludicrously dressed undesirables. As Norman often reminded his errant son, when he was Rick's age, he was training as a Spitfire pilot leading up to the Battle of Britain. Rick was squandering the chance of greatness, Norman moaned, and the opportunity to influence the shaping of an exciting new world. What possible influence would scruffy musicians and artistic types ever apply to the modern world? That bunch of hooligans, the Rolling Stones, Larry and the Pacemakers. Alan Faith. The Beatles, my God. He wouldn't put it past Wilson to knight them in the future. That hideous gyrating American, Presley, although he had at least served his time in the army like a man, so he couldn't be all bad. Rick's world was one that would soon fade into oblivion, at which point Norman would be there to pick up the pieces, and steer Rick onto the right path. The whole modern entertainment business was built on foundations of clay. Even Alf loved all those long-haired degenerates and the ghastly noise they made, so no point in seeking any kind of good sense from that quarter.

"Who's going to remember Presley, Lennon and that foul boy Jagger in fifty years?" Norman asked aloud. "No one! Politicians are the ones whose names are immortalised by their achievements and by their dedication to the nation." Norman reflected upon the names of his former Cabinet colleagues in the Douglas-Home government. Ernest Marples, Henry Brooke, Joe Godber. Names that will resonate throughout history, he reassured himself, long after Jagger, Presley, Faith, and all the rest of this generation's shower of talentless so-called entertainers have been long forgotten. And if Rick's not careful, he'll slide down the dust pipe of ignominy with them.

"Not that I'm in a position to shape anything now, myself," Norman sighed, as he quietly contemplated his total irrelevance; an opposition backbencher with few prospects, under a leader that he well knew couldn't stand the sight of him. The feeling was largely mutual. His gaze fell on two photographs framed on his desk. One was his great-uncle Piers, the other, his father. The two previous generations of MPs, and giants of the Conservative Party. Even seven years after his father's death, Norman's feelings of grief remained, at times, inconsolable.

Richard Armstrong's death was still essentially a mystery. How did a man who had never had a single day of ill health in his life suddenly collapse from a heart attack while doing some light pruning in his much-prized rose garden? But then, Norman knew that he had never really recovered from the death of Fiona, Norman's mother, three years prior. He looked at his favourite photograph — father and son grinning and shaking hands on the day that Norman had been elected to the family constituency. With a slightly increased majority; a fact about which Norman never missed an opportunity to lovingly tease his father.

"You just never know," Norman contemplated, thinking just how much he needed his father now. The elder Armstrong understood the fickle world of politics. He would have known just what to say to buck up Norman's spirits.

It was several months since the election, and still Norman hadn't yet come to terms with actually being out of government. His only other experience of opposition had been the brief period between the 1950 and 1951 elections, after which he went straight to the Treasury; Assistant Economic Secretary under Rab Butler, then under Harold Macmillan, then eventually accompanied Macmillan straight to Number Ten as his PPS. Followed, of course, by his short but eventful stint in the Cabinet as Alec Douglas-Home's Home Secretary.

Observing her husband's general bewilderment, Eileen had suggested that he rediscover reading for pleasure; after all, she pointed out, the extensive library in the Armstrong's Knightsbridge pied-à-terre would keep even the most voracious reader busy for years. For months Norman had toyed with one volume or another, but now his boredom and lack of general resolve were becoming genuinely worrying, for someone with such a disciplined and focused mind.

Norman finally decided that Charlotte Morris was as good a place as any to start, as there was almost an entire shelf of her various works, fiction and non-fiction, in the library. There was an intriguing connection with the author and Norman's grandfather. What was to be made of the very warm dedication to Colonel Fforbes Armstrong in her history of his regiment, *QONR — The Honour and the Glory*, Norman mused. And then of course, her famous literary creation, the sleuthing red-coated soldier, Richard Fforbes, star character in a series of murder mysteries, set in exotic locations throughout the empire, and written between the turn of the century and the end of the Great War. If nothing else, the name of the principal character gave an unmistakable clue that old Charlotte had held the Colonel in high regard; having named her hero after the Colonel himself and his young son.

Norman scanned the volumes, moving beyond some of the non-fiction titles. Her contentious book on Kitchener — not published until after both were dead, but even then, it had caused a major controversy in the twenties. There was her biography of her grandfather, Captain Charles Speers, *Nelson's Own*, as well as a volume the size of the family's leather-bound King James Bible, *The Honourable Company*; a history of Speers Shipping and Speers Colonial Holdings, of which Charlotte herself had been principal shareholder, and from where the Armstrong's own secret family fortune had begun.

Richard Armstrong had been deeply uncomfortable about aspects of the Speers history in the colonies and had sold out the family's interest immediately following the death of Piers himself, a lifelong company man as well as being an MP. Richard's divestment was timed fortuitously just prior to the economic calamity of 1929, which saw the company's value plummet and large swathes of its global operations laid to ruin. This at least provided some comfort for Norman. Even if his own son was intent to squander his life with pointless pursuits, the family's financial future was at least assured.

Norman ultimately settled on the first of the Richard Fforbes novels, *The Colonel's Dilemma*. It was an immaculate first edition, dated 1904. No wonder it's pristine, Norman thought. Who'd want to read that blasted thing all the way through? He wondered if it had even been down from the shelf since it had first been placed there, sixty years ago.

He scanned the synopsis. A young officer of ill-repute; a gambler and drinker; serving in the fictional First Natal Regiment of Foot, stationed at a southern African garrison around the time of the Zulu Wars. There was also, predictably, the beautiful, innocent and naïve young wife. The caddish young officer dies in unexplained circumstances; suspicion immediately falls upon his ill-treated young widow. But what was the involvement of the much-revered Colonel of the Regiment? Did he play any part in the young officer's death? Was it a duel, or something more sinister? Can Captain Richard Fforbes get to the truth, save the poor young widow from disgrace, and possibly even the gallows, and at the same time protect the much-loved Colonel, and indeed the entire regiment, from dishonour?

Gordon Bennett, what a load of old cobblers, Norman thought. He looked up at his grandfather, who returned his gaze. Norman considered the family resemblance. "You wouldn't have got yourself mixed up in anything resembling a wholly unbelievable caper like this, would you?" Norman asked him aloud. Colonel Fforbes Armstrong regarded his grandson with such intensity that Norman actually shivered. The ghosts of the ancestors were always there, Norman knew. Sometimes it was enormously comforting, other times acutely unsettling.

Well, even this old claptrap was more convincing than *Iceberg Right Ahead!*, the penultimate in the Richard Fforbes series. Did people really go out and buy that kind of thing?

They did apparently, in large numbers. No accounting for taste, Norman thought.

A few years earlier, Dick Billings had alluded to a missing manuscript. That's right, Norman remembered, closing the book and replacing it on the shelf. There was a photograph of Charlotte Morris with Lloyd George, in one of the reception rooms at Number Ten. Lloyd George had honoured her for her devotion to shell-shocked officers in the Great War. Dick had hinted to Norman that she knew a lot of secrets, thanks to her business and family connections, and her close and long friendship with King Edward VII; secrets so potentially devastating that the government, even the monarchy could be at risk even now, should the much-dreaded papers ever come to light.

But what did she really know about anything? Norman thought. Buggering sod all, I expect. A courtier and gossip monger, old Tum Tum had plenty of those in his life, it was common knowledge. Imagine surrounding yourself with a bunch of gossiping women. And as well as that, Charlotte Morris was a very bad writer of even worse stories that, had she not been wealthy beyond most people's wildest dreams, and a friend of the King, wouldn't even have made it into a series of penny-dreadfuls. Norman scoffed, and scanned the other Fforbes Stories on the shelf; *The Officer's Mess, Transvaal Adventure, Murder in the Pavilion, Pirates of Zanzibar.*

"Pirates of Zanzibar? Bloody Hell!" Norman muttered contemptuously, then scanned on, giving up in disgust when he reached *Sunrise over Suez.*

I'd rather read the hysterical leftist rantings of Comrade Alf, he pondered, then gently touched the spine of Alf's book on the Jarrow March, featured on the shelf below the long line of Charlotte Morris volumes. Norman smiled as he remembered the brief dedication Alf had written on the inside cover. It simply read: *marras always*.

He then walked over to the television, turned it on, then slumped into his easy chair. It was time for the news. As he waited for the set to warm up, he thought again of his unlikely, but much-loved friend.

Marras always.

Perhaps things weren't looking so bleak after all.

AUTHOR'S NOTE

All our principal characters and corporate players are wholly fictional and are not intended to be representative of the real office holders, nor other protagonists in the true events referenced as our story progresses. Likewise, although a number of real-life occurrences form the backdrop to the narrative, and some real people make cameo appearances, a degree of dramatic licence has been taken.

Although the storyline surrounding the death of the minicab driver and undercover police officer is inspired, in a general sense, by real events, the location and the characters involved are entirely fictional, as are the ensuing legal proceedings and general aftermath.

Reports on the confrontations between police and travellers, known as "The Battle of the Beanfield", were sourced from a number of eyewitness accounts as reported in the news of the time.

Additional material, including interviews, observations and commentary surrounding the aftermath of the Miners' Strike and the political fallout from football hooliganism incidents, was adapted from a number of sources including, but not limited to: official and unofficial websites, news reports of the day; BBC radio documentaries including

Witness (BBC World Service), *Desert Island Discs, UK Confidential*, and *Report* (BBC Radio 4), also newspapers including *The Times, The Guardian* and *The Independent*. Gwynne Fielding's comments and other aspects of the Orgreave defendants' trials were inspired largely by those of miners' defence lawyer, Gareth Peirce, and also Michael Mansfield QC, contributors to Channel Four's 1985 documentary, *The Battle for Orgreave.*

Our Wigham Commission into the behaviour of police during the Miners' Strike is purely fiction, and neither the nature of the enquiry nor the fictional Mr Justice Wigham are intended to represent any real people or events.

Sir Archie Prentice's involvement in the search for NUM funds for sequestration is based loosely on real government actions. Sir Peregrine Walsingham's memo expressing concern over the use of surveillance to this end is based upon sentiments expressed by Sir Robert Armstrong, Cabinet Secretary to Prime Minister Thatcher, and revealed in Cabinet documents made public after the thirty-year embargo. (Reported by BBC Radio 4, *UK Confidential*)

Previously Published Works

The Banqueting Club (2019)
ISBN: 978-1-78830-194-7

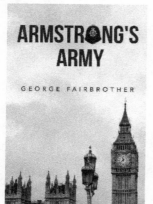

Armstrong's Army (2020)
ISBN: 978-1-78830-319-4

CPSIA information can be obtained
at www.ICGtesting.com
Printed in the USA
LVHW110742140720
660468LV00007B/83